WHEN I WAKE UP

JESSICA JARLVI

HEAD
ZEUS

An Aria Book

This is an Aria book. First published in 2017 by Head of Zeus Ltd

This paperback edition first published in 2018 by Head of Zeus

9 7 5 3 1 2 4 6 8

A catalogue record for this book is available from
the British Library.

ISBN (PB): 9781786698025
ISBN (E): 9781786695451

Typeset by Divaddict Publishing Solutions Ltd

Printed and bound in Great Britain by
CPI Group (UK) Ltd, Croydon CR0 4YY

Head of Zeus Ltd
First Floor East
5–8 Hardwick Street
London EC1R 4RG

WWW.HEADOFZEUS.COM

To Mark, Julia, Leo and Max

for your love and support, always

She staggers backwards, her back ramming into the car door. There is no sense of time. Instinctively, she puts her hand to her head. There's blood on her fingers. She stares at the dripping redness, amazed. Bewildered she looks around. Did anyone see?

She's about to speak when another blow strikes her head. Her back bangs into the door again and this time she falls over. She immediately tries to get back up but a boot explodes into her stomach and she screams, or at least she thinks she does; nothing comes out as she gasps.

She feels dizzy, her eyes won't focus; they're getting increasingly damp and sticky and she wipes them, only to see her hands covered in even more red. It looks like paint. Another boot and it sounds like something breaks. She hopes it's a tree branch and not her ribs but the agony is unbearable. Despite the pain, she clambers to her hands and knees. A blur of movement and her head smashes against cold metal.

Then everything turns eerily quiet.

PART ONE

1

Erik

March 2016

TEACHER OF THE YEAR BRUTALLY ATTACKED IN SCHOOL PARKING LOT.

Life-threatening injuries... coma.

No eyewitnesses.

Erik tries to make sense of the words in the newspaper. They read like badly written lyrics. He's holding Anna's bruised hand; her fingernails are raw and scraped for evidence. He feels sick, emptied of emotion; he stares at his wife, he stares at the white walls.

Then a rainbow of colours. Her wedding ring catches the sunlight, cascading beams of light across the dull room, and he's reminded of the beginning, seven years earlier, when he sold a collection of records to pay for the diamond. Her calm, grounded and responsible nature made him feel loved.

He needs to hang onto that feeling. The beginning. Not the end. Not even the in-between when life rushed past and he sometimes struggled to remember why they were married.

"There was still cash in her purse," the police say. "Money isn't a likely motive."

"Of course not," Erik says. "We live a modest life."

He's not sure if this adds value even if it's true. They live in a small, white-brick house from the sixties and share a second-hand Volvo V70. They bought the station wagon when they left Stockholm for the southern countryside with its widespread, yellow colza fields. Anna had just accepted a job at a local school. He was between assignments and followed her lead. That's when her career started to dictate their lives. The students became her life and he was left to create his own.

The words 'rape kit' bounce harshly against the sterile walls. He switches off, stares at Anna instead, trying to read her: *why did this happen to us?*

Her body is heavy on the white bedding, the long dark hair arranged in a neat ponytail. He feels an urge to pull it out, to make it messy. They've made her look different.

If he squints, she could be someone else. Half her face is dark red, almost purple, her right eye swollen, reflecting the attacker's anger. His insides tighten.

"Her head injuries are consistent with the damage on the car door."

"So it could have been an accident?"

"Not likely. Her ribs are bruised, her right arm broken, the head... it hasn't just hit the car door once... sorry... we understand you need time."

"For what?" he says. To cope? To grieve? To hope? What is it that they want from him? He looks around the room, bewildered. There's no one there to respond to. Just Anna. They've left him alone.

The respirator next to her bed dominates, its overwhelming sound filling the room, reminding him that her chest is no longer rising on its own. Oxygen flows through a mask. As if she's in the sea, deep under water.

They did a test dive on their honeymoon in the Maldives; she wanted to become a certified diver but then the twins were born. He imagines the machine next to her bed as a gas cylinder and the tube a diving regulator. Her head could be filled with the colours of the ocean. In her dream-like state she might be happy.

Tears form in the corners of his eyes, one by one. Blurring.

The doctors haven't told him much. Or maybe he didn't listen properly. He finds the whole hospital machine intimidating: the overwhelming smell of disinfectant, the physicians in their unbuttoned, sloppy white coats, the nurses annoyingly officious. There is this unspoken requirement of him to behave a certain way but he has no idea how to conduct himself. This is not something you can prepare for.

He is immature. Anna has always said so and she's been right. When they first started dating, she found his juvenile nature endearing. "You can get away with anything," she would laugh. Although her patience seemed to diminish as time went on.

He blames her bloody job. Being a teacher is a calling for her. She is consumed by her students – people she isn't even related to!

Now he must nod and say 'yes, she's a great teacher' even though he secretly thinks she should have been a better mum. Then she would have been at home.

He keeps it to himself, must act maturely.

There's a monitor next to her bed that measures her heart

rate, her vitals; a reminder that she is alive... just. A flick of the switch and the machines go quiet; her chest won't rise again. It feels like a threat, like he's God.

A vibration in his pocket and he pulls out his phone.

WhatsApp now

Pernilla Arvidsson: How are you doing? Thinking of you... Sebastian and Lukas can stay late if needed. Hugs

His heart jolts. He's forgotten to pick up the children from day care. They don't know about the attack. Only that mummy is sick.

He writes a response.

Thanks. Thinking of you too.

He stares at the screen. Yesterday he would have clicked 'Send' without much thought. Now it feels inappropriate. He retypes it.

Thanks. See you.

*

"Erik?"

His mum is at the door. At the sight of her, the tears start to fall more heavily until he breaks down completely. The chair shakes under his unstable frame.

"Oh, Erik." She hugs him tightly.

Tears and snot run into a single stream but he doesn't care. "Any improvement?"

He shakes his head. Mum's eyes are teary when she hands him a bag but she doesn't cry. She always remains strong and calm.

"Clothes," she explains. "I'll get the boys."

He wishes she would scream instead of being so organised and practical. That at least someone would react. Everyone is too peaceful; they speak in monotonous, slow voices, as if he's retarded. The doctors, the nurse, the police. Has the world not stopped while his wife fights for her life? It feels like it should.

"I agreed with the teacher that we would keep their routine normal," Mum continues. "Is her name Pernilla?"

He nods and wipes his face with the back of his sleeve. Anna would have hated that. He smiles faintly. If she wakes up, he's going to be the husband she deserves.

2

Anna

September 2015

"Erik collecting the boys?" Kent asked, handing Anna a cup of coffee.

She looked up from the paperwork, happy for the interruption.

"Yes, I'm marking exam papers."

It was a cold and bleak afternoon; autumn was on the doorstep with woolly cardigans making an appearance in the teachers' lounge. She wrapped her fingers tightly around the hot cup.

"How's it going with the new student, Daniel?" Kent made himself comfortable on the corduroy couch next to her desk. "Is he still testing the limits?"

She shrugged. "Basically, yes. I've tried reaching out to the parents but there seem to be a number of problems at home."

"What about the school counsellor?"

"He won't talk to 'a shrink'. His words, not mine. I've explained that it's confidential but he doesn't buy it. He's very private, on edge, you know."

Living in a small town did make it harder for people to open up. Students and parents were often worried that everyone would know their business.

Kent sipped his coffee, nodding. "Should we involve social services?" he asked.

She smiled at him, relaxing her shoulders from the stressful day; she loved that he cared, not just about his own students but also about hers. Their friendship kept her coming back to this school every year.

"I'm not sure," she said.

"Anna, you can't save every child on your own."

"I know," she said defensively. "I'll think about it. I don't want to cause him more harm. He's obviously just trying to get attention."

"Causing fights will definitely achieve that."

"That's why I need to find a way to reach out to him."

She wanted to tell him about the letters Daniel had written to her but she couldn't. Kent would worry, and although it wasn't her job to protect him, she was determined to deal with this on her own.

She had received the first letter in August, when school started after the summer break. As was always the case with new pupils, she had secretly hoped for a studious and conscientious addition, although this had quickly turned out to be a fantasy.

I hate school and I know I'm going to hate you. People like you think you rule over me, but you don't. No one does. If you understand that, we have no problems. If you don't... you'll see what will happen.

At first she had felt threatened. Scared even. Then she had

taken a step back and viewed it from a different angle. After all, it was ridiculous to be intimidated by a seventeen-year-old. She was nearly twice his age. He was simply reaching out to her. That's what her years of experience told her, that it was a cry for help.

The next letter had been similar in nature but then they had become milder.

I hate you. You think I can't read. That's why you don't write back. You think I'm stupid?

He wanted her to reply. So far she hadn't. Was it ethically correct to correspond with a student in this way? Didn't it mean she was showing favouritism? She wanted to ask Kent's advice but she had a feeling he would object to any written communication with a student.

"His writing is good," she said. "Above average actually."

"Well, at least that's something." He looked tired. The stress of the new school system was getting to him. "Good thing I'm retiring soon," he would say. "Let me know if I can help in any way."

"I will," she said.

She had fancied Kent once. Even though he was much older and his khaki trousers and check shirts weren't obviously sexy, his clear blue eyes had made something stir in her. He was an attentive listener, unlike Erik, who had the attention span of a two-year-old.

"You're very ambitious and extremely caring," Kent said, tilting his head. "I admire that, but there's a life outside of this school as well. Don't let the students get to you."

They exchanged a knowing glance. He knew that her troubled students reminded her of her own upbringing.

"I know," she said.

"Anyway, I have to go," Kent said and got up. "Taking Märta to the cinema."

She watched him leave, feeling an unexpected surge of jealousy. It wasn't Märta, a fifty-three-year-old accountant who dressed like a seventy-year-old; it was the feeling of being cherished the way she was. Kent adored her.

Sighing, she leaned back in her chair. It was half-past five. Outside the window, birch trees were bending in the strong wind, the sky thick with clouds. Sebastian and Lukas would be inside, eating dinner. She picked up the phone to call them but decided against it. They would be busy telling Erik about their day. The thought made her smile. She needed to focus on the two wonderful boys they had given life to. Somewhere, there was a video of the twins as babies, highlighting the joyous moments as opposed to the sleepless nights and arguments about whose turn it was to load the washing machine. She should watch it to revel in the smiles and snuggles. Her boys made her happy, and Erik had too. To bring her back to the early days, she often reminisced about his proposal, which had been unexpected and therefore highly romantic: slumped on the couch in pyjamas one evening, he suddenly got down on one knee. No ring, but still.

After Kent's exit, other teachers started to leave and soon she was on her own. She welcomed the ensuing silence. Picking up the red pen, she inhaled the serene school air: paper, newly sharpened pencils, old books, cardboard boxes, gingerbread and coffee. She loved the late afternoon and evenings when everyone had left the building.

"Hi, Anna."

The raspy adolescent voice cut through the air. Surprised,

she looked up. The doors had automatically locked at five o'clock. But there he was, in his worn-out, small denim jacket, backpack thrown over the shoulder, shoelaces undone.

"Daniel?"

3

Erik

March 2016

Anna's parents haven't visited their daughter in the hospital yet but instead of feeling bitter, Erik is relieved. They would only make the situation worse. Like a drama train they would pull in and off-load their own issues. Erik needs to focus on his own family now, on his children.

"I think it's scandalous," Mum says, and it's the closest he has seen her to being upset. "She could die, for goodness sake!"

"It's a long drive for them," Erik says.

He's in the doorway, taking his jacket off. It's been a long night, sitting by Anna's side. This morning he was told to go home, to take a shower and sleep. The nurses promised to call if there were any developments.

"They could get a train," Mum says. "That would only take a few hours. It's not as if they live in a different country."

"They're just busy with their own lives."

He wants the conversation to be over.

"If I had a daughter like Anna…" Mum says and her eyes momentarily tear up.

He's not sure if he should put his arms around her. He hesitates. Mum likes Anna a bit too much sometimes. When he first brought Anna home, he was happy that his mother approved. But when he realised that she had taken the top spot on the likeability chart, with him dropping down to second place, then it became… well, not a competition, but definitely annoying.

"Anyway," Mum says. She wipes her eyes and is back to her normal self and there is no need for a hug. "The boys don't have any clean underwear. Doesn't anyone do laundry in this house?"

*

Erik walks up the stairs to take a shower. Mum has promised to visit Anna this morning so that he can rest. The sun outside is radiating an annoying sense of warmth and happiness, not reflecting his mood. He feels cold and out of place, like this is no longer his house, the bed no longer his, the shower foreign. He glances at Anna's shampoo and scented soaps. Should he throw them out or leave them where they are?

Before Mum leaves, she pops her head into the bathroom.

"Please hang the washing in the drying cabinet when you wake up," she says. "I will pick the boys up from day care this afternoon so that you can go back to the hospital."

"Thanks," he says.

"Oh, and Erik?"

"Yes?"

The hot water burns into his back.

What is it now? Just leave me alone.
"Everything is going to be okay."
"Sure."
Whatever you say. Just go.

*

With the washing machine whirring in the background, Erik pulls out Anna's laptop from her school bag and places it on the kitchen table next to a strong cup of coffee. He pulls the blinds down to block out the neighbours and anyone else walking past. Even though it's still cold outside, the town seems to come alive when the sun is out. It's all very formal and polite. People walk and talk and nod with a high-pitched "*hej*" when they pass each other. Anna loves how friendly this place is but Erik thinks it's fake. He prefers bigger cities where you mind your own business. At least their house is on the main street of Mörna which means they're not tucked away in a cosy neighbourhood with weekend barbecues and coffee mornings. They only have two immediate neighbours: a ninety-year-old woman they hardly ever see and a family with grown children who they're only required to wave to every now and then. The mother has made an appearance since the news about Anna broke. With sad eyes she offered to help Erik with the children or food shopping – "anything at all" – but he has politely declined. He can cope. He *will* cope, and for now, Mum is here.

He should be sleeping as per the nurses' orders, but he can't. No one knows that he has Anna's laptop and it makes him feel guilty. That night when she had to "dash down to school", she left it in her workbag at home and when his band-mate Rob hurriedly drove him to the hospital, Erik grabbed the bag on his way out. It was parked by the door, as if she had forgotten it.

"She might need her bag," he told Rob.

"What the hell is wrong with you?" Rob said. "You don't even know what state she's in, mate."

"Yeah, but it can't be that bad. Otherwise, they would have said, right?"

How wrong he was.

"I wasn't thinking," he said. "I'm... I mean... she's going to be okay though, isn't she?"

He started crying then, the full waterworks. Obviously she couldn't use her laptop. He ended up leaving it in Rob's car and by the time Rob gave the bag back to him, the police had already searched the house. He should have handed it over but something held him back. It's not that he doesn't trust the police; he just doesn't think they will prioritise it. Too often, he reads about the lack of resources in the newspaper, people having to look for their stolen goods themselves. Only last week, two teenagers had to turn investigators and search for their stolen mopeds. That's just wrong. Erik can't leave this in someone else's hands.

*

He flops onto a white, Danish designer chair, the motion sparking a recent memory of Anna's persuasive decision-making. She insisted they buy these chairs.

"They're expensive *and* uncomfortable," he said at the time. "That's a bad combination."

She bought them second-hand. Avoiding conflict but still getting her way.

He grabs a pillow and places it behind his back to make himself more comfortable while also delaying the inevitable: logging on to her computer. It doesn't feel right. Yet it's necessary. The police will need his help.

"Anything you can think of, let us know," they said.

He wants to be obliging and more importantly, he wants to be involved.

Pressing the start button on Anna's laptop, he realises that he has never used it before. The children haven't even been allowed to play games on it. "My work laptop", she called it, even though she had bought it with her own money.

A blue screen stares at him, requesting a password. He tries various combinations. The usual ones. Birth dates, mother's maiden name, name of the pet she had when she grew up.

Please try again.

He tries again and again but has no luck. He snaps it shut. It was a bad idea anyway.

That's when it hits him. The whole situation. It's completely surreal! His wife is in a coma and he has no idea when – or even *if* – she will ever wake up. It's indescribably painful, this limbo… His knuckles whiten as they press hard around the edges of the laptop. There's a cramp inside his chest. He slams the computer down and punches the table, releasing the pressure. What the hell is he going to do?

He breathes deeply, composes himself the way Mum would do. Takes a sip of coffee "to calm his nerves".

"Bloody hell!" He burns himself on the Filippa K mug that's been designed without a handle. Stupid invention.

One of Anna's classes gave her a whole set for Christmas. Looking around, he realises that Anna is everywhere.

Even the furniture is a reminder of her. The few pieces he contributed when they met have slowly been replaced with eclectic ones that Anna has either recycled from flea markets or bought via online auctions. Will she ever do that again?

He calls Rob, the only friend he can truly be himself with. "I'm so fucking frustrated," he says, not just referring to the failed login to Anna's laptop but to everything that has just happened. "I feel so lost. I don't know what's going on. Will she get better? Why can't someone answer that simple question? And the police... I don't know, they expect me to tell them stuff but... but then they don't tell me shit!"

Spitting the words down the phone makes him realise how true they are. How can they exclude him like that? They are married; he is her next of kin.

"I'm sorry, man," Rob says. "I know that sucks but you've got to keep faith. Anna is strong. And maybe the police have been really busy. I read in the paper this morning that someone was murdered in the city."

"And that's more important, you mean? Anna is still alive so why should they keep writing about her in the papers?"

He knows he's pushing it too far but it feels good to take his frustration out on someone else.

"Look, Erik," Rob says. "Perhaps it's just that this other case has left Anna lost within the pages. It doesn't mean no one cares."

Erik rocks back and forth in the chair. The plastic creaks. Another thing he hates about this chair. It's irrelevant, though. Is Anna going to wake up? That's the important question.

Rob clears his throat. "It's really tough, Erik. I know. I mean, obviously I have no idea, but I can imagine. Anna is a gem... I really wish I could help." He stops rambling and sighs before starting again. "Hey, why don't you call that policewoman I dated last year? Big hair, bad breath? Eh... Tina. I'm sure she could, you know, give you some info, tell you what's going on."

Erik starts to listen. He has no idea who Rob is talking about but it gives him hope.

"I don't want to get pulled into something messy though," he says. "Why did you break up?"

Rob coughs. "It's totally cool," he says. "I mean, it wasn't like that. She agreed that I wasn't the one for her. She needed too much attention, you know, always creating drama."

"Well, I prefer drama to no info," Erik says and makes a note of her number.

As soon as he's put the phone down, he calls this Tina.

"Erik? Rob's friend?" She doesn't sound impressed but the moment he tells her about Anna, she changes her tone. "That's your wife? I'm so sorry. Look, from what I can tell, there's not really anything new."

"I see." He starts to cry but he doesn't mind that she can hear him. He wants sympathy.

"Look," she says more quietly. "I'm not supposed to tell you this. They spoke to her colleagues and rumour is she was very close with one teacher in particular... Kent."

"Yes, I know." Because of course he knows. But her tone... is she insinuating something else? He pictures Kent, his greying beard and hawk-like nose pressed against Anna's, the two of them kissing. He laughs through the tears. What a ridiculous idea! Plus there's Märta. Anna has mentioned what a great marriage they have. He does listen sometimes.

"He's happily married," he says even though she hasn't asked.

"Well, they're going to talk to him again. Now, I have to go."

"That's it?"

"Look, I don't have to tell you anything."

Fine. He needs her. "Thanks," he says. "I mean it. I appreciate your help."

*

He walks upstairs and surveys Anna's desk. If he can't get into her laptop, then what else can he look through? The next time he talks to the police, he wants to have something useful to say, and if he can't find anything, perhaps he will have no choice but to give them the computer.

The old IKEA unit from Anna's student days is constantly cluttered with papers; there must be something he can go on, something the police have missed? He imagines them searching her desk in a rush. The house wasn't particularly messy when he arrived home, but then Anna is only a small-town teacher, not an important politician or businesswoman. Mum thinks he's cynical but he's just realistic. This isn't a big city; it's a claustrophobic little town where no one gives a shit about anyone else. Anything out of the ordinary turns to gossip. He imagines the whispers that must be going around about Anna and it makes him ill.

Erik pulls out the wooden swivel chair in front of Anna's desk and sits down. There are a couple of books and he picks them up, thumbing through them. It's mostly fiction. He recognises a few of the authors' names, such as Selma Lagerlöf, August Strindberg and Karin Boye. Anna would be proud of him for knowing his Swedish literature, but unfortunately nothing is hidden inside the hard covers. Not that he had really expected there to be.

Under the books are a number of notepads with scribbled

sentences. *War and Peace intriguing enough? Presenta-tions – Monday – book projector. Renaissance essays? Kent and Märta – Strindberg play Saturday.* He remembers not wanting to go to the play and feels bad.

He tosses the notepad to the side and picks up a stack of papers instead. It's mainly bills, which makes him realise he has to pay them. It's always been Anna who logs in to the Internet bank to pay their bills. He has no idea how it's done. Maybe Mum can do it for him? Another realisation: they have many bills. Electricity, water, waste, phone, broadband, TV… His salary as a house painter doesn't stretch far. They need Anna's income. What will happen now that she can't work? Will she still get paid? He realises he can't ask that question. It will seem insensitive.

He flicks through the bills, his heart growing heavier with each one. Then a note. He finds himself holding a personally written note, not a bill.

That was a nasty thing to do, Anna. You know I'm smarter than that.

It's so small, no wonder no one has seen it. Erik looks closely at the words. The handwriting is tiny and neat. He reads it a few times, trying to understand if there is a hidden message. Who wrote this? A colleague? A student? Her sister? Anna has had her dramas through the years. She's firm with people around her, but fair. At least that's what she used to say. He's not sure anymore. He stopped listening a long time ago.

4

Iris

1983

*B*illie Jean is not my lover, Michael Jackson belted out, making the crowd go crazy.

Bille Jean is not my lover.

But are you?

Iris watched as a woman with red hair navigated her way through the dance floor. She looked older, late twenties perhaps, tall and voluptuous, a cheeky fringe above green eyes. Iris parted her lips, raised her glass and slowly drank the cold white wine, conveying sophistication.

"I'm Hanna."

The woman brought an air of perfume with her and gracefully stretched a hand out. Iris took it. It was soft but firm and she held it slightly longer than was customary for a handshake.

"Iris," she said.

"Are you here alone?"

She was tempted to make up a story about a date

abandoning her but Rolf wouldn't have approved. *Stay as close to the truth as possible.* Their arrangement was so new, she didn't want to let him down.

"Yes. And you?"

"I'm here with friends." Hanna nodded in the direction she had just come from. "They're about to leave though. So... what do you do, Iris?"

The casualness of the question was an emotional U-turn.

"I work in a library," she said drily, anticipating a yawn from Hanna. That was generally the reaction her profession generated. Instead, Hanna's eyes lit up.

"A lover of books!" Her smile broadened. "I'm an actress and also a lover of books."

"Really? What are you reading at the moment?"

"A play I'm rehearsing, *No Exit*."

"By Jean-Paul Sartre?"

Hanna tilted her head slightly. "You know it?"

"Of course. Who are you playing?"

"Inez."

They looked at each other knowingly: Inez, the woman who ended up in hell for seducing her cousin's wife.

*

Walking down a cobbled street with multi-coloured buildings on either side, they talked about the play; leaving the comforting, smoky buzz of the club behind.

"Inez sings as well," Hanna told her. *"They've set trestles in a row, with a scaffold and a knife..."*

Her voice was beautiful and the intimacy it brought made Iris slip her hand into Hanna's. Warmth spread through her

23

palm. It was a crisp summer evening and still light outside. Iris loved the months of the year when it never grew dark; the optimism that filled the air, the love, the hope...

"... *Come, good folks, to Whitefriars Lane, come to see the merry show!*"

Iris clapped while still holding Hanna's hand, not wanting to withdraw it. Hanna bowed.

"Thank you," she said. "It's always been my dream to be on stage."

They walked past a small harbour and a row of shoreline restaurants that were busy closing for the night. Iris let Hanna lead the way, not knowing where they were heading. She had travelled to another city, wanting to remain anonymous, and no street felt familiar. It was frightening but mostly thrilling.

"What about you?" Hanna asked. "Are you living your dream?"

"I'm happy." She didn't want Hanna to know that this was her first job out of university. "I love literature and now I'm surrounded by it every day."

"Good for you."

Hanna started singing again and soon they reached a modern, whitewashed apartment building, each window frame displaying potted St Paulias, hydrangeas or orchids. One day, Iris was hoping to have a large garden filled with flowers. Hanna fished out a key from her handbag.

"*So here we are, for ever,*" she said dramatically, opening the door. "Inez's famous last words."

The apartment on the third floor was a contrast of white furniture and colourful cushions, drapes and curtains. Vibrant and inviting, the open plan space was covered with candleholders: on tables, dressers and shelves. Hanna slipped out of her heels and retrieved a lighter. Barefooted, she elegantly leaned over furniture to light candles, gradually making the room glow. Iris silently watched her while taking her own heels off. Hanna was so graceful.

"Nice moves," Iris said but the words came out all wrong. They sounded like Rolf's. Cheesy. It wasn't a line for her, she meant it. The words needed to be her own to sound authentic. "I mean, did you train as a dancer?"

Hanna nodded and kissed her. Just for a second, their lips touched, before Hanna removed Iris's coat from her shoulders.

"Here, let me take that," she said, her cheeks rosy. "Red or white wine?"

"Red, please." She liked variety.

Iris stepped into the area designated as kitchen. It consisted of a small oven and a cooker, a fridge and a microwave. Hanna pulled out the cork from an already opened bottle on the counter, and poured two glasses. The wine felt like a formality, their eyes observing each other over the rim of the glass as they took a couple of sips. Iris slipped her arm around Hanna's waist, pulling her close. *Quickly take charge.* She pressed herself against Hanna's soft lips, their tongues meeting in a playful kiss. Then Iris pulled away.

"Let's slow down," she said.

Hanna smiled but instead of releasing Iris, she pulled her closer. This was really happening. *Go with the flow.* Iris's hands travelled over Hanna's curves, caressing the firm behind, stroking her muscular back and shoulders, grabbing a handful of the long hair, pulling it back. Hanna moaned as Iris's lips brushed her neck.

"Turn around," Iris said as she moved the glossy, red hair out of the way, hooking her finger around the zip in Hanna's short, patterned dress. She pulled it down, revealing pale, smooth skin and gently slipped the dress off the shoulders. Hanna wasn't wearing a bra and Iris stretched her hands around her front, cupping the generous breasts, gently tugging at the hardened nipples. Pressed against Hanna's back, her own breasts tingled at the warmth of another body. She felt her insides contract.

"I want you," she said.

5

Anna

September 2015

Daniel didn't call her "Miss", he insisted on calling her Anna. She normally preferred it, but the way he pronounced her name, long and drawn out, was uncomfortable. Aaaa-nnn-a.

He was in the teachers' lounge after school hours yet again, wearing the same well-worn clothes, shoelaces undone; his gangly frame hardened by the muscles of adolescence. It was the second time in a week that he had appeared uninvited. Last time, Kent had turned up to fetch his keys and Daniel had bolted before she got a chance to speak to him. Now she seized the opportunity.

"How did you get in?" she asked.

Perhaps he had managed to sneak in when Kent left? The door did take a while to close. Or had he been hiding in the shadows since the bell rang, eavesdropping on their conversation?

Daniel's smirk unsettled her. Had she revealed something to Kent she shouldn't have? She was happy that she hadn't mentioned the letters even though she had received another one.

His gaze was intense. "I just did," he said casually and threw himself on the couch, resting his muddy trainers on the table.

She made no comment; she had to choose her battles.

"How can I help you?" she asked, trying to sound upbeat.

Daniel studied the floor, a bored look on his face, and wiped his nose with the back of his fist. His dirty blond hair always appeared messy, even though a large amount of gel was probably involved.

"There's no one at home," he said, as if the teacher's lounge was the most natural place to be instead.

"And you don't want to be alone?"

He didn't respond, his eyes wandering around the room, seemingly soaking in every detail: the shared hot desks, the out-dated computer, the grey monster copying machine, the hat rack with a number of multi-coloured caps on it, the umbrellas next to the door.

Eventually he turned towards her.

"You haven't responded to my letters," he said, the words hard yet lined with a slight vulnerability.

The last handwritten note, like the others, had been short and to the point.

Homework is a waste of time. I'm not learning. Do you actually want to teach me something?

He was obviously trying to provoke her into responding. Choosing her words carefully, she said: "I'm really happy that you express yourself in writing." The fact that he had used a pen to write, instead of throwing it through the room like an arrow, did please her. "Although I'm not as good at writing as you are. I prefer to talk."

This wasn't entirely true but conversations couldn't be used against you the way letters could. She still wasn't sure it was appropriate to write back.

"I'm not interested in talking," he said. "No one listens."

"Try me."

Normally, she had everything under control. Discipline had never been an issue in her classroom, but Daniel was different. One minute he was an insolent child, the next he expressed depth. She often caught him reading between classes.

"I could kick your head in," he said, jolting her out of her thoughts.

Her spine straightened, her eyes trying to gauge if he was serious. His clenched fists suggested that he was. She wondered if the janitor was still in the building. Although he was notoriously unreliable, he was someone, an obstruction, a witness.

Dread mixed with uncertainty. Did she know what she was doing?

"Daniel," she said, trying to sound calm. *He's only a teenager.* "You have the potential to do really well." She cleared her throat: "If you just apply yourself."

He seemed to relax his hands.

"Who cares?" he said.

"I do," she said, too quickly. She needed to be more constructive; no student was going to learn for her sake.

"Did your parents care?"

Again, he turned the tables, making it about anyone but

himself. At least it was easier to handle it here, where it was just the two of them, as opposed to the classroom where another twenty students were watching.

"It was important to me to have an education," she said.

It felt too personal to divulge that her parents barely noticed when she moved out to go to university.

"My brother beats people up," he said.

Already, they were onto a new topic. His way of jumping from subject to subject unnerved her, as much as his obsession with violence. Not a week went by without him being involved in a major fight. Perhaps he did have a diagnosis. Could she force the counsellor to get involved?

"That doesn't sound nice," she said.

"My mum couldn't care less." He shrugged. "Can I just stay here, while you work?"

There was the child again. She could deal with him.

"You should go home," she said gently and although she made an effort to sound kind, her words seemed to bring back the callous Daniel. His eyes grew dark and he didn't move. He just stared at her, leaving her no choice but to start packing up: papers neatly slid into her bag, pens and pencils went back in their case, her laptop zipped up in its cover.

"Right," she said, standing up. "I'm going home now."

He didn't get up immediately but she could feel him watching her. To distract herself, she fussed with her jacket, putting it on slowly to give him time, changing her shoes; taking the ballet flats off, stepping into her boots. She needed to get out.

"Anna..." he said then and inwardly she sighed. Not only had she missed her precious preparation time, he was making her feel uncomfortable. He needed to understand that while at school, she was in charge. Not him.

She turned to him, her strict teacher's face plastered on. "Yes, Daniel?"

Standing up, he was bigger than her. His face was symmetrical, the cheekbones high and the forehead tall. She could easily picture girls falling for him. Daniel's eyes were firmly on his trainers, as if he was mounting up the courage to say something. She waited patiently, cautious.

Then he raised his head and looked at her. She couldn't quite read his facial expression.

"I have decided..." he started.

"Yes?"

"...that you're going to be my new mum."

6

Erik

March 2016

"Has your wife got any enemies?"

Erik has been asked to the police station in the city to assist with the investigation. Or to be questioned? Either way, the female police officer gains his full attention with her compassionate eyes. The policeman at her side, on the other hand, looks less sympathetic. Erik appreciates that he's asked about enemies, not his alibi. Perhaps that's because the policewoman, who's introduced herself as Linda Johansson, is new. She looks young. Or maybe he's told them already? He has a vague recollection of someone at the hospital asking of his whereabouts. He can't remember what he answered.

"I don't know," he says. "Did you talk to the people at her school?"

Did you talk to Kent?

"Yes, we talked to her colleagues," Officer Johansson says, but she doesn't mention any names.

It irritates him. They should tell him every single lead they might have. He needs to remain calm though. Otherwise he will achieve nothing.

"Why do you ask?" says the policeman whose name he can't remember.

Erik debates whether he should mention Kent, but if he does, they will wonder why. All he knows is that Anna really respected the guy. That's it. He can't imagine the two of them together.

He shrugs. "Just want to make sure no stone is unturned," he says.

"Were you aware of any conflicts at school? Difficult students?"

Erik shakes his head, although there's a nagging feeling he might have missed something during all those daily conversations about school. The note he found on Anna's desk comes to mind but would it make him sound paranoid? It could be completely irrelevant.

"You sure?" asks Officer Johansson. "Nothing that was bothering her?"

Anna has an annoying habit of rattling off every event of her day, he thinks, every single evening, and with time he has learned to nod and say the appropriate amounts of okays and a-has to get through it. Now he wishes he had paid more attention.

"Well," he says, taking a chance. He'd rather share the note than give up the laptop. Tina has explained that electronics are put in storage, labelled as "evidence" and then pretty much forgotten about. "I'm not sure if it will help, but I found this."

He puts the handwritten note in front of Officer Johansson whose interest peaks.

33

That was a nasty thing to do, Anna. You know I'm smarter than that.

"Could be a student," she says. "Someone who wanted a better grade?"

"Sure, I mean, of course."

"We will look into it."

The note is bagged and he imagines it being tested for fingerprints. What will they find?

"How has Anna been lately?"

Officer Johansson leans back in her chair and he tries to look equally comfortable. He's just not sure what to tell them. If only he had something tangible to share. The last couple of months Anna didn't really talk about school anymore. She didn't talk about anything.

"She was always busy," he says honestly.

"On Tuesday, did you speak to her in the afternoon?"

He nods. "Yes, she called and asked me to pick up the children from day care, even though it was her turn."

"Is that unusual?"

"Not exactly."

He remembers the phone conversation well; has had that same talk many times over in different versions.

"What if I'm busy?" he said, tired of being taken for granted.

"You don't have a paint job today."

She was always so aware of his schedule. No, he didn't have a job that day, but Rob had the day off and they were jamming in his garage.

"Are you with Rob?" she asked.

"No," he lied, signalling to Rob to stop tuning his guitar.

"I'll see you later then. I need more time to plan my lessons for tomorrow."

If it wasn't lessons she needed to prepare for, then it was exam papers, photocopying or whatever boring stuff it was she had to do.

"Or she needs to drop a student home who's missed the bus," he complained to Rob. "As if that's even her responsibility."

"She cares, man," said Rob. "If I had a wife like Anna, I'm sure I would change underwear more often. You know what I'm saying? I would make an effort."

"What do you know?"

"Nothing. Can we play now?"

"No," he tells Officer Johansson. "It wasn't unusual."

"Did anyone see you pick up the children?"

Ah, there it is: his alibi.

"Pernilla Arvidsson saw me."

Officer Johansson makes a note and he realises someone will contact Pernilla. What will she say?

"How is your marriage?"

How is their marriage? Erik looks at the male police officer. Is he that transparent?

"What's that got to do with anything?"

"Were you happy?" Officer Johansson's voice is softer.

"I see what you're doing," Erik says despite himself. "You're playing good cop, bad cop."

He wants to laugh but he can't. How would that look? His wife may never wake up. This is real life. The policeman scoffs but Officer Johansson leans in closer and asks: "Was Anna happy?"

"Yes, she was happy." What kind of a question is that?

"She was frustrated at work and she would get annoyed with me, just like any other wife would, but she was happy."

He slumps back into his chair, feeling tired.

"Coffee?"

He nods. "Yes, please."

"I understand it's hard," Officer Johansson says.

Erik looks at her, suppressing the urge to shout: "Do you really?" It wouldn't help. He knows that. Instead he sips the hot coffee, burning his tongue.

"We haven't been able to locate Anna's laptop or mobile phone," the policeman says. "They weren't in the car, at the school, or at your house. Have you seen those items or do you know where she would keep them?"

Erik doesn't appreciate his tone. He doesn't have her phone.

"She would have had the phone with her," he says.

"There was no phone in her handbag or in the car."

"Right." *Well, you're the police, you figure it out: prove your worth to the taxpayers who pay your salaries.*

"Where were you that evening?" asks the policeman. He's annoyingly arrogant, as if he wants to catch Erik lying.

"I'm sure someone has asked me that already," Erik says. "After we arrived home from day care, the boys and I were home all afternoon and evening. No, wait." Erik thinks back to that afternoon. They were out of milk. "I went to the supermarket when Anna got home." Maybe he left that out last time.

"Anna was at home?"

They both lean forward, as if this is really interesting. Except it's not.

"Yes, she came home briefly," he says. "Cooked dinner and then she had to go back to school."

"Why?"

"No idea. To prepare something or pick something up maybe?"

"And while she was at school, you were home alone with the boys?"

Erik nods. "There was no one else to watch them," he says. Isn't that obvious?

"They would be sleeping by what? Eight o'clock?" the policeman asks.

"Yes, that's about right."

"And around ten o'clock, where were you?"

"Getting ready for bed probably."

"So you didn't step out of the house?"

"I might have been in the garden briefly, but that's it. You can't leave sleeping children home alone," Erik says. Stupid man probably doesn't have children of his own.

"Can anyone else verify that you were at home?"

The policeman grins. He wants blood.

"We have to ask," Officer Johansson says.

"Rob," Erik says, at once grateful that Rob decided to come by that evening. "My mate, Rob. He knows I was at home."

They make a note and the policeman leaves the room to check this new fact out, returning within minutes. Rob has confirmed via phone that he did see Erik. He exhales. Finally, this is over. Erik gets up to leave.

"I need to get back to the hospital," he says.

7

Anna

September 2015

The boys were already in bed when she got home. Disappointed to have missed them, she tiptoed into their bedroom to kiss them goodnight. Every time she saw them sprawled across their beds, carefree and peacefully asleep, her heart felt warmer.

"Little rascals," she whispered, quietly kissing their soft cheeks.

How amazing that she and Erik had been part of their creation. That thought always astonished her, that they were their children. Before she left the room, she lingered by the door for a few seconds, watching them. Snoring mouths and blond tousled hair. Miniature versions of Erik.

"It took forever to get them to sleep," he complained when she returned downstairs.

She sighed. He didn't enforce any rules, so what did he expect? She bit her tongue though, but the spell of love she had just felt was broken.

"I'm going to Rob's." Erik grabbed his jacket and headed for the door.

"I only just got home." She couldn't help herself. "What about dinner?"

"Leftover sausages in the fridge."

She heard the front door open.

"Wait, Erik. Please." She ran after him. Couldn't he spend at least five minutes with her? "Please don't leave me alone."

Not tonight. He was already halfway out when he turned around.

"What's going on?"

"I just... There's this student..."

She sat down on the chair next to the hall table. Maybe she could talk to him about Daniel. Erik was a child at heart, perhaps he would understand and provide some insight.

"Right." His face tightened. "It's about work. Not: how were the boys today? Did they get up to anything fun at day care, did they behave, do we need to send extra clothes?" He was really going for it and she let him. He clearly needed to vent. "You care more about your students than your own children."

A clear violation. She wanted to fight back but chose not to. It would only escalate; she had learned that the hard way.

"Come on, Erik," she said.

"Students and parents call you twenty-four hours a day, Anna. How the hell do they even have the right to have your number?"

"Let's not do this."

He was jealous. She had a purpose in life and he didn't. He busied himself painting houses while dreaming of a music career. They could be stuck in this argument for ages. She needed to distract him.

"Kent and Märta are going to the theatre next weekend. Should we join them?"

"I won't sit through another four-hour *Hamlet*, if that's what you think?"

"I have apologised for that enough times, Erik. I didn't realise it was going to be so long. This is a Strindberg play…"

"How great. No thanks."

"Come on."

"Unless it's bloody sex on stage I'm not going."

Where did that come from?

"Not everything is about sex, Erik."

"Don't I know it?"

She didn't want to discuss it. He knew she felt insecure about her weight gain, but it was also something else, something she couldn't explain. She just didn't feel *that way* when she looked at him. A painful truth that she needed to deal with. But how? His behaviour didn't exactly encourage her.

"What happened to us?" she said, depleted.

He came back in and stood in front of her, still angry but calmer. Then he put his hands on her shoulders, the physical contact almost making her cry. She reciprocated by wrapping her arm around his leg, resting her forehead on his thigh.

"I have no life," she whispered.

"What does that even mean, Anna?"

He sounded exasperated and her instinct was to get annoyed. He didn't understand anything! Her arm squeezed his leg tighter but she felt him back away.

"I work hard to provide a good life for us. But sometimes I feel like no one really cares about me, Erik."

"Anna, stop it."

"I mean it." She looked up at him. *See me.* "The boys prefer you. You're the fun dad and I'm the mean mum. My boss no longer appreciates my efforts, he takes them for granted. The students... they're sucking me dry."

She was specifically thinking of Daniel, who had opened up a whole new problem for her to solve.

"You just need validation," he said. "Reality check, Anna, you were Teacher of the Year last year." He spat it out as if it was an accusation. "I hate to break it to you but everywhere we go, you receive praise."

She knew this bothered him; parents and previous students telling her how wonderful she was. This was superficial though: comments said in passing. And she hadn't asked to be named Teacher of the Year. It was one of the principal's new incentives that was supposed to make her feel valued instead of underpaid. The truth was, she felt empty. Erik needed to know. To understand.

"Everyone thinks I'm a terrible mother and that you're a great father."

"That's not true."

"Really?" she said. "If I were to leave early to pick up the children, my boss thinks I'm a bad employee. If one of my male colleagues on the other hand has to pick up his children, he's a good dad. You see? Even though we supposedly live in a modern society, there are still these preconceived ideas. I'm sick of it. I can never win..."

"I don't agree." He broke away from her, forcing her to let go. "Anyway, if that's all, I'm off to Rob's."

She looked at him, perplexed. How could he be so callous?

"Erik."

"Yes?"

It was pointless. She grabbed her bag and the car keys

41

and shot out the door before he got the chance. That would teach him.

"Anna!"

He followed her out to the carport but only caught up with her when she had already slammed the car door shut and locked it.

"Anna! I have to go." He was knocking on the window. She ignored him, started the car and sped off. He wanted her to join him in a screaming match but she wouldn't. In the rear-view mirror she saw him standing in the road, arms up in the air. A mixture of triumph and sadness hit her.

Her phone rang almost immediately. Erik's name flashed on the screen. She didn't pick up. Nothing either of them had to say would be constructive now.

She needed to get away from him. From everything. If only she had made an effort to make friends, she would have somewhere to go. Apart from university friends who were now all over the country, she didn't really know anyone well enough to call in an hour of need. No shoulders to cry on. A fleeting image of Kent. Could she? No. Their friendship seemed to be put on hold when they left the school building for the day, to be reignited when the next day began. Her mother wasn't a viable alternative either. They hadn't spoken for months and when they did talk, her father's grunts and demands in the background kept her mother distracted.

*

Anna drove around for a while, wasting petrol, passing green sprawling woods interlinked with horse paddocks and vast fields, the sea revealed in the distance, the moon sparkling on its dark surface. When they first arrived in

Skåne County, she had found the southern countryside breathtaking. They had moved down in summer, when everywhere you looked was lush and green; the lavender blooming, bumblebees hovering, the ice cream kiosks busy, and families biking to the beach. That first Midsummer had been precious, the tradition from the Middle Ages brought to life in a nearby meadow, celebrated with a few hundred people from Mörna, their new town. Children and their parents had clad the maypole in birch leaves and brightly coloured flowers, a man played folk songs on an accordion while they danced around the pole. It was before Sebastian and Lukas were born and she had made a mental note to bring her future children there. They had continued to celebrate each Midsummer in that same meadow but other than that one time every year, they didn't make use of their beautiful surroundings. She couldn't even remember the last time they had gone for a walk. *There's a life outside of school.* There was indeed.

Erik kept calling. She could imagine his words: "For fuck's sake, Anna! Come back!" He definitely wouldn't be calling to say sorry because he wouldn't know what to apologise for. He didn't understand her, couldn't read her emotional barometer. She kept ignoring him.

When she had met Erik on holiday in Gran Canaria, he was the tall, handsome bartender from the north of Sweden doing a gap year in the sun. She had fallen for his gentle ways, how he was charming but neither pushy nor arrogant. His golden hair glowing, his lips plump. Kissable. She remembered her friends quarrelling because she chose to spend a large part of the holiday with Erik. "We came to have fun, not hang out with boys!" It was true, the purpose had been to get away from their studies. But she had been too exhilarated and had shrugged it off, thinking they were just jealous.

After she had returned to Stockholm, Erik had also moved back and soon they lived together. They had been madly in love and so it hadn't felt rushed. Plus they had their own circles of friends and would sometimes party separately and at other times, together. Since moving to the south, however, they had become overly dependent on each other. It felt like they were this one compact unit, which at first had felt exciting (it was them against the world) but then she had started to feel that every time she broke away from him, she was made to feel guilty.

She drove back into Mörna but the imminent darkness and dimly lit streets didn't welcome her. Instead, she kept driving past their house, along the main street, Mörnavägen, which sliced the town in two: the "right side" meaning the part that was closest to the sea, and the "wrong side", where they lived. She exited the town, passing a long stretch of dense fir forest followed by more farms and fields. After a few kilometres, the next town's lights and rows of houses appeared. She felt herself exhale. It was good to create distance between herself and the town that her whole life seemed to revolve around. She drove down to the sea, passed a small harbour and thought of going for a walk, but it felt chilly and in her rush to get out, she hadn't brought a jacket.

Aimlessly, she drove up and down the small windy Hågarp roads with their doll-sized houses. It was getting dark and most homes were equally submerged in darkness, the majority of the residents being summer guests only.

She managed to get back to the main road and was surprised to see there was a library. How could it possibly survive in such an underpopulated place when most small-town libraries in the county were closing down? It was an old dilapidated building in red brick that had probably been grandiose once upon a time. The word LIBRARY hung precariously above a glass door, glowing like a vintage cinema sign. She stopped the car, welcoming the distraction. Without a plan, she got out and walked up the steps towards the sign. The notion of reading spurred her on. Memories as a child of escaping reality through adventure stories.

Next to the door was a notice with the opening hours: the library would be open until nine that evening. In fact, it was open late two nights a week. She made a mental note as she pushed the heavy glass door. There was a muffled sound of a bell as she stepped into the otherwise quiet hallway. A couple of students were typing on computers, a man was reading a newspaper. She moved inside, sucked into the centre where rows upon rows of books welcomed her.

"Hi there, can I help you?"

A lady behind the counter eyed her up and down. She was chic-looking, in a French sort of way, with a dark bob, pale skin and bright lipstick.

"I'm not sure," Anna said.

The woman viewed her quizzically over the red-rimmed reading glasses, before resuming her typing. Anna noted how slender her fingers were, like a pianist's. She was wearing a black jersey dress, a big arty necklace in silver decorating her neckline. How simple it could be to make an effort. Her own jeans and stretchy jumper could have done with some adornments. When had she stopped caring about her looks?

"Actually," she said. "I do know. I'm in need of some escapism but I don't know where to begin."

The woman looked up, a broad smile on her face.

"You've come to the right place then," she said and stretched out a hand. "I'm Iris."

8

Daniel

September 2015

Dan loved writing. His mother knew this but his brother would tease the shit out of him if he knew. At night, he would compose stories with the aid of a flashlight, hiding the unfinished work at the bottom of his box of comics. It felt childish but satisfying, the blue ink on lined paper, stories created out of nothing, the sense of accomplishment. *She* liked that he wrote. Lying on his back he stared up into the cracked ceiling, following the lines like it was a treasure map. *I'm really happy that you have expressed yourself in writing.* He had memorised Anna's words.

He turned on his side and picked up his phone. No messages, which was no surprise. This was bullshit, moving from town to town.

"I have to follow the work," Frida said, like she was some important businesswoman whose services were indispensable.

"You follow the fucking men, Fri-i-i-da," he said. He couldn't bring himself to call her Mother or even Mum.

"Shut your mouth."

His name had been Emil. Ten years her junior. Martin had beaten the crap out of him after catching them fucking on the couch and that had ended that. The police had picked both Martin and Emil up and Dan hadn't seen either of them since.

Dan missed him. Martin hadn't been the best brother but he had protected him. Now he had to fend for himself and that included keeping Frida in check.

"She needs a good beating from time to time, to keep her head clear," Martin would say. "Or she will be getting up to some dumb shit, start drinking again or smoking weed or worse…"

Dan understood, had seen her at her worst. Memories of no food, uninvited guests, the smell of smoke and vomit, no space sacred. He would sleep on the cold stairs of whatever apartment block they lived in at the time, his backpack filled with books, pens and paper. When the noise got too much, he would hide between the pages and create his own world.

At one point they had been dangerously close to being handed over to a foster family, but Martin had taken charge. At fifteen he had started going to the gym, which had made the junkies an easy win for him. Then he had locked Frida up in her bedroom after first beating her up. Once detoxed, she had tried to start over, moved them to a new town, and secured herself a job. She was scared of Martin but she kept looking for a new man and they followed whomever she had caught in her net, thinking he would bring money, stability, a home somewhere.

Martin's father was dead but Dan's own father had left. He had never even known Frida was pregnant. At least that was the story she told.

"We are the men of the house," Martin would say. "The

others are just temporary." He was right. It turned out none of them wanted to play daddy, they were only interested in getting Frida's knickers off. Early on, Dan had realised that men liked his mother. If she had stayed away from mind-altering substances, she would be truly beautiful. His late grandmother had given him a picture of her as a teenager, showing a striking girl with long blonde hair, a cheeky grin and a slender, tanned body. He kept the photo in his box as a reminder of her youthful innocence.

Emil was gone but Frida would meet someone else of course. That's why Dan had been forced to make a plan. He had formulated it with great ease and it was now as clear in his head as it was on his lined paper. While executing it, he made sure Frida behaved. She needed to stay off the booze and she needed to stay employed.

He hoped she would hook up with a man at the factory. That would mean they could stay for a while. It was a small town and there wasn't much to do, but it wasn't like the shithole they lived in before. Here, they rented a one-storey house with a miniature garden. The rooms were damp and draughty and freezing cold but that didn't bother him much. At least they didn't have to share walls with another family and the area was peaceful. He could walk through the woods, down to the sea, or cycle around in the countryside. Not many arseholes hassled him and the ones who had at school, he had already shut up. They stayed out of his way now.

It felt gratifying getting into fights. He wasn't likely to get kicked out of school for it but he knew he couldn't keep it up without social services getting on his case. He just needed to do it long enough to get Anna's attention.

9

Iris

September 2015

"I guess it's just the two of us, then?"

As the heads of the municipality and county librarians left, Lena Blom, chairman of the social welfare committee, made herself comfortable. Leaning against the reception counter in the middle of the library, she kicked her shoes off and let the silk Hermès scarf slide to the floor.

"I'm opening up to the public again after lunch," Iris said.

"I know."

Iris loaded the coffee cups on a tray and wiped the white, circular sixties' table clean, before heading to the kitchen. Lena quickly followed, her bare feet running up behind Iris, soft on the wooden floor.

"It was a good meeting," Lena said. "You like Britt, don't you?"

"I think she's someone who will deliver on her promises," Iris said. "That's what we need. We need to create a hunger or our local libraries will have to shut down."

"Not yours."

"You never know. Who knows who our anonymous beneficiary is? He or she might run out of money."

"I don't think so."

Iris didn't respond. Lena didn't understand the value of money. Born into a rich family, she lived an affluent lifestyle many would envy. Despite this, she was, however, dedicated to her government job and Iris did respect that.

"How much do you really like Britt?" Lena asked. "Just so I know."

The insecurity wasn't becoming and Iris chose not to reply. Instead, she unloaded the cups and washed them in the sink, handing them one by one to Lena.

Lena dried them, somewhat reluctantly.

"I thought…"

"Not today," Iris said. "It's… we work together."

"We have done for a long time."

Iris handed her the last cup and rinsed out the sink, watching the foam disappear into the minuscule plughole. She needed more time.

"That's exactly it," she said eventually, turning to Lena.

Lena awkwardly held the dishtowel between her hands, as if she might drop it. She looked adorable and out of place, her sparkly jewellery a sharp contrast to the old kitchen décor. Iris found herself losing her thread.

"We will just…" she started, but before she could finish, Lena's mouth was on hers and Iris gave in. She grabbed Lena's waist and pushed her up against the wall, expertly unbuttoning her trousers. Her skilful hand slipped inside Lena's knickers with ease, reaching a rich wetness. Her fingers circulated and played. Lena's moans echoed into the kitchen, spurring her on and Iris quickened her movement, going faster and faster until her fingers almost cramped. They met in a stormy kiss; Lena's hand travelled up Iris's dress, then inside her tights. Lace stretched, the right buttons were pressed; their breathing heightened, their bodies pushed together, the friction intensifying. Groans exploded off their lips as they climaxed. Lena leaned into Iris, panting. Satisfied, Iris held on tight, wrapping her arms around Lena. Just for a moment. Then a brief kiss followed by disentanglement.

Iris felt that although she deeply cared about Lena, their meetings had become a rehearsed routine, it was too familiar. This needed to be the last time, Iris thought. The relationship needed to go back to being a professional one, or perhaps even a friendship if possible.

"Wow," Lena said.

She buttoned up her trousers, grinning.

"I have to go back to work," Iris said.

"I know." Lena combed her hair and checked her make-up in the kitchen mirror. "By the way, I went to your husband's exhibition last weekend."

Iris felt herself tense. "Really?"

Pride mixed with dread; she was immensely proud of him but she wanted him as far away from her colleagues as possible.

"The paintings were extremely dark," Lena continued. "Mysterious."

"I'll pass on the message," Iris said and opened the back door.

"See you next week."

Lena skipped down the steps like an adolescent girl and then she was gone.

*

Iris unlocked the main door, noticing a slight drizzle, which made the newly laid asphalt in the parking lot glisten. One of her regular visitors, Tore, had already pulled up. She waited for him by the door as his eighty-year-old body and accompanying umbrella shuffled up the stairs.

"It's cold," he said, sneezing.

"It's a glorious day though," Iris said.

From the top of the stairs, she could just about see the ocean. It was chilly and windy but fresh, the waves foaming, the seagulls squawking.

"Just come to read the newspaper," Tore said, reaching her.

"You're always welcome here."

While Tore settled in, Iris relaxed back into her day. This was her library, her domain. She breathed in the smell of paper and started to push the trolley down an aisle, returning books to their rightful places.

Then two hands, hugging her from behind. She was about to turn around when she spotted the familiar pair of Converse on the floor. "Excuse me…" said the voice, hands sliding up her stomach, cupping her weightless breasts. She closed her eyes, enjoying the touch for just a moment. "…I'm looking for my wife."

Rolf pressed himself against her back, nibbling her ear, an erection against her spine. Back in the day, she would have giggled.

"I want to fuck you," he hissed into her ear.

"Not here," she said, pulling away.

"Come on, Iris. Where's your sense of adventure?"

When she didn't respond, he released her.

"So…" he said grumpily. "How was your meeting?"

"It was fine, thank you." She turned to face him. "What are you doing here?"

"I wanted to see you."

"I thought you disliked this non-creative environment. I believe you called it 'conventional and uninspiring' the last time you were here." It had upset her and she wanted to get him back. This was her home away from home.

"Iris…"

"Perhaps you don't like it because it's not displaying your art?"

"Anyway…" He stroked her hair. "Who was that woman I just saw leaving?"

He had seen Lena even though she had left through the back door? Was he spying on her?

"Lena," she said. "She's part of the council meetings."

"Right. She's hot. Available?"

"No."

"That doesn't normally stop you," he said, stroking her cheek.

She gave him a disapproving look. "Rolf, don't."

"Right, you don't talk about it anymore, I remember."

He scratched the Jimi Hendrix moustache, sulking, and she pulled his ponytail to lighten the mood, just like she would have in the old days.

"Get out of here," she said playfully. "I've got a group of second graders coming any minute."

"Oh, baby." He kissed her intensely; his relentless desire for her was still arousing. "If only people could see you like this… this wild thing. Everyone thinks you're so fucking polished."

She laughed.

"Let's not tell anyone."

"So this Lena…?"

"She's a colleague. You're not getting jealous with old age, are you?"

He winked at her. "Just making sure everyone appreciates you as much as I do."

She picked up a book and demonstratively placed it on a shelf. *I have a job to do.*

"Okay, I will leave you to it," he said. "I'm sure you have your reasons."

The mood changed as he backed away. He was upset about being rejected, but she knew he wouldn't want to fight. No matter how much he loved starting debates in the media, he despised conflict with her.

"I should mind my own business," he muttered.

"You should."

She glanced at him as he left, the flamboyant shirt disappearing around the corner, acknowledging that she still loved the man she had married over twenty years ago. Her mother hadn't been quite so thrilled at the time.

"I give you one year," she had said. "He's too elusive."

It gave Iris immense pleasure to prove her mother wrong. At the time, however, she had felt disappointed and upset, especially since her mother had been a rebel herself. Brought up in Ireland, she had run off with a Swedish sailor at a young age and her family had never forgiven her.

Iris hadn't intended to live an alternative life with Rolf. It was just that with Rolf, you had to take it or leave it. And so she had agreed to take it.

10

Erik

March 2016

An agonising week and a half has gone past without Anna's condition changing. She's not better but she's also not worse; Erik is supposed to seek comfort in this. Only the colour on her face has changed, from a bruised purple to a yellowy green.

She's in the same ward, the same room, the same bed. Everything is unchanged, even the depressing view of the two-storey parking garage, the dreary cement cold and uninviting. Every time he looks outside, it's as if the world is grey, even the clouds look like they're mocking him with their greyness.

Anna also remains in the same position. Don't they move her?

Her still frame unnerves him. If only she could wake up and argue with him. Anything but this silence.

"She looks kind of weird, Daddy. When is she going to wake up?"

The doctors keep saying "if" but the boys stick to "when".

It worries him, because no one knows for sure. Despite this, he tries to remain optimistic in front of the boys.

"Her body just needs to heal, buddy."

Sebastian kisses her cheek and tells her to please get better soon.

"We need you at home," he whispers in his mum's ear.

How will Sebastian cope if Anna doesn't make it? Lukas, on the other hand, is handling it better. He seems more oblivious, driving a car down Anna's leg, pretending it's a road, her knee a mountain. At least until his grandmother tells him to stop. Mum's big cuddly arms can be deceiving, her wagging finger turning her into a total killjoy. Give Lukas a break, he wants to say, but he doesn't. He is too tired to argue. Being in the hospital with the children is exhausting.

*

When they arrive back home, the white postbox with daintily painted flowers on it is filled with "get well soon" cards from people in the town, mainly parents, students and colleagues.

"People prefer to send a card than to come over," he comments.

While he thinks people are cowards for hiding behind their precious wooden doors, he's secretly happy. If someone did visit, he wouldn't know what to say. Even the short conversation with the neighbour was awkward.

"Well, maybe they don't know how to express themselves," Mum says. "That's understandable after all. At least a card is better than nothing, it shows they care."

He shrugs. "Sure."

The boys ask to watch TV and Mum lets them without asking his opinion. It's okay, he doesn't mind too much. He's used to Anna calling the shots and making up the rules.

Mum has more or less moved in and handles Sebastian and Lukas. Out of the hospital, the boys and Mum are good at sticking with the program of "business as usual". The counsellor has suggested this approach. Erik tries to adopt it himself but he feels a constant unease, an unreachable scratch under his skin. The continuity that surrounds him helps though. The day care hours remain the same, everybody must treat the boys as they did before, and at home... well, Erik probably hugs them more than normal.

He does that now, even though they are heavily invested in Tom chasing Jerry. Competing with the cat versus mouse race, Erik kneels down and holds Lukas. "I'm here for you," he says.

"Mm," Lukas responds, his eyes on the screen.

Erik inhales the scent of his son, a mixture of washing powder and dried ketchup. Then he lets him go. Time to switch. The never-ending battle with twins: giving the children the exact same amount of attention.

"Come here, Sebastian," he says.

Sebastian hugs him hard, burrowing his head into Erik's chest. His hair smells of baby shampoo. Anna hasn't wanted to upgrade to adult hair products yet.

This is my life, he thinks. *These children. I am never letting them go.*

But in that moment, he has to, because Lukas is laughing so hard that Sebastian withdraws from Erik's embrace to see what's so funny. It's comforting to see that they're still able to be carefree children.

Erik leaves them to it and joins Mum in the kitchen. She's busy making coffee.

"I can't compete with cartoons," he complains.

"They'll grow out of it," she says, amused.

Outside the window, a few boys are making their way home from ice hockey training, their sticks slung over their shoulders as they cycle down the road. It looks unsafe but also very normal. It's as if nothing has changed out there. The world continues as if Anna wasn't attacked.

In that moment, Erik decides not to go back to the hospital. The band has a gig this evening. He hasn't told Mum and the guys aren't exactly counting on him but maybe he could go? Be normal for one night.

Mum puts two cups of coffee on a tray together with a plate of rye bread covered in soft prawn cheese. His favourite. Mum knows how to look after him. She carries the tray into the living room where they both slump into a Poäng armchair each, rocking back and forth a couple of times. They're both feeling drained.

The police interviewed Mum today. Apparently she told them she couldn't think of anyone who would want to harm someone as "truly wonderful" as Anna.

"It won't be easy for the police," Erik agrees. "Everyone loves her."

"I know," Mum says gravely. "I really don't understand what could have happened. How could someone like Anna be attacked? I mean... I don't know. I just..."

"You don't have to understand everything," he says.

"But it's such a small town," she continues. "This isn't Malmö or Stockholm. Surely everybody knows everything about everybody? I mean, someone must know who did this. And why. She's so caring, Erik. It doesn't make any sense."

"I know." But he doesn't know about everybody knowing everything.

He puts the bread in his mouth, chews and looks out over the garden. The hedge bordering onto the road and the neighbours' plots needs cutting. Normally Anna would remind him of this.

"This is Mörna," Mum says. "Only what… ten thousand people live here?"

"It's a sleepy town," Erik agrees. "But we're not particularly friendly with anyone. Maybe because of Anna's job we've been quite private."

He's always hated the weekend trips to the supermarket, when they would have to stop every five minutes, bumping into parents who would want to discuss their child's progress. Anna didn't mind and would happily chat while he disappeared down an aisle. Even though he also worked locally, few people seemed to recognise the guy who painted their house.

"The police will find the person who did this," Mum says confidently. "They have to."

"Maybe it was just a random act, a criminal travelling through town who happened to see her alone?"

Have the police thought of that possibility?

"I'm sure they are looking into it, Erik. You need to let them get on with their job."

Linda Johansson hasn't revealed any possible results related to the note he provided them with. There's a need for "confidentiality during the preliminary investigation" apparently but she "thanks him for his cooperation". Fucking fantastic. So he must just sit here and do what exactly? He can't stand it.

"Mum, tonight…"

"You're going to the hospital?"

He drinks up his coffee and wipes his mouth on a flower-clad napkin.

"I thought maybe I would hang out with Rob... I feel like I'm going nuts."

Mum raises her eyebrows and he can tell what she's thinking.

"Sure, whatever," she says and gets up to do the dishes, her back to him.

"I mean, I think it would be good to..."

"Fine."

She doesn't sound "fine" and so he doesn't go. He doesn't want to deal with Mum's disapproval. Not now. Until he's found a new routine, he needs her. Should he drive back to the hospital? The thought of Anna being there alone makes him feel guilty, and what if she wakes up and he's not there? It's unsettling. But at night, when the ward is eerily quiet and only the disheartening sound of machines can be heard, it scares him, the tense white walls and the stretched over-washed linen adding to the intimidation. Everything around Anna has been set up to look perfect, masking her frailty.

When the boys are bathed and in bed, he stays in his room and flicks through the TV channels. He ends up watching an old war movie, *Where Eagles Dare*. Anna used to like it, especially Clint Eastwood's performance. She would fall asleep of course; she rarely made it through an entire film. He imagines Anna next to him, her head resting on the pillow, gently snoring. But all he can see is her swollen eye, the cut lip, the cheeks covered in a gradient of yellow and green.

He turns to face the wall and goes to sleep.

*

In the morning, while Mum and the boys go about "business as usual", he drives to the hospital. There, he sits in Anna's room, on a stiff wooden chair, watching his wife. He would feel better if he could do something, help in any way. Everyone treads so damn carefully around him. They feed him coffee regularly but then they go about their day while he simply sits there, his eyes darting from Anna, to the muted TV, to the window. Green city buses and yellow long-distance buses pick people up and drop them off. That's the most exciting event there is. Cars drive past too. Mostly Volvos. Sometimes he counts them.

Mum pops in to see him, which breaks the monotony. She has a habit of disturbing the staff however, asking them a million questions about the respirator, Anna's position in the bed, her brain activity, the bruising, her ribs – are they healing? – and her hair. Is someone washing her hair? Mum has also inquired about the security measures at the hospital.

"What if her attacker comes back to finish the job?"

"We're taking it seriously," they were told, but there's no guard outside Anna's room.

"Maybe that only happens in the movies?" he tells Mum.

When Mum leaves, the nurses sigh with relief, and so does Erik but he does have a few questions of his own.

He asks the nurse: "What's the security really like here?"

"People can't just come and go," she says. "We have tight controls."

That sounds true. Thinking about his own visits, he realises that no one can enter the ward without buzzing the door first. A nurse needs to tick your name of a list before he or she can let you in.

"What if someone asks for her, someone who isn't on the approved list?"

"That's unlikely to happen. No one should know where exactly she is," the nurse says. "She's been registered as an anonymous patient." She smiles faintly. "Just like a famous person would be."

"Right," he says. Comparing his wife to a celebrity doesn't feel particularly appropriate. Still, he's content. He's asked and has received an answer. That's responsible.

Perhaps as a result of Mum's constant nagging, the nurse is washing Anna today, revealing the bruises on her body. It's the first time he witnesses these.

"I'm sorry," she says, looking up at him. "Maybe you should wait outside."

"It's okay, I just…" He can't finish the sentence.

He's thinking: it's just that I haven't seen her naked in so long. The skin is so white, creating a sharp contrast with the vast, blood-filled patches where she was beaten. He wants to turn away but he can't. He forces himself to look, to follow the lines of the veins as they merge with the discolorations. His eyes linger by the scar from where the twins were born. Under her navel, close to the dark pubic hair. He closes his eyes, remembers the birth. The failed epidural, Anna's discomfort at the doctor's tugging hands. Her pain but then also their joy. Two healthy boys. He loves his sons.

He opens his eyes and watches the nurse's caring hand sweep up and down Anna's legs with a sponge, the flesh melting into the mattress.

"Can she… feel anything?" he asks. "I don't want her to feel any pain."

"I'm very gentle," the nurse assures him.

Gentle. He was a gentle lover. Anna appreciated that; it made her feel safe and adventurous. She often made him blush. Not that he would ever admit it, not even to Rob, but he was pretty straight-laced. Anna, however, wanted to try everything "at least once". It made them grow closer and stronger, and when she returned to Sweden from her week's holiday in Spain, he quit his job and followed her. He told her his contract was up even though it wasn't. He was in fact giving up the opportunity to join a local band. He just couldn't let her get away.

After the C-section, they waited two months to have sex, as per the doctor's recommendation. Then another month and yet another. Anna wanted to lose the weight first. She was worried it was going to hurt and she didn't want to risk another pregnancy, yet she no longer favoured birth control. Abstinence seemed to be her new preference.

"You would be a really good nun," he said once, a joke she didn't appreciate.

Perhaps he didn't try hard enough or he didn't compliment her enough. All he knows is that the few times they did have sex, she didn't let go as fully as the girl he married. He hasn't been able to discuss it with anyone.

The nurse moves up to wash Anna's chest. *She has amazing breasts.* It's wrong. He can't stare. Sitting quietly, he glares at the walls instead. He doesn't feel like getting up, just wants to sit here, in the same room as his naked wife. Him and his thoughts, the splashing of sponge in water, sponge on skin, sponge back in the water, soothing him.

"I love her," he says to the room.

"Of course you do," the nurse says. "I'm really sorry about what happened."

He doesn't want to think about it. Instead he concentrates on the landscape someone has carelessly framed and stuck on one of the walls. It's completely uninspiring. Not a person in sight. Just grass and water, a cloudy sky. He squints, looking for life. A bird even? But no. The painter obviously had a bad day. Just like he is right now.

When the nurse finally leaves, the overpowering respirator takes over the room again. The sound of the machine gets on his nerves. He stands up and paces around the room, the plain décor not stimulating in the least.

Everyone tells him he must be patient, that he must wait for a sign of improvement. They don't understand shit. Erik's eyes rest on Anna's motionless face.

"Are you in there?" he says, his voice breaking. "Can you hear me?"

It's torture. He needs to talk to someone who won't just give him the standard "hopefully she will wake up soon". He picks up the phone to call Rob, but notices he has a missed call from Tina. He immediately phones her back. Maybe she has more information?

She answers on the second ring. "They spoke to Pernilla Arvidsson," she says so quickly the words fall on top of each other and he struggles to understand. Pernilla? "She says you're together."

"Together?" He thinks for a second. "I only see her when I drop the children at day care."

"According to her it extends to outside of day care."

"I'm sure we see each other at the supermarket from time to time."

"She says it's more than that."

"It's not." What the hell?

It was only the one time, but he's not keen to tell Tina or anyone else about it.

Rob had begged him to go out and he had agreed, a boys' night was probably not such a bad idea. Except it had been. They had drunk far too much and when he went to the bathroom to piss, Pernilla had been in line to the ladies.

"Hey there." Blue eyes, sparkling along with her smile. "Fancy seeing you here."

"Hi."

It felt good. To be looked at that way.

"Do you want to have a drink?" she asked.

"Sure, I just…" he pointed to the bathroom.

She smiled and giggled. "Me too."

They reunited in the bar. He looked for Rob but couldn't find him. Knowing him, he had probably left with someone already. Another night, another girl, he laughed. The joke was getting old. He knew it. Erik knew it too but sometimes he felt jealous. Of the attention Rob got, the variety, the excitement of flirting and sealing the deal.

"So what's the occasion?" she asked.

"Boys' night out."

"You're such a good dad," she said and punched him gently on the arm.

She was drunk, her words slightly slurred.

"Thanks. I guess."

"So sweet."

They spoke about the children, about the town, the weather. Anything really. Soon the eyelids that had batted at him seductively, started to move at a slower pace, as if she was about to close them altogether and fall asleep.

"Are you okay?" he asked.

"I'm tired. I want to go home."

"Where are your friends? Should I get them for you?"

"They've gone home," she said, now leaning her nose on his shoulder. He felt her go heavy, her head sinking into his arm, her body closing in, pressing against his chest.

"Don't fall asleep!" he said. "I'll put you in a taxi."

"I can't afford that," she mumbled.

"I'll pay for it."

He couldn't just leave her. After hailing a taxi and placing her in the backseat, she pulled him in.

"Please stay, I think I'm going to be sick."

The taxi driver refused to drive. "Get out, I don't want puke in my cab."

"Are you sure your friends aren't still around?" Erik asked desperately. If he took her out of the taxi, where would he leave her?

She didn't reply; she was leaning against the headrest, fast asleep. He needed to get her home.

"Look," he said to the taxi driver. "Please just get her home. She hasn't had that much to drink," he lied. "She's just tired. Been working a lot."

The driver didn't look convinced but he too needed to get her out of the car and agreed to drive if Erik joined them. Luckily, he had managed to get her address before she started snoring.

When they arrived at her apartment block, he had to pay the taxi driver and get out to assist her. She could barely get the key in the lock. He could have asked the driver to wait. He could have... but he didn't.

Tina clears her throat, alerting him to the present.

"Pernilla says that you are," she tells him.

He hates the excitement in her voice and wants to tell her to fuck off. But right now, she is the only link he has to the latest news and he needs to maintain it. It's what's keeping him sane.

"She's mistaken," he says. "I mean, we get on really well and we always talk when we see each other but that's it...

I'm married," he adds even though he realises that isn't a foolproof defence.

"Okay," she says.

Okay? That's it?

"Not sure where she got that idea then," Tina says and he imagines her twining her hair, biting it between pink lips, enjoying pushing him into the corner just a little bit further. Then he remembers Rob's comment about her bad breath and that makes it easier: now she's a frog barfing down the phone and he almost laughs. Almost.

"Look," he says, thinking hard. "We've got a good rapport. We talk when I'm picking the children up. Have I bumped into her outside of day care? I'm sure I have."

Why does Pernilla have to complicate matters? He hasn't seen her since Anna was hospitalised. Mum is like a taxi driver, taking the children back and forth. While he sits with Anna, Mum does the shopping, cleaning, washing, ironing and cooking. Sooner or later, Dad will need her back of course.

"They might want to question you again."

"What? Why?"

If you were seeing someone else, you could have a motive for hurting her. Is that what they're thinking? He tries not to panic.

"Someone is going to call you," she says.

"Wait, please… Tina." She can't hang up just yet. "What about the note I gave Linda Johansson? Do you know if it's led to anything?"

"Eh, hang on." It sounds as if she's ruffling through some papers.

"No, sorry. I don't know."

"Oh…" That's disappointing.

"Well, it's not your fault. Thank you."

As soon as he puts the phone down it buzzes, alerting him to a new message. Pernilla's name appears and two perfectly shaped, round breasts fill his screen. What on earth is she doing? He doesn't respond.

He sits down and moves his chair closer to Anna's bed. Her translucent skin is fresh from the sponge bath, which makes her look somewhat thinner, paler, camouflaged in the sheets. He leans forward and whispers in her ear:

"I'm sorry."

11

Anna

September 2015

Spit was hanging from the ceiling in Anna's classroom. The girls were pretending to vomit while the boys broke out laughing. Daniel just looked at her, his light-brown eyes defiant and intense.

"Daniel, please can you step outside with me?"

Anna detected a faint smile, which annoyed her. This wasn't meant to be a reward. She just couldn't deal with him in front of the others, ignoring her every request. He stood up and she was glad that at least he was doing as he was told. The boys whistled as he made his way to the door, papers went flying. Chaos was breaking out in her orderly environment. It had to stop.

"The rest of you read from page twenty-five. If you don't settle down, you will all get detention." At least it worked with the majority of the class.

As she followed Daniel out of the classroom, she thought of his latest letter, which could be likened more to a note, only containing one line: *I need a mum, okay?* No threats.

And her heart did ache for him. At the same time, she wasn't sure if she could trust it. Was it just a game for him? It was also the way he chose to communicate: she still wasn't sure how he managed to get the letters into the teachers' lounge.

In the corridor, she pushed her hair back, folded her arms and applied her serious voice.

"This can't go on, Daniel," she said. "If you don't stop disrupting my lessons I will request that you are moved to another class."

This wasn't as easy as it sounded but hopefully he wouldn't know about school procedures. She wasn't sure how his last school had operated and despite numerous attempts, hadn't been able to speak to a former teacher.

"You can't do that," he said.

"I can," she said. "The principal trusts my judgement and if I suggest you're better off in another class, he will consider it."

Now he didn't look so sure anymore. He was biting his lip, shuffling his feet from side to side, hands deep in his pockets.

She had spoken to the principal, not about moving Daniel to another class but about additional support.

"I don't understand," Johan had said while vigorously looking through a pile of papers. "What is the issue exactly?"

"You know Daniel is the reason for the fire alarms going off and all the fights?"

Johan had nodded, his greasy hair and penguin-decorated tie making it difficult for her to take him seriously. He kept searching for something and his eyes lit up as he found it. With a piece of paper in his hand, he quickly glanced up at Anna – as if to check whether she was still there – and said: "Anna, you're the best person to deal with a boy like that."

He might as well have added: "there, there, off you go now."

Johan had only been in the position for a year and during that time he hadn't managed to gain the teachers' confidence. His focus seemed to be on his bosses at the council office. MÖRNA SCHOOL SAVES MONEY UNDER NEW LEADERSHIP read the headline in the local paper, except nowhere did the article mention that new books hadn't been ordered, that the courtyard was in desperate need of repair, or that staff training was on the backburner. Anna had kept an open mind, not wanting to judge too soon, but she felt her patience weaken.

"Daniel needs help," she had explained. *I need help dealing with him.*

"Speak to the parents."

The oblivious look on Johan's face, his hands up in the air. She had stood up and excused herself, realising that she would have to sort this out on her own.

Now standing in the corridor, Daniel whisked his growing fringe out of his eyes. In the fluorescent light, the reflection of emerging stubble was just about visible on his upper lip. It made him look older.

"You know what I want," he said. "And if I get what I want, you get what you want."

"I don't really understand. You want a mum? You already have one."

"She doesn't give a shit about me or my brother. She's a total slacker. Martin was arrested last week and she did nothing about it."

"Maybe she's giving him tough love?" she suggested.

You're way out on a limb, Kent would say. *Keep it real, Anna. The students respond to that.*

"Okay, so what do you want? You want to talk to me?"

He hesitated.

"I want to live in your house," he said.

The words didn't sound like a naïve boy's wishful thinking. She braced herself. "Daniel, it doesn't work like that."

"I know you like me," he said.

"I think…" she started, sighing. What could she possibly say?

"Don't," he said then, his eyes narrowing. "Don't give me sympathy, that's not what I want."

"We can't always have what we want."

She took a deep breath. There had to be a solution, a middle ground.

"Let's talk to your mum, together? In the meantime, please can you wipe off the ceiling, then sit down and listen?"

A compromise.

He shook his shoulders, either he couldn't care less, or he was agreeing. Then he nodded and headed back towards the classroom. Hopefully his mum would profess her undying love for her son. Hopefully. If not, she would talk to Kent and ask his advice.

*

At the end of the school day, she sat in the teachers' lounge with a couple of other teachers. They all had their heads down, working away. Kent had left early and she wished there was someone she could call, just to talk. These days, it felt like phone calls with old friends had to be scheduled. When they were younger, her sister Helen would phone her regularly with various issues, but she wasn't someone Anna in turn could call for support. Now they hardly ever spoke; Helen was wrapped up in her new family.

Erik had a close family. That had added to the attraction when they first met. He seemed so secure and she was sure it was as a result of all the love he had been surrounded by growing up. Her own parents had been strict and controlling, at least in some ways. If she started eating before everyone was served, forgot to put something back in its place, or didn't say "thank you", then she would be shouted at, but if she was out late with her friends, no one seemed to miss her. Helen had rebelled as a teenager but Anna had kept her head down and counted the days until she could leave.

She wished that her family had been closer. Although she had read that once you passed the age of thirty-five you could no longer blame your parents for the mistakes that you made. She had two years to go.

She wondered about Daniel's family. Did he know his father? What little she had found out had revealed that he lived with his mother, Frida, and his brother, Martin. There were no notes about the father. It was a sad situation and she just knew she couldn't turn her back on him. Too many children were left disappointed by adults in their lives, whether it was parents, teachers or government officials, and they tended to end up in a downward spiral of criminality. Daniel's brother was a perfect example of that and she didn't want Daniel to follow in his footsteps. Although he obviously could not move in with her. She felt relieved to have found a line that could not be crossed.

She left work early to spend the rest of the afternoon with Sebastian and Lukas. Erik was working and she decided to bake something with the boys. They loved getting messy in the kitchen and she tolerated that better than Erik, even though he wasn't exactly a neat freak.

"We had muffins at day care today," Sebastian told her.

"Really? I didn't think parents were allowed to bring cake?"

She was sure a health-consciousness note had been sent out proclaiming that only fruit would be served at children's birthdays.

"Pernilla brought it."

"Oh."

The young day care teacher with the long eyelashes. Anna had only met her a few times but it was as if the teacher was assessing her every time, eyeing her from top to toe.

"Is she nice?" she asked.

Lukas shrugged his shoulders. "I like her," he said.

"Good, that's the most important thing," she said.

Twenty-four chocolate muffins later she made spaghetti Bolognese and then rounded the children's evening off with a massive apple-flavoured bubble bath. Sebastian and Lukas put white foam on their chins, pretending to be Santas, singing Christmas songs even though it was only September. Anna joined in, both in the singing and the Santa look-alike competition.

"Mine is better."

"No, mine is."

"No," Anna said. "I believe mine is best."

There were bubbles everywhere, even on the ceiling, but it wasn't a big deal. It could easily be washed off. Listening to the boys' laughter was more important.

Being with her children, Anna could think of nothing else. Not work, not Erik, not even the latest book she had devoured, *Affinity*, which had been recommended by the librarian. Time with Sebastian and Lukas was like a soothing tonic much appreciated after a long day at work.

When the children were in bed, she went downstairs and

waited for Erik. He was late even though he had promised to be home in time for her to go out. She had planned to go to the library, which was open late that evening. He didn't answer his phone so she called Rob.

"Is Erik there?" she asked.

"Sure, do you want to talk to him?"

Bingo.

"Yes, please."

"Anna?" Erik's voice. She said nothing. Would he figure it out by himself?

"Oh, sorry," he said and she felt relief. That meant she wouldn't have to sound like a nagging wife. "I completely forgot. You had something on?"

"That's right."

"On my way."

"Thanks."

While she waited for him, she opened her wardrobe to get changed. Did she own anything that didn't scream "teacher"? Perhaps something that would flatter her figure? Erik always used to compliment her breasts and so she picked out a black V-neck jumper and added a pair of dark grey figure-hugging trousers. It didn't look too shabby. She stood in front of the mirror, deciding which necklace to use. The white moonstone pendant or the silver Bismarck chain? She opted for the moonstone. What about shoes? She mainly wore trainers, boots or ballet flats. There were only a few heels in her wardrobe since she felt awkward increasing her height. She opted for a pair of leather boots with a low heel and sprayed Calvin Klein One on her wrists.

"Fancy."

Erik stood in the bedroom door, his eyes taking her in. He was dressed in loose hanging, low-cut jeans and a dark green hoody, a classic staple Erik outfit that most likely consisted of famous brands. When they first started dating, she found his style to be cool and stylish. At that time he had a wide collection of trainers as well. It was casual but fashionable. She walked across to him and planted her lips on his. He tasted of beer.

"So where are you going, looking so dressed up?" he said, grabbing her waist.

"Work do," she said.

He wouldn't be talking to her colleagues anyway and he didn't need to know about Hågarp's library; he wouldn't appreciate that she yearned to go back for more books. Books were apparently boring, unlike movies.

"You smell so good," Erik said, burying his nose in her hair.

He kissed her ear, her cheeks, her neck; his hands slid down over her curves and she tensed.

"Not now, Erik," she said but he didn't stop and so she stretched her hand out and flicked the lights off.

She tried to think about the tanned, muscular bartender, lovemaking under a whirring fan, his laughter, their bodies sticky between warm sheets; flamenco music from a nearby bar, tourists laughing, the slight breeze from the open window.

His tongue pushed into her mouth and the bitter taste of alcohol made the visualisation more difficult.

She took a step back. Her body wasn't able to cooperate.

"Another time," she said. "Please."

She switched the lights back on.

"There never is another time." He sighed. "I have needs, okay?"

"So do I," she said.

They stood quietly for a while, their bodies no longer touching.

"Can we just cuddle?" she asked.

She could sense his annoyance but it was a decent compromise.

"I'm not..." he started. She waited and eventually he succumbed, sounding defeated: "Sure, why not?"

She would have to visit the library another time. Peace at home came first. She didn't take her boots off, just laid down on her side of the bed. Erik did the same and then they moved closer to each other, eventually embracing. Erik had a way of making her feel protected, the way he held his arm around her. Anna focused on the closeness, the warmth, the feeling of being loved; evoking that tingling feeling you felt on a date.

In the dark, he could be anyone. But it scared her that she wished just that: for him to be anyone but Erik. If only there was someone she could confide in.

12

Iris

September 2015

The sun was up, yet cold winds were banging on the library windows. Iris was unpacking her latest book delivery – a source of joy every time – when the phone rang.

"Hi Mum, it's me."

"Karin?"

She was about to say "you don't usually call me at work" but her daughter started crying before she got the chance.

"What's wrong?" she asked.

Since her daughter had started university she only ever cried if she had failed an exam but Iris suspected it could also be boyfriend trouble. Iris pushed the new book delivery to the side and sat down while Karin blew her nose on the other end of the line.

"I don't know, maybe I shouldn't say it," Karin said.

Iris waited patiently, wondering why Karin hadn't called her father. He was normally the one she turned to. Rolf and Karin had always been close, often leaving Iris feeling like a distant aunt. She wasn't bitter about it but she tried to keep an open door for her daughter, their only child. Karin continued to cry and Iris didn't want to frighten her away by being pushy. She absentmindedly picked up a book, attracted by the dramatic cover, a red title stretched across it like a colourful tattoo, and started reading the blurb.

"Mum…"

She could tell that Karin was mustering up courage to tell her something, and she recognised that she needed to be more receptive.

"I'm listening."

She loved Karin and wished that she could tell her that more often. Her own parents had never told her they loved her. Not once. She sometimes caught herself wondering why they hadn't. Rolf's theory was that their own parents hadn't said those magic words, that they were simply repeating the pattern. It made sense but Iris was intent on breaking that trend.

"I spoke to Granddad," her daughter said.

She could tell where this was going. Her father had been in a home for a few years now and was growing increasingly bitter.

"He said that you're a whore," Karin said. "He said it over and over again. I couldn't stand it."

A whore? Surely her father didn't know about her lifestyle? Not that it made her a whore but in her father's old-fashioned world perhaps it did. She and Rolf had always been discreet, even more so after Karin was born.

"He's… don't listen to him," Iris tried. "His dementia is getting worse, you know that."

Karin started crying again.

"He said that you and Dad don't take your marriage vows seriously. What does that even mean?"

Iris sank back into her chair. So he knew.

"Is it true?" Karin asked, her voice weak.

Iris tried to construct a sensible sentence. They were silent for a while, the seriousness of the revelation sinking in. If Karin were to ask Rolf, she knew he would tell her the truth.

"It's not as simple as that," she said. "We just don't believe in owning each other."

"So, what, you have *affairs*?" The last word was spoken with such distaste. Iris chose to ignore Karin's bitter tone. She had to remind herself that her daughter was only nineteen. An adult by law but still a child in her eyes; not old enough to judge her own mother.

It was hard to admit, but: "Yes, that sometimes happens. I can't speak for your dad but not very often for me."

"Mum…" Karin said. "It's like… it's like I don't know you."

Karin sounded sad rather than accusing and Iris felt compassion for her daughter.

"Are you seeing someone at the moment?" Karin asked.

Iris squirmed in her seat, glad that she hadn't opened for the day.

"No," she said eventually.

She was going to end it with Lena anyway so it wasn't exactly a lie. Getting involved with someone so intricately linked to her work had been a mistake.

"No more secrets," Karin said. "Please."

"Of course," Iris said, feeling like the child. "Those days are sort of over anyway. It was more… when we were younger."

She had still been the model mother, attending parent evenings and football games, taught her daughter how to cook and had spent countless hours supervising her driving. There were just certain compromises involved in her marriage.

Just then, the alarm on her phone went off. It was ten o'clock, time to open for the day.

"I love you but I'm sorry, I have to go," she told Karin. "Why don't you call your dad and speak to him about it? Really though, it's no big deal. We were young and free and now we're getting older and more... sensible."

She sighed when she put the phone down. They had spoken about this, her and Rolf.

"What if Karin finds out?" she had said.

"Then we explain to her that it's fair to let someone be who they are."

"Shouldn't we promote monogamy to our daughter?"

"Why?"

He had a point. It wasn't for everyone. She hadn't even realised she would consider a no-strings-attached marriage until Rolf proposed it. She had been offended at first (was she not good enough in bed?) but when he had explained that he loved only her, that no one could ever replace her, she had opened up. They had agreed on set rules and she had found it to be liberating. At least at first.

Now, with Karin knowing, those memories became tainted. It felt like being exposed while masturbating. For the first time, her choices didn't make her feel quite so open-minded and progressive.

She continued to unpack her new books, pushing the phone call with Karin to the back of her mind. She would discuss it with Rolf later and they would solve it together.

Iris concentrated on reading each blurb even though she had carefully handpicked the newly purchased books herself.

These were her babies, her trusted companions. Once she received a new order, she would read all the books to be able to recommend every one of them.

The first title that took her fancy had been chosen by none other than Lena. It had been a bit of an inside joke, but she had still ordered it. *Delta of Venus* by the avant-garde writer Anaïs Nin was not a recent release but it was an erotic classic. Lena could wait for it. This was the perfect book for Iris to get past her daughter's judgement and to re-engage with her true, sexual self. She slipped it into her bag.

The bell above the door sounded, notifying her of a new visitor. She looked up and saw a curvaceous woman with long dark hair walk towards her. She recognised her from the other day. Already? She smiled to herself. She remembered her name. Anna.

13

Anna

September 2015

It was Saturday morning, the sun had broken through the grey clouds, and Anna had successfully built the tallest Lego tower with Sebastian and Lukas.

"It's as tall as me, Mummy," Sebastian announced proudly, standing next to it.

Lukas quickly got to his feet.

"Me too!"

Erik appeared, looking equally excited, although it wasn't related to the multi-coloured creation on the floor.

"We have a gig," he said. "It's small, but it's in a bar in the city, so it's good. Really good."

"Good for you," she said.

His childish excitement was almost contagious. She wanted to get up and hug him the way she used to, assure him that it was truly amazing, but that closeness seemed to be gone, and she held back.

"I know you've got something on this morning," he said, his voice soft. "I'll rehearse with Rob later."

"Yes, thanks. I'm going to the library."

He scrunched his face up, in that characteristically annoyed way.

"Not to work," she added quickly. "For myself. I just finished a really good book and need a new one." He still looked doubtful so she tried to open up: "I miss reading for pleasure as opposed to what is in line with the curriculum. I guess you could say that I have rekindled an old passion."

He looked like he was going to refer to another old passion they should rekindle. Thankfully he knew not to say anything in front of the boys, who were now busy destroying their tower, Lego pieces flying across the room.

"I wonder who they get their destructive behaviour from," Erik said and left the room.

She detested his way of dropping a grenade and then leaving. Why was she always to blame? He gave her no credit for anything. Who did all the cleaning, the washing, the ironing? She was the mother of their children, the breadwinner and also his maid! If anyone was destroying it all, it wasn't her. But looking at her watch, she realised there was no time for pointless arguments.

"Bye, boys." She leaned down and kissed them both, making exaggerated smacking noises, which often made them giggle.

"Come on, Mum," Lukas said, pushing her away.

They didn't have time for her affection, they were already in the middle of a new creation: a space station. Once upon a time, she had been creative too. What happened to people when they grew up? Why did they lose their sense of fun and adventure?

"I'll see you later. Have fun!"

She slipped out and drove towards Daniel's house. If she had time, she would still go to the library but she couldn't tell Erik the truth. Between her need to borrow books and visiting a student on a Saturday, he was less likely to understand the latter.

*

The house was only a ten-minute drive from Anna's house, straight through town along Mörnavägen, past the sprawling school area on the right and then down a hill towards the seaside. This area used to be taken up by multiple summer-houses, the gardens overflowing with wild flowers. The last few years, people had built larger family homes on these plots but the odd red-painted summerhouse was still visible here and there. Daniel's house was one of those exceptions. A small, quaint-looking shack that had seen better days and most likely lacked insulation.

Daniel's mother, Frida, opened the door; untidy blonde hair, no make-up and dressed in a pair of baggy sweatpants and a top without a bra. She seemed sleepy.

"I'm sorry," Anna said. "Did I wake you up?"

"No, I just forgot that you were coming."

Anna had sent her a text message as a reminder but she must have missed it.

"Is Daniel home?"

"Dan!" Frida screamed, rather than called, into the house. A minute later he appeared, looking newly showered but dressed in the same clothes as the day before. With his hair wet, he looked sleek and less rebellious.

"Come in," Frida said. "Sorry, it's a bit messy."

Anna stepped into the living room, which indeed was a

mess and reeked of something unidentifiable. Bags of crisps, drinking glasses, Coke bottles, scraps of paper and videos were strewn across the table and the floor. No sign of alcohol though.

She found a space on the denim-covered sofa and sat down. Frida flopped down on a swivelling chair on the other side of the table, looking like an exhausted teenager who was about to be reprimanded by her mother.

Except Frida was older than Anna. She was at least forty, the lines on her face reflecting a hard life. With a little effort, however, she would be pretty.

"Thanks for coming on a Saturday," Frida said and Anna appreciated the acknowledgement.

"No problem," she said. "I know you're working a lot during the week."

"Have to do extra shifts where I can."

Frida worked at a local factory, sewing bags, if Anna had understood it correctly. On paper, she didn't sound like a "slacker".

"Daniel, why don't you join us?" Anna said and he motioned closer but didn't sit down.

"Is he in trouble?" Frida asked. She looked fatigued rather than angry.

"Daniel is very bright," Anna said, avoiding the question since she didn't want to lie. "Although I feel he could use more support."

"Can't the school sort that out?"

Daniel grimaced behind his mother's back as if to say "see, I told you".

"I mean from home."

"Look, honey." Frida leaned forward in her chair, assuming

a condescending look. "I'm sure you mean well but I have to work and his father isn't exactly around."

"Where is his father?"

Frida threw her arms in the air, finally showing some energy. "With another woman, God knows where."

"Right." Anna nodded knowingly. "Anyway, if you could perhaps…" *Take an interest in his education.* "Work with him to get his assignments done."

"He's not five," she snapped.

"Oh, I know," Anna said. "He can do it by himself. But perhaps you could acknowledge that he's done it."

Behind Frida, Daniel sighed and Anna couldn't help herself. She turned to him and said: "You don't have to like the work, you just need to get it done."

"*You know what I need,*" Daniel mouthed quietly.

Frida cut in: "Wait, what?" she said. "You want me to pat him on the head like a dog and say 'bloody well done'?"

The way the conversation was going, it would have been better for Daniel not to be there. Then Anna could have been tougher, more forceful, to make the mother see that Daniel needed her badly. Now she had to tiptoe around the issue.

"Encouragement goes a long way," she said, ignoring Frida's sarcastic tone.

Frida turned to her son. "Dan, can you please make your teacher a cup of tea?"

He reluctantly disappeared into the kitchen and Anna was relieved. Now she would take the bull by the horns, except Frida leaned forward, revealing a large, oval bruise on her left arm. Frida must have seen the shock in her eyes because she quickly pulled her sleeve down and whispered:

"Look," she said before Anna could think of anything to

say. "I don't understand the stuff Dan is studying. It's going to make me look stupid."

Frida's tone had changed. It was softer. Anna forced herself to shake off the deep purple image on Frida's arm. It could be work-related. A machine gone wild.

She cleared her throat. "Frida, if you could just ask him a few questions, such as 'what are you studying at the moment?' or 'have you got any tests this week', then that would be encouraging in its own way."

"He will lie."

Anna nodded.

"Possibly. Look, he's really bright, he just needs motivation. If he thinks you're going to be proud of him, he's likely to pay more attention."

Show him you care! That he needs you.

Just then, Daniel turned up with only one cup of tea and Anna drank it self-consciously while they watched her. She tried to keep the conversation going but it was hard work; Frida mostly answered "yes" or "no" to her questions. Daniel seemed pleased though.

*

Anna felt lighter as she drove out of town towards Hågarp. She tried to enjoy the scenery along the road, cast in glorious sunlight. Autumn colours were slowly making their appearance in the midst of the greenery; the cool deep-blue ocean on her right making her feel free. Daniel and his mother soon became distant characters. Finally, she would be going back to the library. She was determined to leave work and Mörna behind. It bothered her that most people knew who she was there. It made it difficult to get close to anyone, in case they should gossip.

When she parked, her phone alerted her to two new messages from an unknown number.

You see? She doesn't give a shit.

The sender's face took shape in her mind. Messy blond hair, upturned nose and intense brown eyes. A disparaging message from a lost young man. Her heart heavy, she read the second message.

You turned up. That's what someone who cares would do.

She leaned against the headrest and took a deep breath. It seemed she could do nothing right. He chose to misunderstand. She should notify someone. She should but she wouldn't. The new principal had clearly shown he wasn't interested in problematic issues, he was too green for that, and Kent would try to talk to Daniel, which would make the situation worse. She had toyed with the idea of speaking directly to the counsellor but her hippie style put Anna off; she was too aloof, someone who wanted to be the students' buddy. Daniel wouldn't respond to that. Erik was right about one thing: she cared too much. That was the problem. But how could she not?

She needed a breather, to recharge and come up with a new solution. That's why she was here. She looked up at the library as Iris flipped the "Closed" sign to "Open". *Time to escape*, she thought, and got out of the car.

No one else had arrived by the time Anna stepped through the door. She felt transported into a capsule, the air warm and inviting, the rows upon rows of books giving off a sense of culture and history. She walked straight to the counter where Iris had her hands in a large cardboard box.

"Hi," Anna said.

Iris was removing a pile of books. Perhaps she was disturbing her. Should she browse on her own first?

"Hello," Iris said then, putting the books down. "You're back already?"

She remembered her.

"I finished *Affinity*," Anna explained.

Iris's lips curled. "That was fast. What did you think?"

"It was great," she said, immediately trying to think of something deeper to add. "It took me by surprise." That's all she could come up with? She groaned, but any standard interpretation she was used to sounded too pompous, too rigid and boring. *A linear story with a feminist heroine.*

"Would you be interested in another book by Sarah Waters?" Iris asked and Anna nodded.

"Sure."

She followed Iris as she steered the way, feeling like a kid, walking behind her. The ancient bookcases gave the place character and the soft glow from the overhead lights made it feel like someone's living room.

"By the way," Iris said, turning to her. "We're starting up a book club. Would you like to join?"

Her instinct was to say "yes" but insecurity overcame her.

"I'm not sure," Anna said honestly. "I probably won't be able to add much value."

"Don't worry about that. The other women aren't literary geniuses."

Without the reading glasses on, Iris looked younger. She was probably in her late forties or early fifties. It was hard to tell. She was wearing another stylish ensemble, a tight black knitted dress, oversized silver bangles and fashionable ankle boots.

"I'll think about it," Anna said.

"Please do. We start on Wednesday at seven."

Iris stopped and eyed the uneven row of spines.

"Ah, here it is." Pulling out a book, she said: "*Tipping the Velvet*."

Anna held her hand out but Iris didn't give her the book at first. Instead, she looked at her seriously.

"This book," she said. "It's a bit… erotic. Just so you know."

Anna broke into a smile and then a giggle. It sounded like Iris was reading out a health warning. MAY CAUSE HEARTBURN. Although Iris didn't seem to get the joke.

"No problem." Anna composed herself. "I think I can handle it."

"More books?" Iris asked and Anna nodded.

"Yes, please."

*

When they had compiled a stack of books and were ready to scan them, the library was still quiet. It had a wonderfully calm atmosphere, making Anna feel completely stress-free.

"Does your husband read?" Iris asked.

It was an odd question. Anna had enjoyed not thinking about Erik, to just *be*. Yet there seemed to be an expectation of her to say something.

"Not really," Anna said. "He's a painter," she added as if that would explain his lack of interest in books. The truth was, he didn't have the patience.

"So is mine," Iris said and Anna was relieved to meet someone else who wasn't married to a doctor, lawyer or schoolteacher for that matter. "Maybe Rolf knows him. What's his name?"

"Erik…" Anna started before she caught on. Iris's husband was an actual artist and she thought Erik was as well, because obviously, there was no way someone like Iris would be married to a house painter. "… but he paints houses." Her cheeks reddened.

"Well, that's being an artist in a way too."

It was kind of her. "What about your husband?" Anna asked to deflect from herself and Erik.

"He's Rolf Sören."

"Oh, I've heard of him…" She stopped herself.

Now Iris smiled, even showing her teeth.

"That's all right, I know what you were going to say. The troublemaker."

Anna smiled. Rolf Sören didn't do anything conventional according to the papers. His reviews varied but he seemed to thrive on attention. There had even been rumours about him using body parts in his artwork.

"He only used fingernails," Iris said. She grimaced as if to say "what can I do?".

"Didn't they detect blood in one of his paintings?"

Anna regretted her words immediately. Being nosy was no way to make friends and it wasn't like her to pry. It was just that Iris fascinated her and this information added a new dimension.

"That was pure PR," Iris said. "Most rumours are spread

by Rolf himself. It makes sales go up, not that I agree with it."

"But you obviously support him?"

"I do. I adore him."

She *adored* him? If only she could say the same about Erik. In that moment, Anna truly wished that she could. At the same time, Iris didn't seem like the type of woman who would adore anyone. She came across as independent and headstrong, someone to *be* adored.

"Can I help you with anything else?" Iris asked.

Anna tried to think of new topics of conversation to stay a bit longer, but a woman had made her way over and the moment was lost.

"I hope you will be back soon," Iris said. "I would love to hear what you think of *Tipping the Velvet*. And don't forget. Wednesday, seven o'clock."

14

Erik

March 2016

"She wasn't raped," Erik tells Mum.

"Oh, thank God."

"Although…"

Mum puts her coffee cup down. "Although what?"

"This could mean nothing but her shirt had been pulled out and her fly was undone. It's possible that someone… that someone started…" He doesn't continue the sentence.

"Poor Anna."

Mum stretches a hand across the table, comforting him.

"I just get so mad," he says. He clenches his fists, bangs them on the table. "Nobody gives me the full picture. Are the police twiddling their thumbs?"

"They're busy, Erik. There have been two murders in the city, just in the last fortnight," Mum says. "That's highly unusual for this part of the country, isn't it? That must be draining their resources."

Mum always has an explanation for everything.

"I'm still upset," he says.

"I know, honey. I know. But right now we need to focus on Anna getting better."

"There's no improvement."

"Have you spoken to the doctors?"

Of course he has. Every day. "Nothing is better."

"Something must have improved, Erik, even if it's minor. Her bruises, for example, they were better when I last saw her." She moves closer, takes both his hands in hers. "Honey, do you remember when you were kids, you and Jonna? When you had trouble with friends, we used to focus on one good thing?"

"Please don't talk about Jonna, Mum. Not now."

"We can't just pretend she never existed."

"Mum, I can't lose a sister and a wife before I'm forty. That would be cruel. I will stop going to church. I will."

He knows this will upset her and she doesn't need to know that he already stopped going. What kind of God would make his sister fall off a cliff and die at the mere age of twenty-three?

"She died doing something she loved to do," Mum says calmly.

"Why do you have to be so damn accepting all the time?"

He gets up, his hands slipping out of hers, the chair falling back onto the tiled floor. He stomps his feet.

"My wife might die, Mum!"

His body feels heavy and drained. Mum gets up, waddles over to him in her indoor slippers and wraps her arms around him, embracing him properly. He bends over to reach her shoulders, leans in. She strokes his hair and as if he's a little boy again, she starts to sing: "*When I find myself in times of trouble, Mother Mary comes to me. Speaking words of wisdom, let it be, let it be…*"

"I'm not a baby, Mum," he sniffles half-heartedly.

She keeps singing and it feels good, soothing. He inhales the musky scent of her cardigan.

*

When Erik is back at the hospital, holding Anna's soft, pale hand, Rob calls him.

"Just checking in, man," he says. "The gig went well. Thought you'd want to know."

Great. Now they're having success. Without him.

"I'll join you soon, I promise. Once this… this mess is sorted out."

"Of course, no pressure. We all know you're going through a tough time."

Do you? Do you really know? He stops himself. Rob's his mate, he's been supportive.

"The police came to my house," Rob says. "To ask about that night."

"I know. Sorry about that," Erik says. "They're just doing their job."

He hates that his friends are pulled into this.

"Of course, Erik. But they asked how long I was at your house for and I wasn't sure. You know me and time."

Why does Rob sound so nervous? Did he say something he shouldn't have? Did he mention the laptop? No one has been in touch with him about it, so probably not. Come to think of it, Rob might not know that Anna's laptop was in that bag. It's probably better not to bring it up. Anyway, Erik just needs to try and access it a few more times.

"It's okay," Erik says supportively. "They're obviously happy with whatever you said. Also, I owe you for putting me in touch with your ex, Tina. She's been helpful."

"Oh, good. Maybe she still has the hots for me? Tell her I said 'Hi'. No wait, don't do that, she might get ideas. Don't say anything."

"You done?"

"Yes, and Erik... I know I haven't been around and haven't said much but I'm really sorry." He takes a breather, collecting his thoughts perhaps, which undoubtedly would be a first for Rob. "You know I have a soft spot for Anna. If there's anything I can do, let me know."

Erik knows how much this means, coming from Rob.

"Thanks," he says.

He should call Tina. The police haven't contacted him regarding Pernilla and although that should bring relief, it makes him feel worse.

He takes a deep breath, pours a glass of water from the jug on Anna's bedside table, psyching himself up to call.

Tina picks up almost immediately.

"Hi, Tina, it's me. Erik."

"Hi, Erik."

She sounds happy to hear from him, which makes him relax. He fiddles with his paper, the questions he has written down.

"I'm sorry to bother you again, but have you... um... heard anything more about Pernilla?" He has to ask.

"Sorry, no."

He decides not to push it.

"Okay," he says casually. "What about Kent? I haven't heard anything."

"This is between us," she says in a hushed tone and then there's what Anna would call "a theatrical pause" before she continues: "They were definitely close."

Right. That could mean many things though. Kent has tried to get in touch with Erik but he hasn't called him back yet. It seems easier not to.

"He also mentioned a difficult student," Tina continues in her hushed voice. He wonders where she's calling from. A quiet corner in the police headquarters? "I'm sure she must have talked about it at home?"

Quite possibly, he thinks and ransacks his brain. Nope, there's nothing apart from the note that really could mean anything. It might not even be from a student.

"Anyway," Tina says, now sounding bored. "I don't know much more."

He can sense she is about to hang up and he can't blame her. At the end of the day, why should she tell him anything?

*

That evening he opens Anna's laptop again. What is her password? He needs to work it out, or at least try to. Her computer must contain emails about the student Tina mentioned. In what way was he difficult? Would he have a reason to hurt Anna? If he can find a possible suspect, then the police will understand that he's helping them and perhaps include him more. It would make him feel less isolated. They will probably be upset about the laptop being withheld but he will come up with a reasonable explanation. It was at a friend's house and he only just received it. Something like that.

Mum is proud of him for being proactive but she thinks he should leave it to the experts.

"But I want to do my bit," he says. "They might be missing something."

Mum is doing the dishes downstairs when he tries the first password combination. This time he is better prepared and has written down a list of possible options. The children's names, their surname, birthdays, anniversaries. He starts to type them in, one after the other, together and apart. Try again. Forgotten your password?

He's about to give up when Mum pops her head into the bedroom.

"Erik, I have to go home for a couple of days. I need to make sure your dad is taking his medication. Will you be all right?"

"Sure." He has to be.

Mum hovers in the doorway. "Is that Anna's computer?"

He nods, feeling like he's been caught. "I'm just, you know... looking."

"Is that wise?" she asks. "Shouldn't you hand it over to the police?"

She clearly disapproves, but what else can he do?

"I know what I'm doing. They're not prioritising Anna because she's still alive."

"I'm not sure about that, Erik."

That really frustrates him. She needs to be on *his* side.

"Have they caught anyone yet?" he says. "No, they haven't. I will give them the laptop if I find anything, okay? Goodnight, Mum."

She leaves him to it but he puts the laptop away, out of guilt. To keep himself occupied, he brushes his teeth, flosses, gargles with mouthwash – all the things that would make Anna proud – before returning to the bedroom to put a pair of pyjamas on. But the laptop beckons to him and he yields to its invisible powers and picks it up again. Like an addict, he just can't stay away. Three more tries and he's going to bed, he tells himself. First one. The year the twins were born. SebastianLukas2010.

Try again.

The place and year Anna was born. Gothenburg1982.

Try again.

The place they got married. Lund2009.

The computer kicks into action. Astonished he watches as the screen changes colour. He's in!

Where to look first? He feels like he's entered a maze. He opens Outlook and goes through the folders, clicking on the one labelled "School". There are a few messages from Kent but they are all of a practical nature.

Are you booking the restaurant for Anne's leaving do? There will be fifteen of us…

I think *War and Peace* is a bit advanced for the students but I know you like to try new methods so I will bring the book tomorrow…

If you need me to assist during the test, I will be available from 10-11am. Does that work?

Hands-on and friendly. He should call Kent; he's obviously been a good support for Anna. The guy has just always made him feel awkward. Like he's not a good enough husband for Anna.

There is no mention of a difficult student, though. Only one email could be interpreted as possibly being related.

Anna, I'm here if you need me. Don't take too much on by yourself.

It could also refer to her workload.

He goes back to the list of folders. Nothing looks all that interesting. Instead he clicks on "Deleted". Perhaps she didn't want to keep certain emails, especially if they were related to problematic students? He stops himself. No. If that were the case she would want to keep them. She would be collecting evidence. Anna is sensible. He's about to leave the deleted folder when an email address catches his eye, only because she has deleted numerous emails from that same address: blackadam4321@hotmail.com. Is it junk? He opens one of them at random.

Hi Anna, it has to be you. No one else.

The sender has mentioned her name. Surely that can't be junk? There is no mention of a company at the bottom. There is no signature at all. This could be anything. Erik opens another one.

Hi Anna, I need someone who listens to me.

Huh. Erik leans back in the chair. What is this? He opens one more.

Hi Anna, I'm sick of this. How about the basement?

The basement? Which basement? The one under their house? He reads it again. It sounds like a response to another email but there is no message from Anna further down. What did Anna say to this person for him or her to send this? He looks in the "Sent" folder and scrolls down but can't find a single one from Anna to this blackadam4321.

He goes back to the deleted folder and opens one more.

Hi Anna, I can't take it anymore. Fucking agree, will you?

He feels as if he's stumbled onto something significant, he's just not sure what it is. Can he bring this to the police?

He calls Officer Johansson and tells her he might have found something.

"I would prefer to meet in person," he says.

He wants to form a connection with her. The police and him should be a team. They can't keep leaving him in the dark.

15

Iris

September 2015

Iris watched as Lena pulled her fingers through her blonde, highlighted hair, and applied the same pink lip-gloss she had used for the last five years. Eventually, Lena picked up her handbag and slid it over her shoulder.

"See you next week," she said, planting a kiss on Iris's cheek.

"Maybe."

Lena turned to Iris, her smile dead. "What do you mean, *maybe*?"

"I mean that all good things must come to an end."

Her words were friendly but firm. This was unavoidable. She had been sucked in once more but it ended here. Lena had become too persistent, calling unnecessary meetings, which could jeopardise her position.

"Must they now?" Lena crossed her arms defiantly, her tone sharp. "And why is that?"

"I will see you at the next meeting," Iris said, heading out of the kitchen, away from the sweet smell of sweat and sex, away from drama.

Lena hurried after her, her heels *clip-clopping* on the hardwood floor.

"When we have our monthly meetings, am I supposed to act like nothing happened?"

Iris was upset with herself. Why had she become involved with someone so close to home?

"Lena," she said, the sweetness in her voice perhaps a tad too exaggerated. "That's what we have done so far. Because we're professionals."

She kept walking, but Lena caught up with her.

"That's because it's been exciting, Iris, knowing we share this... bond. I don't want it to end."

"I care about you," Iris said. "But you have always known I have a husband."

"And I'm sure he would love to know what you have been up to!"

"As I'm sure your husband would," countered Iris calmly.

Lena stormed out; the bells above the door dangerously close to smashing onto the floor.

Iris didn't wish to hurt Lena but there seemed to be no other option. They couldn't keep seeing each other. Lena would hopefully calm down.

Iris wiped evidence of the meeting off the table, crumbs from cinnamon rolls and ginger biscuits falling into her hand. When she had restored order, she went to the bathroom and reapplied her lipstick. It was important to remain professional. She needed to go back to being Iris, the reliable librarian. The task for the day: to discard long-forgotten books that had lost their shelf appeal.

Shaking off images of Lena's gym-trimmed body and her dramatic exit, Iris commenced the much needed weeding out process. In order to make space for new additions, some books unfortunately had to go.

She picked up a short novel that only one person had ever borrowed. Stefan. He had asked her to order the book two years previously. Even in a small town, known for being desolate during wintertime, her customers did have refined literary tastes. Stefan had just moved to Hågarp with his young family. "A fresh start" he had called it, and had quickly become one of her most frequent customers. Keeping her on her toes, they had discussed her favourite authors: Leo Tolstoy, William Trevor, Doris Lessing and Virginia Woolf. Many regarded Woolf's books as women's literature but not Stefan. Gender was irrelevant, he had said and the meeting of their minds had been the foundation of a wonderful but short-lived friendship.

Stefan's new start had ended in divorce and he and his wife had moved away. No one else had borrowed the book since. Iris had read it of course: a story about an older woman in a home for the elderly who became sexually involved with a young male carer. A controversial subject and well worth reading.

Just as she decided to keep the book, a group of teenagers arrived and parked themselves by the computers. They greeted her politely.

"Let me know if you need any help," she said but before she had a chance to strike up a conversation, her phone rang. She normally didn't answer it during working hours, but it was Karin and after the last phone call, she felt she should.

"Hi, Mum. I spoke to Dad."

"Oh." Iris felt anxious. What had Rolf actually said? Had he explained that their arrangement was his idea? That she had been reluctant but had gone along with it to avoid losing him?

"He said the same, Mum. That it was when you were younger, that he loves you and that it's just the two of you now."

Did he now? Perhaps he wasn't so honest after all.

"Great. I'm glad we're all on the same page," Iris said, putting on a cheerful tone. "I have to go now, lots of people here."

"Yes, I can hear that," Karin laughed and they hung up.

More teenagers arrived and while the library got swamped with young voices and laughter, she could feel the phone in her hand vibrate, alerting her to a new message. Lena's name appeared on the screen. Iris would have preferred no contact for a while but they did work together. She opened the text message.

Dear Iris, I thought you would enjoy the first lines from this poem by Natasha Trethewey. Heard of her? I'm guessing you haven't.

The lies I could tell,
when I was growing up
light-bright, near-white,
high-yellow, red-boned
in a black place,
were just white lies.

If I don't hear back from you, I will contact Rolf.

Angry and revenge-seeking. Iris hadn't expected Lena to take the break-up quite so badly. She had assumed they were both fairly casual about it, but she realised now that Lena thought this was a one-off, worthy of telling Rolf if she didn't get what she wanted. Iris clicked "Delete".

Lena was right about one thing. It was white lies. Not real lies.

16

Daniel

September 2015

Dan was busy writing his own story. It had a happy ending.

"Where are the bottles?"

Frida was banging on his door, disturbing his creative process. He ignored her, continuing to form words, transfixed by the paper absorbing ink. But her furious knocking didn't stop, which resulted in a Stephen King inspired moment: suddenly a woman died in his story, buried alive in the foundation of a construction site, her screams muffled by the wet cement. He decided to call her Frida. If she ever read it, that would teach her.

Dan liked that every door in their house had a key. Locking his room made him feel safe. No matter whom she brought home, he was untouchable. And it also kept his mother out when necessary.

"You little shit!" she shouted. "She didn't suspect a thing, so bring them out."

"I poured them down the sink," he said calmly.

He hadn't. Instead, he was going to sell every bottle. Vodka could fetch a good price, he reckoned. Better than beer. There were plenty of under-aged buyers around. Every town had them, even this seemingly perfect one. There was nothing else to do but get together with your friends and drink illegally. That was considered "cool".

The door vibrated as she kicked it. Screaming.

"Focus on your bloody job, Frida," he shouted back.

He remembered the last town they had lived in. His mother at the central square that had become her home away from home, where all the drunks hung out together, making it feel okay to drink a beer at nine in the morning. He had tried to bring her home several times. She had screamed but he had pulled at her top, told her to shut the fuck up and be a mother for once. Everyone had heard them. Her newfound buddies had laughed. It had been humiliating every time but he couldn't give up on her, could he? Then nothing would improve.

He and Martin confiscated her booze regularly. This time, with Anna visiting, it had been different. She had willingly agreed to hide the bottles.

"Why the hell is your teacher coming over anyway?" she had asked. "As if I don't have enough fucking problems!"

He had calmed her down, told her Anna was cool.

"Then why are we getting a home visit?"

"It's a sort of welcome to the school thing," he had said.

On the other side of the door, she continued her pleading.

"Just one fucking bottle, Dan! One!"

She hadn't known that he had hidden the other bottles too, the ones she kept at the bottom of the ironing pile, behind the cleaning products under the sink, in the shed, under the seat in her car. Martin had always been one step ahead of her and with him locked up, Dan had to act the detective.

The best thing about this town was that Frida had to drive to the liquor store. *Systembolaget* was too far away for a walk or even a bike ride. He was hoping that would make the binges less frequent. She really needed to keep this job until he had Anna wrapped around his finger.

Luckily, Anna had witnessed the unbearable living conditions. He had added to the mess, but so what? No one cleaned up around here, it wasn't that far from reality. It would have looked even better with the frosted vodka bottles lined up on the table, but he wasn't stupid. Then she definitely would have contacted social services.

"Dan!"

He continued to ignore her and after a while the kicking stopped. Sobs could be heard through the thin door.

"Fuck off, will you?" he said, feeling like his big brother.

"What's happened to yo-u?" she stuttered between the cries. "My ba-a-by."

"I'm not your fucking baby," he muttered.

I'm somebody else's baby.

17

Anna

October 2015

Anna had decided to stay late to prepare the next day's classes but she kept checking the time. She had to be at the library in Hågarp at seven.

"Everything okay with Daniel?" Kent asked.

"I spoke to the mother," she said.

"Good. How did you approach it?"

Kent already had his coat on but he didn't seem to be in a rush. The teachers' lounge was unusually busy for this time of day but thankfully no one was sitting in their corner. She didn't want to discuss Daniel openly. No other teacher seemed to have any real issues with him, and she didn't want them to start looking for problems if there weren't any.

"I wanted Daniel to be there," she explained quietly. "I wanted him to hear that she cares, because she must do. All mothers who stick by their children and raise them care to some level."

Not the right choice of words, she realised, but it was too late. Kent already looked concerned.

"Aren't you letting this get too personal? Daniel is not your son."

"You would have done the same."

He nodded contemplatively. "Perhaps."

"It didn't go well," she revealed. "She seemed distant. I can't explain it."

"Depression? Drugs? Alcohol?"

"Not sure." Anna hadn't seen any evidence of drugs or alcohol. Maybe she was depressed? It would make sense, with Daniel's father leaving, her sons getting into trouble, the responsibility to make ends meet.

"Anyway, I'm sure you're expected at home," she said. "We can talk some more another time."

She valued Kent's advice but something about this situation made her feel weary. Kent followed the rulebook and she wasn't sure that was the way to get through to Daniel.

"Don't stay too late," he said.

*

It was already dark when Anna headed out of Mörna. Dim streetlights guided her out of town as she followed the windy road to Hågarp. Reindeer were known for making an appearance in these parts and so she held the steering wheel in a tight grip, her eyes constantly darting from left to right.

Eager to get to Hågarp, she also felt uneasy and slightly guilty. As a mother she felt that she should be at home with her children, that every moment away from work should be spent with Sebastian and Lukas. That was the reason she hadn't picked up a hobby since they were born, to always be there for them. But by the time she walked up the stone steps to the library, she had convinced herself that she deserved this, that a book club would in fact make her a better mother.

Through the glass she could see that the library was deserted. She pushed the door open and stepped inside, drawing in the welcoming smell of books and perfume, which seemed to linger in the air. Once again she moved into the centre, the hub where all the borrowing and returning activity took place. Iris was behind the counter, crouched over a plastic crate.

"Hello," Anna said.

"I'm just busy closing," Iris said and Anna thought that perhaps she had got the date or the time wrong.

"Sorry, I thought... book club?"

"Oh, yes. That's still on. I just need to get this delivery packed and lock up. Do you mind getting the coffee ready?"

Iris was just as stylish as she had been the last couple of times and Anna was pleased that she herself had made an effort. She was wearing a matching black outfit with a multi-coloured scarf loosely wrapped around her neck.

Anna followed Iris as she showed her to a small kitchen at the back. There was a sink, a coffee maker, a fridge, a small table with two chairs and an ugly photocopier, not unlike the one they used at school. Still, it was cosy.

Iris directed Anna to the coffee filters and Zoegas beans.

"How many people am I making it for?"

Iris took the reading glasses off and paused for a moment.

"Let's see," she said. "There were going to be four of us but one is working late and the other one just called about some car trouble."

"Oh." Anna felt disappointed. "So you want to cancel?"

"No. We can still have a chat. You've come all this way and you've read the book, haven't you?"

Anna blushed. She had and she had to admit she was

petrified of discussing an erotic, lesbian relationship set in the 1800s. Although perhaps it would be easier without other people there?

"I'm sure you have better things to do," she said. "I can come back next week."

"I need a cup of coffee," Iris insisted. "I've been on my feet all day."

"All right then. I'll just stay a short while."

Anna got to work straight away: she put the filter and beans in, added water and switched the coffee maker on. While she waited for it to brew, she located a couple of mugs and some biscuits in a tin that she placed on a plate. Once ready, she loaded everything on a tray and carried it into the library.

Where should they sit? It wasn't a large space but there were a number of reading chairs and low tables around.

"Over there," Iris called and pointed to a couple of comfortable-looking orange reading chairs. Next to the chairs stood a wide, square pillar that had an old-fashioned, ceramic fireplace in it.

Anna placed the tray on a small table and sat down. The ceiling in this room, the main hall, was exceptionally tall and when Iris turned the lights off, only leaving a couple of floor lamps on, it almost felt spooky.

"This is how we switch out of work mode." Iris said as she lit the tea candles on the table and the mantelpiece.

"So this doesn't feel like work to you?"

"Not really. I may work with literature but it would be sad if I couldn't also enjoy it for what it is."

Anna found herself wishing that Iris would smile. Was she disappointed to be left with only one person to discuss the book with? *You just need validation.* Erik's words hurt.

"Thank you for inviting me," she said.

"Thank you for coming." Iris slipped her shoes off and pulled her feet into the chair. "We don't have to discuss the book if you don't want to?"

Iris eyed her quizzically over the red, moon-shaped glasses.

"It was just very different to the books that I normally read. Similar to *Affinity* of course but well... different all the same."

"Different how?"

"I think, because of being a teacher, I have been stuck on the classics. Shakespeare, Sartre, Austen, Tolstoy..."

"Wow, I had no idea." Iris did a dramatic bow to Anna and it made her laugh.

"Oh, no. I'm not... I mean it's basic stuff. I'm completely hopeless when it comes to contemporary fiction."

Iris seemed to view her with new eyes and although it felt good, Anna wanted to lower the expectations. Everything she covered at school *was* basic; she never had the time to delve too deeply as she tried to cover a broad spectrum of time periods.

"You mean you're not used to reading such explicit books? You don't cover D. H. Lawrence's *Lady Chatterley's Lover*?"

"I don't." She smiled. "I have to admit, the sex scenes in *Tipping the Velvet* made me feel slightly uncomfortable."

She had never been promiscuous. Erik was only her third sexual partner but when they first met he had made her feel that it was safe to explore.

"That's good," Iris said. "Makes you feel something."

Anna picked up a biscuit, which crumbled dryly in her mouth.

"Do you often feel uncomfortable?" Iris asked.

Anna coughed. She certainly couldn't accuse Iris of being predictable.

"You obviously don't," she said, finding her voice.

"Of course I do," Iris said. "I hate large groups of people, for example."

"Me too. I don't understand the politics and the games. I thought getting older would make that easier but often I just can't break the code."

"Too many personalities in the mix, I think. Equally though, I don't like being the centre of attention," Iris continued. "It makes me feel self-conscious. I couldn't be Nan or Kitty in *Tipping the Velvet*, on stage."

"I agree," Anna said. But then there were a lot of things Nan and Kitty did together that she couldn't imagine doing.

They sipped the coffee, the sudden silence feeling comfortable at first but then Anna had to fill it with words. If only to maintain interest. She wanted to be invited back.

"They had a tough life, Nan and Kitty," Anna said.

"The past shapes us, just like it shaped them."

"I know what you mean," Anna said. Her past had definitely shaped her and perhaps she wished they were talking about that.

Iris looked at her deeply then, as if she understood. "People, both in literature and real life, have all sorts of drama in their lives," she said. "Everyone has had a dysfunctional upbringing to some extent."

Anna nodded.

"Although it's what you do with your baggage that really matters," Iris continued.

"That's true."

Iris took her glasses off and wiped a tired-looking eye, a black mascara smudge appearing underneath. Anna felt that perhaps she should be heading off and not overstay her welcome.

"So what are we supposed to read for the next meeting?" she asked.

"I was thinking," Iris said. "That perhaps we should meet weekly? A month seems too long. Don't you think?"

Anna agreed. A month felt like a long time. It felt good to sit there; like inhabiting a warm cocoon.

"What about the others?" Anna asked. "Won't they mind?"

"I'll just inform them. They're easygoing."

Iris put her glasses back on and pulled out a book from a basket on the floor.

"So," she said. "This book will be uncomfortable on a whole other level. This author caused a representative of the Nobel Prize academy to resign, stating her work was 'unenjoyable public pornography'."

Anna wasn't sure in which direction this book club was heading but she felt strangely excited.

"I'm always happy to try something new," she said.

18

Erik

March 2016

Mum has gone home and Erik is relieved for about five minutes. It's nice to have the house back. No pretending that everything is A-okay, no looks of disapproval, no dissecting what could have happened. With Mum gone, he will also be able to look at Anna's emails more closely. Having slept on it, he feels he needs to get his head around them, one way or another.

The day before, he had sat in front of Linda Johansson at the swanky police headquarters, on a blue upholstered chair with wooden armrests, trying to connect with her. Except he struggled. She looked tired and uninterested and he wanted to ask what her problem was? He didn't though. He reasoned she could have a number of issues that were unrelated to him and Anna. Perhaps she was distracted by another case or it could be personal problems?

"I want to help," he said. "For the sake of my children."

She looked pleased. "Good," she said and in a softer voice, she added: "How are the children coping?"

And there it was: her compassion, and... some sort of connection.

He rested his arms on the table between them, to change position – he seemed to be sitting an awful lot lately – but also to be closer to her.

"They're dealing with it the best that they can," he said. "Thank you for asking. It's not easy."

"I'm sure it's not."

She put a pad and a pen in front of her and said: "We talked to Pernilla again, the day care teacher."

He should have expected that but he still felt himself grow hot.

"She verified that you were at day care Tuesday afternoon."

He nodded, waiting for her to continue, but she didn't say anything else. *That's it? She wasn't going to ask if they were an item?* Although it would be uncomfortable to talk about, he wondered why she was holding back. They obviously suspected that he was seeing her. Should he deny it even though she hadn't asked?

"Did you find out who wrote that note?" he asked. A new topic felt safer.

"I can't discuss that with you, Erik."

"Come on." They had to give him something.

She appeared to think. "Fine. We know who wrote it but it appears to have been work-related and is of no further interest."

He sighed. Right. Okay.

"Does Anna have a student called Adam?" he asked instead.

Officer Johansson made a note.

"Why do you ask?"

He hesitated for a second. Shifted in his seat.

"Did you speak to the people at her school again?" he asked.

Are you going to tell me if you spoke to Kent?

"Yes, we have spoken to her colleagues."

She insisted on keeping it vague.

"And no one said anything about an Adam?" he asked.

"I will have to check. What do you know about him?"

"Anna might have mentioned someone with that name," he lied. What else could he do?

He could have shared the email address with them, he had the printout in his pocket, but he held back. They would want the laptop and he wasn't done with it yet. They obviously wouldn't reveal their full hand, so why should he leave the police with all the cards? He decided to email Black Adam himself. To take control, collect more evidence and make sure it got done. Then he would hand any findings over to the police.

"Can I just ask you something?" Officer Johansson said.

"Sure…"

"In your opinion, is Anna a good mother?"

"Of course." Aren't all mothers viewed as the superior parent?

"So you don't feel like she was working too much?"

He shook his head before answering. "No, of course not. She was doing that for her family."

He felt satisfied with his answer. Soon, Linda Johansson would surely have new evidence to deal with and would stop questioning his wife's mothering skills. Why would they even care about that?

*

Erik emailed blackadam4321 when he got home but he is yet to receive a response. For now, he hasn't used Anna's email address in case this person knows that Anna is in the hospital. Instead, he has set up a new, vague email account. He wrote:

Hi Adam, Anna has told me about you. Let me know if I can help in any way?

He toyed with the idea of signing it as Kent but that felt naughty and could become messy. Instead, he signed it as

someone who cares

He will give the guy two more days to respond before he sends a new message.

Right now he is busy. The downside of Mum being gone is that he has to take on the responsibilities she has shouldered for him.

First stop: day care. Having managed to get the boys dressed, a harder task than he remembers, especially with emotions running high, they buckle up in the V70.

Mörnavägen is lined with cycling children so Erik maintains the thirty km per hour speed limit that applies during school hours. They could have cycled themselves, or even walked, but he doesn't want to be forced into any conversations. What do you say when you know your family is the target of gossip?

"When is Grandma coming back?"

Erik glances at Sebastian in the rear-view mirror.

"Hopefully end of the week, buddy."

The boys have sour faces and the drive feels like an eternity, even though it's only a few minutes away.

"So what's new at day care?" Erik asks, trying to sound cheerful.

"We have a new teacher," Sebastian says.

Could this new teacher be a replacement for Pernilla? Not having to face her again would be magic.

"So Pernilla... is she still there?"

"Yes," Lukas says. "I don't like her though."

"Really?" This is a surprise. "I thought you loved her?"

"She's kind of mean," adds Sebastian.

Erik immediately pulls the car over to the side of the road, stops and turns to face them. Fear. He feels fear.

"What has she done?" he asks.

They look at each other, in that twins sort of way. *Should you tell him, or should I?*

"She says Mummy is going to die," Sebastian says and looks down. He can hear the tears in his voice.

What the hell? "She doesn't know anything," Erik bursts out. "Don't listen to her!" Fuck.

"Is she going to die, Daddy?"

Lukas looks at Erik, his eyes big and hurt. He doesn't cry as much as Sebastian but he looks so defeated.

"No, buddy, she's going to be fine," he assures him. "She just needs time. We don't know how long it's going to take, that's all."

He collapses onto the horn, accidentally hooting at a passer-by who starts gesturing rudely towards him. He doesn't care.

"She's doing fine," he tells them. "She's just sleeping. I'm there every day, checking on her."

"Grandma says you have to start working soon," Lukas says. "Who's going to watch her then?"

This astounds him. They know about work and they worry about that?

"Are you sure you're only five?" he jokes, his face not

quite looking as jokey as he would have liked. How did they grow up so fast?

"We're almost six," they say in unison.

"That's right, in three months. How could I forget?"

He turns and smiles at them.

"Boys," he says, choosing his words carefully. "We're the three musketeers. We stick together, sending Mummy love every day."

They nod. "One for all, all for one." He's taught them well.

He gets back onto the road, thoughts of Pernilla now filling his head. What is he going to do? He just doesn't understand what's got into her.

He could speak to her supervisor but what if she tells her about their night together? Then he will be asked to move the boys elsewhere. It's almost impossible to get a new place anywhere nowadays, let alone two. He must talk to her, try and fix things.

When they arrive, a teenager on a bike is cycling around the parking lot, doing tricks. He's got a denim jacket with a faded print on the back and his shoelaces are undone. *They could get caught in the wheels*, Erik thinks, *make him crash*. That's living on the edge, being cool. Erik remembers what that was like, how carefree he himself used to be. Life was uncomplicated back then.

"Nice jacket," he says to the boy as they pass him.

He looks at them intently, then cycles off without a reply.

"Who was that?" Lukas asks.

"No idea, but I used to have a jacket like that when I was growing up." They look impressed. "It made me feel like a rock star. Like on *Idol*."

He wishes there had been programmes like that on TV when he grew up. Stardom within his grasp.

"Maybe you should sing to Mummy?" Lukas says and Sebastian agrees: "That would make her feel better."

They look so sweet. Anna would hate a rock or eighties repertoire but she does love the good old 'Hotel California'. He could sing that.

"Maybe."

He follows them inside, hoping to catch Pernilla. Maybe he can gain her sympathy, make her back away at such a difficult time in his life?

Other parents are also heading towards the door. He has always hated this part of the drop-off and pick-up: the chit-chat. The mums are the worst, with their sympathetic glances and parrot-like comments: "Anna working late again?" Now, with Anna in hospital it's intolerable, as if he's going to break out in a rash there and then.

A man taps his shoulder and Erik freezes.

"I'm Sophie's dad," Sophie's dad says. "My wife tells me Sebastian has a crush on our daughter?"

Erik stops, grateful for how normal the words sound. No mention of Anna, no mention of coma.

"Really?" Good boy.

"Keep him away from her," the dad jokes, hitting Erik's arm with his fist, a little too hard, before bouncing ahead of him, through the door.

Erik shakes his head. Bloody idiot.

"Sophie is really funny," Sebastian says.

"Good for you, son." Even though her father is a prick.

Erik's phone starts to vibrate. It's Mum.

"Hi, Erik," she says. "Are you coping okay?"

"You only just left."

"I know but I worry about you."

"We're okay." *Apart from Sebastian and Lukas's teacher*

telling them that their mum is about to die. "I've got to go, I'll call you later."

"I was just reading the paper on the train," Mum says, ignoring him. "About the police being criticised."

He stops in the day care playground, at once concerned.

"About Anna's case?"

"No, it was just a general attack on the police's operations in rural areas."

"Oh."

His interest wanes but Mum reads out loud from the article: "*We might need to look at changing the lighting in some areas.*" She pauses. "That probably would have helped Anna. It's awfully dark in that parking lot."

That's useful, Mum. "It's too late now."

"It also says that they don't have enough staff and that they can only do so much."

"So?"

"I just mean that they're doing the best that they can."

The boys are about to go inside and he's spotted Pernilla through the open door.

"Thanks, Mum, for that very helpful information... got to go."

He doesn't wait for her to say goodbye.

Pernilla is in the cloakroom, helping another child hang his jacket up.

"Hi," he says nervously as he enters.

Her eyes meet his, glossy lips turned at the corners.

"Hi," she says.

"Go on, boys," he says. "Put your bags away and off you go."

He pats their heads and they run off. With the boys out of sight, he asks Pernilla if they can talk.

"Sure."

"Somewhere private."

She opens the door to a storage room and they squeeze in between brooms and buckets. Before he's had a chance to speak, she's wrapped her arms around him, pushing those lush lips against his. At first he lets it happen, soaks up the affection and feels comforted, welcoming the feeling of being close to another person's body. Then, a couple of seconds later, he resurfaces and pushes her away.

"No, Pernilla. Please. Stop."

Blue, wounded eyes.

"What do you want from me?" she asks, arms folded.

He sighs. *I could ask you the same.*

"Pernilla," he starts. He's older, he needs to explain maturely. "Anna is in a coma. My *wife* is in a coma."

"I know. I'm not stupid. But she's not likely to wake up though, is she?"

"She might." For the love of God, why does she have to make it so difficult? "Stop telling the boys their mum is going to die. It's not fucking okay."

"But what if she doesn't make it?" she says. "You're going to need someone to help you look after the boys. I know them, Erik. They're practically like my own."

He stares at her, the words alarming.

"And you," she continues, her hands caressing his hips. "You will need a lot of love and attention." A hand strokes the front of his trousers and he's torn, wanting to get out, to get back to life, another part wanting to escape into nothingness, to forget, to stay here, away from it all, postponing reality. His cock wants him to stay. She snuggles closer, kissing his neck and it's so soothing. He lets her hold him, leans into her body, hands himself over. Just for a short while. He's going to leave. Soon. Then, his brain poking him: he has something else to say, something important.

"Erm, Pernilla... you told the police we were seeing each other," he says, trying not to smell her newly washed hair. It's still wet, she must have rushed to work after showering. Lavender?

"I just..." she whispers. "I want us to be seeing each other."

"I know, but we can't."

"Just one last time. Please. I'll take care of you."

A loud bang outside the door and he pulls away.

"I have to go," he says. "Don't say anything stupid to the police, Pernilla."

"If we can just... talk. Can we talk, Erik?"

He nods. Sure. If that's what it's going to take.

"I'll come over to your house this week," she says. "Before your mum comes back."

She knows Mum's plans? Of course she does. Mum speaks to her every day.

"Do you know where I live?" he asks.

She nods and he wonders, what doesn't she know?

19

Iris

October 2015

Iris cracked four eggs into a ceramic bowl and whisked them absentmindedly. In the background of her country kitchen, Ella Fitzgerald encouraged Iris to fall in love. *Let's do it, let's fall in love.* Outside the window, the overgrown garden reminded her of how long they had lived in this house, with its white-stained walls and red window frames. Far away from any affairs. Just the two of them, surrounded by serenity, the garden bordering onto kilometres of farmland.

It had been their first house after years of being cooped up with Rolf's paints and canvases in a sparsely furnished Linköping apartment. A big step, but then, her new job had also been a huge leap. Heading up a library had been her dream and it didn't matter that it was a quaint library in the middle of nowhere. Rolf had supported her; he had told her he could work anywhere, as long as they were together.

"It's picturesque," she had told her mother, in an attempt to get her to visit, and just as she thought that, Ella's voice appropriately filled the kitchen with *Heaven, I'm in heaven.*

Iris smiled and pulled out a frying pan. She felt a sense of peace as she melted butter on the cream-coloured AGA cooker, pouring in the eggs, adding fresh thyme and basil from the pots in her kitchen window.

"... *dance with me, I want my arm around you...*" she sang along.

"Of course I will," a voice said behind her and she felt Rolf's arms wrap around her waist, holding her tight. He nuzzled her neck. "You making enough for two?"

"Might do," she said and turned to kiss him.

He had paint on his cheeks and she rubbed it with her thumb in an attempt to remove it. She had felt him slip out of bed early that morning, which wasn't uncommon. When inspiration struck, it didn't matter what time it was, he would be outside, in the red-painted wooden extension that housed his studio.

Rolf slipped his hands inside her robe; he found her breasts with ease, his erection poking her stomach.

"Right here?" she said.

"It's nice and warm by the cooker," he said and pushed her back.

He smelt of turpentine, a smell she had come to associate with lust, and she pulled him close. Their tongues sought each other out; kissing Rolf made her feel like a teenager. His passion shot through her and she was wet before his hand even cupped her sex. He knew how to touch her, knew exactly which buttons to press. She shivered under his touch, reciprocating through his open robe, his naked body moving closer to hers. He painted in the nude, at least when no one was around. When she was ready for him, she spread her legs and he pushed himself inside, the AGA hard behind her back. She wanted him; her hands grabbed his behind and pulled him in deeper. Behind them the eggs were burning.

"You're mine!" Rolf cried out as he came. "Mine! Mine! Mine!"

Afterwards, when their bodies relaxed into the aftermath of the great orgasm, Iris tightened her robe and cracked four new eggs into a bowl.

Rolf had never been domesticated but he did value mealtimes. He would always eat with her if she was at home. They had shared many treasured moments as a family around the kitchen table, the three of them. The house felt empty without Karin.

"Will you join me for a gallery opening this evening?" Rolf asked when they sat down to eat.

"Are any of your pieces showing?" she asked.

Although her support for Rolf was unwavering, the older she got, the further removed she felt from his circus.

"Not exactly," he said. "But we should go. The owner is interested in my religious series."

They exchanged a glance over the near empty plates. He knew that she strongly opposed his latest creative efforts. They were both atheists, so why play with fire?

"I'm sure you will be fine without me," she said.

She wanted to avoid lecturing him about cultural sensitivities. Her dislike would only spur him on. When she had opposed a series of art projects that incorporated human blood, she had spoken up. Except, instead of backing down, he had become more excited than ever.

"If that's your reaction, Iris, imagine the world's reaction!"

He wasn't known across the world but she hadn't pointed that out.

"I need you there," he begged.

"I have book club this evening."

He stopped eating. "Book club?" A cheeky grin. "Since when?"

"We have our second meeting tonight," she said, maintaining a serious look. "You were away last Wednesday. Out of town, remember?"

To see a woman? The less she knew, the better.

"I thought you wanted to keep your distance from the public?"

"Just trying something new."

"This Lena involved?"

"No." Thank goodness.

Lena had sent her another text.

Dear Iris, you're familiar with the poet Karin Boye but I'm 100% sure you haven't read this poem: "From a bad girl".

I hope you're having a rotten time.
I hope you're lying awake like I am,
and feeling strangely glad and stirred
and dizzy and anxious and very disturbed,
and suddenly you'll hurry up
to settle down and sleep like a top.
I hope it takes you longer than you think...
I hope you don't even get a wink!

Why couldn't Lena move on? For now, Iris opted for silence. It was the tried and tested method.

"You spoke to Karin?" she asked.

"I told her I love you," he said.

"That's all?"

"That's all she needs to know." He started singing. "*I can't give you anything but love.*"

He pulled her up and they moved slowly to the music; Iris rested her head on his shoulder. The floor creaked, birds sang outside and in the distance a tractor was pulling a plough through a field. It felt peaceful. Until Rolf stopped dancing. Holding her in a firm grip, he asked:

"Do you remember our rules?"

"Of course," she said.

"No matter what, nothing or no one comes between us," he said. She nodded, not sure if it was a statement or a threat.

20

Daniel

October 2015

While Frida was engrossed in a strenuous fuck aerobics session with a long-haired man with a ridiculous moustache, Dan started to pack. The walls transported every moan into his bedroom, and he furiously threw his few belongings into a backpack. Books, comics, paper, pens, the school folder, clothes and a toothbrush were all the things he needed. He just about managed to pull the zip closed in his inherited Fjällräven backpack.

When he walked through the living room, Frida looked up from the tattered old couch, only a blanket covering her naked body.

"Where are you going, hun?"

"As far away as fucking possible."

The man pulled her back down, as if shielding himself. Fucking loser.

Dan slammed the door shut, not bothering to wait for her to protest.

Martin would have thrown the guy to the kerb by now.

They hadn't visited him in prison. It wasn't exactly Dan's fault. He had no idea where he was held and Frida refused to tell him.

Martin was due to get out soon and would probably deal with Frida's moustache-dude then. Except Frida had said he wasn't welcome back home.

"He's old enough to get his own place. I may have done some stupid shit but I have never been arrested."

"We have forgiven you plenty, Frida," Dan had said but she didn't seem to get it.

He kept asking her if she had spoken to the lawyer but she couldn't get her facts straight. Dan wasn't even clear about why his brother was locked up. Surely it wasn't just because of that stupid fight? The rumour at school was that Martin had been busted for drugs, but Dan refused to believe that.

Tears stung, but he clenched his jaws and made them go away. He was resilient; maybe not a superhero but he could make a decent villain. Nekron or Eclipso. Someone tough. He knew it was childish to still read comics but no one needed to know. Superheroes had been his trustworthy buddies for a long time; they made him feel invincible, like there was nothing he couldn't get through. For Anna, he could be Black Adam, a reformed villain.

Dan unlocked his bike and rolled down the hill towards school. It was past six o'clock but Anna was most likely still there. When she realised he had no intention of going back home she would have no choice but to let him stay. "Just one night," she would say and then it would be another and yet another. He envisioned dinners around their wooden table. Her family, soon to be his. There was a chance she would notify someone, but so what? Nothing ventured, nothing gained. He had to at least try.

Except through the windows of the teachers' lounge, he could see that it was empty. Where was she? He cycled down to the parking lot when her car pulled out. Shit! His feet trampled hard, pushing his bike forward with such speed, his lungs ached from the cold air. At the top of the road he expected her to turn left, to go home, but instead she turned right, exiting town. He tried to follow her but she was too fast and he had to give up. How could she? She was meant to go home, to receive him.

He took out his notebook and read through the story he had written earlier, in amongst the secret pages at the back. It was never out of his sight, it was sacred.

She greeted him with open arms.

"Come in, let me take your bag."

"What about your husband?"

"Dan, let me tell you a secret." She lowered her voice. "I don't love him."

"You don't? So what, you're going to leave him?"

"Yes. For you."

She held him close. He could feel her heart beating through the sheer fabric of her blouse.

Dan looked up, still feeling the smooth silk. It had seemed so real. What was he going to do now?

21

Anna

October 2015

The book on the coffee table sat between them, the letters in red pulsating from the cover: *Greed*. They were waiting for the other members of the book club. Anna tried to think of something to talk about. Small talk. Why was it so hard?

"Do you have children?" she asked.

After the twins were born, Anna had discovered that this was a great ice-breaker, provided the other person answered "yes".

"A daughter," Iris said. "She's at university already, she wants to be a graphic designer, much to her father's delight. He's constantly visiting her."

"That's good. My husband is also a very involved dad. He's good at playing with the children." She thought for a moment. "I probably don't tell him that often enough. I don't know, we tend to get stuck on the small things, argue about who's picking them up or putting them to bed, who's turn it is to cook dinner."

Iris seemed to contemplate this. "I don't think we have ever argued about that," she said. "We have been very clear about our roles from the beginning."

Anna watched as Iris poured the coffee into two yellow Höganäs Keramik cups. They were sitting in the same spot as the last time, their feet free of shoes, legs pulled underneath them. The room was glowing in the candlelight, the sky dark outside. In the distance, she could hear the gentle rise and fall of the ocean.

"I guess I thought we were clear about our roles," Anna said. "But then, when the boys were born... I don't know, they're my life and being a mother is everything I expected it to be, but we don't seem to have found a rhythm since. It's like we're constantly chasing our tails."

Iris added a dash of milk to her coffee.

"Having children isn't easy on any relationship," Iris said. "Our world was completely turned upside down after Karin was born. It gets easier." She stirred her cup. "The trick is to focus on the good parts. Those are the things you end up remembering."

Iris was right. It was just that something had changed. Was it Erik? Or was it herself? Parenthood had definitely altered the dynamic between them.

"So, what did you think of the book?" Iris asked.

She picked it up from the table, as if to remind Anna which one they had read.

Anna hesitated: "What about the others?"

It was only the second book club meeting but no one else had turned up this time either. Anna didn't mind. It made it easier for her to express her opinions, especially when she felt out of her depth. "A Nobel prize-winning author is pressure," she had told Kent, who had chuckled, not knowing who Elfriede Jelinek was. "You know your litera-ture," Kent had said. "You'll be fine."

"They're a bit unreliable," Iris said. "They probably won't make it."

She reached for one of the cinnamon rolls Anna had bought from the local bakery and Anna took one too. Accor-ding to Kent, his wife's circle "read, discussed, drank coffee and ate pastries" and so after last week's dry biscuits, Anna had wanted to bring something more inspiring. Next time, she would perhaps even bake.

"I wish this smell could be bottled," Iris said between bites. "Cinnamon, dark roasted coffee and books. It would be a bestseller."

Anna nodded in agreement. It was a pleasant thought.

"Of course, you would have to add sweaty feet to make it realistic," Iris added and wriggled her toes, the red lacquer on her nails glowing.

She chuckled and Anna joined in, relaxing into the large chair. Iris's dimples deepened, making her look youthful, girlish almost.

A couple of weeks earlier, Anna never would have ima-gined herself sitting here, at the library in Hågarp, laughing and enjoying herself. It was as if a new window had opened in her life, fresh air streaming in.

"So," Iris said. "What did you think of *Greed*?"

Anna sipped her coffee. Where to start?

"It's quite sad… depressing even," she said. "I mean, a man who exploits women is not uplifting."

"Although he's described as pathetic," Iris retorted. "That's vindicating, don't you think?"

"I guess so," Anna said, tugging at her floral maxi skirt. "But the women are so vulnerable, so… I don't know, sad?"

She regretted having used the word "sad" twice in such a short space of time and quickly added: "These women, they're constantly seeking approval by men. I wish they would be stronger."

Iris nodded.

"And what about the violence?" Anna continued, daring herself to take charge. "One of the women asks the man to avoid hitting her in the face. As if she accepts the abuse as long as the world can't witness it. I mean, she asks him, almost politely!"

She was getting too emotional; she should hold back. This wasn't about her, although she had a brief vision of her mother, running away, over and over, always returning. Hiding behind a heavy green curtain, Anna would sit on the cold wooden floor and watch her parents argue. She was not going to have that type of marriage. Ever.

"It's supposed to be ironic," Iris said.

"But he really hates women."

"The narrator hates him," Iris corrected her.

"I just wish the women were stronger," Anna said and to her horror, she started to cry. "I'm sorry," she said, embarrassed, wiping the tears away. "I'm not sure what came over me."

"You're passionate about the book," Iris said. "Or the subject at least."

She stretched a hand across the table and took Anna's in hers.

"It's okay," she said. "Every feeling is allowed in this library."

"I'm just…" Anna started but was interrupted by a loud knocking.

Even though they were in the heart of the library, away from the door, the banging couldn't be ignored.

"Is it the other members of the book club?" Anna asked.

She wiped her face with the sleeve of her top, her fingers tracing under the eyes, clearing the skin of smeared mascara.

Iris shook her head and got up. "I don't think so, but I should check to see who it is."

She stood up and made her way towards the door. Anna decided to join her. She couldn't just let Iris go alone, what if someone was trying to break in? Bringing her phone, she followed a few paces behind, wiping her face once again, making sure she looked presentable.

When they had passed the reception, Anna could make out a woman through the glass. She felt as if she recognised her, but was distracted the moment Iris opened the door and the woman started shouting.

"I called Rolf!" she said, her high-pitched voice piercing through the evening. "He said you were here. It's a bloody book club and I'm not invited?"

Anna decided to hang back, the situation feeling personal, as if she were intruding. Except the woman had seen her and barged in.

"Who's this?"

"This is Anna," Iris said calmly. "She's borrowing books for her class. She's a teacher in Mörna."

"Lena?" Anna asked, now realising who she was. "Lena Blom? I think you know my colleague, Kent."

Lena eyed her. She appeared to be collecting herself. "Why aren't you borrowing books from Tania Svensson in Mörna?"

"Because she's not as familiar with Karin Boye," Iris interjected.

"You're teaching Boye?" Lena asked, looking suspicious.

Anna had no idea why Iris would say that because they

hadn't discussed the twentieth century Swedish author once, but she quickly found herself. Reciting the beginning of a Boye poem, she said: "*Yes, of course it hurts when buds are breaking. Why else would the springtime falter?* That's my favourite."

Lena fiddled with the strap on her handbag, the atmosphere in the room feeling awkward.

"I see," Lena said. "Well, Iris is the perfect person to help you. She loves Boye's poems. Especially 'From a bad girl'. That's *her* favourite."

She turned to Iris, who showed no reaction to Lena's bizarre outburst. Lena smacked her glossy lips, her feet moving around like a boxer about to take the next swing. "So, Iris, should I wait until you two are finished?"

"No, Lena, I think it will take a while. We have only just started."

"So you're saying I have to share you now?"

Lena glared at Anna.

"Lena," Iris said firmly. "You better leave."

Anna wasn't quite sure what was happening but she was impressed that Iris managed to keep her cool. Lena didn't move at first but eventually she opened the door, letting the cold October air seep through. "Say 'Hi' to Kent," she said in Anna's direction.

"Oh, sure." She nodded, perhaps a bit too enthusiastically. "I will."

Iris closed the door and turned the key.

"I'm really sorry about that," she said. "We work together and recently had a disagreement that involved Boye. I didn't want her to join us."

"There's no need to apologise."

Lena's presence wasn't welcomed by her either.

22

Iris

October 2015

After the unfortunate drama with Lena, Anna asked for the bathroom and Iris worried that perhaps she felt the need to escape.

"This way," she said and escorted Anna back through the hall of books, past the central counter that was submerged in darkness, all the way to where the small kitchen was. "Right through there," she showed Anna.

This part of the library had been an apartment once. A small one-bedroom that was now merged with the large hall. The kitchen and the bathroom had been left intact, however. Charming but in need of an update.

Iris remained outside the bathroom door, invisible in the unlit room, allowing her thoughts to form. She felt dizzy, as if she had been drinking a few glasses of wine. What was she doing?

For some reason, she thought of Hanna, who had been one of the very first women in her life. Everything had been easy, from start to finish. When she had left Hanna, no numbers had been exchanged; they had been happy to meet but equally happy to go their separate ways. Through the years, she had floated around, like a ghost, from bed to bed, withdrawing satisfied. The women: artistic, rebellious, passionate and living life to the full. She wanted no regrets, for either party. Anna was different altogether. Nurturing rather than adventurous, reserved, clearly inexperienced, young, a wife and mother.

When Anna opened the door, she walked straight into Iris.

"I'm sorry," Iris said as she took a step back. "I didn't mean to scare you."

She should shut down the book club, withdraw. Old age had obviously blurred her sense of realism.

Anna didn't respond. They were simply standing in the dark, aware of each other's presence but barely able to make each other out.

Then Iris made a decision. She took a cautious step towards Anna, drawing in the scent of soap and cardamom, wrapped her arms around Anna's back, bringing her into a hug. Anna moulded into her embrace. She was taller; Iris could feel her heart beating on her shoulder. The thought of not wanting to let go was intense and frightening. Closing her eyes, she tapped into her instincts and immediately felt her heart jolt. This wasn't lust.

At the realisation, she withdrew, opened her eyes and held Anna at arm's length. She cleared her throat.

"I just wanted to make sure you were okay," she said.

A streetlight switched on outside the window, stretching its glum fingers into the room. Iris observed Anna's face, soft and serious.

"I'm sorry," Anna said. "I don't normally cry, at least not in front of people I have only just met."

"Don't worry. I prefer emotions to no emotions." *She's strong, yet vulnerable*, Iris thought. *I need to lighten the mood, make her feel comfortable.* "Now we'd better read Karin Boye," she said.

Anna laughed. "I guess so. In case I bump into Lena!"

"Which I sincerely hope you don't," Iris said quietly, as she led Anna down one of the aisles.

Together, they located the dystopian Boye novel *Kallocain*.

"It was her last novel and I dare say the most read one," Iris said. "It's dark, a mixture of sci-fi, horror and drama."

No sex or intimate relations, but Iris did enjoy the experimental premise in Boye's novel.

23

Erik

March 2016

Shaking his arms out, Erik wakes himself up. He's spent hours going through the documents on Anna's laptop. It's tedious and hasn't been fruitful so far, and as much as it is an intrusion into his wife's private life, he feels he is entitled to do it. They're married, right?

Tina has told him there was no Adam in any of Anna's classes. Yet he feels this Adam could be important. It's his tone of voice, his outbursts. Erik feels he needs to find him.

Almost everything on Anna's laptop seems to be related to her job. His eyes have scanned through files as mundane as tests to passages from books. Literature. Her newfound love.

"I'm a teacher, Erik. I am expected to read."

"You always read."

"I stopped reading fiction for pleasure, Erik," she said, as if that was his fault. "Now I have found my way back."

"I wish you could find your way back to my bed."

"Everything isn't about sex," she said.

He doesn't want to think about his wife's rejections.

It's easier to think about the early days, when she had no inhibitions.

He's had enough of her boring documents. He clicks back to Outlook. Maybe there will be a new email from blackadam4321? There isn't, but he goes to the "Deleted" folder, opens the emails from Black Adam and reads all twenty-six of them. Every single one starts with Hi Anna. Most of them are one-liners (This is bullshit, I'm going to quit). Most of them are demanding (You need to listen, you need to talk to me). Only a couple of them are longer (You know what it's like. You have seen it. Please will you just help me? I want to be like everyone else. Normal, you know?). And one is truly revealing (I wish I had done better in the test, I wish I had made you proud. You deserve that.) He refers to a test. So it definitely must be a student, except his name can't be Adam since Tina hasn't seen him listed in Anna's file. Who is he then?

Erik has made some notes and has almost picked up the phone to call Kent several times. Instead he tries to think of other teachers he could contact. Anna invited a bunch of them to the house once. End of year drinks. It was totally lame. Someone pulled out a guitar and encouraged Erik to play along to their folk songs. It was like sticking rusty needles in his eyes. And he can't remember anyone's name.

He decides to write another email to blackadam4321 instead. Time is ticking; the police seem sidetracked and he needs to move them back to the real issues. He needs to help. He writes: I know you cared about Anna. The guy wanted to make her proud so he must have cared? I cared about her too, he continues. I did well in her tests. She appreciated that. Would that rile him? Get him to respond? Knowing there was someone else who wanted to be her top student? Or would it be viewed as entrapment? He looks at his words. Entrapment is awesome in the movies but very illegal in Sweden. Boring square Swedish Government doesn't think it's fair. He erases the last two sentences and writes: Please can we talk? I need to talk to someone else who cared about her. I feel so alone.

He feels fairly pleased with the words. Writing was never his strength but this isn't bad. Erik clicks "Send".

He's so engrossed in the email that he's almost late for pick-up at day care. At least the teachers don't raise their eyebrows now. He has a reason not to follow the rules. His wife is in a coma. Thankfully, no one wants to talk about it. One must maintain a cheerful attitude: "the boys were so good today" or "the boys ate really well". Even though Sebastian and Lukas have a tendency to fight when surrounded by other children. They are also fussy eaters. Therefore, he can't trust anything they say. It's all bull.

*

The boys are missing Grandma and so is he. Although he is trying to stay on top of it, the house is already a picture of total chaos. He hasn't had time to do any dishes so the sink is now full. Clothes, toys, mail… He will deal with it. Later.

"Did you sing to Mummy today?" Sebastian asks.

Shit, he forgot. He only spent a couple of hours at the hospital this morning before heading home to Anna's computer. No one can blame him. It would drive anyone insane to wait by a hospital bed. Sometimes it feels like a wake, she's so still.

"I will take my acoustic guitar to the hospital tomorrow," he promises. "I don't think the nurses will like the sound of my Gretsch."

Sebastian giggles. "She will love it," he says confidently, although Erik isn't sure that Anna will enjoy it as much as the boys would. She never attended any of his gigs anymore. Only a few months ago she promised to be there but then something came up. As usual. Stupid book meeting probably.

*

That evening, when the boys are finally sleeping, Erik attempts to clean up the kitchen. Filling up the dishwasher seems to be the best use of his time. Then a knock on the door and the dishes remain in the sink.

His heart sinks when he opens it... Pernilla.

"Now is not a good time," he says but either she's deaf or she's ignorant because she's already on her way in, pushing him to the side, sliding her leather jacket off her shoulders.

"Seb and Lukas in bed?"

Seb? They hardly ever call him that.

"Yes, Sebastian and Lukas are sleeping," he says.

"Good."

She walks into the kitchen as if she's been there before, opens the fridge and pulls out two Pripps Blå.

"Opener?"

He can't believe it. What is she doing? He is about to tell her to leave but the sight of the cold beer makes his taste buds stir; let's face it, no one likes to drink alone.

"Just one beer," he says and digs out the opener from a drawer.

"Sure," she says and hands him one.

He expertly opens it, takes a swig and closes his eyes, relishing the cold bubbles, the dark malt slipping down his throat. Sighing, he opens his eyes again, slightly more relaxed than a second ago. Pernilla holds her own beer out, still unopened.

"Oh, shit. Sorry," he says.

She doesn't seem the least offended. While he opens her beer and hands it back to her, she keeps smiling. She doesn't even comment on the visible mess. They clink their bottles and take a couple of sips.

He has to talk to her about the police. Their suspicions are creating an unnecessary stress. Pernilla twirls her curly hair with one finger, a cheeky grin on her face. She's wearing a white summer dress even though it's only just spring and still chilly outside. No bra, he notices. Just two straps holding her large bosom up. It was only the one time, he reminds himself. One time. One beer. That's all.

"Let's sit down," he says. He'll think more clearly then.

"I'm here for you," she says as soon as they're parked on the much too comfortable navy linen couch. Her fingers rest on the sleeve of his shirt.

"Thank you." He clears his throat. "I appreciate it, but Pernilla, you're making it difficult..."

Her eyes, wide like a reindeer's.

"I don't understand," she says.

"You can't tell the police that we're seeing each other." He feels himself getting worked up. "I mean, it's not even true. And I need to focus on Anna, on her getting better. And the boys."

"Like I said," Pernilla says calmly. "I'm here for you and I won't say anything." She hesitates. "If..."

"If what?"

"If we, you know… keep meeting up. No strings attached if that's what's bothering you."

"I don't want to cheat on my wife."

"Too late."

Touché. He leans back, takes another swig, swallows, gaining time. Her fingers are squeezing his arm, moving up towards his shoulder.

"Pernilla…"

"Yes?" Her other hand is now working his crotch; she's leaning in, her warm breath on his throat. Soft lips against his. *I should throw her out.* He's just so tired; he closes his eyes, lets her playful tongue into his mouth. Then her body moves in, straddling him, her breasts in his face, her perfume intoxicating.

The doorbell. Somewhere in the background he can hear it, the annoying tune like a cheesy song.

"Just ignore it," she whispers, but it's persistent.

He can't block it out; he sits up and pushes her off.

"Have to get that," he says, rushing to the door, hoping it's Mum. She won't approve of him getting cosy – or even just sharing a beer – with the boys' teacher but he doesn't care.

"Hey, man."

"Rob?"

His mate is looking dishevelled; spiky hair held down by a well-worn Arsenal cap.

"Sorry to just come over without calling first. It's just, well… there's a football game on…"

"Come the hell in!" Erik grabs his arm and pulls him in.

"Okay, okay," he laughs. "I'm coming. Have one of those for me?" He points to the beer.

"Of course."

"Hi there." Pernilla is standing in the doorway, seductively leaning against the door frame. Is she hitting on Rob? He can't be jealous. He has no right to be.

"Hi." Rob's tentacles are out.

"Pernilla was just leaving," Erik says. "She's the boys' teacher. We were just discussing… the boys."

He takes her jacket from the hallway and hands it to her.

"Another time," she says.

Then she's out the door, leaving it open, the cold evening air washing over Erik, finally waking him up.

"That's the boys' teacher?" Rob's eyes follow her down the street. "I need to get some children, man."

*

Six beers and a football victory later, Rob leaves. Erik feels restless. Perhaps it's the beer or it's Pernilla's fingers, still etched on his cock. Going to sleep is out of the question. He needs to do something, perhaps watch a movie? The TV is still on and he zaps through the channels. Except he can't hear anything. The mouths on the screen are moving but it feels as if he's accidentally pressed the "Mute" button. Nothing registers.

He switches the TV off and opens Anna's laptop instead; clicks on Safari and logs in to his new Gmail account. There are still no emails from blackadam4321. Anna's Outlook folder doesn't contain anything new either, not counting irrelevant junk mail. He clicks back to her folders and scrolls down the list. He's looked at most of them already. It's all pretty dull apart from the emails from blackadam4321. There are a couple near the bottom of the screen, which he hasn't seen yet. One is called "House" and another one simply "Other". The first one is full of bills and maintenance issues, everything predictably related to their house. He opens "Other" instead, expecting it to contain random messages that don't fit anywhere else. Except it only contains messages from one sender xeroxwed@gmail.com. Nothing about the name is familiar. He opens the first email.

I can't wait to see you this week. To be near you, to taste you. I miss you.

An uncomfortable feeling takes hold of his body. It's a total body freeze. He doesn't want to read this. He closes it down. Then opens it again.

What is Xeroxwed?

Despite himself, he clicks through to another message at random.

Your fingers clasped around my nipple, tugging. I can still smell you on my fingers. What have you done to me?

He stares at the screen. Then shuts it down. All of it. Power off.

PART TWO

24

Rolf

November 2015

A naked woman was strapped to the bed. Pale arms above her head, heavy breasts with mole-like nipples; dark-blue nails harsh against the skin. Another woman, dressed in a PVC corset, a stereotypical German bun on her head, bore down on the first woman, a leather whip entrusted to her strong hand. Muffled sounds of lashes hitting bare flesh; slivers of red across thighs, stomach and breasts. Rolf watched the two women, their perfectly shaped bodies and immaculately made-up faces, making the right noises, their aim to arouse him. Finally, the dominant woman pleasured the submissive with a dildo, bringing her to a climax that was restricted due to the straps holding her down.

"How original," he said.

He felt bored, his erection separated from his mind.

"Well, I'm turned on," Måna said. She mischievously took the remote control out of his hand and clicked "Pause".

He turned to Måna, her bronze-coloured cheeks, abnormally plump lips, the brown ringlets of hair reaching her full bosom. She was a goddess and there was no way he wouldn't finish what he had started.

He tied her up, her bed the perfect set-up: a black wrought-iron four-poster with leopard print throws and pillows. The scarves were strong and Måna agreeable.

Once his work of art was complete, Rolf admired his own skills along with her spread-eagle position. Grabbing her long hair, holding it in a firm grip, he bore into her. She gasped, laughed and moaned, but after a while he felt like it was merely skin rubbing against skin, rather than fucking. He couldn't climax.

Måna was loud when she came, a trait he loved in a woman, but he had to focus, close his eyes and think of... Iris. Pressed up against Lena in the library kitchen, their bodies barely visible from the street. That did it. He groaned and exploded into the condom.

Climbing out of bed, he felt hot and sticky and quickly started to get dressed.

"You're not staying the night?"

He smiled sweetly, leaned down towards Måna's rosy face and kissed her long and hard (leaving a lasting Rolf impression). Then he stood back and studied her intently, taking a mental picture. He wanted to remember them all.

"Your hair is incredibly shiny," he said. "Would you let me cut a lock off to remember you by?"

It wasn't unusual for women to appear in his work in one form or another, each piece a sample of DNA. Måna chuckled, so obviously comfortable in her nakedness, her glistening body crumpling the bed linen.

"If anyone else had said that, it would sound creepy," she said. "But I know your work so I will agree."

This threw him. He never told anyone his real identity.

He was Fredrik, the journalist, or Niklas, the art critic. There had been a time when he had chased the fame to pay the bills, but then he had chased the fame for fame. Iris had warned him about the added exposure, how it could compromise their lifestyle, but he had told her she was paranoid. Should the papers get hold of his personal affairs, then well… bad press was also good press. As long as it was all legal. Kinky was legal. For the most part.

"Don't worry," Måna said. "Your secret is safe with me."

"Scissors?" he asked.

She nodded her head towards a desk in the far corner, and he walked across the carpeted room, opening the drawers until he found a large pair, probably meant for sewing. Her eyes were gleaming with excitement as he cut into the brown hair.

Then he kissed her one last time and made to leave.

"Are you not going to untie me?"

Her smile faded.

"You got yourself into this," he said. "I'm sure you can get yourself out of it."

*

Rolf walked through the streets, making his way back to the car. He would tell Iris that his meeting with a gallery owner had gone well and she would congratulate him. Or he would be honest. He wasn't sure yet. Perhaps it was old age but he felt jaded after a life of sexual exploration. He had tried everything except monogamy: having Iris all to himself.

The air was cold, the pavements lined with drunk youngsters, beers in their hands, shrieks of laughter, open jackets revealing skimpy outfits. He walked past them, not even noticing the young breasts on display.

He stopped at a bar and ordered a whiskey on the rocks and downed it.

"Tough night?" the bartender asked, a tattooed snake wrapped around his muscled arm.

If only you knew, Rolf thought. *You would be jealous as hell.*

"I miss my wife," he said instead.

"Gotcha."

Tattoo man poured him another whiskey. "On the house, mate."

"Thanks." Kindness offered by strangers always surprised him.

"So, you're on a business trip?"

"Something like that," Rolf said distractedly, the fingers in his pocket wrapped around the silky smooth hair.

"Your wife couldn't join you?"

He imagined Iris standing next to him, the two of them on a weekend trip. No more women. No more extramarital sex. Was that really what he wanted? He nodded to himself: yes.

Rolf looked up; the guy's eyes were a bit too inquisitive for his liking.

He was tempted to say that his wife was dead, to make him squirm. Except he couldn't say the words "Iris" and "dead" in the same sentence.

"I've got to go," he said.

25

Anna

November 2015

Anna parked on the dusty gravel and walked up to Iris's house. It was fairly large, with an extension to the left, three doors facing the courtyard she was standing in. She stepped up to what she assumed was the main entrance but couldn't find a doorbell. Instead she knocked hard, small flecks of red paint peeling off, landing by her feet.

After their last meeting had been interrupted by Lena and her adolescent attitude, Anna's excitement about book club had been dampened slightly. She had passed on Lena's greeting to Kent and his reaction had confirmed her gut feeling: "She's a nutcase," he had said. "Don't involve yourself with her unless you have to."

Iris had called Anna, which at first had surprised her since they had never swapped numbers, but then she had remembered that her contact details – much to Erik's annoyance – were publicly listed.

"Would you mind if we meet at my house next week

instead?" she had asked. "The vents are being cleaned at the library."

Anna's enthusiasm had immediately been resurrected. She would have the opportunity to soak in Iris's home atmosphere, to learn more about her, and that was exciting. Although she had to admit she was nervous about potentially meeting Iris's husband. Rolf Sören had featured in the newspaper over the weekend after it was discovered that one of the paintings in his "Red Series" was painted with one hundred per cent pig's blood. He had claimed it was from a local butcher's shop but the art critics had had a field day, claiming he had killed the pig himself.

Iris was barefoot when she opened the door, wearing a multi-coloured kaftan. It was the first time Anna had seen her in anything other than black.

"There you are," Iris said, opening up her arms. "I hope you didn't get lost."

They embraced in a typical greeting. It was genuine but quick.

"I almost did," Anna said. "It's so dark out here without streetlights."

"That's what I like," Iris said. "It's almost as if we don't exist, it's so deserted and tranquil."

Anna held up a golden-brown sponge creation. "I baked a banana cake," she said.

"Lovely. Come on in."

Inside, there were a number of lanterns and tea-lights, creating a truly wonderful ambiance.

"I simply love candles," Iris said. "Don't you?"

They sat down in the living room, the walls made up of unpainted terracotta-coloured bricks, the furniture random, the sofas covered in blankets. Books were everywhere: stacked on the coffee table, lined up on shelves, in piles on the floor. Various paintings were either hanging or leaning up against the walls. Anna didn't understand what most of them portrayed, but then she wasn't that interested in Rolf Sören's art.

"Welcome to our creative chaos," Iris said.

They sat down, sinking into a couple of deep armchairs with batik-patterned cushions. Anna was about to ask one of her pre-prepared small-talk questions (*How was your week? Have you read* War and Peace? *Can you recommend any new Swedish authors?*) when Iris said: "You look amazing."

"Oh…" She looked down on her grey shirtdress. "This old thing?" she said, even though it was brand new. It looked so plain in Iris's vibrant living room.

Iris wasn't wearing her reading glasses this evening, only a hint of mascara framing her green eyes.

"I really enjoyed *Kallocain*," Anna said.

Iris poured the coffee and handed Anna a knife and plates for the cake.

"What did you like about it?"

Anna felt self-conscious, as if her role as a teacher had been exchanged with that of a student. At the same time, she couldn't help wanting to perform well.

"It was scary how the state really controlled the people in the book," she said. "How they couldn't think for themselves."

"I think the idea of the truth serum is fascinating," Iris said. "How Leo Kall uses it on his wife because he thinks she will reveal that she's in love with someone else."

"Only he finds out she fantasises about killing him," Anna said.

"Exactly. It works against him."

"Can you imagine?" Anna said, sitting back. "Living with someone who wants to kill you?"

"This is delicious!" Iris exclaimed as she bit into the cake. "Leo and Linda's marriage isn't real of course," she continued, wiping her mouth on a small square napkin. "The purpose of the marriages in the book is to produce children, nothing else."

"I know. It's a strange set-up," Anna agreed.

"Not all marriages are the same," Iris said, chewing on the cake. "I wouldn't want to harm Rolf but he's not enough for me."

He wasn't enough for Iris? But she *adored* him? Anna processed the new information, shocked but intrigued. She took a piece of cake and sipped her coffee, not quite sure how to respond.

"I'm going to make more coffee," Iris said and stood up. "This is cold."

Anna moved in her seat, pulling at her dress. She wanted to be friends with Iris and that meant communicating.

"What do you mean exactly?" Anna said. "About him not being enough?"

"I mean," Iris said, picking up the thermos. "I mean that I'm not monogamous."

It sounded so matter of fact; Iris's face open, the personal divulgence like a trap released.

Anna's heart beat fast.

"You're not?" she said. "What about your husband?"

"Neither of us is," Iris said simply. "Not that we broadcast it."

Anna nodded. "Wow."

"Anyway, that's not for everyone. Do you want more coffee?"

Iris made her way to the kitchen and Anna quickly got up

to join her, a feeling of wanting to normalise the environment in which the bomb had landed.

"I don't think Boye was monogamous either," Anna said, catching up to Iris. *Let's talk literature.*

"Actually, I think she was," Iris said. "Just because she lived with a woman doesn't mean she cheated."

"Maybe, I don't know."

Working in tandem, Iris pulled out a new filter and filled it with coffee while Anna measured the water.

"Boye was modern that way," Anna said. "Living with a woman even though it was against the law. I admire that. Everyone should be brave enough to be who they are."

Iris nodded, pouring the water into the coffee maker.

Contemplatively, and without thinking, Anna continued: "And you're not monogamous."

For a moment, Iris looked unsure. She switched the machine on and as it kicked into gear, water started spluttering out. They both turned their attention to the glass pot, filling up with the tar-like liquid.

"Does that mean you see other people?" Anna asked.

They didn't look at each other; still transfixed by the fresh brew.

"It does," Iris said eventually.

"I shouldn't pry," Anna said, apologising. She rinsed out their mugs and put them on the sink, next to an amazing AGA cooker. "I can't remember, do you take milk?"

"It's fine," Iris said, resting a hand on Anna's arm. "Don't worry about it. I never talk about it because, well, it's a small town and I don't want people to judge me."

"I won't tell anyone."

"I know you won't. And yes, I do take milk."

26

Iris

November 2015

After a deep but lively discussion about the permeated darkness in *Kallocain*, Anna made to leave. She started stacking the plates and the coffee cups and Iris had to stop her. "I'll do it later," she said.

She didn't want the ordinary to overshadow the mystery too much.

Anna put her coat on, a warm woolly creation, and leaned in for their farewell hug. Iris couldn't resist closing her eyes, feeling Anna's curves, assured that the thick fabric wouldn't give her away. Anna lingered longer than normal, her ear warm on Iris's cheek.

Iris knew that she had opened the door of possibilities. All she needed to do now was invite Anna in. *Always follow your instincts*. And so she did. Leaving the warmth of the embrace, she pulled back and faced Anna. Their eyes locked and Iris could sense her uncertainty. Then, very gently so as not to scare Anna away, she put her hands around Anna's glowing face and leaned in.

Soft. Her lips were soft.

Anna seemed puzzled yet she didn't pull away so Iris brought her closer. Their bodies were touching now, the kiss growing intense; lips explored, strong flavours of dark roasted beans mixed with longing. Anna wrapped her arms around Iris, showing an enthusiasm Iris hadn't expected, which made her heart beat stronger. The minutes got lost; Iris wanted Anna to stay. For a long, long time.

"Wait," Anna said, breaking away. There was panic in her voice. "Rolf?"

"He's not home," Iris said. "He will be back very late."

"You're sure?"

Iris held Anna's face in her hands. "Anna, I have never brought anyone to my home before."

Anna's face relaxed.

"What happens here, is no one else's business," Iris continued. "It's just between you and me."

She removed Anna's coat, then kissed her neck, her cheeks, her nose, her forehead. Her lips.

Anna looked down. "I'm nervous," she said quietly.

So fragile. Iris would need to be gentle.

She opened the buttons in Anna's dress, one by one; her breasts warm against Iris's own body. She could sense Anna handing herself over, her body weightless, lithe and willing.

They moved smoothly from the hallway to the living room, transporting their bodies from up against the wall, to the couch, to the floor, like two characters in a silent movie, their bodies entwined. As they moaned, caressed and kissed, clothing began to fall to the floor.

27

Erik

March 2016

When Erik married Anna he never imagined she might die before him. They never signed a pre-nup, nor did they draw up wills. Naïve perhaps but they never even discussed it. Only when they bought the house, did they arrange life insurance. That way the mortgage would be paid off, should one of them die. It felt morbid, signing those papers. Although necessary of course. Mature. It made him feel responsible.

Anna isn't dead. She's still in this limbo-land where she might wake up or she might not. When people ask him about her condition, he gets annoyed, and to deal with it better, he's come up with a standard reply: "All we can do is wait."

He has learned not to show too much emotion. Sometimes his emotions can be beneficial of course. Like when he called the council office about new day care placements for the children. He's still in a queue but someone now cares enough to work on it. Soon, it will be resolved – "to give Sebastian and Lukas a fresh start" – and he will never have to see Pernilla again.

Anna once insinuated that he had cheated. It was the night he had been out with Rob. For weeks, he felt nervous every time Anna dropped or picked up the children at day care but at the time, Pernilla seemed to regard it as what it was: a one-night stand.

Erik cheated. Only once. It barely counts but he recognises that he did. With Anna it is different. He never expected her to be unfaithful. Especially since she no longer seemed interested in sex. Yet she did cheat. He knows this. The question is, how does he notify the police? He could show the emails Anna was sent from Xeroxwed, but they could be viewed as harmless. Internet chats done in the comfort of your own home, without the exchange of bodily fluids.

That's when he has a "light bulb" moment.

*

As soon as Rob steps over the threshold, Erik lashes out: "Did you fuck my wife?"

He slams the door shut behind Rob, locks it. Now there's no escape.

"Dude, what are you talking about?"

The offended look on Rob's face.

"Took you by surprise, did I? Thought I wouldn't find out? You have to have all the girls, don't you?" Erik grabs Rob's collar and shoves him up against the wall. Coats and bags come crashing down, landing in a heap on the wooden floor. "Including Anna."

He's spitting and Rob angrily wipes his face.

"Get off me!" Rob shouts.

He takes hold of Erik's shirt. A button pops.

"Just bloody admit it, will you?" Erik shouts back.

"You're one to talk. Having a beer with the boys' sexy teacher while your wife is in a coma."

That does it. The pain goes deep into Erik's stomach and he wants Rob to feel that same throbbing soreness. He lunges at him and Rob buckles and ends up flattened on the floor. There's a distinct look of contempt on Rob's face as he gathers his limbs. Erik's anger subsides momentarily but he can't stop now. He grabs hold of Rob's shoulders to head-butt him when Rob shakes him off, sweat running down his furrowed brow.

"Get the fuck away from me!"

"Just admit it..." Erik starts, his voice trailing off.

Once again, the fury makes room for something else. Rob is his best friend... Fuck. Tears push against his eyelids but he won't cry in front of Rob. He leans forward but instead of hitting Rob, he embraces him. Hard.

"What the hell is going on?"

Rob's voice is angry but it also sounds concerned.

"Did you sleep with her?" Erik asks.

"Of course not! Who do you think I am?"

"A womaniser?"

Erik is half-serious, half-joking but Rob is clearly beyond offended.

"Your best pal's wife is off limits, man."

"I'm just so confused right now," Erik says.

"Then talk to me. Don't fucking attack me."

"Sorry. Come here, I need to show you something."

He pulls Rob into the kitchen.

"Whatever you say," Rob says, following him. "I know

168

168

you're upset but don't ever do that again."

Instead of answering, Erik opens Anna's laptop and logs in. He opens the "Other" folder and picks an email at random. "Read this."

Just thinking about you makes me wet. Your moans. Tender, passionate, wild. You're insatiable. And I love it.

Erik studies Rob's contorting face.

"What *is* this?"

"An email."

"I can see that. Who's it from? Your little teacher friend?"

"What? No! It was sent to Anna."

Rob's eyes widen, his mouth a big dark hole. "Anna?"

Erik relaxes, his own feelings justified.

"Wait," Rob says. "You thought I sent these? That's why you just accused me of...?"

"I'm sorry, I just don't know what to think anymore. This has completely thrown me."

"I'm impressed," Rob says, smiling and looking like his old self. "You thought I had written this? That is way too poetic for me. I would be like 'you make me wanna come'. Straight to the point, you know?"

"Rob, we're talking about my wife."

"Sorry, but how could you possibly think I wrote that?"

Rob scratches his head and they both stare at the screen.

"So who sent it?" Rob asks. "Are there more?"

Erik nods. "There are loads. I have no idea who sent them. It must be some sick joke, or... I don't know. We weren't, you know..." He squirms but clears his throat and says it: "... having sex all that often."

Although he's allowed himself to be vulnerable, Rob

doesn't seem to notice. He's busy clicking back to the folder to open another email.

"Have you shown this to the police?"

Erik shakes his head. "Not yet. They're sort of accusing me of cheating so I don't want them to think that I made this up."

"It's evidence, though. Black and white. This could be a motive. Jealous lover attacks... or something. It's just that I can't believe that Anna would cheat. She's so... perfect. But it definitely seems that way." He looks at Erik with compassion. "I'm sorry, man."

"Thanks. I'm just... Maybe you could mention it to the police?"

"Me?" Rob looks like it's a crazy idea. "I would have to tell them you showed it to me and then they would wonder why you're not telling them yourself."

"No, I thought that perhaps..." Erik thinks carefully about what he says next. "... that perhaps you could tell them you suspected she was cheating."

"But they will ask who with and I won't know. I mean, I want to help but I... Oh, wait a minute..." Rob stands up straight, his hand is in the air as if he's asking for permission to speak.

"What?"

"What I said earlier, about the emails being poetic," Rob says. "Do you think a teacher could write something like that?"

"I'm not sure..." Where is he going with this?

"Maybe what's-his-name, her colleague, wrote it? Kent?"

Erik nods slowly even though he doesn't agree.

"Maybe you need to pay him a visit," Rob says.

"If I do, will you go to the police?"

"Let's see what you find out first."

Rob looks like he's playing a part in a soap opera but Erik isn't stupid. He knows what he has to do.

*

Kent and Märta live in an art deco house at the outskirts of town, accompanied by an unruly garden. Erik navigates through the tall grass, where there used to be a tiled path.

The moment Märta opens the door he thinks: *I would cheat with Anna if I were Kent.* He would need a bit of fun on the side. It's not that Märta is ugly, she's just tense, the lines in her face deep, making her look grouchy. That would put them in the same boat. Him and Märta, bobbing on the ocean of adultery victims.

"I'm here to see Kent," he says.

She shakes his hand. "I'm so sorry about Anna." Her lines soften, a sympathetic smile appears.

"Thanks. And... thank you for the flowers you sent."

Kent and Märta sent white lilies to the hospital. Kent obviously knew they were Anna's favourite.

"There you are." Kent shows up, giving him a manly, albeit uncomfortable, hug. "I've been trying to call you. How is she?"

"The same." Erik clears his throat. "All we can do is wait."

"She's strong, Erik. She will get better."

Erik nods. *What do you know?*

"Come in, sit down."

They draw him into their home, filled with old-fashioned farm cupboards, flower-patterned cushions and figurines, making him feel like he's in his mother's house. A cup of coffee is placed in his hand, accompanied by a Vanilla Heart on a plate. He takes a bite, the sweet custard filling his mouth.

"How are the boys?"

He swallows and takes a gulp of the coffee. They need to get through the pleasantries so that they can get down to business.

"They're okay," he says. "Dealing with it, you know. They're brave. Sleeping right now. My mate, Rob, is at the house."

The words seem to disappear into space, like puffs of smoke. He felt more sure of this when he left home. Confrontation is never comfortable, especially not with someone like Kent. Erik reminds himself that Kent may have been Anna's support pillar at work but he did not father Anna's children. *He* did. He is the man.

Kent stands up and pours Erik a whiskey.

"You look like you need one."

Erik agrees and takes a sip as soon as it's placed in his hand. It's strong and smooth.

"So, I just need to ask you some questions," he finally says, mounting up the courage. "Was Anna... happy at school?" Let's start there.

"You know she loves her job."

"Yeah, I know. But were there any problems?"

Kent seems to think about this.

"She had a tough start to the year," Kent says. "I'm sure she's told you about the new boy. He had some issues and Anna wanted to help him."

Erik racks his brain, searching for a point of reference? Did she talk about having problems with a student?

"What kind of issues did he have?" he asks.

"He was getting himself into fights."

"Right, had no problem beating people up, did he?"

"Erik." Kent seems to understand what he's getting at. "We can't jump to conclusions."

"Why not?"

"Erik, she did her best and he did calm down. Anna definitely had something to do with that, which is exactly what I told the police. He respected her and wouldn't have attacked her, is my opinion."

"His name isn't Adam, is it?"

"No, and you really shouldn't go chasing after her students, Erik."

"Okay, what about you then? Were you a support to Anna?"

"Of course, we talked about it regularly."

"After hours."

"Sometimes."

"Right."

Silence descends on them. They look at each other, tension prevalent in the air. Until Märta speaks: "Are you insinuating something here?" She looks intrigued rather than upset.

"Is that so strange?" Erik defends himself. "Anna fucking loves Kent. It's always 'Kent this' and 'Kent that'."

Kent looks baffled. "We are very good friends, Erik."

The way he says it makes Erik feel dirty. As if he has dragged something pure and beautiful through the mud that will never be completely clean again. He's already crossed the line though. No point turning back.

"That's it? You sure?"

"Erik, I am one hundred per cent sure. I'm flattered that

you think she would be interested in an old bloke like me, but I am not on the market." He exchanges a smile with Märta. They're so textbook. Happily ever after.

"So who do you think attacked Anna?"

"I honestly don't know," Kent says. He's resting a hand on Märta's knee, as if he needs to reassure her that he is there for her, no one else. "I feel like Anna has been so happy lately. A bit withdrawn perhaps but radiant, I would say."

Radiant? Erik nods. "So you think she was cheating on me?"

Kent looks perplexed. "Not at all."

Shit. Why doesn't anyone cooperate?

"But it's possible?" Erik probes.

Kent shakes his head. "I think she would have told me."

Do you now? What else would she have told you? Erik imagines Anna and Kent after work, heads close together, her soft voice complaining about her husband, gaining Kent's sympathy. It burns his ego as much as his heart.

"Have you been helping the police?" Erik asks.

Kent takes an annoyingly long sip of his whiskey. "As I already explained, I have spoken to them, yes. But I don't think I have been all that helpful." He looks Erik in the eye. "I can't think of anyone who would want to harm Anna."

28

Daniel

D an cycled around town, past Anna's two-storey house and its empty driveway. The lights were on and he could make out her husband and their two small boys at the kitchen table. A white ceramic lamp dangled from the ceiling, lighting up their plates of meatballs and mashed potatoes. "Lingonberry?" he imagined their father asking them as he passed them the red jar. They shook their little heads, stretching their hands out to the bottle of ketchup instead. Anna had probably hand-rolled the meatballs and made the mashed potatoes from scratch, or maybe her husband had. Frida only ever bought the supermarket's readymade super-savers pack. She would eat the meatballs with her fingers, often dressed in only her underwear. Occasionally, if she was sober and her payday didn't end up at the liquor store, she would actually cook. His favourite meal was *fläskpannkaka*, a thick oven pancake made with pork.

A car came driving down the road and he quickly hid

behind a bush. A station wagon passed him; it wasn't Anna's black Volvo but a navy-blue Volkswagen Passat. He felt like throwing a stone at it but thought better of it. He didn't want to draw attention to himself. Inside the house, dinner seemed to be over. While the boys ran out of the kitchen, their father took care of the dishes. Dan promised himself to help clear the table when he lived there. Anna would smile and thank him for being so helpful.

Except Anna wasn't there. Where was she? He waited for another hour, then cycled down to the town centre where he bought a hot dog. He was starving after seeing Anna's family eat. With the hot dog in his hand, he continued on to the church. Not only was it clad in scaffolding while it was being painted, making it easy to hide; it was also strategically placed between two roads, both acting as entrances into Mörna. From here, he would be able to see Anna's car. But it didn't show.

An hour later, he went back to Anna's house. Now the lights were out and goodnight stories most likely read. A faint blue flicker, perhaps from a TV, could be seen from the room next to the dark kitchen. Nothing else. He toyed with the idea of ringing the doorbell.

"When will Anna be home?" he would ask. "I have a question about an assignment."

But what if her husband looked at him with disgust, a misplaced nobody who interrupted his evening? He couldn't take that risk.

In the end he had no choice but to go back to Frida. She was snoring on the couch but at least the dickhead was gone. He preferred it when her shags didn't stay the night. No smug or guilty face eyeing him up in the morning. Both scenarios were equally excruciating.

He went into Martin's room. Soon it would be packed up. Not that his brother had many belongings. Next to the wardrobe there was an old hockey stick and his second-hand ice skates. They hadn't been skating in a while. His brother had outgrown most of their regular activities. Dan wondered why his brother hadn't moved out sooner. *Because of me.* He had stayed to protect his little brother. The realisation made him head for the door. He felt guilty, the weak sibling in need of babying. Dan would make it easy for Martin. He would move out and create his own future.

Back in his room, he flopped down on his bed, his shoes still on, and stared at the now familiar ceiling. He had thought about sneaking back inside the teachers' lounge but he wasn't sure. That first time, Kent had unfortunately snuck up on them and he had been forced to escape into a closet down the corridor before running outside. The second time he had had Anna to himself but she had been on edge and that wasn't the way he liked her. He wanted her to hug him and stuff, tell him everything was okay, that she loved him.

In his notebook, he continued his story.

"Where do you want me to sleep?" he asked.

"In the basement, so that my husband doesn't get suspicious."

"Does he... touch you?"

She looked alarmed.

"No, we never have sex anymore," she said. "I'm leaving him. Plus we have young children so that wouldn't be appropriate."

He felt pleased.

"I'm going to take care of you," he said.

"Oh Dan!" she said, her eyes happy.

She seductively undressed in front of him, revealing an

hourglass figure. Pulling him close, her hand started knea-
ding the growing bulge between his legs.

Dan stopped writing, his cock hard, his mind filled with confidence. Now he knew what he needed to do. He had to either catch Anna outside of school or her home, where there was no one else; just the two of them. The next evening he would be better prepared. If Frida's car was back from the shop, he would drive. He might not have a licence but he knew how to get around. Otherwise, he would "borrow" the neighbour's moped. That way she wouldn't escape.

29

Iris

November 2015

Anna was on Iris's mind the moment she woke up. She dared to admit she felt happy. Anna on the other hand, would probably be feeling guilty right now. *Love them but leave them*, Rolf would have said. He had always offered so much advice. Too much. There had been times when she had toyed with the idea of leaving Rolf, but she felt she owed him too much. They had met at a time when her confidence was at rock bottom, and he had made her feel worthy. Would she ever feel like she had repaid him?

With Anna, Iris felt she had achieved the impossible. Anna was so unlike anyone she had ever wanted, so unpretentious and real. There was nothing remotely flaky about her. The fact that they had made love amazed her. If Rolf knew, he would have felt proud, pulled her close and wanted her, right there. He got off on her affairs, had encouraged them from the moment they met. But he didn't know about Anna and neither would he.

Iris felt she needed to get to know Anna better, explore...

She sighed and shook her head. Anna was much younger. She had a family. It was most likely already over.

"Coffee?" Rolf handed her a cup and sat down on the bed. "Fun night last night?"

"I should be asking you."

She had smelt perfume on him as he crept into bed. He used to think that turned her on: "It's a reminder that although others find me attractive, I'm still yours at the end of the night."

"Last night was actually quite boring," Rolf said and gently stroked her cheek.

Then he got back into bed and spooned her. It was the last thing she had expected.

"You're going to make me spill my coffee," she said.

"Sorry." His right hand was cradling her breast, the left hand playing with her hair.

"Are you okay?" she asked.

"I missed you last night, and I was thinking… perhaps we should, I don't know, renew our vows?"

He stroked her nipple through the sheer fabric of her nightie. She tensed even though she enjoyed the sensation his touch caused her body.

"Why now?" she asked.

"Because I want to start over."

At that, she gently pushed his arm away, rejecting his words.

"I want us to be exclusive," he said. "Not see other women anymore."

She laughed. "Is it April Fool's Day?"

He pulled himself up on one elbow and looked at her. "I mean it." His facial expression looked hurt and for a moment she felt sympathy for her husband of twenty-two years, a sporadic sense of pity. That was until the bleaker memories of their marriage resurfaced, the feelings of inadequacy, of being shared.

"But it was your idea," she said.

"I've had enough, Iris. You're the one I want to spend my life with."

"You must have had a bad evening, Rolf. What did she do? Did she talk too much? Did she criticise your art? Did she turn out to be male?" She forced a laugh, trying to be overly humorous to distract from her own emotional evening. *Anna on the floor, her eyes filled with affection.*

"No, Iris, it wasn't like that. Anyway, you don't want to know."

"Normally I don't, but I can make an exception since this one seems to have given you some sort of an epiphany."

"It wasn't her. She was fine, attractive, great hair." He pulled out a brown, shiny lock from his bedside table and showed it to her.

"That's disgusting."

"She gave it to me willingly."

She sipped her hot coffee.

"Lena called me to tell me about your affair," he said.

That didn't surprise her. Lena had been mad.

"I thought as much," Iris said. "Did you at least pretend to be upset?"

"Of course. She wants to meet me to tell me all about it."

She felt calm although it was clearly a problem that needed to be solved. Lena was part of her work life.

"Maybe," she said and turned to Rolf. "You could... I don't know. Pay her some attention? So that we can end this."

"Really? What about being exclusive?"

She stroked his chest. "You know you don't really want

that. Anyway, you think she's hot, don't you? And this one time, I don't mind sharing."

"Why not?"

She wasn't sure exactly but most likely because there was someone else, a woman who made her feel something new entirely.

"I stayed with her for too long," Iris said. "She's all yours."

He seemed to contemplate this. "She *is* a knock-out," he said. "Want to fuck?"

He looked so excited, she felt she needed to reward him for agreeing to her plan, and so she embraced him and fucked away, her closed eyes imagining someone else. A woman who quite possibly would break her heart.

30

Erik

March 2016

When Erik returns home from Märta and Kent's house, Rob is asleep on the couch. He opens a beer and sits down next to his mate. To clear his head. He wishes he could put electrodes on either side of his brain and flick a switch, go back in time. Then he would have been a better listener, more attentive; he would have been a musician, not just a wannabe doing gigs at near-empty bars. He would have kept his dick in his pants, been an amazing husband. Fatherhood should have made him grow up. He worked that out too late.

"Isn't life a bitch?" he says to Rob. "When you finally realise what you have, it's gone?"

Rob snores and Erik takes another sip. The beer goes down with ease. He gets another bottle, then another. He switches the TV on, zaps through the channels. It's all so boring, so far removed from reality.

Rob wakes up. "Sorry, did I fall asleep?"

"Yeah."

He sits up, rubs his eyes and yawns.

"So, what did he say?"

"Not much." Erik leans back. "Something about a bratty student."

"What about him and her? I mean Anna and Kent?"

"Nah. Don't think so."

"Look, I've been thinking," Rob says.

"Really? Hurt your head?"

Rob does an uppercut under Erik's arm.

"Careful!" He laughs. "No, but seriously. I could call Tina. Maybe tell her that Anna was cheating?"

"Maybe."

Erik thinks. Actually, that might be a brilliant idea.

"She can pass the info on to whoever is dealing with the case," Rob says.

"Won't she say it came from you?"

"She loves me, man. She's been calling me and stuff. I'm sure she will be cool with it."

"That would be great. Thanks."

Rob doesn't even wait. He takes out his phone and calls Tina straight away.

*

The next day, Pernilla sends several explicit photos. Erik keeps the phone far away from the boys these days and clears it of anything inappropriate. Pernilla isn't just satisfied with pictures. She also sends many, many messages:

When can we meet up? Let's have some fun. You and me = forever.

He responds to none of these. Although it makes it particularly awkward to drop the children at day care.

Today, however, the boy with the denim jacket and untied shoes is outside the day care gate. He cycles towards them.

"My dad used to have a jacket like yours," Sebastian says.

"Anna is my teacher," he says. This time he speaks. "I hope she's getting better."

"Thanks, pal. I appreciate it."

The boy nods his head and cycles off but Erik spots an opportunity.

"Hey," he calls after the boy. "What's your name?"

"Da... David," he stutters.

"Can I ask you something?" Erik says. "Please."

The boy stops his bike and looks at them. His hair is dishevelled and although his jacket is still cool, Erik can now see that it's in need of a wash, the denim no longer blue.

Erik takes a leap of faith.

"Is there a boy in Anna's class called Adam?"

Erik thinks of the emails from Black Adam. Unstable. Possessive. Direct. Does this boy know who Black Adam is?

The boy looks puzzled. "Eh, no," he says.

Erik takes a couple of steps towards him. "You sure? What about in another class at your school, is someone, anyone, called Adam?"

"Maybe," the boy says. He adjusts the folded sleeves on his jacket. "It's not an unusual name." He pauses. "Why do you want to know?"

"Nothing really. I just thought that perhaps she had talked about someone called Adam."

"Oh. Like, what did she say?" The boy is holding onto the handlebars again, ready to cycle off. "I mean, maybe I can help?"

"No, that's okay," Erik says. This was perhaps not the best move. "Anyway, nice to meet you. I'd better get the boys inside."

"Sure."

Erik watches his back swerve around a corner.

"He's cool," Lukas says, awe in his voice.

"Yeah," Erik says.

Inside the day care building, the cloakroom is almost empty. Thank goodness. The boys put their backpacks away, hang up their coats and put their shoes on the rack.

"Good job," he says to them, sounding like Anna.

"There's Sophie!" exclaims Sebastian and he's off, running inside to the action, where children and teachers sing and play instruments. Lukas joins him and Erik is sure he's rolling his eyes at his brother.

He sighs with relief. He can't see Pernilla.

Back in the Volvo, he calls Linda Johansson for an update. Hopefully Tina's news has reached her fast, but she seems rushed off her feet and doesn't mention anything.

"I'm sorry," she says. "I know this is very difficult for you and your family but unfortunately we can't share information about the investigation with you. We'll be in touch."

"Trust Tina," Rob said. He hopes his mate is right.

31

Rolf

November 2015

Rolf put his heart and soul into fucking Lena. He hadn't expected any bells or whistles but anger could apparently be converted into the wildest passion. She really wanted to get back at Iris.

"You're not Iris, but you're pretty good," she said, her hair sweaty, perfectly round, fake breasts resting above a trim stomach.

Iris's ongoing affair with Lena had endured for too long and he emptied himself into her, marking his territory. Then he stood to leave. He didn't ask for any hair, didn't clip one of her nails or ask for a drop of saliva. It was a revenge fuck, not a piece of art.

Exiting the motel room, leaving a satisfied Lena in bed, he got into his car and called Iris.

"It's taken care of," he said.

It seemed to take a while for her to register what he meant.

"Oh, good. Thanks."

"See you later?"

"I think so."

"Have something better to do?"

"Don't start, Rolf."

It was obvious that she didn't want to change their arrangement and although that frustrated him, he couldn't blame her. He still remembered having to convince her to have an open marriage in the first place. Just because it didn't suit him anymore, he couldn't realistically expect her to flick a switch. At the same time, he didn't like taking no for an answer.

"If you change your mind, I'll be in the studio," he said.

They hung up and he started the car.

Driving out of the city, down the familiar roads to their house in the countryside, his headspace was occupied with images. Iris and that woman, together. Normally, such a sighting would have meant a heightened sexual experience for the two of them later, or at least for him when he was on his own. There were times when he would go back to his car and pleasure himself, his eyes closed, his mind on Iris and her passing partner. Not last night. He had opened the door, seen the fireplace lit up (which in itself was unusual), the glow reflected on their naked bodies. It had been a shock. He recognised that perhaps it shouldn't have been but this was their home, which meant Iris had broken the rules and that had stunned him, then momentarily mesmerised him. *I like rule-breakers*. He had silently moved closer until he had seen them. Really seen them. The tenderness, Iris's hands caressing the other woman's face, her eyes glowing with desire; the other woman tentative, fully under Iris's spell. Jealousy had hit him, quite possibly for the first time, his gut on fire, his heart bruised.

At that point he had backed out of the room, an immediate

need to block out their moans, urgently escaping. He had stayed in the studio. He had tried to paint. He had tried to drink. He had tried to listen out for that woman's car leaving.

Who was she? Her ridiculously common Volvo V70 parked in their courtyard.

He had waited. And waited. He had poured the wine down the sink, the taste bitter and off. He had grabbed the car keys and left. A need to curb his boredom had made him call Frida. She was wild and a lot of fun. The way Måna had been. Although Måna had been a one-off, he had met Frida twice already. It wasn't forbidden but it was against their set principles that Frida was single and wanted him, not only as a lover, but all out. That wasn't allowed. You couldn't "complete a transaction" under those circumstances because then you would risk hurting someone. He distinctly remembered this being Iris's one and only request. But she seemed to have rewritten the rulebook since then, so what did it matter?

He had felt a strong need to get back on the horse, so to speak, to ride someone hard. And so what if Frida wanted him? At least someone did.

32

Erik

April 2016

At the hospital, a new bunch of flowers sits on the table next to Anna.

"They arrived this morning."

The nurse's words startle him. Erik turns around, he doesn't remember her name. He should know them all by now. Should recognise their faces. At the same time, he doesn't want to get too familiar.

"Maybe they're sent out of guilt," he says.

"You think whoever put her here sent her flowers and added his or her name on the card?"

She's mocking him. He turns away. There are too many thoughts in his head, crowding his frail brain. He wants to punch something. Hard. He waits until the nurse is gone and then he packs one into Anna's mattress. Her body barely moves but he still feels guilty.

The red roses are squashed together in the vase, there are so many of them. He reaches across and reads the card.

Your husband needs me. P.

He rips it out from the bouquet. Stares at it for another second to make sure he's read it correctly. Has anyone else read it? He rips it into miniature pieces and sprinkles them into the bin. Only he gets paranoid and starts to pick them out again.

"Lose something?"

The nurse is back in the room, watching him bent over the wired basket attached to the wall.

"My ring slipped off," he says.

"Oh, dear, can I help you?"

She's already standing next to him and he blocks her by grabbing hold of the basket with both hands, pretending to retch. "I'm going to be sick."

"But your ring?"

"I'll get it…" Pretend retching. "Later."

"Let me get you something else to vomit in," she says and she's off.

He manages to get the plastic bag out from the bin and ties a knot around it in time for her to return.

"I just need some fresh air," he says and shoots out of there.

*

Erik fires up the car engine and heads back home, although "home" is a loose term these days. It's where he used to live with his wife and children. Now it feels like a temporary place. Maybe they should move? He feels like they're stuck in time. Apart from the police having moved through the house like phantoms that first day when he was still at the hospital, everything is the way Anna left it, yet she's not there. The white-and-blue furniture runs through the house like a pulsating vein about to explode in his brain. If he moves anything or paints a wall, she might get upset if she comes back home. If he doesn't change anything, he might go crazy.

Inside the house he takes his shoes off and goes straight to the laptop, which he now keeps in a kitchen cupboard. He checks the emails regularly. He has composed at least twenty more emails to Black Adam but he hasn't sent them. He has also done some research on Kent to understand him better. After their meeting, he doesn't want the guy to think he's paranoid. He wants them to be cool, which means he might need to see him again, strike up a form of friendship. Not that he could find much out about Kent. From the Internet, he has learned that Kent attends theatre premieres and council meetings from time to time and that he has worked at the same school forever. Boring stuff. They don't have much in common.

Now he looks Pernilla up. Sometimes you need to know your enemies and she's obviously got it in for him. She's extremely active on social media, which doesn't surprise him. They're not friends on Facebook but he can still view her profile. Privacy doesn't seem to bother her. There are photos of Pernilla wearing sunglasses, Pernilla dancing, Pernilla drinking shots, Pernilla with her arms wrapped around friends in bikinis. Posing, her lips kissing the camera. He lingers a bit too long. It's like porn though, once you look, you can't stop.

It's harmless voyeurism but it makes him feel he can deal with her. Eventually he forces himself away from Pernilla's photo gallery to check Anna's emails. It's become a habit, to make sure he doesn't miss anything. Her inbox still receives subscription mail but no longer messages from her personal contacts. People obviously know about her coma by now. Does Black Adam also know?

It's a tedious task, checking emails all the time, but it keeps him sane to have a routine. Today, however, he notices a new email and it's not from Black Adam. He opens it, the feeling of surprise quickly replaced by total disbelief: it's from Anna's own mother and she most definitely knows that her daughter is in hospital with only a fifty per cent chance of survival.

Hi Anna, when you're back on your feet, I hope you will read this. Please know that I wanted to visit you but you know what your father is like. There's not much going on here. Helen's daughter is almost two now and she's such a little chatterbox. She has a real bond with her granddad and I think she has softened him somehow. Anyway, I hope the boys are well.

I miss you, Mum.

Apart from being completely disgusted, Erik isn't sure whether to also be utterly pissed off or if he should laugh. *Back on your feet?*

"She doesn't have flu, Gerda."

He feels a sudden loyalty to Anna, the way he used to when they first started dating, the two of them conquering the world.

"Just stay where you are," he says to the email. "That makes my life easier."

He feels angry and unsettled. What he would give to let

rip on his guitar with the band. Lately, they have excluded him from any jamming sessions. At first, it felt respectful but now it's infuriating. He's even heard rumours about some guy replacing him. He picks up the phone and calls Rob.

"Any gigs coming up?" he asks. No point wrapping it in cotton wool.

"Ehm, no."

"Are you jamming?"

"We know you're busy, Erik."

"Don't shut me out, I need to play." He realises he sounds too desperate but the words are flowing. "Come on, Rob. Please. It's the one thing I'm..."

No, he stops himself. He can't say it. *The one thing I'm good at.* He needs to sound less whiny. There's no need to alienate Rob. He needs his friend and music buddy.

"Did you speak to Tina?" he asks instead. "Did she deliver the information about Anna?"

"She's here," Rob says cheerfully.

"Really, you're what, back together?" That's a shocker. Erik has a bad feeling about it.

"Yeah, sort of," Rob says.

Thinking about it, Erik isn't sure he cares. Having Tina even closer might be good. He still has to ask: "I thought you said it was too much drama?"

There's giggling in the background and absentmindedly, Erik logs into his new email account. This is another routine. He does it every day, sometimes several times: opens and closes the inbox. Occasionally he receives emails about money he is supposed to have won or about penis extensions, the usual junk.

Rob resurfaces. "It's all good," he says. "Why don't you come over and meet her?"

"Wait..."

There's an email from Black Adam.

"I'll talk to you later, Rob."

Excited but nervous, he puts the phone down and opens the email.

Hi there, thank you for caring (whoever you are). I loved Anna. I still love her. Whatever I can do, please tell me. I will do anything.

Anything?

"How about revealing who you really are?"

And he "loved" her? Was it really a student? Erik had assumed so because of the mention of a test but perhaps it had been a different type of test? The thought makes his muscles tense.

Then he gets an idea.

Thank you. That's very kind of you. Do you know Xeroxwed?

If he doesn't get a response, then it's possible that Black Adam and Xeroxwed are one and the same. He's searched for emails that Anna might have sent to this Xeroxwed but hasn't found any. Maybe she deleted them. Or did she not reply at all?

It's such a mess. He rests his head in his hands, closes his eyes and wishes he were somewhere else, the emotions tearing him in different directions. Nothing means anything.

But then again, anything means something. Like a Rubik's cube, he twists and turns, hoping it will all come together. He needs to get everything back to normal.

33

Anna

November 2015

The road lay deserted in front of Anna as her old running shoes hit the asphalted pavement. The air was chilly and her lungs sore. Her body already wanted to give up but she kept going. The aim: to eliminate intrusive thoughts. Thinking would mean taking responsibility for her actions. It would mean entering reality where she was a wife and a mother and... a lesbian?

She stumbled, a tree root protruding through the cracked tarmac, briefly making her think of marriage. She shook her head at the absurdity and kept putting one foot in front of the other. Moving forward.

What had she done?

As she ran past the closed-down flower shop, the memory of Iris's feminine scent hit her, strong and sensual. That feeling of longing wrapping its arms around her chest. Desire.

Her run slowed to a walk. It wasn't just the way Iris smelt or how safe she made Anna feel, there seemed to be invisible ties pulling them close. They were so strong they scared her.

Her sex had been entrusted to Iris whose fingers had been soft but firm. Anna recognised that she had reciprocated, the arousal making her brave. All the way home, she had lifted her right hand from the steering wheel to smell her fingers, to remind herself of what had actually happened.

She picked up her pace again. Her heart was aching. Never in her life had she imagined doing what she had done. It had just felt so natural, like something she couldn't have stopped from happening. But she had cheated on Erik.

She ran faster.

The darkness closed in on her. Only a few lights were on in the town's houses. Most people were asleep. Her feet moved forward while her brain raced at an even faster speed. She ran past the small supermarket that was now closed, signalling that everything had shut down for the day. It was like a ghost town, eerily quiet without the sound of traffic.

Then a car came from behind. She could hear its wheels slowing down and braced herself, waiting for it to pass. Out of the corner of her eye, she noticed a dented bumper and paint peeling off. The car didn't pass by, instead it stopped and a dirty window was rolled down.

"Excuse me, is there a petrol station around here?"

A man in his fifties or sixties, sporting a moustache. A familiar face that she couldn't quite place. A student's parent?

"You need to turn around and go back," she said. "Then take the first road to your right. About fifty metres down you'll find a self-service station."

She started running again, feeling vulnerable. Most likely she was being paranoid but she wanted to keep moving. The car followed her and soon it was level with her again.

"Do you live around here?"

The question was unnerving and so she ignored him. She kept looking straight ahead as her feet ran forward but he kept driving next to her. Why hadn't she brought her phone? Her heart was beating double beats. Could she cut through the bushes to her right or run into someone's garden and ring a doorbell? While she was debating what to do, he sped off.

Had he really left? She waited for him to turn around and head towards the petrol station but instead he drove straight ahead as if exiting the town.

After a hundred metres or so, she stopped, out of breath. She looked over her shoulder but there was no one there. Yet she couldn't shake the feeling of unease and pushed herself to keep running no matter how much her throat hurt.

When she returned home, she needed a few minutes in the hallway to digest what had just happened. Was it just a weirdo trying his luck? She wanted to tell Erik about the man and the car but he was engrossed in an action movie and barely looked up. She hesitated for a moment, hoping he would turn to her and ask about her run. He didn't and so she decided not to bother him. He would probably tell her she was paranoid anyway.

In the bathroom, she undressed. Her pulse slowed down and she felt calmer, her focus now elsewhere: on Iris and their night together. Her fingers tracing Anna's curves, making her feel beautiful.

Anna viewed herself in the mirror. Her body felt different, it felt new. Her skin was glowing instead of looking loose and flabby and her breasts appeared shapely as opposed to sagging. As she stepped into the shower, hot water warming her up, she closed her eyes and stroked her arms, her hips, her waist, the same way Iris had done. She transported herself to Iris's living room, imagining her fingers were Iris's, following the line of her breasts and belly, down between her legs. Opening her eyes with a jolt, guilt overshadowed the sensation of lust: could she really see Iris again?

Then again, how could she not?

34

Rolf

November 2015

Frida's moody kid had just arrived home and Rolf wanted to smash his head in. The way he spoke to Frida was completely unacceptable. Except he didn't want to get involved. As soon as Dan slammed his door shut, Rolf got out of Frida's bed to dress.

"See you soon, lover boy," Frida said.

Her limbs were spread out on the flimsy duvet cover, her long, blonde hair floating around her head. She resembled an angel but she sure as hell wasn't one. He knew all about her financial difficulties as well as the liquor induced ones. It didn't worry him. She had never asked him for a single krona – he actually thought she genuinely wanted him to love her – and the booze… well, it made her one hell of a spirited lay, so no complaints there.

"Not sure when," he said because he worried that perhaps it was becoming a bit too regular.

The feeling of being with a woman who was in love with him was attractive and gave him comfort, but he wasn't going to throw his marriage away. Iris was his. At home, he had a rare painting with actual human blood in it, his and Iris's. The red blotches he had managed to squeeze out of their fingers on their wedding day had quickly dried to a dark brown on the canvas, but it served as a reminder of their eternal union.

Rolf left Frida's converted summerhouse and drove through Mörna. It was completely deserted, as most small towns after ten o'clock tended to be. That's why he was surprised to see a woman jogging along the pavement. It was always worth slowing down, especially when a woman was alone.

He rolled down his window and asked for a petrol station even though his tank was almost full. When she leaned down and peered at him, he couldn't come up with another single line. It was *her*. The woman who had screwed his wife on the Turkish rug in his living room. She gave him some directions to which he didn't listen and then she kept running. He couldn't just let her go and so he followed her. Did she live around here, a town that was only twenty minutes from his and Iris's home? He had to know if this woman, who made his wife irresponsible, lived so treacherously close to them. And perhaps not too tactfully, he asked her this directly.

"Do you live around here?"

She ignored him and he had no choice but to drive off and leave her and his resentment behind. He had to go home and reclaim his wife.

35

Anna

December 2015

The temperature had dropped below zero and the road was perilously icy, but Anna had to see Iris. She drove carefully to the library, and by the time she got there, it was almost closing time. She hurried inside and walked towards the counter, where Iris normally was; her heart racing, nerves and excitement making it difficult to concentrate.

Just then, Iris appeared from the back although she didn't seem to show any signs of recognition and that made Anna even more nervous. When Iris reached her, Anna had no idea what to say but Iris beat her to it.

"It's not Wednesday," she said, eyeing Anna over the reading glasses. "Did you finish the book already?"

The book? She couldn't remember what it was called. Had Iris even given her a new one?

"Jodi Picoult?" Iris clarified. "*Sing You Home?*"

Now she remembered. She had agreed to read a book in English, since the book was yet to be translated into Swedish.

"I haven't started it," she said truthfully.

Of course, she should have. She was at a library, meeting her librarian. Whether it was book club or not, she should be there because of books.

Disappointed, she made to leave. In the time they had been apart, she had obviously attached more importance to each and every little word that had been said in Iris's house, every touch, every moan. She had got it all wrong.

As she opened the door, the sky heavy with snow, she heard Iris's voice behind her.

"Wait."

Anna took a deep breath and turned back to face Iris, bracing herself for her words: "I think you misunderstood", "it was a mistake" or "it can't happen again".

"Why don't you make some coffee while I lock up?"

It was impossible to interpret Iris's gaze but a sense of relief still established itself in Anna's heart, making it lighter.

"Are you sure?" she asked.

"Yes. I'll just be a minute."

Anna walked through the familiar library, hoping everyone had already left so that they could be alone. No matter what was to come.

*

When Iris finally entered the kitchen, Anna was leaning on the counter, waiting for the coffee to brew. They faced each other and although Anna had spent the last ten minutes telling herself that she had no expectations, the moment she saw Iris, her sleek black jersey dress and silver bangles, she realised that she did.

Iris opened her mouth. "I…" she started and in sheer panic, Anna took a step forward, reached her arms out and pulled

Iris towards her, resting her chin on her shoulder blade. She closed her eyes and felt the softness of Iris's velvety dark hair, the droopy earrings shaped like black rain drops cold against her face, arms plaited into a tight embrace.

Then Iris pulled away. She was still holding onto Anna's arms as she raised her head. She had removed the glasses, her green eyes deep and naked. Butterfly wings touched the delicate lining of Anna's stomach. Iris parted her lips slightly, as if to say something, but instead she leaned forward and kissed Anna.

Iris's tongue was warm and eager and Anna's insecurities vanished, confusion laid to rest. Iris clearly wanted her. With her hands firmly on Iris's waist, she pulled her close. Anna could feel Iris's fingers stroking her back, nestling their way in between the lining of her skirt and her jumper, touching the bare skin. More. She wanted more. She wanted to feel Iris's hands all over. Should she remove her clothes? Or undress Iris? Her inexperienced hands pulled at Iris's dress when she took Anna's hands in hers and whispered: "Slowly".

"Sorry, I just..."

Iris's lips silenced her, the soothing sensation making her close her eyes and hand herself over. She leaned backwards and hit something hard. Turning her head around, she realised it was the photocopier.

"It's okay," Iris said. "It won't break."

From the moment they had met, Iris had been in charge and it was comforting in a way. Anna would go with the flow and not force it. At least there was no rushed kneading of the breasts and wham-bam-thank-you-maam, as was the case with Erik these days. Iris seemed to treasure every part of Anna's body, her hands gliding over her waist, her bottom, her hips. Lips nuzzled Anna's neck, kissing it tenderly. Through her clothes, Anna felt the outline of Iris's small round breasts, the hard nipples pressed against her body.

"Spread your legs," Iris commanded.

Without hesitation, Anna moved her feet, sensing the vacuum between her thighs as they parted, filled with feverish anticipation. Iris intimately touched her belly button, caressing the soft skin on Anna's stomach, taking her time before gently nudging the skirt down. Her hand slipped inside the lining of Anna's carefully chosen black lace knickers, softly stroking the pubic hair before moving further down.

Their eyes exchanged a silent agreement, saying this was okay. This was good. This was better than good. Anna nodded her approval and Iris was on her knees, caressing the inside of Anna's thighs, her lips soft between her legs. Still leaning against the photocopier, Anna rested her hands on Iris's head, wrapping the short hairs around her index fingers, enjoying the sensation of Iris making her way inside of her. Anna groaned as Iris's tongue and fingers expertly tipped her over the edge.

Afterwards, even though Iris had done all the work, Anna felt exhausted as she slid onto the floor. She held Iris's face in her hands and kissed her hard.

"Thank you," she said. She really meant it.

"You have amazing breasts," Iris said and burrowed her nose in Anna's cleavage.

Anna felt euphoric but also unexpectedly shy: she wanted to make Iris feel equally ecstatic but didn't know how to start. As if sensing this, Iris took Anna's hands in hers, showing her the way, under the hem of her dress. Anna's fingers fumbled but she learned to follow Iris's moans and used them as a guide. Her confidence growing, Anna leaned down and pressed her lips against Iris's sex. A taste of earth on her tongue, in her mouth. Iris came fast, a rattling in her throat confirming her climax, bringing on an even deeper satisfaction than Anna's own orgasm had.

Later, when they were lying on the floor together, Anna leaning her head on Iris's outstretched arm, Anna's mobile started to ring. Dull signals vibrated in her bag, reminding her that there was a world out there. She shuffled across the floor and fished out her phone.

Erik's name appeared on the screen. "When will you be home?" His voice sounded tired.

"Not sure… eh, in an hour?"

"Sebastian won't go to sleep. He wants you."

She sat up, her mummy autopilot on. "Is he okay?"

"I think he might have a fever."

"Might have? Did you check?"

Iris moved behind her and Anna stopped herself. She had no right to be upset with Erik even though he clearly should have checked Sebastian's temperature.

"I'm on my way," she said instead.

After she put her phone back, she turned to Iris.

"You have to go," Iris said simply.

Anna nodded. "I'm sorry." She hurriedly got dressed.

"Before you go…" Iris said, the words trailing off as her mouth met Anna's, the kiss deep. Anna's steps were unsteady as she backed away, reeling.

"I'll be back next week," she promised.

36

Iris

December 2015

Iris wanted Anna. Not just for a few hours or a day. She wanted her for an entire week, a month or more. To discover each other and to talk and make love. Anna was so pure, so inexperienced and sweet, yet also intelligent and passionate. There was so much she wanted to teach her, the way she had once been taught. A holiday together would be incredible.

Iris had only ever taken a woman on holiday once before. Rolf had thought she was scouring the stands of a foreign book fair when in actual fact she had been walking down the streets of Berlin, hand in hand with a woman. They had enjoyed art museums, bratwursts, beer, an operetta and sex shops in between long sessions in their hotel room. It had been love.

Back home, however, the woman had chosen her husband and had ended the relationship. From then on, Iris had never disclosed any of her affairs to Rolf. It was as if she had crossed a forbidden bridge that had then collapsed behind her. There was no way of going back.

Iris realised that Anna had a life. A life that she would most likely go back to after she had experimented with Iris. A holiday would perhaps be too much to ask for? Also, Anna had children.

Iris had never planned to have any. She had been on the pill when she accidentally fell pregnant. Rolf had wanted a child, a protégée of sorts. Now, she couldn't imagine her life without Karin but at the time it had brought up too many bad memories: the pregnancy at sixteen and the miscarriage, which had turned out to be a blessing in disguise since her mother had refused the abortion, but traumatising nonetheless. Just thinking about it put her on edge. Her mother would have preferred to throw her out on the street than be humiliated. The fact that Iris later wanted a university degree hadn't gone down well either, but thankfully university was free and didn't require her parents' consent. She had been a very different type of mother to Karin. She encouraged her to dream big.

Rolf's advice would have been to end it with Anna immediately. *If you start to invest your heart, pull out.* But she couldn't end it. Anna was unique. Rolf would have laughed at that. *What a cliché!* She had to smile. It was perhaps ridiculous but, with or without children, she was determined to have Anna. And, she thought, if that meant losing Rolf, then it had been a long time coming and would be worth the sacrifice.

Anna had a different life, with children and a husband and an important job. She wasn't like Lena, rich and bored, seeking excitement wherever she could find it. Anna was a good person and sooner or later she would have to make a choice. A good girl's choice. How could Iris convince Anna that this was real, that she was worth it?

37

Daniel

December 2015

Dan recognised the dude's car as soon as he arrived back home. An old and bashed-up Nissan was parked dangerously close to the row of leaning trees by their drive-way. What if one of them fell on his car? That would be funny. With that awful car, the dude obviously wouldn't be bringing them money anyway. It didn't matter. He kept Frida busy and that wasn't so bad. Dan couldn't stand it when Frida turned needy. *Sit on my lap, Danny boy. Bring me a beer, will you? Let me hug you. Just for a second.*

He went straight to his room. Frida's car was still in the shop since she couldn't afford the repairs and the moped next door hadn't been parked in its normal spot for three days. He had taken a chance and had waited for Anna out-side the school building on his bike but both afternoons she had walked to her car with Kent. The guy was creepy. Dan had tried to cycle after her but she hadn't headed straight home. Maybe she had gone food shopping or to visit friends? It was possible. He didn't know much about her life. At least not yet. They needed something to talk about over Sunday dinners.

It was almost five o'clock and Anna would be leaving school soon. Perhaps he could borrow the dude's car? With an ear to the wall, Dan tried to listen to any sounds. Were they fucking? He could hear voices. Perhaps it was some sort of foreplay? He sneaked out to the living room to see if the keys were there. He looked through the pockets of a worn leather jacket but apart from chewing gum wrappers they were empty.

He went outside. You never knew, maybe the dumb fuck had left the keys in the ignition? It was a pretty safe area where people were known to leave their houses unlocked. Nope, not there either.

Back inside, he grabbed a snack. Cheese crackers without cheese. That fucking summed up his life. He sat down and poured himself a Coke Zero (Frida lived on the stuff, usually mixed with vodka of course).

That's when he saw the dude's jeans, thrown over the side of the couch. They had obviously started out here. Not as eager as last time then, when they hadn't even made it to the bedroom.

The car key was in the pocket.

*

Dan swerved into the school parking lot. Anna's Volvo was there. Score! He parked on the other side, behind a bus. Out of sight. Then he waited. Every now and then he would check her status on WhatsApp. Had she been online recently? She rarely was but he had nothing better to do. He didn't want to contact her via WhatsApp anyway. He preferred to send emails from a nondescript email address. Although she had only responded to a couple of his initial emails, then she had stopped. That needed to change. He needed to make her listen.

Black Adam wanted to rule the world and, like his super-hero, Dan had been patient. He might not have spent five thousand years travelling to earth, but he had waited three whole days and this was his chance. Together with his superpower: a trashy old car. He laughed because it was kind of crazy. But according to some ancient writer, all was fair in love and war. Anna would be pleased if she knew that he listened during her classes.

After about half an hour, she emerged from the school building (alone!) and started walking towards her car. He waited a few seconds before he followed her.

38

Anna

December 2015

Daniel had stopped leaving Anna notes, which was just as well, since she had started to discard his handwritten scribbles. She did not want to be caught in a compromising position. Except now he had turned to email, and the ease of sending an email, compared to delivering a note into the teachers' lounge, meant the volume of messages had risen considerably. His email address was blackadam4321@hotmail.com and curiosity won her over. She emailed him back asking about the name. Perhaps she would better understand him if she asked questions he could actually answer.

Hi Anna, he was someone bad who turned out to be good.

Every email started that same way. Hi Anna. He not only loved saying her name, he loved writing it.

Hi Anna, I need someone who listens to me.

She sighed. It wasn't an unrealistic request. Once again, she tried to direct him to a counsellor but that only angered him.

Hi Anna, I don't need a fucking professional. I need you. I want to live with you. I need a family.

She deleted the message immediately, even going as far as emptying it from the trash folder. It was better to pretend he hadn't written that, but still, he kept writing.

Hi Anna, I'm sick of this. How about the basement?

The basement? Even if he knew her address, he would have had to see her house to know she had a basement. It was unsettling and she debated whether she should go as far as to report this. But once again she reasoned that he needed her help, not authorities treating him like a criminal.

She shut down the emails and switched to Google. After much hesitation, she keyed in l followed by e s b i a n. It had happened twice, sex with Iris, and she needed to understand.

On the screen, a number of words flashed at her like a red-light district: lesbians, fuck, porn, sex novels. She had the urge to erase them, wanting to resist their harshness. They didn't represent her experience. She added the keyword l o v e. It looked oddly surreal on the screen but she clicked "Search".

Sexual how-to books and pages and pages about lesbian women's sexual habits stared at her, as if to say: is this what you need? It wasn't.

She had never been with a woman before, so why did she feel this way? Would she be forced to make a choice? Leave

Erik and be with Iris? How would that affect the boys? Would they hate her? Would Iris even want to be with her so permanently? She too was married.

She longed for Kent's straightforward advice but there was no way she could confide in him.

She examined the options on the screen again, then changed the search. Sex wasn't the goal, only a consequence. In Google, she added the words y o u n g e r and o l d e r. News about discrimination against lesbians and reading tips about forbidden and unrequited love in black and white. A sign?

She really wanted to talk to someone and speaking to Iris about what had just happened felt like ruining the magic. To Iris everything seemed so simple and obvious.

What would her friends from university say if she told them? *I've slept with a woman.* Most likely, every single one of them would feel the need to share such yummy gossip. This wasn't just any news, it was dynamite. She couldn't take that risk. Anyway, how could she expect someone else to understand when she didn't even understand it herself?

Her mobile notified her of a message and she picked it up, both dreading and hoping that it was a message from Iris.

It was from Kent.

Didn't see you today. Daniel's last school called.
Please call Maria Bergman.

The woman's contact details popped up on her screen.

Daniel. A headache came on. Reality had a way of penetrating her fantasy world. Except Iris wasn't a fantasy. She was real.

At least the school had finally called.

Maria Bergman sounded strict. That was a good sign. It would mean no nonsense and Anna liked that.

"I was Daniel's humanities teacher," Maria Bergman explained. "The principal told me you had enquired about him."

"That's right. I just…" Where to start? "I'm worried about him."

"Really, why? Has something happened?" Maria Bergman asked but Anna didn't pick up on any real concern in her tone.

"Well, a few things," she said. "He likes fighting a bit too much, as I'm sure you know."

She tried to laugh but it sounded stiff.

"Fighting? The Daniel I taught was always sitting quietly at the back of the classroom. Clever boy though, always did well in exams."

Now it was Anna's turn to be puzzled.

"Daniel Persson? Tall, blond, could do with a haircut and seems to have a dislike for tying his shoelaces."

"Yes, sounds about right. And you said he's getting into fights? Are the other students picking on him?"

"Not exactly. It's more… the other way around."

Maria Bergman was quiet, as if she pondered this. "That sounds odd. I mean, he's had it tough. His brother was known for getting into trouble with the law and his mother… well, she drank apparently."

"Are you sure about that?" Anna asked. "About his mother? I'm only asking because I've been to his house and didn't see any signs of that."

"Well, that was the rumour."

Rumour? Anna felt she needed to push this teacher a bit more. "Did you find out for sure?"

"No, I didn't..." She sighed. "Look, I have many students."

Didn't they all? Anna was speechless.

"I wish you the best of luck," Maria Bergman said, sounding as if she had had enough. "I wouldn't want him getting into trouble."

"Why not?" Anna quickly added: "I mean, did you become attached to him?"

"He made no trouble for me. Always love students like that, don't you?"

I love all my students, Anna wanted to say, but for an easy way out, she said: "Sure."

She wanted to get off this call. This woman clearly didn't know the Daniel she knew. Whether that was good or not, she wasn't sure. Something had made him change though and she couldn't quite figure out what.

*

Anna wanted to see Iris. It was more than an escape, she was that friend she had missed, someone to talk to. So far, Anna hadn't spoken about work but perhaps it was time to open up. Knowing the library closed early on Tuesdays, Anna hurried out of the school building.

It was just past five o'clock and the roads were busy with people heading home from work. That was probably why she didn't notice the car behind her, at least not until she was about to turn into Hågarp. She had to look twice to realise it was the same sedan that had stopped her when she was jogging. Was it a coincidence?

She looked in the rear-view mirror to catch sight of the driver. Did the guy have a moustache? It was too dark and therefore impossible to make him out but it was such a wreck of a car (with the bumper knocked, paint coming off) that surely there couldn't be two of the same?

She turned into Hågarp as planned but instead of going straight to the library, she turned right. The car behind her also turned right. She turned left and drove down a residential street. Again, the car behind her went down the same road. Why was he following her? She stopped her car and got out, feeling safe amongst all the houses, ready to confront him.

He drove past her, an arm in front of his face, clearly wanting to shield himself from her. It was odd. Who was he? She got in her car again and drove back to the road she had come from but he was soon on her tail again. That's it, she thought, I have to lose him. She drove up and down, turning left and right, then she exited Hågarp and drove to the next town, where she did the same manoeuvre: up and down the streets, oblivious to parents and children in ski suits building poor snowmen from the wet snow about to melt away. Finally, she noticed he was gone. She was on her own and she could drive back to the library. Except by the time she arrived, it was too late. The door was locked and Iris most likely already at home. With her husband.

39

Rolf

January 2016

Christmas was over.

"Thank fucking goodness for that!"

Rolf had always hated traditions. Iris went through the motions every year for Karin's sake but even Karin had felt that the last Christmas had been lame. She had kept asking her mother if she was okay and Rolf had whispered in Iris's ear: "Missing your fuck buddy?"

She hadn't taken the bait. That was the most unnerving thing about his wife. She could ride any argument out through silence, her eyes calm but serious, her back straight, her lips always perfectly painted.

"Someone seems to have forgotten about our rules," he said through clenched teeth. "No one comes between us."

She stared at him, looking fascinated by his outburst.

"How many women have *you* fucked through the years?" she asked.

She rarely used the f-word but he didn't let that throw him off.

"A gentleman doesn't count," he said.

"Well, I have never butted into your affairs," she said. "So stay out of mine."

Then she walked off. He resented arguing with her. The whole situation was frustrating. There had been limited action in the bedroom. Needless to say, it hadn't been enough. He had seen Frida a couple of times. She was Iris's polar opposite, screaming and threatening him but also fucking him with a heated passion. He knew it would end, but he needed her. At least for the time being. There was no pretence with her. She turned herself inside out, she was raw and vulnerable and real.

"I also hate Christmas," Frida said.

They were still lying in bed.

"That's because you make no fucking effort," the kid shouted.

"Stop eavesdropping!"

"Where's his father?" Rolf asked. Couldn't he buzz off to his dad for a couple of weeks?

The sun was up, causing water to drip from the icicles by the window. Rolf should be heading home.

"I don't know," she said. "He ran off and I've never heard from him since."

To be fair, the kid had been away a lot. Rolf wasn't sure where he spent his time, with friends most likely, but it was a bloody godsend when he wasn't there. He was negative energy.

"He's writing a book," Frida whispered in his ear.

"Oh, really. What's it about?"

"Some girl. I think he's in love. I don't know."

This was good news. That was obviously who he was spending his time with.

"Have you met her?" he asked.

That seemed to crack her up: "Do you honestly think he would bring her home to meet me?"

"But aren't you curious about who she is, what she looks like?" If she's got firm breasts, a thin waist, long hair?

"I've looked for photos but I couldn't find any. He's only got photos of his teacher, printouts from the Internet, loads of them. I think he's kind of obsessed with her."

Ha. The older woman crush. "Maybe that's who he's in love with?"

She shook her head. "I've met her and I don't think so. She's not exactly.... I mean, she's kind of average looking, plus she's like my age."

She pulled out a folded A4 from her side table, opened it and smoothed out the creases.

"Judge for yourself."

He sat up. "That's his teacher?"

She nodded. "Why? Is she an axe murderer or something?" Her laugh was raspy.

He shook his head. "Hopefully not." But it's *her*, he thought. Again. He got up. "I have to go."

Her lips pouted: "Already?"

"Gotta love you and leave you," he joked.

"You love me?"

Oh, shit. He looked at her, weighed his words. He needed her now, more than ever. In fact, he needed the kid.

"Sure," he said.

40

Daniel

January 2016

Thankfully, Frida's latest dude hadn't realised that Dan had used his car. If he had, he hadn't said anything. The problem was, Anna had realised she was being followed so after that fiasco he needed to find another way.

A couple of weeks later, the moped next door had been replaced by a new one, quite possibly a Christmas present, judging by how spoilt those children were. It was perfect and if there was such a thing as a God, he was smiling at Dan right now, as he got down on his knees to hotwire it.

He wasn't likely to get caught by the police in a small town like this; he had never seen a single patrol car circulate Mörna, so he felt confident. This time he was going to corner Anna and talk some sense into her. She needed to understand that she couldn't turn her back on him, a young man in need, that he craved the stability of her home, her love and care, even her firm hand at times. She would see this, one way or another.

Dan stationed himself behind the school gym, at the outskirts of the school area next to the parking lot, and waited for Anna to emerge. He prayed that she would have ditched the creep and that she would be alone. She wasn't and he cursed silently. Kent and Anna strolled down past the basketball court, appearing to have a serious conversation. What were they talking about? Did they discuss Dan? His letters and emails? He bloody hoped not. He needed to trust Anna.

As luck would have it, Kent left before her. Anna stayed in her car, her head bowed down (over a phone maybe?) as Dan waited. If she were headed home, he would catch her in the garage and if she was going elsewhere, he would talk to her there, wherever it was.

When Anna drove out of the parking lot, he followed her at a distance. She turned right and then right again, heading out of town, the same direction as the other day. Although the moped had been suped, it still couldn't quite keep up. At least Dan had an idea of where she was heading this time. He was going to drive up and down every street in the two towns she had been to the last time if he had to. He was as determined as determined could be.

Was she going to someone's house or a shop? He felt like a secret agent, sweeping the assigned territory for Anna's car. Every now and then he stopped and looked for her. Many times, he felt furious; stuck in new housing areas with slow-growing hedges and white flagpoles. How could she just go off like that? Vanish into nothing? Yet he couldn't give up. This was quite possibly the only time he would be able to use the moped. If they realised the petrol tank was low, they would most likely lock it up.

So he kept going. He needed to live with her, to get away

from Frida without ending up in some fucking foster care or youth facility.

"It's just one more year," Martin had said. "Then we'll get a place together."

Martin had said that right before he ended up in prison. He would be out soon, but while Martin had been away, Dan had worked a few things out: his brother was caring but he wasn't the brightest, he would keep breaking and entering rather than getting a nine-to-five job. He surrounded himself with losers. "Only because no one else will have me," he had said. It was a pretty lame excuse. Dan wanted "normal". Before it was too late, he wanted what he deserved: rights. Anna was his and he was going to prove to her how true that was.

He decided to plead with her, cry if he had to.

Renewed with energy, he kept going. Luckily, there was still plenty of petrol in the tank. Another five minutes went past, ten, twenty. He couldn't stop. His life depended on this one night.

About thirty minutes later he found her car.

"Yes!" he shouted, his arms in the air. "Victory!"

The car was parked outside a red brick building. A library, apparently. He walked up the steps and pulled at the door but it was locked. He looked around. Where else could she have gone?

There was an old post office next door that still had the post office sign hanging outside but was clearly converted into a home. White crocheted curtains decorated the windows. He liked that. It was homely.

He walked around the library building. A light was on in one of the windows at the back. Was she there? Maybe some sort of a meeting? A séance or a Bible study group or a book circle. The last one obviously made the most sense.

He walked up to the door, a brown wooden one with a heavy handle. Should he try to open it? Or knock? He hesitated. What would she say if she was actually in there? She would think he was crazy. He pulled his hand back. He needed to see what was going on through the window first. How many were they? The parking lot only had two cars in it so he suspected there weren't many of them but people could have walked or cycled there. There was a bike parked up front.

He walked over to a lamppost and climbed onto the rock wall behind it. From there, he had a pretty good view. There was Anna and another woman. They were talking. Could he interrupt them? She would know he had followed her and that would look bad. There was no good explanation why he had accidentally ended up by the back door of a library in the next town, was there? Maybe he should wait until her meeting was over and corner her then?

He was about to jump down from his viewing spot when something changed. The woman leaned forward and… kissed Anna? He strained his eyes to see better. Had he been mistaken? But no, Anna was kissing the woman back. Not just a friendly kiss. A full-on snog. Both jealousy and excitement hit him like a force. How could this be happening? He imagined Anna's arms wrapped around him instead, her soft hair against his face.

Then he emerged from the dream. This was a fucking pain in the arse. A mega-bump in his road to happiness. He started laughing. This was ridiculous. How could someone as innocent as Anna end up in the claws of some woman?

Ah. That's when he saw it: *the opportunity*. Now she would have no choice but to move him in. If he had to blackmail her, then so be it. He could totally do that.

41

Erik

April 2016

Black Adam is now corresponding with Erik. He is extremely direct and he causes Erik some concern:

> Who the fuck is Xeroxwed? You know, you should get out every now and then, let someone babysit the children. Take care of yourself.

It is signed someone who cares. Erik isn't sure if that is supposed to be sarcasm? Is he making fun of Erik's first email, which was signed in that same way? And how does he know they have children? That's a worry. He is debating whether this is worth pursuing but then he thinks about Tina.

He met her at Rob's and she wasn't exactly what he had expected. Just like Rob had said, she was a whole lot of big hair. When she leaned in to hug him, she smelt of spearmint chewing gum and strong perfume. She wore gold bracelets and many rings and had an excess of make-up. He couldn't imagine her patrolling the streets, dealing with criminals or even working on a high-level investigation. Then again, one shouldn't judge.

"So, what's your role at the police station?" he asked, his thoughts becoming unprocessed words.

She looked surprised. "I'm a police woman," she said, while tickling and kissing Rob, which was distracting.

"Did you, eh, tell the team about... you know, that Anna might have cheated?"

This was hard.

"Yes, of course," she said.

Oh, great. He felt lighter. "Is it being taken seriously?"

"Totally."

Her hands were under Rob's shirt, her long nails scratching his back. He purred like a kitten. Erik had never seen him this ridiculous before.

"Right," he said. "So are they looking into it?"

"I can't really tell you that."

He needed more information. Flattery? That usually worked.

"You must be really good at your job." Too much? "I mean, your job must be fascinating."

"Oh, it is!"

That got her going. She told them about a murder investigation in the city, the "slippery eel" suspect, an mc gang bust where stacks of money and guns were found, and the large supermarket fire that had featured in the papers recently.

"It could be arson," she said.

"Should you really be telling us this?" Erik asked. "Isn't that, like, classified information?"

"I completely trust you," she said, an offended look on her face. "You won't tell anyone, will you? I know Robbie won't."

A smile and a shower of kisses on Rob's blushing cheeks.

"Of course not," Erik said. *But what are you telling people about Anna's case?*

He felt nervous and no reassurance from Rob could make him feel at peace.

"She won't talk about your case," Rob said later on the phone.

"You don't know that. You heard her, she was telling us way too much. Inside stuff."

"Come on, don't be like that. She's helped you, hasn't she?"

"I know."

Yet he can't stop feeling anxious, which is why he needs to keep the correspondence with Black Adam up. He needs alternatives. He writes:

Thanks for the concern. I will take that into consideration. Were you Anna's student?

Right down to business. Black Adam's response is immediate:

Anna had many students. Your question should be: was I special? The answer to that would be YES. She loved me.

This annoys the hell out of Erik and he wants to send this to the police faster than fast. Instead he calms down and composes another email. He needs Black Adam to keep talking.

I'm sure she did love you. The question is, in what way? She was, and still is, married.

So far, it's been as if Black Adam is sitting by the computer, waiting for Erik's emails. But this last email is like hitting a wall. There are no more responses.

*

That evening Erik sits with the boys at the dinner table, imagining that this is going to be their life going forward. Can he do this on his own?

"Everything okay today?" he asks the boys as they tuck into the ready-made ravioli. It's been luxuriously poured from a can and heated in the microwave.

"How's Mummy?" Sebastian asks, picking at his food with a fork.

"She's getting better, I think."

Mum would give him a blasting for that one. We don't know, Erik, she would tell him.

"Really?" Lukas looks up. "When is she coming home?"

"Oh, I don't know yet. She has to rest."

Even though he wants to move, maybe they're not ready just yet. Mum has promised to help him with the mortgage if needed, so he can't use that as an excuse. Something needs to happen though.

"How would you feel about going away for a few days?"

Sebastian scrunches his face up. "And leave Mummy?" He shakes his head.

Shit. "You miss her." He says it more as a statement than a question but they both nod.

His pocket vibrates and he takes his phone out. Unknown number.

"Erik?" A vaguely familiar voice.

"Yes?"

"Linda Johansson here. We need you to come down to the police station."

Her words are abrupt which alarms him.

"Why? What's happened? Did you find the attacker?"

Or did they finally find out who Anna was sleeping with?

"We have a few questions."

His chest starts to burn. She offers no further information and he's afraid to ask. She hangs up and he has to go into the other room, dread filling him.

Shaking, he keys in Tina's number. Rob was right. She's been helpful, he shouldn't be ungrateful.

"I'm sorry to call you but I'm scared, Tina. Why do they need to see me? I haven't done anything."

Tina takes a second to catch up. "Slow down," she says. "I'm sure no one is accusing you of anything."

"But you've heard something?"

"Shit, Erik, don't do this to me. I can't..." she pauses. "They know about the baby."

"What baby?" Then he understands. "Anna was pregnant?" But they hadn't... not in months. The punch in his gut. He can't breathe.

"Anna isn't pregnant," Tina whispers down the line. "But Pernilla Arvidsson is. With your baby."

PART THREE

42

Rolf

January 2016

The kid's favourite food was kebab pizza, so Rolf had ordered two large ones. The kid could eat and Rolf needed him to open up. What were his vulnerabilities?

Rolf and Frida sat on the couch like a united team while the kid was draped over an armchair, the pizza boxes balancing on a pile of crap on the coffee table.

"What's your job?" the kid asked, drenching his first slice in garlic sauce.

Look who's talking already?

"I'm an existentialist," Rolf said. He took a small slice of pizza even though he didn't normally eat such vulgar food but he wanted them to feel like he was one of them. "I believe that we are all individuals," he explained. "And that each person is responsible for giving meaning to his or her own life."

"Are you a fucking philosopher?"

"Language…" Frida said half-heartedly, kebab meat spilling out of her mouth.

"So how do you make money?" the kid asked.

"Dan!" Frida looked horrified.

"It's fine, babe." Rolf turned to the kid. "I make money by interpreting life and making it accessible to others, or sometimes, I guess I end up doing the opposite. I love to shock people. That's the truth."

"And this turns into cash?" The kid didn't look convinced. "Your car looks kind of cheap."

Rolf started laughing. "I'm not into material things," he said. "What about you, kid. What's your purpose? What do you want out of life?"

The kid shrugged. "What's *your* fucking purpose? To be a creative loser?"

"Dan!" Frida hissed. "That's enough!"

"Leave him," Rolf said. "This is a good conversation."

The kid actually smiled, which was a huge step.

"You know, I had a great teacher at school," Rolf said, now that they were getting somewhere. "She helped me find my purpose. That one person changed my life. For once, someone believed in me."

He studied the kid's frozen smile, trying to interpret what was going through his young cranium. The kid didn't give anything away; he simply wiped his mouth with the back of his hand and drank his Coke.

"School is good that way," Rolf continued. "The special teachers stay with you for the rest of your life."

"Please don't." Frida seemed to cotton on. "Rolf, don't." She pulled at his shirt but he yanked his arm back. Why did she have to spoil it?

"Just having a conversation about life, babe."

The teacher's name was Anna. Frida had been helpful but her knowledge didn't stretch very far. He needed more.

"Have any teachers like that?" Rolf asked.

The kid looked down, shook his head and put the rest of his slice away. He stood up. "Thanks for the pizza." And then he was out the door.

"Leave him alone," Frida begged. "He hasn't done anything."

Rolf smiled and grabbed hold of her arm, twisting it upwards. "If I leave him alone, I will also leave you alone."

"I'm sorry," she said, cowering under his touch. "I'm really sorry. I'll find out more, I promise."

43

Anna

January 2016

Anna finished reading *Sing You Home*, a book about two women falling in love and wanting a baby. She wondered if Iris was trying to send her a message. Perhaps not the baby part, even though she clearly loved her daughter, but the two women, one a lesbian and the other one previously married to a man, had fallen in love.

Was it love?

She had only just come to terms with living in the moment and not put too much pressure on herself.

"So what did Daniel's old teacher have to say?"

Anna looked up from her desk as Kent handed her a cup of coffee. The book slipped into her bag.

For once, Anna didn't want to talk about work. She wanted to discuss her complex feelings, the tigress trapped inside her body. She wanted to discuss the meaning of love, lust and the two combined. Was there such a thing?

Kent looked at her expectantly.

"Actually, I feel more relaxed now," Anna said, packing up

the remainder of her belongings: pens and papers, her laptop and phone. "He was apparently quiet and fairly studious at his last school."

"Oh." Kent sat down, making himself comfortable. "That's odd. Isn't it?"

She glanced at her watch. Book club started at seven but she wanted to have dinner with the children at home first. At least, she assumed there would be book club. There had been no messages from Iris.

"Ehm," she said. She looked at Kent, focused on his blue eyes. He was always there for her; she needed to be more generous with her time. "It's probably just a case of him struggling to fit in. I mean, this place is so homogenous."

Kent nodded.

"Maybe."

"I'm sure he will calm down," she rattled on. "At least now I know that he wasn't always like this."

Kent understandably looked doubtful. She just didn't have time to discuss it right now.

*

At home, Anna was watching Erik over the dinner table. He was engrossed in his tablet, a headphone hanging loose around his neck, the other one in his ear. Instinctively, she wanted to tell him he was setting a bad example for the children but who was she to talk? *Thoughts of Iris's hands.* She closed her eyes as if to reboot and then she opened them again, thinking: *Iris is a woman, a female friend whom I am simply very close with.*

Perhaps that's all it was? There had been no time to talk the last time they had seen each other since Anna had rushed home to Sebastian. Only, he hadn't been ill. As soon as she had arrived home that night, Erik had announced he was going to Rob's.

"You're using your own son to make me come home?" she had asked.

"I need to rehearse," he had said. "Not that you would know that."

He had been upset because she had missed his last gig.

"We didn't have a babysitter that night," she had defended herself yet again.

"You could have sorted that out, if you really wanted to be there."

"Why couldn't *you* arrange the babysitting for once?"

And just like that, they had been back on the treadmill of arguments. Anna had felt she needed to hit the stop button but Erik had beaten her to it by slamming the door in her face. It didn't matter. And yet it did. This wasn't how life was supposed to be. You got married, had children, worked, spent time with friends and family. And you were happy. Weren't you?

"Found it," Erik said and gave the boys an earphone each. "What do you think?"

"They're five," she muttered. How refined did Erik think their music tastes were? She realised she was being grumpy. The look on Lukas and Sebastian's faces, bums happily dancing in their seats to the beat. They were having fun. If they weren't going to invite her to join, she would have to crash the party.

"Let me hear that," she said and stretched a hand out but neither one of them was willing to share their earphone.

She sat back, accepting the defeat but feeling left out nonetheless. A dull sound on her phone signalled that she had an email and she picked up the phone to keep herself occupied. She opened her inbox, and found a new message, not from Daniel aka Black Adam, but from a cryptic address. Her stomach tightened. Was it yet another trick? Was it another one of his personas? Apprehensively, she opened it.

I can't wait to see you this week. To be near you, to taste you. I miss you.

She stared at the screen, her mood sunnier. That could only be from one person. Reading the email address again, Xeroxwed, it made sense. Book club had initially been on a Wednesday and the photocopier she had leaned on that time in the library kitchen, Iris's tongue between her legs, was most likely a Xerox. She would check next time.

"Okay, Mummy, you can listen now."

She felt caught, and as she looked up and Sebastian gave her his headphone, she quickly switched back to being Mummy again. Her ear filled with Taylor Swift's girly voice singing 'Bad Blood'.

"It's pretty good," she admitted, humming along to *Now we've got bad blood, it used to be mad love*. She looked at Erik to see if he remembered the mad love they had once shared but he seemed distant. She danced with the boys as they did their moves and she wondered how long this innocence would last. In a few years they would surely find their parents embarrassing and boring. Time would fly by and the boys would leave. What would remain? Herself and Erik, sleeping as far away from each other as possible?

When the song ended, the boys left the table. "Can we go and play?"

"Sure," Erik said and pretended to chase them out of the kitchen.

She was about to remind them to take their plates away but she stopped herself. They needed to view her as the fun mum from time to time. She was going to say to Erik: let's put some music on the speakers so that we can both listen, but with the boys out of the room, Erik was back on his tablet, playing Candy Crush.

She stacked the dishwasher in silence and once she had switched it on, it was Sebastian and Lukas's bedtime.

The boys were in the living room, building a train set in a dinosaur park. She knelt down and picked up what she thought was a T-rex, and with a dinosaur voice, she said: "Time to go to sleep."

Unwillingly, they tore themselves away if she promised to read an entire dinosaur book, and after struggling to pronounce Carcharodontosaurus, Euoplocephalus and Deinonychus, with the children falling over with laughter, she finally tucked them in and kissed them goodnight.

"I love you. Sweet dreams."

Downstairs, she picked up her bag and her library books.

"Book club again?" Erik said back in the kitchen. "Seems a bit frequent."

She stood still for a moment and stared at him.

Hold me. Hug me. Kiss me. Tell me you love me and I will stay.

Her eyes obviously did a lousy job communicating her feelings. Erik put his feet up on one of the new chairs and kept swiping colourful candy across the screen.

"Reading keeps me sane," she said and then she left.

44

Iris

January 2016

Once Anna sat down with her, the smell of freshly brewed coffee in the air, candles lit, Iris felt at peace. Their last meeting had been too brief. This would be different.

"So, how have you been?" Iris asked.

Anna was wearing another maxi skirt and Iris allowed herself to brush her bare feet against Anna's stockings, sliding underneath the floral fabric. A bit of human contact, that's all she wanted.

Anna seemed tense, however. "Were there ever any other members of this book club?" she asked, pulling her legs up and onto the chair.

"Oh." Iris had half expected that question. "Well, yes. Initially there were going to be two more but they dropped out. And to be honest with you... I was pleased to have you to myself."

Anna looked at her intensely. Iris wasn't sure if she was trying to assess whether she was being truthful or if she was searching for something else. Then she finally spoke: "I'm not sure I can do this."

"Right." She couldn't pretend to be unaffected. "That's unfortunate. I mean, I had anticipated that you might not, but I…"

She took the reading glasses off and rubbed her nose.

"Did you read *Sing You Home*?" she asked.

Anna nodded.

"So, then you know how Vanessa felt, how she worried that Zoe would leave her, that perhaps it wasn't real for her?"

"Yes…"

"That's how I have felt since you came to my house," Iris said. Her eyes met Anna's; she wanted the sincerity of her words to hit Anna straight in the heart.

"But you're not faithful to anyone," Anna said.

She sounded calm but her words were tinged with something else. Hurt? Worry? Or was it judgement?

"I can be," Iris said.

Anna picked at something on her skirt. She looked beautiful. Wavy hair, minimal make-up, the natural features pure.

"I'm married," Anna said, as if disclosing this for the first time. "I have children. Having an affair, I just can't…"

"An affair? This is not an affair."

Anna looked up. "It's not?"

"Perhaps it was at first," Iris said.

She felt herself gravitate towards Anna as she got out of her seat and sat down on the floor next to Anna's chair. Uncharacteristically, she rested her head in Anna's lap. It wasn't necessarily a conscious action, to give Anna the power while she exposed her feelings.

"I need to be close to you," Iris said.

Anna's hands stroked Iris's head, her fingers softly combing through the hair. Iris closed her eyes, pacified by the touch. They sat in silence for a long time before Anna spoke.

"I feel confused," she said.

Her words sounded genuine but not exasperated, and Iris lifted her head to meet Anna's gaze. She smiled to show that she understood before leaning forward. Their lips met halfway.

It was a long and sensual kiss.

"Maybe we could go somewhere," Iris said, their mouths withdrawing for air. "A holiday, just the two of us."

Anna shook her head. "I'm not sure," she said. "My children…" She looked away, her eyes watery. "Anyway, we would just be back where we are now."

"What do you mean?"

Iris stroked the back of Anna's hands with her thumbs, the skin young and supple.

"I know I would have a lovely time," Anna said. "It's not that. But I would be back here, in this library, feeling equally guilty and confused. Perhaps even more so."

Iris placed her hands on Anna's cheeks, forcing their eyes to meet.

"I want only you," Iris said. "No one else."

"Why me?"

Iris pictured Lena's face together with the text she had sent after Rōlf supposedly had "taken care of her".

I fucked your husband but I have a feeling you don't care, so I will make you care. My final words to you by Emily Dickinson: "Mine Enemy is growing old, I have at last Revenge." Revenge, such a sweet word.

Iris looked at Anna. "You're different," she wanted to say. Instead, she stood up and squeezed herself into Anna's chair.

Anna was larger and so she had to make do with resting one buttock cheek on Anna's thigh. She just needed to be as physically close to Anna as possible.

"Anna," she started. "I feel as if you're going to question me over and over. I can't change my past but you need to know this." She fiddled with the silver pendant around her neck. "Anna. The way I feel about you, this is new for me. In fact, it's astonishingly complex and incredible and absolutely terrifyingly wonderful." She hesitated before saying the crucial words: "I have fallen in love with you."

Right then, Anna seemed to have given in. Her shoulders relaxed, her face looked almost sad, as if she had lost an internal battle.

"What about your husband?" she asked.

"I'm going to leave Rolf."

45

Anna

January 2016

When Anna woke up in the morning she felt a stab of excitement at the thought of the previous evening, the intense moments with Iris in the small kitchen; their conversation trailing off, the physical taking over. She felt guilty however as she lifted her body off the mattress – the very body that Iris had caressed and nurtured with her touch – and turned to the other side.

Erik's face was squashed on the pillow, his mouth partly open, a gentle snore escaping his throat. It was surreal. This was her life. This was reality. It was as if she had been airlifted into another world the night before, into a delicious vacuum where she had been allowed to just be Anna. What she shared with Iris couldn't be real. Despite Iris's declaration of love, their relationship felt fake as soon as she was back home.

Yet Erik looked like a foreign object in her bed. She always woke up before him and when they had first got together, she would lay quietly, stroking his cheeks, his bare arms, his chest. A feeling of being truly happy made a momentary comeback. The way she felt with Iris, could she once again feel like that with Erik? She lifted up her hand, ready to touch him, to make the memories real, but put it back down again. She couldn't face the rejection. If she touched him, he would probably flick her hand away.

The house was quiet, the boys were either still sleeping or they had switched the TV on, making sure the volume was on mute. They were smart.

She let Erik sleep while she went downstairs to organise breakfast and sure enough, the boys were submerged into their beanbags in front of *Pippi Longstocking*.

"Let's leave Pippi for now and have some breakfast. Otherwise we will be late for day care and I'm sure you want to see Sophie?"

Sebastian was up and out of his beanbag within a second, on his way into the kitchen. She could hear him opening the fridge.

"Lukas, cheese or ham?" he yelled.

Lukas was grumpy when she switched the TV off.

"Come on," she said and kissed his head. "Cheese or ham?"

"Ham."

While they were making open sandwiches for breakfast, Sebastian asked about her evening meeting. "Did you bring cake?"

Her stomach clenched. "Not this time," she said. "But I will bake another one with you soon. I promise."

Lukas stopped drinking his milk. "Chocolate cake?" he asked.

"Absolutely," she said.

She did treasure their time in the kitchen. It was important to teach your sons to cook and bake. Erik wasn't too bad as long as it was basics he had learned from domestic science at school.

"Did the others like the last one we made?" Sebastian asked thoughtfully.

"They loved it."

He nodded, obviously happy about this, wiping his mouth on the back of his pyjama sleeve. Guilt held her back from reprimanding him, aware that she needed to create good memories.

"Is Daddy driving us?"

"No, we will let Daddy sleep."

"Will he pick us up?"

"No, I will."

It wasn't just good memories that she needed to create. She needed to take back control of her life. Only then, would she decide what to do about Iris.

*

That evening Anna was relieved that Erik had gone out. Unless the band was playing, which seemed to be less frequently these days, he tended to stay at home in front of the TV. She cherished having the house to herself. The children were sleeping after a precious moment of bedtime stories. Reading to Sebastian and Lukas had always been her job and every time she did, she thought, I must do this more often.

The tranquillity of the silent house was liberating. She poured a glass of red wine and sat on the couch with the latest book on her lap. Iris had opened up about her own private library, full of English titles that she was campaigning to have translated into Swedish. The collection was stored in a room behind the library reception.

"I haven't been too successful," Iris had explained. "I think the publishers are tired of my emails and phone calls, but at least I can share these books with people who are comfortable enough reading in English."

Anna opened the book: *Loving Her* by Ann Allen Shockley. The title wasn't lost on her and she found herself reading until she fell asleep, the book resting on her stomach, her glass empty on the coffee table.

She woke up when Erik came home, banging into the railing like he was drunk. Instinctively, she looked at her watch: four thirty a.m. That was late even for him. He went straight to the bathroom and showered, which she found odd. Had he been smoking? He knew that she hated that. She would find out the next morning. These days, bars didn't allow smoking so clothes no longer shrieked of smoke after a night out, unless you had actually smoked yourself.

She went upstairs and decided to go straight to bed instead of popping into the bathroom to ask about his evening. If he were drunk, he would be argumentative.

When he came to bed he kept to his side, wrapping his duvet tightly around his body, as if he were upset. Perhaps he had had a fight with Rob?

"Are you okay?" she asked.

"Had a bit too much to drink," he said.

"Fun night?"

"Not bad. Really need to sleep. G'night."

He didn't turn to her for a goodnight kiss. Was he trying to hide his nicotine breath?

The next morning, she pulled out his clothes from the wash basket. They smelled of grimy bar and stale beer, but not smoke. His shirt, a black short-sleeved one from a medium-range clothing chain, had a stain on the collar however, which she tried to brush off with her thumb. Greasy red paint, or… lipstick?

A million thoughts went through her head. Did he know about Iris? Was he trying to get her back? But how could he possibly know? They had been so careful, there was no way he would know, she reasoned.

"Erik?" She went into the bedroom where he was still nursing his hangover. "Erik? I was just going to do the laundry and found this."

He squinted as she held the shirt up to his face.

"It seems to have a lipstick stain on it. Kind of clichéd, don't you think?"

"Oh," he said, looking away. "Yeah, well I bumped into what's-her-name… a teacher from day care. She gave me a hug. That must be it."

"Kerstin?" Anna asked even though she couldn't imagine the fifty-plus teacher in a bar with red lipstick.

"No, oh… I can't remember her name. Starts with a P, I think."

"Pernilla?"

"That's the one."

"So you had a good time?"

"Yeah, I mean. With Rob. Not with her. Felt a bit awkward chatting to her, you know. She's young and hip and must think I'm like ancient."

"So you chatted to her?"

"She really likes Lukas and Sebastian. Had lots of nice things to say about them."

"I heard that she is the daughter of what's-his-name, the owner of that big coffee company. Apparently she only got the job as a favour, she's not even a trained teacher."

"I wouldn't know."

Right. "So you're sure that's it?"

"Of course." A pained look on his face. "Actually, Anna... honey, please can you get me some Ibuprofen. My head is killing me."

Honey? As she went down to fetch the painkillers, she thought about Iris's suggestion to go away for a couple of days. Perhaps she shouldn't feel too guilty after all?

46

Rolf

February 2016

Rolf wanted to paint Frida; a bottle of vodka in one hand, legs spread to the wind. The cross around her neck prominent above the small tits. She was raw and unpolished and not like his other objects. Hair and red nails didn't have a place in this painting. Instead he would sample drool out of her mouth, skin off of her heels, and pubic hair. Lots of it, protruding through the smooth acrylic paint. It would be a large canvas, his central piece in the next collection.

"Dan's teacher is married with two children," she said, visibly excited to have some new information. "She's known for being a fucking Mother Teresa who's generous with her time. She's strict though, doesn't take any shit from her students."

He sat up, not bothering to cover himself with the blanket. The kid wasn't there.

"Want a drink?"

He shook his head but she got up, pulled out a large

packet of washing powder from a cupboard and fished out two beers.

"Keeping the beer clean?" he joked.

"It's my son. He keeps confiscating everything."

She was being dramatic. That could be good or it could be bad.

"So, who did you ask?" he said. "People at work? Other parents? Your kid?"

She took a gulp of the beer, then another. Lost in another world, she started dancing even though there was no music. He needed to reel her back in. Did she need another round of the Rolf gun? He laughed. Iris had found that funny once. His Rolf gun.

"Frida? I'm talking to you."

"I just know," she said.

At that moment, he'd had enough. Forget the painting. Fucking and leaving was better than this pretending to have a relationship shit.

"That's not fucking good enough," he said. "I'm off."

Loneliness was her enemy and he shamelessly abused it.

"Please don't go," she predictably begged him.

Her beer breath was upon him, her wet lips on his.

"You just don't take me seriously," he sulked.

Violence didn't seem to work on her, guilt worked better.

"I do," she said but he didn't budge, and so she sat down and lit a cigarette. "I read about it... in Dan's story."

"Right."

"He's deep," she said. "Writes all kinds of shit. Poems, stories, even comics that he draws pictures for."

"Yes, yes, you've told me already. But maybe what he wrote about his teacher is just fiction."

"It's not a story. He also writes in a special notebook."

"And he just left that out for you to read?"

"Of course not! He keeps notes and shit in a box under his bed but this notebook is always in that stupid backpack. Someone gave it to him, way back. It's got holes and everything but he won't give it up. Anyway, he was sleeping when I sneaked into his bedroom. I didn't have time to read the whole thing, he started stirring, but I think he wants me to be like her. So whatever you can do to get her off my back, do it."

47

Daniel

January 2016

Dan was exhilarated. Excited. Pumped. He wrote the adjectives down in his notebook, wanting to remember this moment. Lying on his bed, a big fat grin on his face, he closed his eyes and imagined Anna. Her lips on his, holding him just the way she had held that woman, in a tight I-will-never-let-you-go grip. She smelt of summer, freshly cut grass and yellow buttercups. "Oh, Dan," she would whisper and hand herself over, her large breasts pushed into his face, his erection hard. Her expert hands would undress him, one layer at a time, until he was completely naked. She would view his body, impressed by his biceps, the almost six-pack and how hard he was. Then she would dig her nails into his back, spread her legs and ask him to fill her up.

He wanked. And instead of the usual guilt that followed his release, he felt happier than in a long time.

"Where have you been?"

Frida had opened the door and was standing at the foot of his bed. He looked at his hand, covered in a sticky white liquid.

"Get out!" he shouted. He quickly pulled a blanket over himself.

"Thinking about your girlfriend?"

"I don't have one." He got off the bed, drying his hand on the rough fabric before he pushed her out of the room. "Get out, I said."

Frida fell backwards but she was quickly back up on her feet.

"Get the fuck away from me!" He shoved her hard.

This time, she slipped on the rug and hit her head on the wall. Her body descended to the floor. A sad pile of bones.

"Leave me alone," she cried.

He was too worked up and had no intention of listening to her pleas. He raised his leg and kicked her, his bare foot hitting the sharp outline of a rib. It hurt but he lifted his foot up again. This time he aimed at her stomach and his foot sank into the fat, the elasticity of her skin accommodating. No one would see the bruises apart from the Nissan dude and he didn't seem like someone who would care.

When Dan grew tired of her whimpering, he stepped over her and went into the kitchen, opened the fridge and took out a snack. The selection was fantastic: plain yoghurt, a dried piece of cheese and half a leftover sausage. He felt hungry and ate all of it, washing it down with Coke Zero, which he drank straight from the bottle. Then he returned to his room. Frida was crying on the floor outside.

"You need to go food shopping," he told her. "I want bananas."

All sports people seemed to eat bananas to keep their energy levels up. He would need that.

He slammed the door shut and pulled out his book and wrote a to-do list:

Step 1 – blackmail

Step 2 – move into Anna's house

Step 3 – become best mates with her kids

Step 4 – fuck her/she dumps the husband

Her husband was clearly not man enough for her. This would be easy.

*

Outside, in the corridor, Frida was quietening down. All he could hear was a muffled groan as she tried to stand up. She would be heading straight for a bottle, if there was one – he'd done a raid earlier in the week and had confiscated three six-packs of beer and two bottles of home brew. If she had been to *Systembolaget* since then, she would soon be passed out on her bed, her limbs floppy and unresponsive, drool trickling out of her mouth. For once, he didn't mind. It would mean peace and quiet and he needed that for two important reasons: to create a detailed plan and to write about his new life. He needed to visualise it. That way he wouldn't lose faith.

I'm really happy that you have expressed yourself in writing.

In his last assignment, Anna had told him he had a poetic streak. He had circled her observation with a red pen and he now kept the paper in the box with his other sacred stuff.

Bang!

He sat up and faced the door. Frida had swung it open

and was swiftly taking the key from the inside lock. What the…? He got to his feet to stop her but she had already shut it. He grabbed the handle but the door wouldn't open. It was already locked.

"Gotcha!" Frida shouted gleefully outside.

Fuck. The key was meant to lock her out, not the other way around.

He banged on the door as hard as he could.

"Open it right now or I will beat the crap out of you!"

"Haven't you done that already?" she said, her tone acidic.

He went over to the window but it was jammed. The owners had painted the house before they moved in and the window had been stuck ever since. The small panes wouldn't be able to let him out, even if he smashed them one by one. He was stuck. Shit, shit, shit.

"Frida… I'm sorry," he said, changing tactic. "I don't know why I did that. Are you okay?"

He leaned on the door and stroked its wooden surface, imagining it was Anna's skin. Soft and cool.

"I'm not fucking okay," Frida said.

She hit the door which made his head bounce. He hit it back.

"Let me the fuck out of here!"

"No. Game over, son."

48

Anna

February 2016

Anna was going to spend the afternoon talking about family, war and death, with *War and Peace* featuring at the centre of the class discussion. But to quote her late grandmother, "the young are not how they used to be." Her grandmother had had a point: the students' attention span was limited. The use of multiple electronic devices was partly to blame and they wouldn't read an extensive piece of work such as Tolstoy's classic masterpiece. She had therefore decided to bring Shakespeare into the mix. Although it had been four hundred years since his death, his work still seemed to resonate with her students.

"*Othello* is about love and revenge," she said and that immediately got their attention. The drama of teenage life meant that everyone could relate. Young love, whether seemingly true or unrequited, was something they all had experienced. Except perhaps Daniel, who didn't seem interested even though there were plenty of girls mooning over the "bad boy".

Daniel hadn't turned up for school that morning. She had received no emails from him and no one had picked up the phone when she had tried to call his house. It didn't exactly worry her, it just seemed unusual. He didn't ordinarily skip school. So where was he? If he was ill then why hadn't the school been notified? Lately he had appeared to be a better listener in class and he was causing less drama. There were still fights outside of the classroom from time to time, but he seemed to have settled in. Apart from his obsessive messages, which she ignored for the most part, things were looking up.

"Othello is a black soldier who falls in love with an Italian woman called Desdemona," she explained. "But her father doesn't want her to marry a black man." She paused to make sure they were listening. "Yet she does marry him behind her father's back. That's how strong Desdemona's love for Othello is."

Many of them smiled, as was expected. To marry for love, that was romantic. She herself had married for love. In the past, Erik had even bought her flowers.

But Erik had changed.

Then again, Othello had also changed.

Anna let the class read the passage where Othello passed Iago over for lieutenant, in favour of the less-experienced Cassio.

"Iago was upset and wanted to seek revenge," she explained. "To hurt Othello, Iago claimed that Desdemona had cheated with Cassio. In fact, Iago was so persuasive that he pushed Othello into insanity. Eventually Othello started to doubt Desdemona's fidelity, and to protect his honour, he killed her."

She looked out at the class, their attention completely on her and Shakespeare's dramatic plot. It was a fantastic feeling, to capture them like this; one of the many perks of being a teacher.

"When the truth finally came out and Iago was exposed as a liar," she said, "Othello couldn't live with himself and took his own life."

"What an idiot," someone said.

"What happened to Iago?" someone else asked. "Did someone kill him?"

Anna thrived. "No," she said. "Iago lived."

That got the discussion going. Everyone was talking at the same time and she had to structure it, divide them into groups and hand out specific discussion points. She loved the energy, how passionate they felt as they tackled anything from fairness, inequality, death and gender roles to racism, love and revenge. While they talked, she glanced at the open book in front of her and caught sight of two lines.

But that our loves and comforts should increase,
Even as our days do grow!

The group's heated debate became a distant murmur as she lost herself in her own world, just for a moment. Loves and comforts, even as our days do grow. As our days grow. The future, what would it bring?

*

As the school day drew to a close, Anna packed up swiftly. There would be no staying behind to mark papers or plan future lessons today.

"Happy weekend," Kent said as she stepped out of her new lightweight heels and pulled the winter boots on. There was a gentle sprinkling of snowflakes outside the window.

"Thanks," she said. "You too."

She had revealed part of her weekend plans, saying it was a book club outing, but hadn't provided too much detail. Kent knew her too well; he might detect holes in her story. He was happy for her, though. Not like Erik.

"An author's visit?" he had said, as if she was going to a sect meeting.

"Yes," she had confirmed. "She's travelling from the UK to do a talk and my book club is going. We thought we would make a weekend of it."

"Yes, but Lund? That's an hour away. What if I need the car?"

"I don't have to drive. I can either take the train, or I'm sure I can catch a ride with someone from the book club."

He had looked unsure. Was it the prospect of being left alone with the children over the weekend that bothered him, or that she was breaking away from him, like a piece of furniture out of place?

"It's good that I've made some friends, isn't it?" she had tried.

"I guess."

She had walked up to him and given him a hug. A friendly cuddle. He had hugged her back, his customary annoyance filling the air, but he had given in.

*

Anna headed home to pick up her overnight bag and to drop the car off for Erik. He would use it to pick the boys up after he arrived home from work.

"Another day, another house to paint," he had said unenthusiastically that morning, but perhaps because of her own weekend ahead, she had tried to show an interest.

"Are the owners nice?"

"They're okay. Bankers."

"Interesting colour?"

She really couldn't think of anything better to ask.

"Grey. Unfortunately it's still very popular."

"At least you're an expert on grey."

He had actually smiled at that.

She had dropped Sebastian and Lukas off at day care that morning and had said goodbye then. They weren't used to her being away overnight and she could tell they had been anxious. She felt guilty but Erik did love them. He might not be the disciplinarian that she had hoped he would be, but he did genuinely care about his children. They would be fine.

*

Iris picked her up at five o'clock sharp, despite the slush that was now sadly prevalent on the roads. The above-zero temperature wasn't giving the snow a fighting chance, which would disappoint the boys. Every morning, they were hoping for an opportunity to have a snowball fight.

They needed to get going. The author's event would start at seven and they had agreed to check into their hotel before then. Anna put her overnight bag in the boot of Iris's Golf and got into the passenger seat.

"Everything okay?" Iris asked, nodding towards the house.

It felt peculiar, to have Iris literally so close to home.

"Erik's at work."

"And what about you?" Iris asked. "Are you all right?"

Anna nodded. "Let's do this," she said confidentially.

Before Iris left Rolf. Before she made such a life-altering

decision, they had agreed to do this. A whole weekend. Just the two of them, together. A trial of sorts.

Loves and comforts, even as our days do grow. What did the future hold?

Could she leave Erik?

49

Iris

February 2016

“It wasn't a holiday but it was close. A weekend with Anna. Iris had signed them up for a talk by the Welsh young adult writer Gwenhwyfar Dunne, an up and coming novelist who she had wanted to listen to anyway. The fact that it was in Lund, an hour away – not too far from Hågarp, but not too close – was an added bonus.

All we have is each other
each other, each other, each other

Iris thought of these few but significant words by the poet Lars Forssell, as she guided them out of Mörna and onto the E4 motorway. The weather was abysmal and at first, small talk filled the silence. Then Anna became braver. She opened up about her work, about the students and her desire to at least help one student better him – or herself every year.

"Hopefully more!" she said.

"You're passionate about your job."

Iris liked that about Anna. That she cared.

"How do you like Mörna?" Iris asked. "Would you ever consider living anywhere else?"

If we actually do this, if we are going to be together, would you be able to do that in a small-town mentality? Or would you move somewhere else with me?

"I find it peaceful," Anna said.

"But life is so transient," Iris said. "Like the poet Theodore Roethke said, 'I learn by going where I have to go.' I think that sums me up at least."

The comfortable silence in between, Anna's hand resting by the gear box, her pinkie almost touching Iris's leg. It was exhilarating, sharing this ride, heading towards an unexpected future.

Love didn't come easily for Iris. To say it out loud to Anna, 'I have fallen in love with you,' had been momentous and out of character for her.

Iris thought about the first time she had fallen in love. She had been sixteen, more than three decades ago. Her mother's strict, religious upbringing combined with Iris being an only child, had created a sheltered life. When she thought back to it now, her own naivety always got her.

*

"Big Mac?" Svenne asked her.

She nodded even though she had no idea what it was, not wanting to admit that she had never been to a McDonald's before.

"American burgers," he had said and that had somehow convinced her.

They sat on opposite sides of a small table, the fake leather chairs hot and slippery. He was everything her mother would hate: long hair, unshaven face and a brand-new tattoo. A black swan. It clashed with his overall look, the beautiful bird so unlike his torn jeans and crumpled shirt.

She picked at the skinny fries.

"Not hungry?" he asked as he shovelled his own burger down. A few bites and it was gone. She offered him hers, not able to eat anyway. The smell made her nauseous.

"My mum wants to meet you," she said and he looked at her, those grey eyes that had met hers at the local video store. He had been renting foreign movies with subtitles. He was deep and different and she liked that.

"You think that's a good idea?" he asked.

That was another thing she liked: his self-awareness. He knew he wasn't everyone's cup of tea.

"It's going to happen sooner or later anyway," she said.

A raised eyebrow. "Is it?" A smile she couldn't quite read.

"Well… I mean…" They had done it. Surely that meant they were serious.

"I've harvested some new weed," he said. "Want to smoke some after?"

He was creative. He wasn't just a dealer like the other boys on the housing estate, he grew his own, trying out new plants, combining them.

"Sure."

She liked the sensation of being someone else when she smoked, of floating, the weightlessness. Except lately she couldn't stand the smell, it brought on that feeling of wanting to hug a toilet bowl.

"Iris," he said and looked at her. "Never compromise who you are."

That made her feel good. She walked him home, smoked

*even though it made her feel sick, and made love to him,
feeling like she was the only person in the world for him.*

*The following Saturday, she went back to McDonald's to
try that Big Mac after all, to remember that precious time of
just the two of them. He hadn't returned her calls.*

"Never compromise who you are."

*The words made something flutter in her stomach and
she turned around, happy to hear his voice. But those grey
eyes were not on her; the words formed by the lips that had
tenderly kissed her were aimed at someone else. A young girl
with pretty blonde hair in braids. Iris ran out, holding her
stomach, the pregnancy test glowing in her handbag.*

*

She cringed at the memory. Love had been so complicated
after that. Then Rolf had swooped in and her perspective
had changed. Was it time for it to change again?

In the corner of her eye, she caught Anna fiddling with her
rings. A sparkling diamond set in gold, next to a plain gold
band. Was she thinking of her husband and the betrayal that
lay ahead?

Iris was glad that she had offered to drive them. Should
Anna suddenly have second thoughts, she couldn't just drive
off; they would be able to give this a proper chance.

"Have you read Gwenhwyfar Dunne's book?" Iris asked
her.

Anna shook her head. "Not yet, but I'm hoping to this
weekend. I know it would have been better to do it before
the talk but I haven't had a chance. Busy at work and with
the boys at home."

"That's fine. I can always fill you in."

They exchanged a smile.

"Tell me about Erik," Iris said then and she sensed Anna flinching slightly. She realised it was an unexpected request but it was better to get the elephant out of the room.

"I've told you about Rolf," Iris continued. "So I would like to hear about Erik. I just want us to be honest with each other. Let's talk about everything, even our dirty laundry, our doubts and concerns."

In the corner of her eye, she could sense Anna studying her, and it felt good, to have her undivided attention. To be with Anna was easy. Not only did they share a love of literature, Anna was a kind and thoughtful woman who made her heart expand. She made Iris feel like she cared again, not just for herself, but also for humankind. She could easily do this. The two of them together. Forever.

"So, what do you think? Should we air the dirty laundry?"

50

Anna

February 2016

I do like the sound of that," Anna said.

It was true, her mind did like the notion of complete honesty, but what could she possibly tell Iris about Erik?

"As you already know, he paints houses," she said. "But he likes to play the guitar. They've got a band, him and his friend Rob and a couple of others. People come and go in that band but Rob and Erik always remain." She was blabbering. "He's a great dad," she added. "Not strict enough, but fun and loving and well, without him, I wouldn't have my beautiful boys."

"And is he a good husband?"

The question was loaded and very personal. How should she respond?

"We were obviously in love when we got married," Anna said. "And in those early days he was very attentive. Then…" she felt like she had already explained this to Iris a long time ago but she told her anyway. "Then we got a mortgage, had children and bought a Volvo. I guess it wasn't what we had expected."

"Have you tried counselling?"

Anna shook her head. Although she urged her students to seek help, she couldn't imagine sitting in front of a therapist with Erik. He would make a mockery of it.

Iris didn't ask any more questions about Erik and Anna felt happy to leave it behind.

*

They were going to share a room. Iris had asked her permission before booking the hotel. It felt completely natural. Like platonic friends, they unpacked, went to the bathroom and got changed for the evening's book talk. Only when they were leaving the room, did Iris take hold of Anna's waist, their hips touching.

"Thank you," Iris said. "For coming here."

She leaned in and kissed Anna, who felt the heat spread from her mouth to her body. If Iris had asked her to stay in this room and not go, she would have. Anything, for this feeling to last. But Iris withdrew her lips.

"Come on," she said and playfully smacked Anna's behind. "Or we will be late."

*

The author was enigmatic. She talked with confidence about her book, a story about telepathic gypsy twins fighting an ancient magic. Even though Anna hadn't read the novel, based on the presentation, she could imagine her students loving it. It sounded like it would transport them to another world filled with drama, intrigue and adventure. There was no limit to the imagination and that's what students needed, to be swept off their feet by books as opposed to video games, computers, apps and all the rest of it. Having said that, the book would most likely become a video or computer game or even an app if it became a hit.

Anna bought thirty books to have them signed. The sales assistant thought she heard wrong.

"Did you say thirty books? I'm just worried we won't have enough for everyone else."

The author, who was signing at a table nearby, heard this.

"Don't worry," she said, catching Anna's eye. She seemed warm and friendly; a beautiful tattoo of a gypsy woman displayed on the arm signing books. "If they don't have enough, they can order more. Just out of interest though, why do you want to buy so many?" She flicked her short, silver-blonde hair. "Not that I'm complaining!"

"It's for one of my classes, they've done really well this year," Anna said.

"I thought students were supposed to buy the teachers presents, not the other way around?"

Erik had asked that same question every single year. Normally, she only bought something small, a bookmark or an Ernest Hemingway or Selma Lagerlöf keyring. She took out her debit card.

"I just want to inspire them to read," she said.

"That's just like her," Iris said. She had appeared next to Anna, holding a book of her own. "She really cares."

"Here, let me sign them for you," Gwenhwyfar, said. She reached out her hands to take Anna's load of books.

"But the queue...?" the sales woman said.

"Why don't we offer them some coffee while they wait?"

Gwenhwyfar said. "Or better yet, wine!" She turned to Anna. "What are your students' names?"

Anna rattled off their names one by one. It took about half an hour, the queue not sighing and muttering as much as she had expected. Drinks had magically appeared and everyone seemed to be chatting and having a lovely time.

"I wish there were more teachers like you," Gwenhwyfar said, as she handed the last book to Anna.

When they left, Iris helped her carry her purchases.

"She was lovely!" Iris said. "One of the nicest authors I've met. And I've met many. So charismatic as well and did you see those grey-blue eyes? Beautiful."

She couldn't explain it, but Anna felt odd. Was this how Iris normally talked about other women? How would she tackle this?

"And she let you pass the whole queue," Iris continued. "She definitely liked *you*!"

This confused Anna even further. She reminded herself that this weekend was about discovery: there was so much she needed to learn about Iris.

They walked in silence to a nearby restaurant where they were generously provided with space for the bags of books.

Tables covered in white linen, candles and subtle tones of jazz in the background made it an intimate setting.

"This is romantic," Iris said as she smoothed out a napkin on her lap.

Anna felt that in order to carry the conversation forward, she needed a few answers. There was no point waiting.

"What did you mean back there?" she asked.

Iris looked curious. "I don't understand?" She tucked her short hair behind her ears, the candlelight reflected in her shiny red lipstick.

"That author might have liked me for buying thirty books," Anna said. "But did you like, *like* her?"

She realised she sounded like a twelve-year-old as the shape of Iris's face changed.

"Oh," Iris said. "No. I just thought she was nice." Her words were stale, which made Anna feel insecure. Had she made a mistake talking about this?

"There's just so much I don't know about you," Anna said honestly. "You're not monogamous, remember. Would you want to..." *do it with her?*

"Anna." Iris placed her hands over Anna's across the table. "I already told you it's different now that I have met you."

Her face softened, her words tinged with colour.

"But can you just change like that?" Anna said. "Overnight?" Surely she didn't have that effect on people; that they could just alter their way of living?

"Anna," Iris said and Anna involuntarily pulled her hands back. The way Iris said her name reminded her of Daniel and he was the last person she wanted to think about. Iris didn't look offended however. She just leaned back in her chair and said: "I love you."

Love. That word, which Anna hadn't repeated back. She looked at the white tablecloth, the uneven threads, the faint stains of spilt red wine. Iris waited. Anna had to give her credit for that. There was no pushing her up against a wall and making her say or do anything. Anna looked up.

"Iris, I don't know how I feel right now."

"I know," she said. "But I'm still leaving Rolf." She paused. "Not for you. For me."

She seemed to leave space for Anna to inject her thoughts on the matter but she had nothing to say.

"I do adore him," Iris said. "I think he's brilliant in so

many ways, but we should be friends, not lovers anymore. Lately, I have found myself switching off. I think he's sensed that because he's become… not suffocating exactly, but close enough for someone like Rolf. He's never been like that before and I can feel myself being tied down."

"I have children," Anna said. "Responsibilities."

"You do. I don't know how we would work it out but I don't feel like that's important right now. We wouldn't even have to live together." Iris leaned forward and Anna found herself stretching her hands out once again. She wanted to touch Iris, to feel the comfort of her warm skin. "But we can't stay married, that wouldn't be fair," Iris said.

"You have slept with married women before."

Iris nodded. "I have, but affairs are brief," she said. "This isn't."

Their eyes met, their hands touching. *This wasn't brief.* Anna affectionately squeezed Iris's fingers, trying to convey her own feelings, the outside world no longer existing.

"Are you ready to order?" A waiter stood next to their table, pen and pad in hand.

They simultaneously turned to him and Anna was about to say, "Can't you see we're in the middle of something?" when Iris patiently said, "I'll have the salmon. What about you, Anna?"

*

They shared a bottle of Sauvignon Blanc and left the relationship and serious questions. They spoke about books and holidays and dreams, realising they were both lucky enough to have jobs they loved.

"Whenever I have a class coming in to the library, I always

feel such admiration for the teacher. How do you cope with so many of them, day in and day out?"

For the hundredth time in her life, Anna found herself explaining that: "Discipline should be dealt with at home." Although she quickly added that her students, for the most part, were well behaved.

Again, Daniel came to mind but she didn't want to tell Iris about him. Two more years and he would either be working or moving on to university, which at the moment didn't seem likely. He was clever, though. That was the frustrating part.

When they walked back to the hotel, Anna carried a plastic bag in one hand, the other hand dangling suggestively close to Iris's. She wanted so badly to hold it, but what if they bumped into someone they knew?

Would it always be like that, if they were an actual couple? Or was it acceptable if it was out in the open?

Just then, Iris grabbed hold of Anna's hand and pulled her into an alleyway. A dark, moist wall behind her back, Iris's lips on hers. Anna giggled, the bags falling to the ground; their hands caressing, stroking, loving. She didn't care that it was cold. Anna had dreamed of being taken like this, with such passionate unexpected force, but she had never thought it would happen in this lifetime. She no longer cared if anyone passed by or if she would know someone here. It wasn't the alcohol, it was Iris, the way she made her feel, like fire on her skin, inside her heart, a longing to stay with this woman at any cost.

Iris hoisted up Anna's dress, her hands expertly inside her knickers, finding a sensitive spot, circulating, applying the right amount of pressure. Anna moaned into Iris's ear as she neared a climax. She wanted to reciprocate but her limbs went numb with pleasure and any feeble attempts to satisfy

Iris were brushed aside. "Later," Iris said. "Later."

She came hard into Iris's hand. Shocked by the strength of her orgasm and slightly embarrassed by the loud sound coming out of her mouth, she adjusted her knickers and pulled her dress down.

"That was incredible," Iris said, kissing her. A soft, intense meeting of lips. "You're so hot."

Anna laughed nervously.

"You make me *feel* hot," she admitted.

They held hands the rest of the way, and once they arrived at the hotel, there were no inhibitions. If she could have an orgasm in a public, albeit hidden, place, then she could do anything.

Clothes fell to the floor, the covers of the bed pulled away. Limbs stretched, backs arched, wet lips searched and discovered new territory. Iris's body became her own; her erogenous zones Anna's, her nakedness less awkward. Lights on or off, it didn't matter.

"Who are you?" Iris asked at one point, laughter bubbling out of her.

Anna laughed as well. This was new. Laughing while having sex. Who knew that could be so good? So comfortable.

No more shyness, no more self-consciousness. Anna could feel how much Iris worshipped her body, including her dimpled behind, round thighs and chunky toes. In fact Iris sucked them. One by one, she pulled Anna's toes into her mouth, her warm tongue circling, causing a tickling but sensual feeling that made her tingle between her thighs.

Iris had taught Anna to tease and delay and to avoid reaching an early climax. This ran through their every meeting, whether it was sexual or not. They seemed to linger in every moment, making the most of it.

Feeling adventurous, Anna pushed Iris off of her and pinned her to the bed.

"Now it's my turn," she said laughing, and she could tell Iris was excited by the changing roles.

Anna separated Iris's slender legs and for a few seconds, she just watched Iris: her perky breasts, hardened nipples, slim waist and tanned arms that were now resting comfortably under her head. Her lipstick had worn off but her eyes were like emeralds, emphasised by the black eyeliner.

"Your body is so young," Anna said. "What is your secret?"

"Lots of sex," Iris said, grinning.

It was a joy to be with Iris. She made Anna feel as if she had the whole future ahead of her. Iris tried to sit up to kiss Anna, but Anna pinned her down again.

"Hey, I wasn't done with you," she said and this time she acted quickly, opening up Iris's sex, resting her tongue in the opening, boring it into Iris. She let out a gasp and grabbed hold of Anna's hair. Anna's tongue slipped out, over Iris's parted lips, wetting them. The satisfaction Anna felt from Iris's moans egged her on. *I can do more.* She had looked at handbooks online that freely showed sample pages and felt spurred on.

Kissing a woman between her legs was like kissing her mouth. Anna's tongue licked and circled and sucked, her hand simultaneously moving up to Iris's breast, tugging at the nipple.

"Oh…" Iris gasped, her breath uneven, her hips rocking back and forth.

Anna lifted her head up briefly. She wanted to witness Iris's pleasure, her relaxed face, widened nostrils, her closed but fluttering eyelids. It was exhilarating to know she could stimulate Iris this way. Encouraged, she placed two fingers on Iris's dark, trimmed pubic hair, moving it up and out of the way, stretching the skin to expose the vulva. A bare rose, pink petals blooming just for her. Her tongue ran over the delicate lining, the skin smooth and silky. Iris's moans intensified. With growing comfort, Anna let her right-hand index finger play with Iris for a while, slipping it over the wetness, licking and rubbing, before slipping it inside of her. She was warm and tight, and Anna was turned on by the confined wetness. She pushed another finger in, slipping them both in and out, watching Iris's body react, the contracting stomach muscles, the upper body almost floating over the bed, the spread legs taut and toes stretched out. It was time to let her come and Anna moved the fingers in and out faster, her eager tongue kissing Iris's vaginal lips. She screamed out her orgasm, sweat (or was it tears?) on her face.

Afterwards, Iris lay motionless, not speaking a word and having felt on top of the world for making Iris's release so intense, Anna now felt concerned. Had she done it all wrong?

Then Iris spoke. "That was… a-m-azing," she said.

She opened her eyes and pulled Anna down next to her, kissing her gently but passionately. At once, Anna felt both exhausted and thrilled. She rested her hand on Iris, caressing her stomach. *I think I am falling in love with you.*

They lay in each other's arms for a long time, Iris's heartbeat comforting, and once they had recovered, they started over. Their bodies moved from one position to the next, the orgasms woven into one another's. With plenty of playfulness and versatility, Anna's body tried new positions: she was on her back, on top of Iris, sitting up, on her knees, in front of, behind.

The minutes went past, the hours; darkness became day, daylight turned to night. They talked, they made love, they showered, they talked some more, they ate, made love again, came and went.

When it was time to go home, Anna had decided. She would need to have a difficult conversation with Erik.

51

Erik

April 2016

It's Walpurgis Night, marking the arrival of spring, and Erik's happy to have Mum back, if only she didn't insist they attend the annual bonfire by the beach. He doesn't want to. Having to see Anna's colleagues, students and their families, Sebastian and Lukas's friends with parents... what if everyone knows about Pernilla? Then he won't just be a sad fuck whose wife is in a coma, he will be a fucking scumbag.

"Don't be selfish," Mum says. "Think of the children."

Her words are sharp and uncompromising and he wants to please her, he just can't face the humiliation.

"I *am* thinking of the children," he says. "I don't want to embarrass them."

"Erik, I have just had enough!"

He shrinks in his seat as he watches her eyes widen, the way they did when he was young and got into trouble.

"You're a grown man," she continues. "I have been quiet long enough. Anna has been more of a mother to you than a wife." She pauses as if grounding herself. "Tradition is important. You grew up in a small town so you should know."

"My wife wasn't in a coma then, was she?"

"And your girlfriend wasn't pregnant, you mean?"

She twists the dagger in his chest.

When he spoke to the police they didn't mention Pernilla and that freaks him out. After first calling him to request that he comes down to the police station, they cancelled the meeting because of "other priorities". Mum reads out loud from the paper every morning, highlighting more severe crimes, which obviously are more urgent than a small-town teacher who is still alive and has no obvious threat to her. When they finally managed to fit him in, it was a brief meeting, the questions hitting him one after the other.

"You haven't come across her phone or her laptop?"

"No." He was too annoyed with them to admit that he had the laptop, and too much time seemed to have passed. What if he got into trouble?

"How long did Rob stay at your house that night? Did you watch anything particular on TV, what did you talk about?"

He tried to answer as best he could.

Then the rough punch: "Were you faithful to Anna?"

"Yes," he said.

He had really thought about it, should the subject arise. If they were going to accuse him of sleeping with someone, he was going to confess, but in the seriousness of the moment, he just couldn't. After all, what proof did they have, other than Pernilla's words? Even if they found the taxi driver, he didn't see them have sex. Quite possibly, the baby wasn't even his. Pernilla most probably slept around. He decided that it was his word against hers.

"Do you have any reason to believe that Anna might not have been faithful to you?"

There it was, finally. "No," he said, because it couldn't come from him. Someone else needed to verify it. Not him.

"Did she mention any particular students?"

"No." She really hadn't.

"Did any students call the house? Was anyone upset with her?"

"Plenty of people called her and who knows if anyone was upset? She was pretty strict."

It was an unsatisfying interview and he really wishes they had asked him about Pernilla straight out. Why play games with him? Are they waiting for a DNA test to see if the baby is his?

The situation is too stressful and he just can't handle Mum's judgement right now.

"I'm not the only one," he tells her. "Anna was also cheating."

"No wonder. A woman needs a man, not a boy."

He can't believe it. "You're defending her?"

"It's time to grow up and start taking responsibility. We're going tonight, whether you like it or not. Otherwise I'm going back home."

Their eyes duel for a few seconds but he knows he can't win.

"Fine," he sulks and heads up to shower.

"Great," Mum says from the bottom of the stairs, back to her old spirited tone of voice. "We leave in ten minutes."

*

They walk even though he would have preferred to drive

282

to avoid the customary greetings along the way. The town's population turns into pilgrims, walking in clusters, a strong current pulling them down to the sea. He puts his head down and pretends to be in an animated conversation with Mum but she greets every person they walk past, even though she barely knows anyone. Sebastian and Lukas wave to their friends and Erik is forced to raise his hand a few times.

Luckily, it only takes five minutes and when they arrive they stay at the outskirts of the crowd. In the middle is a pile of trees and bushes that the community has scraped together from their gardens and outer farms. There is even the odd Christmas tree, dry and ready to be burnt to a crisp.

"Can we go and play?"

He hesitates, Anna wouldn't have been comfortable with the boys roaming around unattended.

"I'm not sure," he begins.

"Of course you can," Mum interrupts and turns to him. "Let them have some fun."

"Mum, the times have changed." What was it Anna used to say? "It's not like when I was young." *They could be kidnapped.*

He used to accuse Anna of being paranoid but now that Mum is the liberal one, the boot has ended up on the other foot.

"It's about to start," Mum says and the matter is dismissed.

He looks to the stage, a temporary wooden platform, where the traditional speech will be held and everyone quietens down: no more small talk about the latest house project or school gossip.

A man in a ponytail and a ridiculous moustache starts to talk into a microphone. He welcomes the spring and launches into the history of the bonfire, the farmers letting the animals out this time of the year and explaining that the fires were used to scare vultures away. He talks about the intricate hide of an animal and of blood. Blood? Erik looks at Mum and whispers:

"What is this rubbish?"

"He's an artist, Erik. I read about him in the paper. He's famous – or infamous is perhaps a better word – for adding blood to his artwork."

"That's fucked up."

"Language."

"The boys can't even hear me!"

Sebastian and Lukas have found a couple of friends and are playing nearby. They seem to be having fun, which makes him feel slightly better.

On stage, the artist drones on about individuality instead of spring and his eyes wander, bored. He scans the crowd, wondering if Pernilla is there. He's going to have to talk to her at some point. Mum has already discussed it with him.

"Don't ask her if the baby is yours," was her advice.

"Why the hell not? Maybe she has had multiple one-night stands?"

"Erik, you will come across as a heartless man."

"Who cares?"

But he realises he needs to think about what he's going to say. At the moment, anger and the notion of child support payments are preventing him from thinking clearly.

People start to clap as the speech finally comes to an end, and two men begin the job of lighting the fire.

"I hope it doesn't rain," Mum says.

Erik wishes it would. Then the fire would be out and they could head home. A couple of people have cracked open cans of beer and his taste buds are longing for one.

"Mum, did you bring…"

"Hi there," someone says and stretches out a hand. It's the artist who did the speech. "You must be Erik?"

"Yes…" He better not be related to Pernilla. Instinctively, Erik takes a step back. "Do I know you?"

Behind them, the fire grows, the heat tickling his back.

"I'm really sorry about your wife. How is she?"

"She's been better." He can't help it, he gets defensive. Who the hell is this dude, turning up asking about his wife?

"My wife knew Anna."

"Right…"

"Anyway, I wish her a speedy recovery."

The dodgy looking artist presses his palm into Erik's before walking off.

"How weird was that?" he says to Mum.

"You can't be upset with people for being friendly."

He looks around, aware that he hasn't seen the boys for some time.

"Can you see Sebastian and Lukas?"

Mum looks around. "They were just here…"

Were they now? *If only you hadn't let them run off!* His pulse is quickening as he looks left and right but there's no sign of them. He searches through the crowd, which at that moment starts to sing about spring, backed by the local church choir.

"They're probably off playing with their friends," Mum says.

"They're only five!"

"You ran around at five," she says but she doesn't understand. *I can't lose them too.*

"What if they're too close to the fire?" he says to get Mum to react.

"Then someone will pull them back."

People are either busy singing or drinking, he doubts they would notice the children. He circles the outskirts of the crowd, words of fresh, playful winds and streams following him around. Every time he sees a little boy he thinks it's Sebastian or Lukas but it's not. They're wearing matching, bright green jackets, bought by Anna during the sales season. They should be visible.

When he's rushed around the fire and pushed his way through the people, no longer caring who knows what about him, he returns to Mum.

"I can't find them," he says, out of breath.

Was Pernilla there after all? He realises that she quite possibly could have taken his children to deliberately piss him off. They trust her and would absolutely follow her if she asked them to.

"They must be here somewhere," Mum says. "Go and look behind the trees. Maybe they're playing hide and seek?"

"Why do you have to be so fucking calm?!"

He storms off.

Where are my boys?

52

Erik

April 2016

E rik runs over the grassy sand dunes, the cold grabbing
hold of him as the distance from the fire grows. There
are other children around and he asks them if they've seen
two boys in green jackets. They shake their heads and run
off. Frustrated, Erik starts running too, like a mad man, he
looks behind, even under, every single pine tree in sight.

"Sebastian! Lukas! Where are you?"

Someone offers to help him look and then there are more
of them. He doesn't have time to thank them, he just keeps
going, and then he hears a voice out of nowhere that sounds
familiar.

"That's cool!"

"Sebastian?"

His heart is beating so fast, it could very well be an
upcoming heart attack, he thinks, and calls again: "Sebastian?
Lukas?" Please.

"We're here."

They brush past a tree branch, grinning mischievously.

"Bloody hell, where have you been? You scared me!" He gets down on his knees and hugs them tightly. "Don't ever run away from me again, okay?"

"Don't worry, Daddy. We were with the boy with the cool jacket."

"Who?"

The boy who was cycling outside day care, the one who knows Mum."

"Oh. Is he here?"

The boy appears from behind a branch and steps in front of Erik and the boys.

"We were just playing. Sorry if you got scared."

"They just don't normally run off like that."

"Well, we were having fun. Weren't we?"

"Your name is David, right?"

The boy nods.

"Thanks for looking after them."

"No problem, if you ever need a babysitter, I would be happy to help."

Erik vaguely remembers someone else suggesting he should get a babysitter. Black Adam? Why are people so obsessed with him getting out?

"That's okay," he starts but Lukas is pulling at his jacket. "Please, Daddy," he whispers. "David loves Lego and he's promised to build a really cool ship with us. You know, for all our Lego people?"

Right. "Why don't you come over and hang out with the boys sometime?"

Maybe he can tell Erik about school, what Anna was up to. He needs to catch up on everything she's told him that he hasn't listened to.

"Sure."

"How about this weekend? Saturday at ten?"

The boy smiles. He high fives the boys and is off.

*

They head back to the fire when Erik's phone starts to ring. He expects it to be Mum, wondering if he's found the boys, but it's the hospital.

"You'd better come," someone says.

This is the call he's been waiting for.

"Has she stopped breathing?"

He tells the boys to quickly get Grandma, his life with Anna passing by like a silent movie.

"I don't want you to get too excited because it's still early…"

Has Anna moved? "Is she okay? Can she talk?"

"We're not quite sure yet."

"You've got to give me something," he shouts. "I can't drive for twenty minutes wondering? Don't you get that?"

"Erik." Mum has appeared at his side, her hand resting on his arm. "Calm down."

But he can't. He's shaking with built-up anger.

"Tell me!" he spits. "Tell me now!"

The person on the other side of the line hesitates. Is it a nurse? A doctor? An administrator? He wants someone with authority, someone who can offer a confident explanation.

Eventually the person on the line speaks: "She is awake."

53

Rolf

February 2016

Frida had become increasingly demanding and Rolf wasn't sure how long he could keep it up. Daily texts and phone calls, often in the middle of the night, was normally the reminder he needed – affairs should be brief – but Iris had gone away for the weekend and although she hadn't confirmed it, he was sure the teacher was involved.

He went over to Frida's to see if the kid knew about his teacher's whereabouts but it turned out he was locked up in his room like some five-year-old being punished for a temper tantrum. Not that he was complaining, it was nice having him out of the way.

"*Hej*, babe."

The place was damp and chilly, as if the heating wasn't working properly, but Frida didn't seem to notice. She was tipsy. And badly bruised. She always did have a few black marks here and there. That was apparently part of working at a factory, but it was worse than normal.

"Get into a fight?" he asked, pulling her close.

"Something like that."

"Looks pretty bad."

"Nothing a bit of love can't heal."

Her manipulation worked. He needed a shag to take his mind off things, and to warm up.

This time he tied her up. She was drunk enough to agree to anything, so it was easy. She was loud though. Louder than normal, and the kid kept banging on the wall. There was a lot of "shut the fuck up" and at one point, Rolf had to really focus to remember that he was having sex with Frida only, because at times it felt like a sick threesome.

He realised that he must be a masochist to put up with this. Frida was useless at getting information out of the kid – all he knew was where Anna lived, that she was married with two children, and that she had been voted Teacher of the Year the previous year. All very ordinary, non-juicy stuff.

"You're leaving already?"

"Gotta go."

The problem with the kid being locked up was that he couldn't talk to him. It would seem desperate to communicate through a door. He needed to come up with another idea.

"Will you come over later?" she asked.

"Sorry," he said. "I have to see my daughter."

It was true, he had planned to go to Gothenburg for a couple of days while Iris was away. If nothing else worked, he wouldn't hesitate to use Karin, who definitely wouldn't want to see her parents apart.

*

When he arrived home, he planned to pack, but first he had

to write an email from Xeroxwed. He would send it to Anna after the weekend. Even though Anna hadn't responded to his earlier emails, he had to assume she was reading them. She would definitely think they were from Iris. Wednesday book club meetings and fucking up against the Xerox copying machine – who else would know about that other than Iris? And should she mention the emails to Iris, which he didn't think she would, but if she did, then he knew Iris well enough: she would keep a straight face and realise how serious he was about hanging on to her.

Xeroxwed wrote:

After this weekend, the sex... well, I'm not sure you're up for this. I don't want to see you again.

54

Daniel

February 2016

While locked up in his room for a whole fucking weekend without a phone or even toilet breaks, Dan had spent his time shitting in a bag. He had tried to break the door down several times but despite his strong arms it wouldn't budge. It was freezing cold as well, the windows specked with ice, the air in his room stale.

Frida would be lucky to be alive by the time he got out. Apart from sinister murder plans which involved poisoning her vodka, he had also put some careful thought into his next move with Anna.

He didn't want to threaten Anna via email, SMS or a handwritten note. That was too much evidence. He would have to see her in person. The temporary school parking lot seemed to be the best place. Mörna School didn't have a sophisticated surveillance system, and there were no cameras in the gravel-filled plot serving as parking while the new canteen was being built.

After having to endure Frida's sexual circus next door

over the weekend and being driven crazy by the smell of shit, she had eventually let him out. On one condition: he would have to agree to hug her for two whole minutes. She would time it with her phone. It had seemed ridiculous and even though he had imagined hugging her so tight she would be strangled, it was still too stupid. He was not a child.

"I don't want your saggy tits on my chest," he had said.

That hadn't gone down too well. She hadn't spoken to him for half an hour. Then she must have got lonely because she had given him a second chance. She was all for second and third and fourth chances, Frida. God knew they had given *her* many.

"Okay, fine." What choice did he have? Soon the saggy tits would be replaced with Anna's full bosom. Her breasts were large. Firm.

"I have one more condition," she had said.

"What is it now?"

"I want to know about your teacher. Anna. The one who came to our house."

Anna's name coming from his mother's mouth had made him feel cold. What the hell did she want to know about Anna for? Had she rummaged through the papers under his bed? The violation of his privacy. Had he mentioned Anna's name there? He believed he had been discreet enough not to. Oh. The photos! She would have seen the photos. Fuck.

He had taken a deep breath to sound calm. "What do you want to know?"

"Is she nice?"

"Yes."

"So you like her?"

"Yes."

She had paused.

"Are you…" She had sounded as if she were about to cry. "Are you in love with her?"

What? No. Please. It had seemed so unbelievable when verbalised. Made up.

"Of course not."

"Are you sure? You just seem to really, really like her."

"Come on, *Mum*." Not Frida this time. Anything was fair in love and war. "You know I like to write and she's very supportive of that in her class."

She had cried then. The word "Mum" had that affect on her.

"Is she messing with your head?" she had said in between sobs.

"No! She's just a cool teacher."

She had opened the door to let him out and she had clung to him as if he were saving her life and for a tiny second he had felt guilty about his plan. What would happen to her when he left? Would the Nissan dude move in? Would they shack up and have more children? Most likely she wouldn't want more mouths to feed. He pushed the image away. From now on, it was her life and she could do whatever she wanted to. He was heading somewhere. Onward and upward, as they said.

"Got to go," he said and peeled her arms off.

*

He waited on his bike. If he was lucky, Kent the creep wouldn't be with Anna and he could cycle right up to her and deliver his blackmail message. Plan B was to go to her house and ring the doorbell. He would ask to speak to her privately and she would have to step outside. Plan C was to take Frida's dude's car and go to the library and deliver the message there. He didn't much care if the other woman saw him. He was in control now.

As he waited, he wondered how Anna would react. He didn't want to anger her after all; his wholesome, down to earth, sexy Anna. But would she cry? Would she beg him not to tell anyone? Would she embrace him, agree to anything as long as he left the matter alone? He had a feeling she wouldn't. She was feisty.

After about twenty minutes, Anna appeared. She had a serious look on her face and her steps were determined, which made him hesitate. Was she already upset with him? Did she know that he had been spying on her? He had missed school and hadn't been able to send any emails. For a brief second he wondered if she was upset because he *hadn't* emailed her.

Less sure of himself, he wheeled his bike towards her. She looked up but kept walking.

"Hi," he said.

"Hi, Daniel."

"Ehm…" Shit, this was not how it was supposed to go. It had sounded so good in his head, so easy. *I saw you*.

She opened the car door and hauled her bags in. As she was about to get in herself, he said: "Wait, I need to talk to you."

She turned to him and said: "Not now, Daniel. I have something important…"

"No," he said. Please don't do this. Why was she being so rude?

The stern look on her face. "I'm sorry," she said. "It's just that I have to go."

But she couldn't go. Not when he finally had her attention.

"Do you like it when I send you emails?" he asked.

"What?" She looked at him quizzically. "I don't understand."

It was as if she was waiting for an explanation. Would he give her one? No.

"I don't exactly mind," she said then. "It's just that you send so many, which can be stressful. It would be good if you slowed down the traffic."

"Okay," he said. "I will do that." Except, no. He realised he wouldn't. "I need your help, Anna. To have a normal life, you know."

"Yes, I do know," she said. "You have written that many times, but I can't help you with that. Not even if I wanted to."

She wanted to?

"So, you mean… you want to help me?"

"Of course."

He straightened up, felt the acceptance, the feeling of a warm comforting blanket, Christmas with a real tree, newly baked gingerbread biscuits.

"Does that mean I can move in?"

She sighed and her expression drastically shattered his illusion: the blanket suddenly with holes, the tree made of plastic, the biscuits stale. And that angered him. Was she trying to fool him?

"Is that a 'no'?" he said, his teeth clenched even though he had meant to portray a calm and mature attitude.

"Daniel, why don't we meet and talk about it tomorrow?" she suggested. "I have to leave, I have an important…"

"Yeah, I know," he interrupted. "Something important." *That doesn't include me.* Before she said anything else – he didn't want to hear her excuses – he said what he had come to say, because there was clearly no other way.

"I saw you," he said. "And now you will do what I say."

"What?" she said. "What are you talking about?"

"You belong to me now!" he said, his words forceful. He needed to make her understand that he was in charge. Not her. Perhaps it had been unrealistic to expect her to shout "Oh, Dan. Fuck me!" at that point but he had at least hoped she would break down in tears and make herself vulnerable.

"Dan," she said firmly, placing a hand on his arm and he looked at her fingers, the light-pink nail polish, the bent knuckles, squeezing his bicep. Maybe he hadn't been too unrealistic after all? But her tone didn't sound loving. The battle within him; the confusion she caused. He wanted to flick her hand away to show her that he was the boss, but he also wanted to move closer, to smell her hair, burrow his nose in it, let her hold him. Could he do that? Would she let him? He leaned his head forward and rested it on her shoulder. Shut his eyes and let her feminine scent soothe him.

He felt her move closer, felt her arms wrapped around his back, holding him. This feeling, he needed to savour it, to mentally lock it in his memory. Then she grabbed his arms and pushed him away.

"Daniel," she said. "I really care about you, but…"

He didn't want to hear "but", and without thinking, he just acted to stop her from speaking. His lips landed on hers and he kissed her. He decided to let his tongue loose, to taste her, really taste her, but she pressed her hands into his chest and shoved him back. Not as gently as before. This was rough. The pressure made her fall back onto her car door while he tripped over his bike and landed on the ground.

They looked at each other. She seemed paralysed, she just

stood there. He could feel her "I care for you" evaporate, her disgust for him taking over.

He wanted to get back at her. He wanted revenge. "I saw you and that woman," he said, spitting the words out.

The horror in her eyes. He enjoyed it as much as the kiss.

"What woman?" she asked.

She clearly tried to remain composed. It wasn't good enough. He needed her to sweat, to understand that this was some real shit.

He said: "I saw you with that woman, at the library in Hågarp."

Her face dropped, her cheeks red. And so he kept going, feeling more self-assured by the second.

"Yes, that's right," he said. "I know you're a lesbo. And if you don't want anyone else to know, you will do as I say."

55

Erik

April 2016

On the way to the hospital, Erik takes out his phone to call Tina.

"You shouldn't use your phone while driving," Mum says.

"I'm calling Tina, to see what she knows."

"We will find out when we get there. Anna is awake, that's what's important."

"You don't understand," he says. "I need to talk to her, to get more information." He hesitates. "It's nice to have someone on your side."

"I'm on your side." Mum's words are sharp and critical. After what's happened with Pernilla, he understands how pathetic he must sound.

"It's not like that," he says but he's too tired to explain.

He scrolls down to Tina's number and presses "Call". She picks up almost immediately and before he's had a chance to say anything, she says: "Have you heard?"

"About Anna waking up…"

"Exactly."

"I'm on my way to the hospital," Erik says. "Do you know anything else?"

"No." Tina pauses. "I guess you won't need me anymore, then?"

Her choice of words combined with her tone makes him feel like shit. She's Rob's girlfriend now, isn't she? How many policemen or women would willingly share information the way she has? He reckons not many.

"Of course not, Tina," he says. "You're a gem. I'll call you later."

"You will?" She seems relieved. "That's great."

He's about to hang up when she adds: "Actually, Erik…"

"Yes?"

"There's one thing I could tell you. About Pernilla."

Really? He looks at Mum. Can she hear the conversation? She's staring out the window so he has to assume that she can't.

"Did you warn her about talking to the police about your relationship?"

Fuck. "We don't have a relationship." He glances towards Mum again but there is no reaction.

"But you slept with her," Tina says.

Once. It was once! "No!"

"Well, she claims that she spoke to you the day of your wife's attack and that you were very upset."

"Ehm…" He needs to think. Did he speak to her at day care that day? Maybe about Anna taking him for granted, that he had to pick the children up even though it was her turn? Shit. He might have talked to Pernilla about that. It was possible. His verbal filter wasn't always switched on.

"Well, now there's a new rumour…"

Not another one! What is it now? Is he fathering more

children? He waits for her to continue, glancing in the rear-view mirror. The boys are fast asleep in the back.

"Yes?" he asks after a few seconds.

"Apparently a colleague of Anna's..." she starts, and there's an excited urgency in her voice that puts him on edge. A minute ago she didn't have anything to tell him but now the information is flowing. "Well... anyway... now there's a rumour that maybe you tried to kill your wife."

He swerves and Mum shrieks, grabbing the phone from his hand.

"That's enough talking," she says.

"No!" he shouts. "I need my phone back!"

He pulls over and stops the car. "Happy now? Give me my phone."

Mum looks at him grimly. In the back, the boys are stirring.

"Please?" he tries.

Mum hands it to him with a condemning frown, but it's too late. Tina is gone and she's not answering when he tries to call her back. He tries three times before he decides it's stalker behaviour. She must be tending to an urgent case. It's just that he doesn't get it. What the hell did she mean? *He* is a suspect? And a colleague of Anna's said what? Did she mean Kent? Or has Pernilla concocted something out of a desire for revenge? He leans his head on the steering wheel and takes a few deep breaths.

"I thought we were in a hurry?" Mum says.

He turns and stares at her, wanting to convey his annoyance, because right now he is a mess. "I know," he says. Anna is awake. A part of him can't wait to get to the hospital, to hold her. Another part is worried. Will she be a vegetable? Or will she be the woman he married?

They drive in silence. Erik thinks about Anna, when they first met. The dimples when she smiled at him, the hair loose and wavy, her lips a soft red. How she caught his eye despite the busy crowd in the bar, how he unashamedly called in sick almost every day after that. When she was on a plane back to Sweden and he was still behind the bar, a job he had just about managed to hang onto, the joy of being a bartender at a resort quickly disappeared. The party was no more.

"I've been such a fool," he says more to himself than anyone else but Mum says: "Yes, you have." Although she squeezes his arm gently and in that moment he feels her unconditional love. Despite his faults, she's still there for him.

They park in the parking garage and half-run, half-walk into the hospital, taking the elevator up to the third floor. Mum tries to chat to the boys but Erik is too tense. He just holds Sebastian's hand and tries to focus on each step he has to take, the grey linoleum floor sticky under his feet.

Inside the room, the first thing he notices is Anna's head. The bed has been raised, and her head is resting on a pillow, her hair flowing over her shoulders. They've let it out of the ponytail. She must hear the commotion as they enter because she turns to them, her eyes open. He gasps. Her brown eyes are looking straight at him. Time stands still, he can't move and doesn't notice the boys running up to the bed, shouting "Mummy!"

When they jump up to her, her eyes are averted, moving

away from him and onto the boys, with an almost terrified look.

"Boys, take it easy." Erik's Mum is there, gently moving the boys down from the bed. "Mummy only just woke up."

"Mu-u-u-mmy?" Anna slurs.

The doctor appears.

"Sorry, I was hoping to speak to you before…"

"Before we barged in?" Mum asks.

He smiles self-consciously and continues: "Well, yes. You see, Anna might be experiencing some initial memory loss."

Erik finally moves, as if he's been released from a stranglehold. He walks up to Anna and leans down to kiss her, closing his eyes to feel the full softness of her lips. *My wife.* But all he can feel is a cold cheek, and when he opens his eyes he realises she has turned her face; her eyes, harrowing.

"Who ar-r-r-e yo-ou?" she says, as if she's only just learned to speak, and her words hit him right in the chest. She doesn't recognise him either?

He feels someone's hand on his arm, pulling him back.

"You don't know who I am?" he asks lamely.

"I'm sorry," the doctor says. "Most likely she will regain her memory. Her head was badly injured, so this is not uncommon."

The boys are crying and Mum ushers them out of the room, her words soothing them along the way: "Mummy needs to rest, she has a headache. We will come back later."

With Mum and the boys out of the room, the doctor asks in a hushed tone if Erik can perhaps bring some family photo albums to help jog Anna's memory.

"She has called for her mother," he explains. "If she recognises her photo, it might be a good idea for her mother to come and visit."

Erik feels the pressure on his chest tighten.

"Right now she is frightened," the doctor continues, his wiry nose hair moving as he speaks. Erik struggles to concentrate. "She needs someone by her side who she remembers."

"I'm sorry, I don't understand," Erik says, meeting the doctor's tired eyes. "She doesn't remember me?"

"Unfortunately, she doesn't seem to recall everyone who was in her life before the attack," the doctor says. "Once she is stable enough, she can go home and hopefully her memory will come back when she is surrounded by her own belongings."

"Come home?"

"Not yet, but hopefully soon."

The doctor smiles, the typical smoker's lines around his mouth deepening. Erik feels terrified. He glances at Anna, who has closed her eyes and looks like she's sleeping, as if she's back in the coma.

"Is she...?" he asks.

"Just resting. This is very traumatic for her."

He says they mustn't rush anything, they must take it slowly so as not to stress her out.

"It might take months to get her back on her feet."

"And her memory?"

"We will have to wait and see."

Erik picks Anna's hand up, puts it to his lips and kisses it.

"I love you," he says.

PART FOUR

56

Anna

February 2016

After her weekend with Iris, Anna planned to speak to Erik immediately. As soon as she stepped inside the house, she put her bag down and called his name. There was no time like the present.

"Erik?"

There was no response. Where was he? She needed to tackle this now, before the guilt overpowered her. Resolutely, she walked inside, only to find him fast asleep on the living room couch. She watched him, debating whether to wake him up or not. He looked so innocent; could she really be so cruel as to rouse him from a dream, only to tell him she loved someone else? She couldn't.

Yet there was so much to talk about. They needed to discuss the children, how they would alternate the weeks that they cared for Sebastian and Lukas. She dreaded being separated from them for seven whole days at a time, but it was only fair. Erik was a great father and he hadn't really done anything wrong. They had simply stopped loving each other. That's what she would tell him.

*

The next morning was buzzing like all other mornings, children needed to be fed, clothed and chauffeured to day care. There was no time to talk. The only line Erik threw her way was: "You must have arrived late last night."

He didn't ask any questions about her weekend.

"I had a great time, thank you," she said, trying to make a point.

It was lost on him.

All day, she struggled to concentrate at work and to make matters worse, she had a meeting after school. Kent was there too, and during a short coffee break, he sat down next to her.

"You look tired," he said. He graciously handed her a cup of coffee, for which she was very grateful. "Did you have fun with the book club?"

"Yes, it was good. Thank you."

He looked disappointed. "That's it? No literary scandals? Didn't anyone get drunk and do something embarrassing?"

"If you're trying to live out your wild fantasies through me…" *then you have come to the right person.* "Then I'm sorry to let you down." She was tempted to tell him about Iris, to share something original for once. "*Actually, Kent, I have met someone and I'm going to leave Erik.*" It would sound too ridiculous; could she really do this without discussing it with someone else first?

"Kent," she said, lowering her voice. "Do you and Märta ever have any problems or are you always happy?"

He moved his chair closer. The teachers' lounge was

unusually busy because of the meeting, with a number of discussions going on.

"You need to nurture your marriage," he said and she couldn't deny that it stung. When had she given up? Then again, Erik didn't try either. Not that it was an excuse. "I've been lucky," Kent said. "We are compatible and have fun together almost daily but sometimes I think people need to accept that they will be happier without each other. Look at our students for example. A number of them have divorced parents but everyone gets along and shares the responsibilities. Then you have parents who stay together 'for the children'..." Kent did quotation marks in the air. "... who have toxic relationships which the children end up suffering from."

She nodded. "Do you think my marriage is toxic?"

She had never allowed herself to get this personal with Kent but he was the closest to a friend that she had. He hesitated, she could tell.

"It's okay," she said. "I appreciate your honesty, you know that."

"Fine," he said. "I don't necessarily think it's toxic but I have always wondered why you're married to him."

She hadn't expected that response, and she wished they were sitting in a wine bar having this discussion instead of a busy teachers' lounge.

"Why?"

Kent put a hand through his hair, looking pressured.

"You seem to have different interests and goals in life," he said.

She nodded. "What if I told you I'm planning to leave him?"

"Then I'd say I'm not surprised. You need to follow your

gut, Anna." He placed a hand on her shoulder. "I'll be here for you if you need me."

She was grateful for his support but she also felt embarrassed about the state of her marriage. Perhaps she shouldn't have opened up quite so much?

"Sorry to drag you into this," she said.

"Anna," he said seriously. "Whatever you tell me, I will not share with anyone, not under any circumstances. You have my word."

His loyalty made her feel better.

"Thank you."

*

Anna just about got through the rest of the afternoon meeting and as soon as she could, she packed to get home.

On her way to the car, her mind was preoccupied with what she was going to say. "We've had problems for a while", "Something has happened, Erik", "I've fallen in love", "This isn't just a fling, it's real", "I'm really sorry".

She could sense someone cycling up to her but she didn't want her practised monologue to be interrupted, so she kept walking.

"Hi."

It was Daniel.

"Hi, Daniel."

She wasn't in the mood for him today, the conversation with his previous teacher reminding her that he was playing her. *But why me?* Why not Maria Bergman? What made them so different?

Before she had a chance to question his motives he ambushed her, and perhaps out of compassion, or perhaps to do the opposite of what he was expecting, she hugged him. He wanted a mother and so she gave him exactly what a son would need. Comfort.

Except he then took it one step further and kissed her. In that moment, for the first time, she realised what was actually going on. He had a *crush* on her? She pushed him away, shoving him harder than intended. They both fell backwards.

"I saw you and that woman," he said.

She froze. Iris? But how? When? It wasn't something he could have made up or even have guessed, which meant he was telling the truth. But how could he possibly have seen her and Iris together? She wanted to defend herself but didn't get a chance, the words now leaving his mouth like a machine gun, one after the other, quick and forceful: "I know you're a lesbo. And if you don't want anyone else to know, you will do as I say. I don't want anyone else fucking you. Do you hear me?"

Panic rose in her. She had completely misjudged him. She was such a fool. When he finally rode off on his bike, he left her with the words: "I move in tomorrow."

*

She drove straight to the library. She hadn't planned to see Iris this evening but there was no one else she could talk to. She called Erik and said she would be slightly late.

"Rob and I need to leave at eight," he said.

She had forgotten that he had a gig. She needed to speak to him but she also needed to talk to Iris first. Daniel had spooked her.

"I will be back by then, I promise," she said, a tremor in her voice.

Could he tell how shaken up she was?

"Okay," he said and hung up. Obviously he wasn't that perceptive.

It didn't matter. Her attention was on the road. Her mind, however, was on Daniel. His glistening eyes, the looming body, exerting his best efforts to be overpowering and intimidating. His words. *You belong to me now*. How could he have crossed the line without her noticing? How naïve she had been. Distracted by the jittery new sensations of love for Iris.

She barged through the library door, the bells clanging together, drawing Iris out from one of the aisles.

"Anna? What's going on? Are you okay?"

"We need to talk," Anna said. Her determined steps reached Iris within seconds. "In the kitchen, please."

"I can't leave the library unattended, it's still open."

"Then close it."

"I can't. There are people…"

"Just two minutes." She sighed. "Please."

"Okay." Iris nodded. "Give me a minute. I'll see you back there."

Anna paced back and forth in the kitchen. She had felt so safe in this small seaside town, like it was just the two of them in the world. The fact that Daniel had spied on them tarnished everything.

Iris entered the kitchen and closed the door behind her.

"Do we need coffee for this?"

Anna shook her head and then she hugged Iris and cried.

"What is it, Anna?" Iris stroked her hair. "Did you tell Erik?"

Erik's name sounded foreign in Iris's mouth. She didn't even know him. *Don't talk about him.*

"Someone saw us together," Anna said. "A student of mine. And now he's blackmailing me."

"What?"

Iris grabbed Anna's shoulders, pushed her back so that they faced each other.

"Who is he?"

"It doesn't matter, just a student." Her voice felt weak. Tired, she slumped down onto the floor, leaning up against the cold photocopier, resting her head on its plastic surface.

"So tell me about him," Iris said.

"Where to start?" She thought for a moment. "He moved to Hågarp during the summer. He has moved around a lot."

She told Iris about his increasing obsession with her, his wish for her to be his mother, but she didn't mention the kiss or his comment about her not being allowed to *fuck* anyone else. She couldn't.

"Why didn't you report him?"

"It's not that simple, Iris. You can't just shuffle children around the system. It has to end somewhere, someone along their journey has to care."

"But does that have to be you?"

Those words were all too familiar. "You sound like my husband," she said.

"Sorry." Iris looked genuinely concerned. "I'm just worried about you."

"So what do we do?" Anna said. This was surely a joint problem?

"You could tell Erik and I will tell Rolf. That way no one is in the dark and there is no one to blackmail."

Iris made it sound so simple.

"I guess that would suit you," Anna said.

She felt angry, not necessarily with Iris, but with the whole situation and she wouldn't be in this mess if she hadn't met Iris.

Iris withdrew, looking as if Anna had physically hit her.

"I'm sorry," Anna said, wishing she had kept her mouth shut. "I'm just stressed out."

She stretched her arms out, reached for Iris. They would find a way.

"You make me sound like a predator," Iris said, staying where she was.

"It's just," Anna said, trying to find a way to explain herself, "there have been so many others for you. I mean, Lena? She was with you as well, wasn't she?"

She realised that this was actually part of the problem, that perhaps she was going through this pain only to lose Iris down the line. Would she be able to overcome her insecurities about Iris's past?

"The important thing for you to know, Anna, is that it's just you now. You and me."

She looked sincere and Anna leaned into her arms, wanting to believe that Iris meant it.

57

Erik

May 2016

Anna is awake but doesn't remember Erik or her children. The police have already been to see her but it appears that she can't remember anything about the night she was attacked.

Erik spends limited time in her hospital room, needing to keep the children away from her. It's a battle: she might remember more if she sees them but it's too upsetting for the boys.

On top of that, Mum has announced that she is going home at this most critical time. And when he thinks it can't get worse, Linda Johansson calls and says she is on her way to see him. He begs Mum to at least stay for that. If he really is a suspect like Tina said, then he will need Mum's support.

"Okay," she says. "I'm sure there is no need to worry but I will stay and see the officer with you. Then I have to go home. Dad needs me."

Apparently his father cut himself the day before; he was

bleeding profusely and Mum feels that something worse could happen if she's not there.

"At least Anna is awake now," Mum says. "Things will only get better from now on."

"Anna's mother is on her way," he says. There is nothing *better* about that. But he realises he needs to be grateful that his wife is awake even if she doesn't recall that she has a husband.

"That's good," Mum says.

"Yeah, great. Her husband agreed to grant her a week's freedom."

"Surely it's not that bad?"

He looks at her, with total disbelief. "I'm sorry, were you not at the wedding?"

Mum nods. "They're just old-fashioned," she says. "At least he's not coming along."

"But, Mum. She's not going to be any help. I'm going to have to babysit her!"

Speaking of babysitting, he needs to talk to Pernilla about her – their – baby. She has stopped sending him messages now that he actually needs to be in contact with her. With Anna being awake, it's essential that he's viewed as someone who takes responsibility for his mistakes. He will tell Pernilla that he can't leave his wife but if she could perhaps move elsewhere, he can visit her and the baby regularly. Not seeing his child would be devastating but he also has a reputation to think about. He will agree to pay child support. If only the jobs were more frequent. Recently, people have been complaining about him being distracted.

Unfortunately, Tina has also disappeared. Not even Rob has heard from her.

"She's probably busy with some investigation," Rob says.

Or she doesn't want to be in touch with a suspect, Erik thinks.

When the doorbell rings, Erik expects it to be Linda Johansson and he puts his best smile on. Except it's that boy…

"David?"

"You said to come by?"

"Oh, yeah. Sorry, I completely forgot."

Shit. He should send him away.

"I've really looked forward to seeing Sebastian and Lukas," David says. "I only have an older brother so it's like they're my little brothers."

Maybe he could let him play with the boys while he talks to Linda Johansson? It would be better if Mum doesn't tend to the children when the police arrive, she could be by his side one hundred per cent.

"The boys are in the basement," he says. "They're playing with their train set. Maybe you could hang out with them for a while? If you could just you know… keep them occupied. I have an important meeting."

"Sure, no problem."

David takes his shoes off, something Anna would appreciate.

"If you wouldn't mind closing the door," Erik says. "I'll get you all some cordial and buns when we're done up here."

"Sounds great."

Is it odd that a teenage boy wants to hang out with two five year olds? No. He shakes it off. He remembers playing with his younger sister, how great it was that he could use her as an excuse to still play.

*

When Officer Johansson arrives, Mum is overly friendly, offering coffee and newly baked cinnamon buns. He just wants to get it over and done with.

"We have tried to interview Anna but her memory loss has made it difficult," she says.

"I know."

He's fidgeting with a napkin and tries to stop.

"A witness has stepped forward," Officer Johansson says.

"Really?"

Someone saw something at the school? It amazes Erik that the inhabitants of their town have been talking to the police, sharing their sightings of her, as if they were spies. He wants to move away so badly in that moment, go far away from this small-town nonsense.

"Does that mean you know who attacked her?" Mum asks.

"We're not sure. If we arrest him, we only have four days to charge him." Officer Johansson looks at Erik intently. "Did Anna really never mention being frightened of anyone?"

He thinks hard, wishing there was someone he could mention, but Anna wasn't easily intimidated by anyone.

"No. I don't think so," he says.

"Did Anna ever have any guest speakers at work?"

He has no idea. "Maybe. You would have to check with the principal."

"Okay." She makes a note. "I also need to ask you... was Anna interested in art or did she do any art modelling?"

"What?" He racks his brain for anything that could vaguely be relevant but comes up with absolutely nothing. "No."

Who are they talking to? Is it based on actual suspicion? Especially after Tina's comments about the police now suspecting him, he would really like to know.

"I know you can't tell me who it is," he says. "But do you think he or she is guilty?"

"We'll see. Anything you can think of would help."

"He's an artist?" Mum asks.

Officer Johansson looks at her apologetically. "I have already said too much," she says.

"Fuck, that's sick," Erik says. He can't wrap his head around this news.

Mum strokes his back. "At least they've found him."

"I guess that means I'm no longer a suspect," Erik says.

"I'm sorry?"

"Yeah, I heard you might have it in for me," he says, forcing himself to laugh.

Officer Johansson arches her eyebrows.

"Why would you think that?" she asks.

"Just someone…"

"It's that woman, Tina," Mum says, her voice shrill.

He looks at Mum and tries to kill her with his eyes, his lips a whisper: "She's put her job on the line for me, Mum. You can't expose her."

"Who's Tina?" Officer Johansson asks.

He shakes his head to Mum. "No one," he says.

"For God's sake, Erik. She can't tell you things like that without any evidence!"

"Who are you talking about?"

Officer Johansson looks as if she's demanding an answer and Mum is all too willing to provide one.

"Tina something. She's with the police. One of your colleagues."

Officer Johansson shakes her head. "I don't know of any Tina and I'm familiar with most staff."

Mum sighs. "Erik?"

He gives up. "I don't know. Tina. Big hair, green eyes, very pink lipstick although perhaps not when she's on duty." Officer Johansson still looks like a question mark. "I've only met her once... eh... small gap between her front teeth." That's all he's got.

"Tina Olsson?"

That sounds familiar. "Think so."

The officer gets her phone out and scrolls through some pictures before she shows him a Facebook photo of Tina. It appears to be from a party and Tina has her arm around a man, a drink in the other hand. "Yes, that's her," he says, relieved. For a second, he thought she was some psycho pretending to be someone she's not.

"She's not a police officer," Officer Johansson says. "She's a cleaner at the police station."

"Oh..."

There's brief eye contact with Mum who seems to be saying "I told you not to trust her" but he's too busy racking his brains. What did Tina actually tell him? She knew about Pernilla and she mentioned Anna's student, and also Kent. She insinuated that Anna had an affair with Kent? Was it all lies?

"This is very serious," Officer Johansson says as she makes a few notes in her notepad. "What exactly did she tell...?"

"Did you ever speak to Anna's colleague, Kent?"

He knows it's rude to interrupt but he has his own thought process and he needs to go back to the beginning.

"I don't understand how that's relevant."

"It's just... I need to know if she was telling me the truth."

"I'm more concerned about her telling you anything."

Right. He needs to play this differently.

"I understand but she... Did you speak to Kent? Did he seem to like Anna a bit too much?"

"Look, she's had no insight into our investigation. It's possible that she has seen some paperwork on someone's desk but..." Officer Johansson rubs her temples. "This is very serious."

She's clearly not going to tell him anything.

"At least you seem to have found the attacker," Mum says. "Just one question. Is there a motive?"

58

Rolf

March 2016

Rolf usually got what he wanted. He wanted a wife who accepted that he slept with other women and he found someone who didn't value herself highly enough. He wanted a baby and he replaced the birth-control pills with sugar pills. He wanted press attention and he stirred up a storm. He wanted a woman and he read her like a book and found her weak spot.

Now, he wanted Anna gone. He had tried talking to Iris but she had built a wall around herself.

Instead, he went to see Frida, bringing a couple of bottles of cheap red wine.

"Where's the party?" he asked and held up the bag.

"Babe!" She was all over him, hungry for his attention.

"I need to see your kid," he said.

"Dan?"

"Unless the other one is out of prison?"

She didn't find that amusing.

"He's out in a couple of months," she said.

Rolf would be gone by then; that one was even more trouble than the young one.

"He's in his room," she said. "Happy as can be. Don't ask me why!"

She too was in an excellent mood.

"Be a dear and open the wine and I'll be right back," he said.

He knocked on the kid's door before he opened it. It was sparsely furnished with only a bed, a chair and a badly built wardrobe. Frida wasn't exactly an interior designer.

"Get out," the kid said, not even giving him a chance.

As much as that pissed Rolf off, he maintained a friendly tone.

"Hang on," he said. "I have something that you want."

The kid, who had been lying down on his unmade bed, sat up.

"I've got everything I need," he said.

He looked a bit too cheerful. "Are you on drugs?" Rolf asked.

"Fuck off, I'm not stupid."

"Sorry," Rolf said, holding his hands up like a bad guy caught by the police. He entered the room while talking. "You know your teacher friend?"

That zapped the good mood right out of him. "What about her?"

"I know you want to fuck her."

"What? No!"

He was a useless liar. Rolf inched closer to the kid's bed and sat down.

"You see, your desire will solve a problem of mine. I need

you to tell social services that she made advances on you."

"No way." He laughed at Rolf. "You're insane. She will never talk to me after that."

Rolf leaned against the wall, making himself comfortable despite the room's overpowering smell of dirt and sweat. It really needed to be aired out. He picked up a book, a notebook of sorts with a hard cover, and threw it at the window. A small windowpane popped.

"What the hell are you doing?"

"You love your mother, don't you?"

"What's going on?" Frida was at the door. She looked at the window. "What happened?"

"Just an accident, babe. I was talking to Dan here about you, and how much he must love you."

Her face contorted into a grimace. "What?" A second later, Rolf got up and held her by the neck, pushing her up against the wall. His life was falling apart, his perfect marriage of over twenty years was coming to an end, and he needed these lowlifes to help him restore it.

"You love your mother, don't you, Dan?" he said. "She's all you've got. That teacher friend of yours couldn't care less about you. You know that, right?"

The conflict within the boy was obvious. He would pick his mother though, all boys did. If Rolf's mother were still alive, he would pick her any day.

"Your teacher is fucking someone else," Rolf said. "My wife, to be precise."

The kid didn't look as shocked as he thought he would, or perhaps he was used to keeping a straight face. Frida was more upset.

"You're married?" she asked, letting out a sob.

"If only you read the papers, babe, you would know that."

The kid stood up. He didn't even try to reach for Frida. He simply stared at Rolf.

"Get the fuck out of our house," he said.

Rolf tightened his grip on Frida's neck.

"If you honour your part of the deal."

59

Erik

May 2016

David is back. He puts his trainers next to the door and hangs his denim jacket on one of the hooks in the narrow entrance hall. Erik notices his jeans are short and his T-shirt has seen better days. Perhaps he can dig out a few old shirts for the guy? Unless that would offend him? Or perhaps it's just the fashion? He wishes Anna was there to clarify.

"The boys are in there somewhere," Erik says.

Erik isn't quite sure why David is here. Did they agree for him to come back and play with the kids? Or is he babysitting? Is he supposed to pay him?

"You've got a really nice house," David says.

"Thanks. It still needs quite a bit of work."

It really does. They had underestimated how much maintenance it needed, a source of endless arguments since Anna didn't favour his DIY skills.

"If you need help with anything, let me know," David says. "I'm good at carpentry."

"Good to know."

Anna must like this student, he's polite.

They locate Sebastian and Lukas. Always together: different but inseparable. They're building a puzzle but the pieces are not quite sticking together the way they want them to.

"Careful," Erik says. "Or you'll break them."

"Here, let me help you," David says.

He patiently shows them what goes where.

"Boys," Erik says. "We're leaving for the hospital in half an hour."

Hopefully David understands that he will need to leave by then.

Thumbs up from the boys. Great. Erik goes back to the kitchen and pulls out Anna's laptop. He hasn't received any emails from Black Adam in about two weeks. He looks at the last email he sent. I'm sure she did love you. The question is, in what way? She was, and still is, married. Why had that upset him so much? Was he harbouring feelings for Anna?

His phone rings. It's Rob.

"Hey, I heard Anna woke up?"

"Yes, it's great." He says that to everyone. Great. Fantastic. What a miracle. No one understands that it's not his wife who's woken up. It's a woman who looks like his wife.

"Look, Erik. I'm calling because... I mean, I know you have a lot going on, especially with Anna being awake and everything but I don't want you to feel excluded, so... would you be up for a gig?"

"We haven't practised in ages."

"It's like cycling! There's an opening tonight. Lead singer of the other band is ill and they refuse to do it without him. Total amateurs, obviously!"

He laughs and Erik can't deny he feels a stir of excitement.

It would feel good to bring the guitar out, to be a musician for the night.

"What about the others?"

"They're in as well."

But. "Shit. I don't have a babysitter. Mum just left."

"Oh." Rob is obviously disappointed.

"Do you have any girlfriends who can babysit?" Erik asks. Joking about Tina makes it less painful. He called Rob as soon as he found out that Tina was a cleaner, not a police officer. Why would Tina even do that? To get back with Rob? Or to stir up someone's life? Rob, however, seemed more worried about Tina being exposed than about Erik.

"I'm sorry about Tina," he says.

"I know. You were just trying to help," Erik says sarcastically.

"That's right, and now Anna is awake so it's all good, right?"

Erik ignores him. Rob still feels bruised about Tina.

"Can't you find someone else?" Rob says. "A neighbour's kid or something?"

Erik does want to play, so he racks his brain. Who could he reach out to? Just then, the boys – all three of them – come rushing into the kitchen, cars on the floor, racing. *That could work.*

"Hey, David? Are you free tonight?"

*

Erik isn't planning to get drunk, it just happens. No one can blame him though; he's been through a lot. He enjoys the pumping music, the smell of beer, the feeling of being "one of the gang", swigging the beers back mixed with a few shots. Not too many. He keeps saying "no more" but drinks anyway, reality breaking away at the seams.

The women crowd around him and the band as they dance, sprinkling compliments about the set they played. He notices that the average age of the audience is older than it used to be. When did he become old?

Someone grabs his arms and he turns around.

"*Hej*, Erik."

Pernilla? She seems like a drunken vision.

"I've never heard you play before," she says. "You were great!"

"Thanks." He reminds himself that she's carrying his baby. This is awkward. He should say something. "What are you doing here?"

"I heard you were playing so I thought I would check it out."

"But I haven't heard from you in ages."

"Right." She studies the floor briefly before fixing him with her blue, blue eyes again. "I wanted to see if you would chase me if I played hard to get."

"Oh." They should talk. "Can I get you a drink?"

"Sure."

They make their way to the bar and he notices that she has slipped her hand into his. He will let that one slide for now.

"What can I get you?" he says. "Coke, water, juice?"

"Vodka tonic, please."

"Vodka?" He attempts to shake the fuzzy drunken feeling. "Shouldn't you drink soft drinks only?"

She laughs. "I'm not an alcoholic."

"But... you're pregnant."

"What?" She's not laughing anymore. "Are you saying I look fat?"

"No, of course not, but you told the police you're carrying my baby…"

Her face distorts. "What the hell are you talking about? I'm not pregnant."

"You're not?"

"No!"

Wow. He looks at her stomach and it doesn't look swollen at all. Why *did* he think she was pregnant? He needs to sober up.

"A vodka tonic for the lady and a Coke for me, please."

"Party pooper." Her palms are on his chest, stroking his shirt. "So, you thought we were having a baby together." She snuggles up to him. "Were you excited?"

The drinks arrive and he pays before downing his Coke.

"Shit," he says, ignoring her question. "You're definitely not pregnant?"

She shakes her head. "No, but we could make a baby if that's what you want?"

It's not what he wants. Not at all.

"I'm mad," he says.

He really is mad as hell. It was Tina who told him Pernilla was pregnant. This whole time, he's felt like shit because of it. He should leave and go home to calm down, but instead he heads back to the dance floor.

Pernilla runs after him. "Hey, wait up."

But he's heading for Rob. He grabs his mate's shoulder and turns him around. "Remember how your girlfriend said Pernilla was pregnant?" he says loudly, talking over the music. "Look, she's right here and guess what? NOT pregnant." He gestures to Pernilla who's clearly not sure how to react.

"Maybe she's lying?" Rob shouts. "Maybe she did tell

the police and now she's getting cold feet?" He throws an unimpressed look at Pernilla.

Erik looks at her. "Did you?"

"Of course not."

She seems genuine and considering that Tina has lied before that seems the best bet. It's all Rob's fault. He's responsible for bringing Tina into Erik's life. At that moment, Erik shuts down his friendly feelings for Rob and activates his fists.

"What the fuck!"

Rob ducks but is quickly back up, throwing him a punch of his own. Erik's face hurts. He will not stand for this. He gathers all his strength and rams into Rob, flooring him. But Rob is quick; he wraps his legs around Erik and they end up wrestling, rolling around on the sticky floor, sweat dripping, strong arms pulling and punching. Erik isn't sure how long they fight. He's just so angry, his hands hungry for blood.

Someone breaks them apart. Erik is accused of being the instigator and he's thrown out, but Pernilla is immediately on hand with a napkin, wiping the blood off.

"You did that for me?" she asks, her body too close, her lips almost on his. He pushes her off.

"Get off me," he says. "I don't know if you lied or not. I was angry about something else."

She stares at him with hurt eyes.

"You will regret that," she says, and storms off.

60

Daniel

March 2016

W*hat a douche bag.*
Rolf was pinning Frida against the wall, making threats.

"There is no deal," Dan muttered as he grabbed his brother's hockey stick and swung it into the Nissan dude's back. Both he and Frida fell to the floor like an old set of dominos, Frida clutching her neck, breathing hard, and the dude holding his hands to his back.

"Getting a bit old for fighting, grandpa," Dan said and swung it again.

"Stop it!" Frida begged. "Don't kill him."

"Just teaching him a lesson."

When Dan was satisfied that the dude no longer posed a threat, he let the hockey stick slide out of his hand. It landed on the floor with a *bang*. The dude was groaning and Frida crying.

Dan quickly filled up the Fjällräven backpack and threw

his toiletries into an ICA supermarket bag. He was out of there.

In the hallway, Frida was trying to comfort her lover but he didn't seem into it. Dan stepped over the sad twosome and bent down to the dude's level: "Nice try, you dumb fuck, but I fucking hate my whore mother."

He avoided looking at Frida's face; the tears rapidly turning her into a hopeless mess of a victim. *I'm doing this to protect you, Mother.* He was confident the dude wouldn't be back after this. But it was a worry that he had it in for Anna. Dan needed to protect her now.

"When you're with me, no one will hurt you."

"Oh, Dan. You make me feel so safe."

She leaned into him and he held her in a firm grip.

"I will never let you go."

Outside the air was cool. He put his jacket on and unlocked his bike. Frida hadn't asked him where he was going. She hadn't even asked if he was okay. Instead she had been huddled over that loser. The choices she made. He spat on the ground. He was over it.

Getting on his bike, he headed over to Anna's.

61

Rolf

March 2016

Despite his best violent efforts, the kid didn't scare Rolf. He was messing with the wrong artist. If he didn't watch it, his life would be portrayed in a series of paintings: "A sad little shit's life" – an epic, dark story told by the world-renowned artist, Rolf Sören. He would happily let everyone see how pathetic the kid's life was: drunken mum, jailbird brother, a childish crush on a teacher. It was depressing as hell.

Rolf decided to end it with Frida. Apart from being beaten up by her son, the final straw was the downward spiral that had become their sex life. He had been on top, deep inside of her, when her body had become unnaturally still, almost lifeless. His concern had barely had time to register. She had been snoring! Asleep in the middle of his winning, circular cock-movement.

He no longer had a use for her, anyway. He had all the information he needed. But Frida had no one, her son's affections elsewhere, and so she incessantly texted and called him.

When he arrived home, he planned to tell Iris about Frida. It would feel good to share, cleansing, and a good way to start over. But before he got the chance, she said: "I'm leaving you."

Iris sat in the kitchen, a cup of tea and an open book in front of her. It was as if she had been waiting for him. Next to her were two suitcases. She had already packed.

"Where are you going?" he asked. "Moving in with your teacher friend?"

"How do you know she's a teacher?"

Ah. She got him. How was he supposed to know that?

"She was Teacher of the Year. I read about her somewhere."

"Right, and you just happened to know that's the same person I'm seeing because there aren't many teachers around?"

"I know what she looks like, Iris, and it matched the photo in the article."

Iris stopped fiddling with her tea cup.

"You know what she looks like?"

"I fucking saw you, Iris. In our own home!" God, that felt good. Like he was justified in his anger. Her face was priceless too. "That's right, Iris, I came home early because I was having a boring evening, because other women just can't give me what you can, Iris."

She stood up but instead of picking her bags up, she gently touched the cut on his face.

"What happened to you, Rolf?"

"Oh." He touched her hand. "Nothing, just a mindless fight."

"Since when do you fight?"

He shrugged, not in the mood to share.

"I'm sorry," she said. She composed herself, kissed his cheek and made to leave. "I'll tell Karin we're taking a break."

"Is that all it is?" he asked. "A break? Because I don't want to die alone."

"You still have plenty of years in you," Iris said, looking amused. "And there's always Frida. She called. She's hot for you, but you should tell her to stop beating you up. You're more of a 'make love, not war' kind of man."

"Frida called you?"

"I've had enough of the drama, Rolf. I'm out. I have rented an apartment and ... well, I will always love you. We have Karin and we will behave in a civilised way."

It was as if she spoke for the both of them, and when he heard her car roll out of the courtyard and onto the asphalted single lane road, he didn't think. He just acted, got into his car and drove to that teacher's school for a heart to heart.

*

Frida had been useful to some extent. She had read the kid's journal and had found Anna's routine written down. That's how he knew she often stayed late at work. He had also found out that her husband was a house painter named Erik. Rolf had seen a photo of him on the painting company's website and he was an attractive man, in a rugged kind of way: blond with a slight stubble. Anna's life seemed perfect. What could she possibly be thinking, wanting to give that up for an adventure with Iris? Even if they thought it was the real deal – love – it wouldn't last. Iris was a free spirit, she wouldn't want to become a stepmother to two young boys. The very thought was ridiculous. Had Iris made any promises to Anna? He needed to know if she really was the reason his marriage was over.

He had printed off a photo of Anna from a school event, thanks to Google Images, just in case. He had obviously seen her but the first time it had been, well... without clothes and the second time she had been sweaty while jogging. She had brown, glossy hair that reached her shoulders, she was larger than Iris's women used to be, and although she dressed like a teacher in rather ordinary clothes, there was an element of pretty to her. He had to admit that. She was shaggable.

When Rolf arrived at the school he wasn't sure whether to barge into the teacher's area or whether to wait for her in the parking lot. Her black Volvo V70 was there, poking him in the eye: hello-I-have-been-to-your-house-before.

Being back at a school was strangely intimidating. Memories of bullies teasing him about his hippie clothes and his cheating, lowlife father and his mother who tried to cover for her husband's mistakes. He found he couldn't go into the school building. He would wait for her here, in the school courtyard.

62

Anna

March 2016

The day after Daniel threatened Anna, she bumped into Kent several times, and every time she was about to say "I have an issue with Daniel." But then what? "He wants to move into my house. I know it's crazy. Well, he wants me to be his mother but he also kissed me, so I'm not sure what his intentions are. Why haven't I reported it? Well, he's seen me kiss, and perhaps even make love to, another woman even though I am married. Yes, I have decided to leave my husband, so who cares about that? It would tarnish my reputation but I could possibly, possibly live with that. But Daniel also stopped me in the corridor today, whispering that he will kill himself if I report him or stop him from moving in. So I'm kind of stuck."

Daniel had slowed down as he approached her, smirking. She refused to turn around, choosing to show no fear. But the moment he leaned in with his threat, she couldn't help it, she let out an involuntary gasp. This couldn't go on. She immediately went to see the principal but Johan was at a conference and could only fit her in the following day.

She felt trapped. Daniel had played her well. It was a classic case of manipulation and she kicked herself for allowing it to become so personal. But then again, that's who she was. Her Teacher of the Year accolade had been a result of her "creativity, pedagogical approach and going that extra mile for her students".

Anna called Erik to ask if he could please pick the children up from day care, blaming lessons she needed to plan. He was off work that day anyway but he was jamming with Rob and got annoyed. Still, he grudgingly agreed. In the meantime, Anna headed to the counsellor but she was off sick. She felt let down, even though she blamed herself. Her idealistic views had allowed this to go on for too long. She decided to leave and instead deal with her situation at home first. Erik had rushed to his gig the night before and not given her a chance to speak.

*

By the time she got home, she felt ready to discuss their marriage but Erik had his jacket on.

"We're out of milk," he said. "I'll just go and pick up some groceries. The boys are watching a movie."

"Okay..." She was so focused on the conversation she was finally going to have with Erik that she couldn't really think of anything else to say.

She went into the living room where Sebastian and Lukas were slumped into their beanbags.

"How was your day?"

She kissed their heads but they were non-responsive, *The Lion King* clearly more captivating. Her heart felt heavy watching the two of them, but it didn't change anything. She loved them.

She returned to the kitchen to start dinner. Twenty minutes later, when the sausages were fried and the potatoes were boiling, she laid the table and finally sat down to wait for Erik. He should be home soon. She checked her emails to make the time go by faster. Thankfully there were no emails from Daniel but there was a new one from Xeroxwed. Excitement quickly turned to shock as she read it.

After this weekend, the sex… well, I'm not sure you're up for this. I don't want to see you again.

Her stomach started cramping and her heart was squeezed so hard that she thought she might be having a heart attack. Had it meant nothing to Iris? Had it really only been about sex and due to Anna's inexperience, she was now going to end it? She hadn't mentioned anything the night before so why this sudden realisation? Anna picked up the phone to call Iris when there was a knock on the door.

Daniel. She had almost forgotten about him. Thankfully the children were still watching TV.

"Is my room ready?" he asked, his backpack slung over one shoulder and a plastic bag in one hand.

He was about to step over the threshold when she physically had to stop him.

"Daniel," she said. "You can't live here."

"Sure I can."

He was in a spirited mood.

"Daniel, I have a family."

"I know," he said. "I want that too and I'm here to protect both you and your family."

He took another step towards her and once again, she had to put her hands up to keep him out.

"I don't want to call the police," she said. "But I will if I have to."

"So? I couldn't care less. By the time they arrive, I will already have established myself in the basement."

That didn't even make sense. "Then they will remove you," she said.

"I have a knife and if they come anywhere near me, I will kill myself."

It was too much. Was he even serious? She wasn't sure how she had ended up in this situation. All she had tried to do was show compassion.

"This is not appropriate," she said. "You need to leave and we will have to talk tomorrow at school." *And at that point, I will have talked to Kent, the principal and social services.* There was no other way.

Just then, she heard the Volvo pulling in to the carport. That would be Erik returning from the supermarket. Daniel wouldn't be able to push past her husband.

"That's my husband," Anna said.

"I'm sure he would love to hear about your woman," he said and made no attempt to leave.

"Don't blackmail me," she said. It wasn't going to matter if he did even though Iris had obviously changed her mind. She would still talk to Erik but she needed to be in control of the communication. It shouldn't come from a student of hers. "That's not what I would expect from someone who wants to move into my house," she continued.

His facial expression changed then, from arrogant to almost sweet.

"So I can move in?"

"Tomorrow," she lied. "I need time to prepare your room."

She could hear Erik opening and closing the car door. He would be there any minute and she needed Daniel out of the way. Otherwise the conversation she was going to have with him would start on the wrong foot. He couldn't stand students turning up unannounced.

Daniel looked at her as if he were assessing her. "Don't mess with me," he said. He grabbed hold of her shirt and when they were face to face, he said through gritted teeth. "I will live here, I will eat at your dinner table and I will fuck you when you're ready to accept that."

His words slapped her in the face and she instinctively pushed him.

"I'll be back," he said and walked off.

When Erik turned up at the door, her pulse was still racing.

"What's up?" he asked.

She felt fear. *I will fuck you when you're ready to accept that.*

"Nothing," she said, her heart beating fast. "It's nothing. I just thought I heard someone."

"No burglars," he said. "Just me."

She sat down, attempting to regulate her breathing, and told Erik she needed to speak to him.

"Sounds ominous," he said. "What's it about?"

He seemed annoyed and a panic attack washed over her. She couldn't do this now. "Let's talk later." She needed fresh air.

"What?"

"I'll just be an hour. Please feed the boys. I need to dash down to the school to collect something."

"School? Now?"

Where else could she go? If she went outside, Daniel might

follow her. She needed to go to her safe haven, where she could unlock a door with her access card and then lock the door behind her. Where no one else would be at this hour. She needed solitude.

She grabbed the car keys and headed out before Erik could say anything further. Driving normally soothed her but she kept looking left and right for signs of Daniel on his bike.

Like someone on the run, she rushed from her car to the school building, quickly swiping her card and entering the building, then pulling the door closed behind her.

But even though she was alone at a desk, with only a dim light on, she couldn't find a sense of peace. She tried to call Kent but he didn't pick up. Should she call Iris? While debating whether she wanted to talk to her, the words in the email still raw and hurtful, Iris called her. Her name flashed on the screen and Anna felt her protective wall give way. She answered.

"Hi Anna, sorry to disturb you. Can you talk?"

"Sure."

"Did you speak to Erik? I don't want to put any pressure on you, I just thought that perhaps you wanted to talk about it?"

"What does it matter?"

"What do you mean? I thought this weekend..." Iris paused and Anna felt the tears on her cheeks. She was already mourning Iris. "I thought," Iris continued. "I guess I thought I was Terry in *Loving Her* and that you were Renay but instead of moving in with your daughter you would be bringing Sebastian and Lukas. Was that naïve?"

Iris's way of sending mixed messages angered Anna.

"Do you always interpret life through novels?" she asked.

"Great novels are a reflection of life," Iris replied.

"Are they?" That wasn't Anna's experience. "Everything seems so much easier in novels."

"Anna, what's going on? Did he take it badly... or did you not tell him?"

Anna scoffed. "Why would I tell him anything?"

Iris was quiet. Did she feel bad about the email? Because she should, especially after such a magical time together.

"Did you have a bet with someone?" Anna asked. "Your husband perhaps. To see if you could make a straight woman love you? Oh no, silly me, you've obviously had sex with married women before, so that can't be it. So why do it?"

"Anna... are you saying that you love me?"

That's what Iris picked up from her outburst? "You're so fickle," Anna said frustrated. "So what if I'm not good enough in bed?"

That's when the dam completely broke and the tears started flooding for real. She grabbed a tissue from a packet on the desk.

"Anna," Iris said. "What are you talking about?"

Iris just didn't get it. Anna blew her nose and said: "Iris, let me translate this into your own language, namely literature. I'm like Anna Karenina to you. You toy with me but when I'm about to ask my husband for a divorce you change your mind, and I'm the one who will be scorned by society. Or perhaps you thought I was Madame Bovary? Well, let me tell you that I am not as desperate as her. I was not just seeking an adventure." She paused and took a deep breath but she wasn't finished. "The fact that both of these women die is perhaps an indication of where this is heading."

"Anna, stop," Iris said. "Please, just stop. I have no idea what you're talking about. I love you and I have left Rolf. I was simply calling to see how your conversation with Erik went. If you're trying to tell me that you changed your mind, then just say so. I'm a big girl."

346

"*Me* changing my mind? You're the one who... oh, wait let me just..." She scrolled through her emails. "Oh, here it is. 'After this weekend, the sex... well, I'm not sure you're up for this. I don't want to see you again.' That's a pretty clear message so there is really no need to call me to see how I'm doing."

She wanted to hang up but couldn't. Deep down she wanted Iris to apologise and say that she hadn't meant it like that.

"Anna, I haven't sent you an email," Iris said. "I don't think I even know what your email address is."

Denial was worse.

"Really," Anna said. "So xeroxwed@gmail.com just happens to be someone who knows about us having sex up against the library photocopier."

"Oh, dear God."

"Exactly."

It was supposed to feel good, to feel justified, but she just felt a permeating sadness.

"Anna, please trust me. That was not from me. I am fully committed to you."

Was that possible? Anna tried to piece it together. If it hadn't been sent by Iris, could it have been from Daniel? Was it one of his other games?

"I've got to go," she said. She needed to call Kent again.

"Anna, wait. Where are you? You sound really upset. I'm coming to see you right now."

"No, don't. I'm at school but I need to go home and talk to Erik, to get it over with."

"Okay. And Anna..."

"Yes?"

"I really do love you."

Anna still felt bruised, and also confused. Had Iris really not sent that email? She wanted to believe that it was from anyone but Iris. She needed to move on. Finding the courage to be true to herself, she said: "I love you too."

Anna wiped her tears and called Kent but there was still no reply. She sent him a text message Call me when you get a chance please. She needed to talk to him about Daniel and brainstorm what she was going to tell the principal the next day.

She stood up to leave. The deserted teachers' lounge felt foreign. Perhaps she wouldn't be coming back here? Maybe she would have to move and start over somewhere else? The thought made her sad.

She went to the bathroom and checked her make-up. Her face was swollen and her hair a mess, and she wanted to look approachable when she faced Erik. She combed through her hair and pulled out a lip-balm from her handbag.

When she left the building and walked towards her car, she heard footsteps behind her. She turned around and saw someone she recognised.

63

Iris

March 2016

Leaving Rolf had been easy. Despite their many years together, Iris had always felt that the time spent with others had meant less time cementing their own foundation. Obviously, she would always care for him; he had taught her so much, most importantly, confidence.

Jealousy hadn't really been an issue when she was married to Rolf, at least not after the first couple of years. By then she had adjusted to the marriage set-up. Now, however, Iris felt an irrational jealousy towards Erik, a man she hadn't even met. She felt threatened by the fact that he was Anna's age and at one point he had obviously made her feel loved enough to want marriage and children.

Niggling at the back of her mind was the fact that Anna hadn't been in touch since the previous evening, when she called her from the school. Despite Anna finally declaring her love, it had seemed under duress. Had she changed her mind since? Had the callous email about the sex not being good enough scared her away? She hadn't explained to Anna that

Rolf was the likely sender; it would have revealed too much about her complicated marriage. At least now Iris was free of her soon to be ex-husband's twisted ways.

To stop herself from worrying, Iris thought about their weekend away. Anna's inquisitive eyes, the mounting passion and how adventurous she had become. There was a never-ending sense of exploration between them.

She hadn't imagined it. They had a connection. Surely Anna would get a divorce? Iris couldn't imagine Anna going back to her loveless marriage, and the student threatening her had actually done Iris a favour. There would be no more secrecy.

Even if Anna didn't leave Erik, it wouldn't change anything with Rolf. She had made her decision, and Rolf would come round. They would be friends, she was sure. No more sex though and she was okay with that.

"Your father and I are taking a break," she told Karin.

"Are you getting divorced?" She sounded unexpectedly unemotional about it.

"Probably."

"At least you won't have to fight over custody," Karin said.

Iris ignored the sarcasm. She wanted Karin on board.

"We're still friends," she explained. "We will spend your birthday together."

"Really? I spoke to Dad and I think you have some making-up to do."

He had beaten her to it then. "I guess."

"I mean, come on, Mum. Are you a lesbian now?" Her tone was growing harder. "Plus she's like half your age. Are you having a mid-life crisis?"

"It's not like that."

"Of course not. It's different, isn't it? Everything is always different with you and Dad."

"We love you."

"Really? But you don't give a shit about my reputation? It's bad enough having a father who is controversial for the sake of it. At least he used to have a message. 'Save the planet, love each other.' But now every painting is a bloody mess! No pun intended. And now you…"

Finally Karin stopped for air and Iris gasped. She had never heard Karin speak badly about her father and although it probably should have upset her, it made her feel slightly better. She needed to capitalise on this new-found neutralisation of their relationship before it tipped over.

"I'm just following my heart," Iris paused. "Her name is Anna. Even if I hadn't met her, I still would have left. Our relationship was once built on a mutual understanding…"

"Of sleeping with others, yeah, I know."

Iris pretended not to hear. "But then it became cheap."

The word "cheap" hung between them like a tattered old T-shirt on a laundry line. They sat in silence but at least Karin didn't hang up.

"I'm happy," Iris said.

"So it's going to be you and her?"

"I don't know."

They promised to speak again the next day. Despite Karin's belligerence, Iris felt closer to her daughter. Rolf could no longer monopolise the time with Karin. Now Iris would form her own bond with her.

Iris had Googled the phone number for the painting company Erik worked for. It was incredible how easily accessible everything was these days.

"I need my apartment painted," she said. "By Erik Berg. I hear he's the best."

The apartment did need painting and someone had to do it.

"I'm sorry, he's on leave at the moment."

"Oh." Anna had never mentioned a holiday. Could she really go from one get-away to another so effortlessly, as if the first one didn't mean anything? Or was it an emergency trip to fix the marriage?

"When will he be back?" Iris asked.

"We're not sure."

"Right... well, how long did he ask to be on leave for?"

"He didn't exactly..."

"I see. Erm... I'm a friend of his wife's and I promised I would only ask for him." A white lie was like a companion, a trusted friend.

She needed to have met Erik, to see whether they would all be able to get along. Even though Rolf was upset at the moment, she knew he would come round. Would Erik?

"Look, I'm really sorry," the man on the phone said. "Anna is in the hospital... she's been attacked."

64

Rolf

March 2016

Rolf brought Iris lunch but she didn't eat, the fork play-ing with the spaghetti, moving it around like a picky child. She wasn't sulking, she was just calm and composed and he realised this wasn't about Lena or Frida or even about them anymore. Iris was really through with him. The realisation was a major blow.

"I don't know what to tell the police," she said. "Should I call them and tell them I knew her? Would that help?"

He didn't like the idea of her getting involved with the police.

"If you don't have to, I wouldn't," Rolf said. "I mean, you can't help them anyway."

Her facial expression was pained.

"There was this… thing she told me about, someone threat-ening her. I should tell them."

Rolf had a different opinion: he wanted them to forget that this woman had ever existed.

"I don't know, Iris. In my experience, you stay away from the police unless they contact you."

"No one knew that we were friends, I don't think they will contact me."

"That's good, Iris. Hopefully that means you won't have to get involved."

"But Rolf," she said. "I want to help."

"I know you do and I'm sorry about her being in the hospital," he said. "But you need to face reality... even if she wakes up, she might not leave him."

At first she didn't say anything but when he reached a hand across to touch hers, she withdrew her hand, saying: "I'm more concerned about her recovering."

"I'm sure she will, she seems like a healthy and strong woman." He paused for effect. "I mean up close."

She looked up and loosened her grip on the fork, which bounced off of the plate and onto the floor. He leaned down to pick it up, letting her wait for an explanation, a strong need to torture her.

"How exactly do you know that?" she asked, her words barely audible.

"I'm just joking," he said.

"Rolf?" She looked as if she was going to attack him, the lines on her face deep, her body tensing. "Where were you that night?"

"Now hold on..."

He realised that it was only now that it occurred to her, that he might have something to do with her lover's attack.

"You had a cut on your face. Was that the night?" she shrieked. "You obviously hate her! Was it you?"

She scared him: he'd never seen her so tortuously unhappy.

"Of course not," he said. "How could you possibly think that?"

She screwed her eyes shut and brought her hands to her face, hiding. Rolf noticed she was still wearing her wedding ring. That was a good sign.

"I don't know what to believe anymore," she said and walked off.

He suspected she was crying and he knew she preferred to do this alone. Yet he followed her, couldn't leave it like this. He needed her. She kept walking down a corridor and into a bedroom. It felt odd, this being her apartment, but he couldn't leave.

She was sitting on a bed, a white quilted bedspread he'd never seen before, pulling under her weight. Her body slumped, his heart ached. Could he enter her private space to comfort her? He cautiously remained in the doorway.

"You gave me your word," she said, as if speaking to the wall. "That you wouldn't tie me down, that you would allow me to be free. That was our agreement. In fact, it was *your* agreement and I adapted."

"I know and I'm sorry," he said. "It's just that we had rules, Iris, and you broke them."

"She didn't deserve this."

PART FIVE

June 2016

65

Erik

Anna's mother is sitting next to her daughter's bed, holding her hand. The sight is astonishing in itself but even stranger is the fact that Anna is talking in a mild manner to her mother. Like an outsider, Erik stands by the door, watching the two women. It feels like a TV set where a director will call "cut" at any time. But so far, the show is rolling on. Erik feels he needs subtitles for the bullshit. "I've been so worried about you" should be translated into "I haven't really cared until now" and "I hope I can help you remember" should be "a week is all I've got, honey, so you better hurry up."

"*Hej*, Erik."

It's the doctor, his coat unbuttoned, revealing a tight, white shirt and pink tie. He looks smart, Erik thinks. He is starting to grow fond of him, not because of his fashion sense but because of how he treats Erik. He is always respectful of his feelings.

"I hear someone has been arrested," he says. "That must be a relief."

"It is," Erik says. "But I don't think he's been charged yet."

Linda Johansson had the courtesy to notify him of the arrest but he doesn't know much more. All he can do is read what's in the papers, which isn't much. Who is it? Can they all relax now? He's desperate enough to call Tina but her phone has been disconnected. Maybe she's been fired? He won't feel guilty about it. She brought this on herself.

"Well, Anna's memory has been getting better," the doctor says. "She may not remember what happened yet but the prospects are good."

"Has she remembered anything specific?" *Like her husband?*

"Not exactly, but it has helped having her mother here. Also, she has spoken of leaving the hospital, which is a good sign. I think that perhaps it's time to start transitioning her back home. Would you be able to cope?"

"Sure…"

"E-e-erik?"

The sound is coming from the bed and they all look at Anna. Did she just say his name? She says it again, with more conviction this time.

"Erik?"

"Anna!"

Erik runs to her bed and holds her hands. He wants to kiss her but he's worried she will turn her head away like the last time.

"Do you remember me?" he says, his words so soft he's not even sure she can hear him. He starts to cry. This is so unexpected.

Anna looks bewildered, as if she's woken up from a bad dream. "I think so," she says.

He turns to the doctor. "I need to take her home."

"I guess I'll go back, then?" her mother says.

Gerda, with her rat-coloured hair tucked behind her ears, the thick glasses making her eyes look comic-like, actually speaks to him. *Yes*, he wants to say, *you can go back to your wife-beating motherfucker of a husband*. But he cordially, albeit sarcastically, says: "I guess your job is done."

He studies Anna: will she react to the exchange between him and her mother? Will she roll her eyes and share a conspiratorial smile with him? Does she remember what her mother is really like, or are they now best buddies? But there is nothing. Just confusion. Still, she's coming home.

*

In the car, his phone rings and it's a woman from the police. Not Linda Johansson unfortunately.

"We would like to talk to you about Tina Olsson," the woman on the phone says.

And he was having such a good day.

"What do you want to know?"

"We need to know everything she told you."

Apparently her information might have compromised their investigation. He wants to yell: what investigation? *You have already arrested someone*. Or haven't they? He should be more helpful.

"I will come down and tell you everything," he says.

*

Erik is excited to pick the children up from day care. They will be happy about Anna coming home. She still may not remember them, but at the moment, they have to take one step at a time.

He used to wonder if Anna would still love him when she woke up. He's been holding her hands, massaging them to keep the blood flowing, etching his touch into her skin so that when she opened her eyes, she would remember his loving touch. And yet when she did wake up, she didn't remember him at all, at least not until now. The question is: does she still love him?

When he arrives at day care and opens the door, he hears someone laughing. He turns his head just as the door to the broom cupboard opens and Pernilla tumbles out. Her hair is messy and she's not alone. She's with... Sophie's dad? Erik stares at the two of them giggling. Although the moment they realise that Erik is there, their faces straighten and they go their separate ways, like two tree branches stretching away from each other. Sophie's dad, whose name Erik doesn't know, has opened and shut the door in less than a second without a glance at Erik. Pernilla makes her way towards the group singing inside, ignoring him. It's almost as if he's invisible.

"Pernilla!" he calls.

She keeps walking and at first, it hurts. Then a feeling of liberation. He might be off the hook. For the first time in a while, he feels what can only be described as hope. Anna is coming home, the police have a suspect for her attack, and he's free of Pernilla.

Just then, Pernilla turns around and winks, before running up to him. She grabs his arm and drags him into the broom cupboard. It feels awkward, especially since she was just here with Sophie's dad.

"I just wanted to get back at you by making you jealous," she whispers. "Did it work?"

Her hands are holding his buttocks in a firm grip.

"No," he says even though he must admit he did feel slightly sidelined.

"Come on, Erik."

"Anna is awake," he says. "I can't do this."

She backs off.

"Unless you kiss me right now, I will make your life very difficult for you."

He hesitates. A kiss is just a kiss, right? He leans in and plants one on her pouty lips. Flash. He opens his eyes and realises she's taken a picture.

"What the hell was that for?"

"Facebook," she says.

"What? Give me that!"

He tries to take the phone off of her but she wriggles out of his grip, laughing. Enough is enough. He takes a firm grip of her body and pushes it up against the wall. "That's enough, Pernilla. Delete that photo now or I will…"

"You will what?"

She seems more turned on than scared.

"What do you want from me?" he says. "You want this?"

He pushes her against the wall, snogs her hard and feels up her boobs, pushing a hand between her legs. He's rough and he's hoping she will cry and tell him she's sorry, but she moans, she bloody moans!

"Fuck this," he says and backs off.

"Come on, that was amazing."

"Just delete that photo, please."

"Fine." She takes out her phone and deletes it in front of him. "But if we don't get together soon, trust me, I will fuck you over."

He leaves the cupboard and goes into the assembly room to collect the boys. If only he had never slept with her. If only he had walked away.

"Sebastian, Lukas..." He's lost his thread. "I have some news."

*

Back at the house, David is waiting for them in the driveway. Erik can't remember asking him to babysit but his life is so chaotic at the moment. Perhaps he planned to jam with Rob? Except they haven't spoken since the incident at the bar. Anyway, the boy has proven himself to be a fantastic babysitter and the children look up to him. He's helpful too, laying the table for dinner and stacking and unloading the dishwasher.

"Our mummy is coming home," Sebastian tells him as soon as he's out of the car.

"Really?"

David seems as happy as Sebastian and Lukas, so Erik feels he can't turn him away. Instead he invites him in for a *fika*. Some defrosted cinnamon buns and cordial never hurt anyone, and the children really do like David being there, even though Erik still doesn't understand what David gets out of this.

The boys talk nonstop about what they're going to do when Mummy comes home.

"Do you think she can bake a cake with us?" Sebastian asks.

"Yeah, for our birthday," Lukas adds.

Shit, they're turning six in a week and he hasn't prepared anything.

"She might not be quite ready for that," Erik says.

"I can bake something," David says.

"You know how to bake?" Erik asks. He just doesn't look the part.

"Sure," he says. "You just need to follow a recipe."

Erik laughs. "You're on."

"Oh, and one more thing," David says. "This is kind of awkward but our house is being fumigated, the owner insists on it, so I was wondering... could I crash here for just one night?"

Oh. It's not that he doesn't like David, he seems like a good kid, but staying overnight? What does he actually know about him?

"Mummy would have said 'yes'," Sebastian says seriously and Erik nods. She would have. How do the boys know about Anna's charitable nature?

"Okay, one night," Erik says.

"Yay, it's like a sleepover!" Lukas says.

"You can sleep in the basement," Erik says. "We have a sleeper couch there." Then he's separated from the rest of them. One whole floor between them.

"What about our room?" Sebastian asks.

"It's fine, buddy," David says. He looks elated. "The basement will be awesome."

"Will Mummy be home for our birthday?" Lukas asks.

"I think so," Erik says. "But no birthday party this year. It will be too much for her."

"What about Grandma?"

"Grandpa can't travel at the moment and she needs to stay

with him, so probably not. She will Facetime you, though."

"And... Gerda?"

"Who's that?" David asks. He picks up another bun and tucks into it with great appetite.

"Anna's mother," Erik explains. They call her by her first name because... well, they have only met her twice."

"Oh, how come?"

It's not really David's business but Erik finds himself telling him anyway. Talking to David is like being friends with your younger self.

"Anna isn't close to her parents," Erik mouths quietly. Sebastian and Lukas don't need to know about this. "Her parents aren't... particularly pleasant."

"Oh, but Anna is so... nice."

"She's worked hard not to be like them I guess."

David nods. "Yeah, that makes a whole lot of sense."

The boys leave the table and run into the living room where Erik can hear them pulling their Lego out. Soon, Sebastian pops his head into the kitchen to ask if David will join them.

"Soon," he says. "Just going to finish this bun." It's his third one.

"My mum isn't nice either," David says to Erik when they're alone again. "I mean, she sort of means well sometimes, but she's..." It looks like he's about to cry and Erik feels panic. He can't deal with any more drama. "Anyway." David seems to pull himself together. "With my brother travelling, he's in Australia right now, she's all I've got. My dad is dead."

"Oh."

Does that mean David sees him as a father figure? He straightens his back, at once feeling respected.

"Where's your mum staying tonight?" he asks.

"She's got a boyfriend," David says. "She's at his place most of the time. I'm usually home alone."

"And your brother, when will he be back from Australia?"

"In about three months or so. It was extended due to... another place he wanted to visit first."

"Sounds amazing," Erik says. "To be so free."

"I guess so. Anyway, I'd better go home and pack."

David puts his shoes on without tying the shoelaces and runs outside. Erik can hear the wheels of his bike skidding on the gravel. He sips his coffee, an unsettling feeling in his stomach; perhaps he's been a bit too generous, agreeing to let the boy stay?

66

Daniel

When Dan unpacks his bags in the basement of Anna's house, it's the same bags he packed only three months earlier before cycling here. Except, that time he wasn't allowed in. Now he's here.

The house smells like a home. He takes out his notebook and writes the scents down: washing powder, coffee, vanilla candles and air-dried sheets. Then he places a tick next to *Step 2 – move into Anna's house*. He's halfway there.

Step 3 – become best mates with her kids

They're getting on quite well already.

Step 4 – fuck her/she dumps the husband

Her husband, Erik, has helped him pull out the sofa bed and provided him with a pile of bed linen, a pillow and a duvet. When Erik is back upstairs, Dan sinks his nose into the sheets and takes a deep breath. At Frida's house, the smell of booze and cigarettes overpowers everything else. This is paradise.

While Dan makes the bed, he can hear the commotions of a family above him. Children playing, fighting and laughing. A father reprimanding them from time to time. The sound of a washing machine whirring in the background together with soft eighties' music.

No sounds of a mother but she's on her way home. He needs to find a way to stay here until then. He's desperate to see the look on Anna's face when she first lays eyes on him. Will she be happy or won't she recognise him? Erik has explained that she's struggling with her memory. Maybe that's good. She won't remember pushing him or that he tried to blackmail her. He can simply be the family friend staying at her house, someone she grows to love. He will be sympathetic and take such good care of her that she will feel as if she can't survive without him. It's an ideal scenario really, her being so vulnerable. It almost feels too simple.

"You're such a special person, David."

He will have to accept that for now, he is David.

"I'm doing this for you," he says.

"Please won't you stay home from school and keep me company?"

"Of course I will."

"Can you lie here next to me, please? I feel so lonely."

He crawls up into her bed and lies on his side, facing her. They lie there together, looking deeply into each other's eyes. She strokes his cheek and that's when he leans in to kiss her. He's a gentleman, he will take things slowly. They kiss for a long time but eventually he grows restless. His hands start to wonder, touch and squeeze. He's so hard now, he needs to get some action.

"Everything okay?"

Dan looks up and sees Erik on the stairs. Couldn't he bloody knock? He quickly puts the notebook on his lap, covering his stiffy.

"Yeah, sure. It's fine."

"Do you want me to help you make the bed?"

"No, that's okay."

"Come on, let's do it together. It will be quicker."

Fuck. He thinks of cold running water, yellow pimples and wonky teeth. That works.

"Sure," he says and gets up.

They work in silence but Dan's mind is in overdrive. He's not sure how he should convince Erik that he must stay. Then again, he hadn't expected the fumigation story to work at all. Erik practically invited him with open arms. Maybe he should make Erik feel like he needs him? That's the one good thing Frida has taught him. "People like to feel needed," she says. The problem is, she's the one needing everyone else. No one needs *her*.

"If you need help with anything around the house, just ask," Dan says.

"Thanks."

Erik smiles and Dan reckons that's a good sign. They tackle the duvet, with Erik holding the cover and Dan feeding the feather-filled comforter into it.

"I mean, with anything," Dan clarifies. "Babysitting, cleaning or food shopping. I'm used to doing housework at home."

"That's nice of you," Erik says and he seems to genuinely consider it. "I might take you up on that. It's been busy here lately."

"I can imagine. It must have been hard... I mean, Anna being attacked."

He glances at Erik, wanting to see his reaction. How much does he love his wife? How hard will it be to eliminate him from her life?

"Yeah," Erik says absentmindedly and they smooth the duvet out over the bed. "That's all done then."

Why can't Erik just open up to him? Should he push it?

"I know you must love her very much," Dan says, hoping to sound like an adult, an equal.

"Mm," Erik says and it looks as if he might cry. "Anyway, I better start dinner."

He turns and walks up the stairs and Dan calls after him.

"Thanks for helping me with the bed!"

When Erik is gone, Dan sits down and thinks about his next move. It's time to stop daydreaming; he needs to make things happen. Frida is a worry. What if she interferes? He wonders if she will miss him when he doesn't come home this evening. Will she call the police? He doubts it. Someone like Frida doesn't trust the police. They came to the school after the attack and before he knew it, he was asked to the police station to answer questions about a note. Since he was a minor, a shaking Frida had to come along. They put the note in front of them.

That was a nasty thing to do, Anna. You know I'm smarter than that.

Dan confessed immediately. There was no point lying.

"Yeah, I wrote that. I regret it now but I was just so upset with my exam results. It was really nasty of her to fail me when I had actually done an okay job. I mean..." He almost started crying here, for effect. "I was trying really hard."

He told them what a great teacher Anna was and that everyone loved her.

"Anyone will back me up on that," he said. "But she was tough, man, and when I first arrived I just wasn't used to that. That's why I wrote the note. I'm sorry. I really hope she gets better soon so that I can tell her that in person."

Frida stayed quiet the entire time, not even mentioning Anna's personal visit to their home. Afterwards, she was hysterical, asking him: "Did you have anything to do with that teacher's attack?"

"I swear, I didn't," he said. "You know I really like her."

She nodded. Yes, she did know that. But she didn't seem happy about it, not even when the exam in question was submitted to the police, and he was in the clear. For now, he just needs to stay out of her way.

He needs to be careful though. Erik and the boys think his name is David. Someone might call him Daniel or Dan but it might be similar enough?

What he needs to do now is make himself indispensable. Luckily, Sebastian and Lukas are already eating out of his hand. They're sweet actually. When they're finally together, himself and Anna, she will obviously want the children to live with them (because that's the kind of mother she is) so he needs them on his side. That's okay though; he really likes Sebastian and Lukas. He could easily be their dad.

That evening he places a tick next to *Step 3 – become best mates with her kids*. He feels he has covered that after just one full day with them.

Now he needs to tackle Erik. What are his weaknesses?

67

Iris

An "Unknown" number flashes on Iris's phone, and she quickly answers it, hoping it's a fully recovered Anna.

"I've been arrested!" a stressed voice says instead. Rolf? "Can you believe it?" he continues. "They're going to search through our house and my studio."

"Really?" she says. What is he up to now? Rolf has been desperately needy lately, constantly calling her. Most likely, the police have simply warned him about his inflammatory art, but she does relish him feeling cornered for once. "And you always think you can get away with anything?"

"Seriously, Iris?" he sulks. "Don't you care?"

"Rolf, what's actually happening?"

She's not in the mood for his theatrics.

"It's true, Iris. I really have been arrested. They're just trying to find evidence to charge me for Anna's attack."

Anna's attack?

"Why?" she says.

"I don't know." He sighs. "They seem to think I had something to do with it."

She doesn't know where to start, what to say. He unequivocally blames Anna for their marriage break-up but would he go to such lengths to get rid of her? She can't believe that he's capable of such a monstrous act but he's Rolf and he can be an enigma. There was that cut on his face. *Did she fight back?*

"Did you have anything to do with it?"

"Of course not!"

Then why would they suspect him? She needs to think. He's the father of her child, the man she has shared her life with for so long. She has to process the information and sort it in her head, go through it step by step.

"Do you have anything to hide?"

"Not really," he says. "Apart from the painting with Anna's hair in it."

"What painting?" *There's a painting?* "With Anna's hair in it?"

This shocks her more than Rolf being arrested. He always sleeps with the women he incorporates into his art. Anna would never...

"I guess they'll charge you in no time," she says, her voice hard.

She's staring out the window, at the lush greenery that's supposed to symbolise summer and love and dreams come true. Why is her world crashing down on her? Anna in a coma, Karin hostile and Rolf... he's somehow involved. How?

"Don't be like that, Iris," he says. It sounds as if he's crying. That would be typical, Rolf making himself the victim. "You make it sound as if you want me to go to prison."

"Perhaps you deserve it," she says. "And just out of curiosity, did you pick a strand of hair off the rug after she had been to the house?"

That would make sense, to get back at Iris.

"No, I didn't."

"Then please do tell me, how come you had her hair in your possession?"

She tries to sound calm but her blood is nearing boiling point.

"I may have met with her to obtain it..." he says.

He what? "You said that you didn't, that it was a joke, a bad one but still, a joke." She had believed him. How stupid of her. He had actually met with her!

"You scared me that time, Iris. I was going to tell you but you were so upset."

"When?" she asks, the anger seeping through.

"It doesn't matter. I've already told them she gave it to me willingly, that plenty of people do, and so far she's not really been in a position to argue about that, has she? Anyway... perhaps *you* should be worried. The police don't seem to know about your relationship with Anna, but maybe they will after going through our house."

"She was only there one time, Rolf, and anyway, so what if they find out?"

"Maybe they feel you should have come forward?"

She is done with this conversation. They may have spent years together but if he gets charged, he only has himself to blame. Still, she has to protect Anna.

"You know that would just upset her husband and anyway, I haven't done anything wrong."

If Iris is forced to speak to the police, she won't reveal the nature of her relationship with Anna. If Anna dies, she doesn't want her husband to know she cheated. She owes Anna that. If anyone asks, they are simply "friends".

"No," says Rolf. "In your eyes you have done nothing wrong."

He always thinks he's better than her, trying to manipulate her into his twisted web.

"Anyway… I heard she might be awake," Rolf says.

Her heart stops beating. "She is?" Or is he just trying to get attention?

"Well, it's a rumour," he says. "I'm sure they don't want me to know."

Iris hasn't heard anything, so Rolf might be lying. She needs to find out for herself. If Anna is awake, it will be the best news. Will she want to see Iris? Especially after the email that Rolf sent her, who knows?

"Why did you send her an email?" she asks.

She expects him to at least try to wriggle his way out of answering but he comes clean immediately. "It wasn't just one email," he says. "I sent many."

"Why?"

"I had to get her to trust me, to believe they were from you. Then I ended it on your behalf."

She wishes she were standing in front of him so that she could hit him with something, or squeeze his neck. "If you weren't the father of my child, I would never speak to you again," she says.

"For fuck's sake, Iris. Listen to me, I did you a favour. Don't you see? She's young enough to be your daughter. It would never have lasted anyway!"

Iris wants to hang up but can't give him the satisfaction of losing her temper. To calm herself down, she thinks back to the first night she met Rolf, how she admired him. It was at a gallery opening where he was the centre of attention, telling stories about a warped reality and being able to exist in the present. She was instantly drawn to him; their eyes met across the room and she probably looked away momentarily, intimidated by his stare.

"You no longer intimidate me," she says.

The words seem to stump him. In a friendlier voice, he says: "I'm just telling you to be prepared, Iris. The police will obviously question you since you're my wife."

"I will tell them the truth," she lies.

He seems to hesitate before he answers. "You will?"

"I have nothing to hide."

"If you tell them the truth you will put me in a very diffi-cult position, Iris. They might think I was jealous and wanted her out of the way."

"That's possible."

"Fucking hell! You see, Iris, what I don't understand is this: if they don't know about your relationship with Anna already, then why would they even suspect me?"

68

Daniel

Dan is reading the paper at breakfast, like a proper grown-up. It's going to be sunny today. Maybe he can take the boys to the beach this afternoon? There's a long stretch of sand with shallow water close by. Every now and then he tickles Sebastian and Lukas and they laugh. It's amazing how they look up to him. He imagines what it will be like to drop them off at day care after breakfast (in a year he will have an actual driving licence if he can work out how to pay for it – maybe Anna will?). Afterwards, he will come back home. Anna will be newly showered and even if she isn't, he will still fuck the shit out of her. She will giggle, then moan until she screams with excitement and comes.

He looks across the table at Erik, who will be long gone by then. Maybe he was cool once but he's a nerd, someone who thinks he is younger than he actually is.

"When is your next gig?" Dan asks. "I would love to hear you play."

Erik laps it right up. "That would be awesome but it will

be in a bar. You're not eighteen yet, are you?"

"Next year," Dan says. *But I doubt you'll be around then.* "I could babysit while you're playing?"

Both Sebastian and Lukas think that's a great idea.

"Please, Daddy!"

"But I'm not playing tonight," Erik says.

Dan ignores him. "What's your favourite movie?" he asks the boys.

"The *Lego Movie*."

"Maybe we could watch it together?"

"Yes, please! Tonight?"

Dan looks expectantly at Erik. "Would that be okay?"

Sebastian and Lukas are doing such funny faces: "pretty please we promise to be so very good." Dan laughs. He's noticed that Erik struggles to say "No" to them and has entered this as a weakness in his notebook.

"Fine," Erik says. "But David, your house is ready to move back into, right?"

"Actually, my mum sent me a message late last night. They recommended another night. Apparently they had to spray twice." Lying is easy. All those years he watched Frida lie has taught him how *not* to do it. She is always annoyingly obvious and adds too much detail, as if that's supposed to make him believe her. *I didn't drink, I promise. I had no money so I couldn't have gone to the liquor store even if I had wanted to. They cut my salary this month, those buggers, some story about me being late too often. Plus I don't need to drink, you know that. I don't really feel like it tonight actually.*

Dan can tell that Erik is thinking about what to do.

"Does your mum know where you are?" he asks.

"Of course. Anna came to visit my house once and my

mum really liked her... so she's totally happy about me being here." He stops himself. That's already too much.

"Anna came to visit your house, did she?"

Dan can immediately tell that Erik doesn't like this.

"Well, Anna was actually trying to do me a favour because my mum doesn't care about school. She would prefer that I work and make some money."

"And did your mum come round?"

Both Sebastian and Lukas are listening too, their little mouths full of cereal.

"Yeah," Dan says. "Anna's a great teacher."

"Okay, well... as long as your mum is okay with it."

"Awesome," Dan says and high fives Sebastian and Lukas. "Shouldn't you two be getting dressed now? But don't forget to clear the table." That's what an adult would say. Frida would tell him to *fucking* clear the table but Dan actually knows his manners when he wants to. Erik looks at him appreciatively over the table. *See, I'm helping. You need me. We're cool*, Dan thinks. But just in case, he has prepared another speech.

"I was planning to learn guitar," he says. "If you have time, would you be able to teach me? I read about your band and it has awesome reviews."

It's true, he has read old reviews online and they did say "okay" and "pretty good" in-between a number of less favourable statements such as "inconsistent" and "all over the place".

Erik's face brightens. His music is definitely another weakness.

"Sure thing. What kind of music are you into?"

"Eh... mainly eighties. My mum plays it all the time. 'Should I Stay or Should I Go' by the Clash and 'Don't You

Forget About Me' by Simple Minds are my favourites."

Both of them were mentioned in the last article about the band.

"Wow, you know your stuff. It would be an honour to teach you. Do you have a guitar yet? If not, don't worry, I have a spare one."

They talk about music for a while and when Dan has exhausted his knowledge of eighties music and guitars, he demonstratively turns over a page in the newspaper.

"I need to keep track of the news for school," he explains.

Erik is now in a great mood and Dan sits back and relaxes. He's so easy to read, that man. This will be a piece of cake.

Dan quickly locates an article about Anna's attack. The papers generally provide a short update, especially now that a suspect has emerged. He reads it with great interest. The suspect isn't named but it says that he's a local artist, and to Dan's great pleasure, a character witness has come forward saying he is a "sadistic swine".

When Dan called the police with the anonymous tip, he told them Rolf was obsessed with Anna and that Rolf's car had been seen following Anna in Hågarp one night. It was risky but he didn't think anyone could have seen him behind the wheel. It was dark and the dude's windows were tinted.

"How do you know all this?" they asked.

He told them he knew Rolf and that he had heard him talk about Anna in a very fixated way, as if he had to have her at all cost. He claimed to be afraid for his own safety and therefore wouldn't be able to come forward as a witness.

"We will look into it," they said but he felt they didn't think it was enough. He needed to tell them more.

"He's into some grisly art," Dan said. "Blood and body parts and shit."

He had been smart enough to do a bit of research on the guy. For someone who was in the paper so much, he should have more money, but maybe no one wanted to buy his sicko art.

"I've heard he's violent too. He's rumoured to have murdered people to display them in his paintings," Dan said. "But I don't know, that's just what I've heard."

He didn't want to sound too confident, or they might think he was framing the guy.

Nothing happened at first. There were no news articles, so he kept busy with other strategies. If truly desperate, he would involve Frida. The anonymous phone call was the seed, however, that would hopefully grow. Now the article says that a school janitor, who had been on holiday since the incident, has stepped forward. "The said artist was talking to Anna in what looked like a heated conversation," he told the journalist, clearly clamouring for a moment of fame. Rolf's name isn't mentioned but it's him, for sure.

The fact that someone has also labelled him "sadistic" is pretty awesome. More people digging the Nissan dude's grave is a good thing. No more poking his dick into Frida and, more importantly, no more trash talking Anna with Frida.

He might have to remove Frida if she stands in his way. It will be easy; he's daydreamed about it enough times. It's just that Anna is not herself at the moment and that's a gamble. He needs Frida as a back-up. No foster care for him.

"David, hello?"

Erik is waving a hand in front of his face.

"Don't you have school to go to?"

"Oh, yes. Of course, I'll just shower and get ready."

"Can I just ask you something?" Erik says and Dan nods.

Go ahead. "Have you heard any rumours at school about me?"

"Eh, no." But this is interesting. "What kind of rumours?"

"No, it's nothing. I just thought, well, people talk, you know, in a small place like this."

"I could listen a bit extra," Dan offers. "And if I hear anything, I'll tell you."

Erik looks pleased about this. "That would be great."

Another weakness. Erik cares what other people think. That could come in handy. He needs to make Erik think they're aligned, that Dan is his buffer from the world outside. That would bring awesome power.

"I won't let anyone talk badly about your family," he says. "I really care about you all."

"Thanks, David. I appreciate that."

Feeling like he's scored, Dan whistles as he showers and gets dressed. Although he realises he will need to do some washing later; he's running out of clothes. Or he could buy new clothes with the money he made from his last beer sale, maybe before Anna comes back? He wants to look presentable so that she sees the potential in him.

She saw him across the room and immediately felt an attraction.

He looks at the line. It's shit. The words are just not flowing. Perhaps he's read too many of his mother's romance novels? It makes him sound like a pussy. He sighs. He needs to decide what he wants. It's so complicated. She has to love him but she also needs to understand that he has a raw urge to stick his cock inside of her. Repeatedly. He's running out of patience. She better come home and spread her legs soon.

69

Erik

Officer Johansson and a young policeman Erik hasn't seen before are sitting on the other side of the table. He doesn't have time for this, but they haven't given him a choice.

"How did you get in touch with Tina Olsson?"

He's not keen to involve Rob but what to do?

"It was my mate, he used to date her. Really, she was just trying to help me." *That one's for you, Rob.*

"Help you how?" Officer Johansson looks at him sternly. "Why would you need help?"

Okay, maybe he shouldn't have chosen those words. He looks back at her, his eyes trying to convey: *remember how you used to think this was hard for me, how you felt sorry for my family?*

"I just felt like you weren't involving me," he says. "That's all."

"Our focus is to find Anna's attacker," Officer Johansson says. "Not to keep you informed."

Wow, that hurts.

"I have an alibi," he says.

"You could have hired someone."

It's the new face sitting next to Linda Johansson. His self-satisfied mug and shaven head makes him look more like a thug than a professional member of the police establishment. Erik feels a violent dislike for him. But he's an adult, so he politely says: "My wife means everything to me."

"Well, we'll see," the new face says.

What does that mean? Erik stares at him, the wide, penetrating eyes uncomfortable. Are they... investigating him?

"You have already arrested someone," he says. "I don't have to listen to this."

"Getting a bit defensive," the new face says.

"I have nothing to hide," Erik says. He holds up his hands. "You want my phone?"

They will find messages from Pernilla but he no longer cares. So what if he made a mistake? *One* mistake. Just because he isn't perfect, doesn't mean he beat Anna up.

"Speaking of phones," Officer Johansson says. "How many times did you talk to Tina Olsson?"

"I don't know, a few times."

"Did you call her or did she contact you?"

He needs to think. "I think I called her."

Even though there's a recording device on the table, they note down everything he says.

"What information did she give you?"

He leans back in the chair to try and feel more comfortable.

"She said that Anna and Kent were very close," he says. "Too close perhaps. Also... something about a student of Anna's being difficult."

"And you never mentioned any of this to us?"

He can't believe it. "I assumed the information was coming from you and that you were checking it out," he says. *God, they're annoying.*

Linda Johansson scribbles something down. "What else?"

"She said that you possibly suspected me…" He's told her that already anyway. But what about Pernilla? Should he tell them? "She also lied to me."

"About?"

"She claimed that I had made someone pregnant."

Linda Johansson's face says it all. She didn't know, which means that Tina made that up, not Pernilla. Stupid cow. Why would she do that? Did Tina get some deep, perverse sense of satisfaction, thinking about Erik's life unravelling? *Kick me when I'm down, won't you?*

"Who?" Of course they want to know with whom he was supposed to have fathered a child but it feels like a test, as if they already know and want to see if he will tell them the truth.

"A day care teacher," he says. "It was just a one-off, a *mistake*." He emphasises the last word to show them that he only has eyes for his wife.

The officer's pen is writing furiously now. It sounds like nails on chalk. He wants to leave.

"You told us you were faithful to Anna," Officer Johansson says.

"Sorry," he says. "I forgot. It was just one time. One!"

The silence is the room is suffocating.

Eventually the new face says: "Did Tina say anything else?"

"No." Erik shakes his head, feeling drained. "That's it."

"Thank you," Officer Johansson says. "We will call you if we need anything else."

"Sure, call me any time." He stands to leave, and to show

them what his life is really like, he adds: "It's my children's birthday today and I have to bring their mother home."

*

Sebastian and Lukas have picked flowers from the garden for their mum, and numerous drinking glasses, turned vases, decorate the home. The best birthday present for the boys is not only Anna being home, but more importantly, that she remembers them.

"Sebastian and Lukas?" she says tentatively and they throw themselves around her neck.

"All right, calm down," Erik says.

He pushes the wheelchair into the living room where he has placed a guest bed for her. She won't be able to climb any stairs just yet.

"Happy birthday," Gerda says.

She hasn't bought them any gifts and stands awkwardly next to Erik, looking at Sebastian and Lukas. The boys' eyes seem to ask the question "why is she here?".

"Gerda is going to stay here for one night only," Erik explains.

Anna panicked when her mother said she was leaving and they agreed that Gerda would stay in order for Anna to settle in. Then she will leave. Tomorrow or the day after, at the latest. Not soon enough.

A nurse will be coming to check on Anna regularly and help monitor her medication. Erik barely listened to her orders. Anna is home and they will be able to get by just fine. He's going to right any wrongs by taking care of her.

He does need to work, however. Summer time is when people want the exterior of their house painted and apparently his boss is desperate enough to need him. It's good. He needs a distraction. Seeing Anna like this other person is distressing. Also, he needs to contribute to their bills. He still has to figure out what's happening to Anna's salary. Is she receiving sick pay and if so, how much is it? Surely it's lower than her normal salary? Finding out means sitting in those phone queues that take forever.

Gerda just exists. She makes no attempt to ask the children any questions and doesn't talk to Erik. All she does is sit on Anna's bed, holding her hand, not talking or engaging with any of them. Considering how she waits on her husband at home, Erik is perplexed. Couldn't she at least make herself useful and clean a bit?

"I've put a mattress in the children's room for you," he says.

Anna looks concerned.

"Don't we have a sofa bed somewhere?" she says. "I thought we did."

Yes, but it's currently occupied by your student, David. He imagines saying it out loud to Anna: "I didn't think it was a good idea at first, but it's great actually. The boy is useful. Not only can he babysit from time to time, but he's also listening out for news about our family. Plus, he just told me his mother had to go on a business trip so she's happy that he has somewhere to stay. It's all good."

The doctor would have disagreed – "don't overwhelm her" – but what does he know?

"We do have a sofa bed," Erik says. "But we have a house guest at the moment, a family friend. You can meet him later."

Before anyone asks any further questions, Erik tells them he needs to go to the supermarket to buy ingredients for the children's favourite dish.

"Lasagne," Anna says.

She remembers. Yet she has a vacant stare when she looks at her husband. Every time he goes near her, she holds on to her mother for dear life and he wants to yell: "Your mother was never there for you, remember that? You used to hate her."

"Will you be okay with the boys or do you want me to take them with me?" The question is aimed at Gerda.

"Of course, but I need to be here for Anna first and foremost," she says and smiles at her daughter, who lovingly returns the smile.

Is Gerda hoping for a second shot at being a good mother? Or is she trying to manipulate Anna's memory loss so that she will appear to be a nice, loving person? Either way, she's a body and she's there when no one else is. David will be home from school later and he's promised the boys to join them for dinner. Hopefully, Anna won't mind.

When Erik is in the car, Rob calls him. He hesitates before he answers. They still haven't spoken since the fight in the bar, but he misses his mate. Maybe he should just answer? He could use a friendly ear with everything being so intense at home.

"Hey, how are you doing?" Rob says. He sounds nervous and Erik finds himself being annoyed all over. Why did Rob bring that ghastly woman into his life?

"I'm fine," Erik says even though he isn't.

"Look," Rob says. "Let's forget about that night. We were both drunk. I'm just calling because, well... have you heard from Tina?"

Tina has apparently split from Rob. Normally, he's the one doing the splitting but her rejection appears to have turned him on.

"I don't ever want to talk about her," Erik says. "Especially now that Anna is at home. Plus, it's the boys' birthday. If you really were my best friend, you would know that."

"Whoa, happy birthday, boys! But Erik, that's great, you should be happy. Your wife is home."

"I'm just so sick of you. Maybe I should find a new band that actually takes music seriously. You're just in the band to attract the chicks anyway."

Erik parks the car but leaves the engine running. Has he gone too far? He's just so pissed off with Rob and the world right now.

"Oh, man. You're on a roll!"

"I'm sorry," Erik says. "It's just… Anna looks at me like I'm a fucking stranger."

"But she remembers your name, right. That's a start."

"I know, you're right." He feels bad now. What's got into him? "Sorry about all that. I didn't mean it."

"It's okay," Rob says but Erik can detect a hurt tone. He really needs to care more about his friend.

"You've always been there for me," he says to assure Rob that he truly is sorry.

"You're right though," Rob says, "I *am* in the band because of the chicks."

They laugh and Erik feels better. "If you're really my friend," Erik says, "then stay away from Tina. She really messed with me."

"Come on, she helped a little bit too. Maybe she didn't have the authority but she meant well."

Erik isn't so sure about that. He felt like she was more interested in placing a bomb in Erik's life, waiting for it to explode, than to assist him.

"Still not coming to your wedding," he says.

He puts the phone down and notices a new message. It's from Pernilla.

I'm waiting to hear from you. I'll give you one day.

He's not sure what to reply and can't exactly give her any further ammunition, so he simply writes: Let's catch up tomorrow. He has no plans to do so but hopefully it will sustain her. He can't deal with her now, not tonight. The rest of the messages, he ignores.

*

When he's back home, Sebastian and Lukas are in front of the TV watching a movie. Anna is watching too, from her bed. Gerda is asleep.

Erik cooks dinner and when David arrives, he bakes a cake as promised.

"Is she here?" he asks in a hushed tone.

Erik can tell he's excited.

"She is but her memory is still a bit shaky," he explains.

"Okay," David says. He leans on the door into the living room so that it slightly opens. He smiles and Erik is about to tell him to leave her for the time being, when he closes it again and says: "If I upset her I'll just go downstairs."

That's considerate of him. "Thanks, buddy. I'm sorry but that's just the way it's going to have to be."

"No worries."

Erik puts the lasagne in the oven. "How was school?"

David shrugs. "Okay. Not the same without Anna, of course."

"I'm sure." Erik clears his throat. "Are people talking about her?"

"Sometimes. People are worried that she's not coming back."

Erik watches David stir the melted butter into his cake mix. Even though he's following a recipe from the Internet, it looks as if he's done it before.

"What about her attack?" Erik says. "I mean, it happened at school. Didn't anyone see anything apart from that janitor?"

He's wanted to ask David this question for a while. Surely people talk?

"Nope," David says. "And there are no cameras in the parking lot."

"I know, the police told me."

David stops in the middle of opening the oven to put the cake in.

"What else did the police say?" he asks.

Erik shakes his head. "Not much."

David proceeds to put the cake in and sets the timer. That's where the conversation ends. Erik doesn't want to talk about it anymore. His attention needs to be on the evening ahead.

When dinner and the cake are ready, Erik puts Anna in the wheelchair and the boys wake Gerda up. Together, they make their way to the kitchen where David is standing by the table like a waiter, his back straight and his hair combed to one side. He's quickly got changed and it looks like he's wearing new clothes. Instead of the ripped jeans and much too small T-shirt, he's wearing a white shirt and blue chinos. Very smart indeed. Someone wants to impress.

"Anna," Erik says. "This is one of your students. Do you remember him?"

70

Iris

Ever since Iris found out about Anna's attack, her life has become suffocatingly small. She avoids seeing people when she's not at work, electing to stay at home. It feels too cruel, to have fallen in love with someone only to have that person taken away from you.

When she's alone at home, she spends her time reading user manuals for the new dishwasher and washing machine, determined to install them herself to keep her mind occupied. She can't concentrate on reading fiction. Everything seems banal compared to reality.

Iris managed to visit Anna in the hospital. The sight of her was painful and her instinct was to gently kiss her while talking to her as if she were awake. Anna's face looked serene on the hospital pillow, but her body looked uncomfortable, the stretched duvet holding her down as if it were a straitjacket. Iris pulled it out, making it fluffier.

At first, she wasn't sure where Anna was. When she called the different hospitals in the region, no one could confirm her presence. It would make sense, however, if Anna had been taken to the one closest to Mörna. Iris predicted that security around her room would be tight but how could she live with herself if she didn't at least try to access it? The security guard would surely need the bathroom at some point? There was also Erik to consider, of course, and so Iris drove around the hospital car park, up through the parking garage, to scan it for Erik and Anna's car. Everyone seemed to be driving a Volvo these days but she knew that the twins' baby shoes adorned the rear-view mirror in Anna's car, which made it easy to recognise. Finally seeing the car on the second floor was a huge relief; it confirmed that this was the correct hospital. Iris parked and waited for Erik to leave.

Iris had never actually seen Erik, not counting the blurred photo on the painting company's website, and when he arrived, she felt guilty. This man was married to Anna. He was the father of her children. His hair was a bit too long for Iris's liking but he wasn't bad looking either.

Once he left, Iris stepped out of her car and walked into the building to ask for Anna Berg. No one with that name was registered. Frustrated but not deterred, she ventured up in one of the many elevators. On each floor she would stop and read the signs outside the wards. It was a case of elimination. Anna wasn't likely to be in the psychiatric or the OB-gyn wards, and so Iris narrowed it down to the third floor. On that level, only one ward was locked, therefore signalling that this was the one. There was a seating area outside and Iris sat down, waiting for someone to exit. Twenty minutes later, she was able to sneak inside.

There was neither security by the entrance, nor down the hallway, and Iris walked in with an air of confidence, as if she knew where she was going. That's how she managed to find Anna's room, the door slightly ajar.

After loosening the duvet cover, Iris sat by Anna's bed and held her hand. At least she wasn't in any visible pain, but her skin was pale and her lips dry. Iris dug out a lip balm from her bag and applied it to Anna's lips. The skin felt rough under her touch but after a few applications the smoothness under her finger made Anna's lips more recognisable. By that point the one-sided dialogue had dried up and instead Iris started to read out loud from *Loving Her*, hoping the words would filter into Anna's inner world.

*

Today is a new day, however, a day filled with hope. Although Iris has lost her job (Lena got her revenge in the end, as promised), she has no need for user manuals. After speaking to Rolf, she went to the hospital and found Anna's room positively empty. That could only mean one thing – she was awake. Any other outcome would have been reported in the newspaper. It wasn't just a rumour. She leaned against the wall in the hallway around the corner from the nurses' station, pretending to be absorbed by her phone, as most people these days were. From there she picked up snippets of a conversation that she assumed was about Anna. Words such as "home" and "awake" lifted her spirits but did they also say "amnesia"?

What's important is that she's on the mend. She's awake! It feels better than a thousand book deliveries combined.

Iris paces up and down in her new living room. Can she visit Anna at her home? She needs to see her, speak to her.

Nothing else seems to matter. Her marriage is over and she's got nowhere she needs to be.

When Rolf calls her, she reluctantly answers.

"One more day or they have to let me go," he happily informs her.

Apparently there is not enough evidence yet. Iris has been questioned but is confident that she didn't speak out of turn or compromise anyone. She and Anna were friends but they hadn't known each other for very long, she told the police.

Should she tell Rolf that Anna is indeed awake? She doesn't particularly want to, but who else can she talk to? No close friendships have formed over the years, unless they involved work.

"I heard about Lena," Rolf says. "Who would have thought she was the anonymous benefactor? She seemed like somebody who would have screamed that from the roof tops, someone who would want to feel important."

"You don't know her," Iris says.

Rolf scoffs. "She fucked you over and you're defending her?"

"I clearly played with her emotions," Iris says. "I have to take responsibility for that."

"So will there be no more library or just no more Iris?"

Iris doesn't actually know. She was simply told that funds were low and that they could no longer afford her salary. Lena will pay her until the end of the month but she was asked to leave immediately.

"Who knows?" Iris says. "She has no interest in keeping it going, especially not for my sake."

"Sorry, I really thought I had made things right with her."

"Well, you didn't."

She can't really blame him but she does.

"Come on!" he says. "Many things are my fault, but not *that*."

There is no point arguing. "I guess you did your best," she says.

For Karin's sake, she's trying to bury the hatchet.

"Anyway, there's something else I want to tell you." She pauses. "She's awake, Rolf."

Her heart is beating fast as she says it. She's excited but she also wonders how he will react. Will he be upset? Worried? Now that Anna is able to speak to the police, what will she say? Iris wants to believe that he's innocent, but he's acted irrationally since their separation.

"Right," Rolf says. "Well, I guess that's good. I mean, good... for her."

"A witness saw you, Rolf," she says. "It was in the paper."

"I know, but he didn't see me in the parking lot, Iris. He only saw me in the courtyard. Then he left."

"That doesn't really mean anything, Rolf. Why were you even there?"

She tries to supress her anger, has promised herself to keep it amicable.

"I don't want to talk about it, Iris."

If he doesn't want to talk, he won't. She can imagine how frustrating it must be for the police to question him. At least she will no longer be married to him. It's amazing how accepting you become when you spend over twenty years with someone. She obviously needed to meet Anna to break free. Anna has a big heart, she's considerate of other people; she's someone who doesn't need to be the centre of attention. She's also generous with her time and her affections. Iris has never met anyone like her. She wants to wrap her arms around her at night, share her inner thoughts and just be with her.

"I'm going to see her," she says.

"I thought you might say that."

He sounds more tired than worried and she decides to hang up. She never tells him what she's really worried about. That Anna might be suffering from memory loss. What if she doesn't remember her?

71

Rolf

Rolf is having the best day. Well, it would be better if Iris was sharing it with him but he's spending it with Karin, which is just as good. Despite her sometimes cynical views on life, he respects and admires his daughter. She is her own person, which is exactly how they raised her.

"We're celebrating," he says. "I'm a free man."

Karin has taken him to a trendy café in the heart of Gothenburg, where they're drinking café lattes in large white mugs and sharing a giant chocolate ball.

"Did you even know that teacher?" she asks him.

"Not really," he says. "She provided some hair for one of my paintings but that's all. Anyway, I'm off the hook. Not enough evidence!"

Karin crosses her arms and views him quizzically.

"Why aren't you more upset about this?"

She's got that "I'm deep and serious at university" look. Black hair and clothes, red lipstick like her mother but no tattoos or piercings. Apparently that's for "losers".

"I don't know," he says. He wants to move on, they should focus on happy subjects, and he vigorously stirs sugar into his coffee. "I can never be…"

"… sweet enough," she finishes his sentence.

"I guess I've said that before."

She nods and he feels ancient.

"I just don't understand," she says. "My dad hates any kind of injustice. And you were treated very unfairly, wouldn't you say? I mean, you were arrested and almost charged!"

"That's the point though. *Almost*."

Karin shakes her head. He knows that she has never understood his desire to experience life to the fullest, whether for better or worse. She once accused him of being "attention-seeking". That hurt.

"Another thing I find odd," Karin says and he braces himself. Why isn't he scared of critics but terrified of his daughter? "That teacher wasn't the type of woman you normally include in your art."

"Oh, so I have a type now, do I?" He laughs. "How do you even know about the women in my art?"

"They've been pretty forthcoming in the press."

Oh, yes. That's right. The accusations have been great for publicity.

"It just doesn't add up for me," Karin says.

"Well, as long as it adds up for the police, that's all that matters."

Karin sips her coffee but her phone rings and she gets up to answer it. The whispered talking suggests it's an intimate conversation, so Rolf leans back and enjoys his freedom, which is now so much more enjoyable than just a few days ago.

It went too far. He shouldn't have allowed himself to get

so emotional. Iris will never come back to him, even without Anna, he realises that now. He has decided that if that means they will only be friends, then he will take Iris's friendship over nothing at all.

He told Iris about his run-in with Anna. There was no longer a reason to hold back. He explained that he did go to the teacher's school the night of her attack, filled with anger after Iris had packed her bags and left.

"I just wanted to talk to her," he said.

He stressed that he was there before her attack and that he in no way was responsible. It was just a coincidence that he was there that particular night. She didn't sound convinced.

"Tell me exactly what happened," she demanded.

"I parked at the school because her Volvo was still there," he told her. "Then I walked up to the school building just as she was leaving."

He left out that Anna recognised him from that night she was jogging.

"*What do you want?*" she asked.

"*I'm Iris's husband.*"

"*Oh.*"

"She let down her guard when she realised I was connected to you."

"What did you tell her?"

"I said you were mine and that she better not mess with our marriage. She apologised and said she hadn't intended for anything to happen but apparently she's dumb enough to love you."

"Did you leave her alone after that or did you...?"

"Iris! You can't possibly think I would do anything stupid."

"Let me think, my husband, Rolf Sören, doing something stupid? No, not at all."

"Okay, there's no need for that."

He had known it would be a tough conversation but now he needed to get it over and done with.

"Iris, I love you. I was simply trying to scare her off."

"And how exactly did you 'scare' her?"

"I might have reached out and grabbed a handful of her hair, but then I left," he said. "That's the truth."

"Sorry, Dad."

Karin is back at the table, her cheeks flushed.

"Good talk?" he asks, winking at her.

"Don't," she says. "Let's focus on you. So, you were arrested. I guess it was just a matter of time before you got into trouble."

"But they let me go, remember."

Karin nods and finishes off the chocolate ball.

"It's odd though, isn't it?" she says, swallowing. "A woman you took hair from was attacked the very same night you saw her?"

72

Erik

Erik looks for signs of recognition on Anna's face.

"David?" Erik says. "Do you remember him?"

"Da..." she says before stopping.

Erik can tell she's working her brain muscles hard. She badly wants to remember, her expression pained.

"You're my favourite teacher," David says, his face lit up.

"What is he doing here?" Gerda whispers to Erik.

"He's been very concerned about Anna," Erik whispers back. "And he's been a great support for the boys."

It's a slight exaggeration but he wants to shut her up. Who he invites into this house is not her business.

"David?" Anna says, studying the boy.

He nods. "That's right."

It's painful to see his wife, Teacher of the Year, not recollect a student.

"Let's eat," Erik says, to avoid any further awkwardness.

He wheels Anna up to the table which has been laid out with blue Höganäs Keramik plates and blue-and-yellow napkins, portraying the Swedish flag. He places one on Anna's lap, and Gerda sits down next to her as if she's Anna's carer. She doesn't offer to help but expectantly waits for her glass to be filled, holding it up to no one in particular. Erik is pleased to see David take charge: he pours Fanta and Coke for everyone while Erik dishes up the lasagne. He can't say it's his best work but at least it's not burnt and no one complains, not even Gerda.

They mainly eat in silence. Sebastian and Lukas chime in every now and then, telling their mum about day care, Sophie, Lego and pirate ships. She nods and says "a-ha" and "wow" which spurs them on. Erik wonders how much she actually understands. Is her brain intact? Can she comprehend what's being said and turn words into something meaningful, something that relates to her old life?

She's different. Milder and more contemplative. Obviously she has no work to stress about, but still. She simply exists. There's grumpiness, which is probably due to her not remembering everything, but she doesn't ask as many questions as he had expected. It's as if she observes them all, which at times can be unnerving. She's also not able to get around by herself just yet. She can walk but her body is slow and quickly gets tired.

Will he need to hire someone to care for her full time? Mum has promised to come down for a few days but not for another week at least. He doesn't want Gerda there and quite honestly he can tell she would rather get back to her heartless husband than stay with her daughter in need. She's constantly on the phone to him, listening rather than talking.

Will the government provide a full-time carer? He probably should have asked. If he needs to hire someone himself, he needs more cash. Maybe he can do more evening and weekend shifts when the pay is better? Would David be able to watch the boys and Anna? Is it even fair to expect that of a seventeen-year-old? Having said that, if he was Sebastian and Lukas's brother, he would have to do his bit. Except he isn't, of course. Living far away from family is difficult when you have young children. That was one of his objections when Anna wanted to move here.

"We have to share the responsibility," she said back then, but her job obviously became more important than his.

Anyway, he can't dwell on that now.

"David says school isn't the same without you," Erik says.

Anna doesn't respond, she just stares at him for a few seconds as if she can't understand what he's saying, before looking down at her food. Erik notices that she avoids looking at David throughout dinner. There is something unsettling about it. Even though David tries his best to make polite conversation, Anna doesn't seem to register his existence. Perhaps he should have kept this meal to family only? Maybe she doesn't want to be reminded of her work life, especially since she has to recover fully before she can return. He should have thought of that.

At one point, David puts his knife and fork down, sighs and says with a dejected look on his face to Anna: "Do you not remember me at all?"

Erik feels his muscles tense. *You shouldn't have said that. Lay low please.* But it's too late. Anna is stirring in her seat. Everyone looks at her, even Sebastian and Lukas. What will she say? Will she be annoyed?

She nods and briefly meets David's eyes. "I do," she says. "At least, I think I do."

"That's great," Erik says, trying to sound positive. "I thought that perhaps you didn't—"

"No," she interrupts. "I remember something about him."
She looks down at her plate again where she's moving pieces
of lasagne around. "I just can't... I'm not sure."

"That's good, though," David says. "A toast to that."

He raises his glass.

"Yes, a toast to that," Erik says, ignoring the fact that
Anna is rejecting his food, and they all say "cheers", clink
their glasses and sing a spontaneous happy birthday to the
children.

Despite drinking only water, Anna seems drunk. It's probably the medication. She's distant, except for when she looks
at Sebastian and Lukas. Then a new energy surges through
her. Apart from fighting about who gets to sit next to her –
if only Gerda would move and let them sit on either side of
their mother – they seem to be having an okay birthday.

"Do you want me to read to you tonight?" Anna asks.

"YES!"

"Are you sure?" Erik says. "You don't want to overexert
yourself."

What if she finds she can no longer read?

"Of course I will," she says and hugs them tightly.

He should be fully content. His wife is back and his
children are happy. He needs to chill.

*

That evening, when the children are in bed and Gerda is in
the bathroom, Anna calls Erik. He sits on her bed, not sure
whether to touch her or not.

"Are you okay?" he asks. "Was dinner a bit too much?"

"It was a lovely birthday dinner," she says. "Thank you for

organising it. But why was he here? Da… David?"

She's already struggling to remember his name. Maybe she won't fully recover her memory?

"I understand that you feel uncomfortable," Erik says, because the doctor has told him to validate Anna's feelings to make her feel heard. "It probably reminds you that you can't teach for a while, but he's staying here, only temporarily, of course." He pauses as he watches her reaction. Will she be happy that he's housing a student of hers, or not? It's hard to tell. She looks puzzled. "He needed somewhere to stay," he explains. "So I offered him a bed for a night or two. I thought you would be happy that I was helping one of your students?" She doesn't react. Maybe she doesn't remember the countless arguments they have had about her work?

She turns on her side and a strand of hair falls over her face. He leans in, brushes it away. "He'll be out of here soon," he says.

Anna puts a finger in her mouth, biting her nail. He's never seen her do that before.

"How many days has he been here now?" she asks, not looking at him, making him feel like a failure. He's just never good enough.

"A week," he admits.

She scrunches up her face. "I may not remember him, Erik," she says. "But there is something about him… I don't want him here."

"Well, I have asked him to leave several times," Erik defends himself. "But he always has a new excuse and, well, I feel bad. I was trying to think what you would do, and I thought you would let him stay."

The latter is a lie but a hugely satisfying one.

"For God's sake, Erik," she says then and in that explosive moment she is his old Anna, the fiery woman he fell in love with. "Talk to Kent if you need help."

"Kent? You remember Kent?"

"Yes," she says. "We work together."

73

Iris

The next morning, Iris knocks on the door of Anna's house. It's a relatively small home, which now has a rather neglected garden. Still, it's cute. The straight panel curtains have a maritime look about them; she can picture Anna choosing them. *Anna has decorated this home for her family*. Iris quickly flicks the thought away and knocks on the door one more time.

Finally, an older woman with grey hair weaved into a plait, answers it.

"Hi," Iris says, not sure who the woman is. "I'm Iris, a friend of Anna's."

"Come on in. I'm Gerda, Anna's mum."

They shake hands. "Nice to meet you." It's a relief that it's not the husband opening the door. He might not know about their relationship but it would still feel awkward. She would be torn between being polite for Anna's sake while also demonstrating to him that she plays an important role in Anna's life. A very important one.

Gerda shows Iris into a living room with wooden floors and tasteful navy and white furniture. Anna is lying in a bed next to a sofa and Iris walks over to her, full of nerves. She has no idea what to expect.

"Anna?" she says.

At first Anna looks as if she doesn't know who Iris is but then her expression changes. Her body softens, her lips part. She smoothens her hair out and gestures for Iris to sit down next to her.

"You came to see me?" she says.

Iris takes Anna's hands in hers. "Of course. I've been so worried about you. I visited you in the hospital but... well, you were asleep but... still so beautiful."

She can't take her eyes of Anna. *She remembers me.*

"Would you like some coffee, Iris?" Gerda asks.

"Yes, please," Iris says, only so that Anna's mum will leave them alone.

"That's my mother," Anna says when Gerda goes into the kitchen. "I can tell that Erik doesn't like her."

"She's not his mother," Iris says.

Even though she has no right to, Iris doesn't like Erik. From the few stories Anna has told her he seems childish with a chip on his shoulder. But he also seems like a good father and, no matter what happens in the future, he will always be a part of Anna's children's lives. They need to get on.

"My husband was accused of your attack," Iris says. She has debated whether to tell Anna but has decided that it's better that the news comes from her.

"I'm sorry," she says.

She can't tell from Anna's expression if she knew about this already.

"Don't be," Iris says. "They don't seem interested in him anymore."

"The police showed me some pictures of a man with a dark moustache and a ponytail."

Iris nods. "That would be him."

Does Anna remember meeting him at the school? Does she recall how he pulled at her hair? Iris feels a knot in her stomach at the thought. Should she remind Anna, to help her with her memory?

"I told them I didn't recognise him," Anna says. "But I also said I wasn't one hundred per cent sure, that maybe I had seen him, I just didn't know when."

Iris feels torn.

"You might have seen him," she says. "I think the two of you met at some point."

"Oh," Anna says. "When was that?"

"He wanted to tell you to stay away from me but you said you loved me and he backed off."

That's his version of the event. Maybe Anna's will be different, should she ever remember, but Iris wants to remind her: *you said you loved me.*

Anna doesn't respond and Iris quickly says: "Anyway, the police interviewing him was a reality check. He needed it."

She kisses Anna's hand. She smells the same.

"It's just that I don't remember what happened that night," Anna says.

"So what have you told the police?"

"I haven't been able to tell them much."

"That's terrifying," Iris says, at once feeling both outraged and alarmed. "That means the attacker is still out there?"

Anna nods and Iris can feel the heat in her veins. Whoever he or she is, she wants to grab that person by the neck.

"What if you're not safe here?" she says. "What if that person comes back for you?"

"The police check in on me regularly. Anyway, it might just have been a random act, Iris. There is no apparent threat. Also, Erik is here," Anna adds, and Iris feels more than jealous in that moment. She wants to be the one protecting Anna.

Gerda brings them coffee and Iris lets go of Anna's hands.

"I will leave you to it," Gerda says. "I need to pack anyway." She heads upstairs and Iris is thankful that she doesn't stay to make trite conversation. It's Anna's mother and she should make an effort. But not today.

"So how much do you remember?" Iris asks.

If you can't recall who attacked you, do you remember that you were going to leave your husband?

Anna doesn't seem to like the question. She sips her water and Iris picks up a coffee cup to give her time.

"I remember a lot," she says eventually, avoiding eye contact.

Has she forgotten about their weekend away? Their intense lovemaking, the laughs, the intimate conversations. The love.

"Do you remember how we met?" Iris asks tentatively.

Anna lies back on her pillow. She looks frail. Maybe she shouldn't probe her with questions?

"You wore a black outfit and silver jewellery," Anna says. "Red reading glasses and matching lipstick. I didn't think you would be approachable at first, but then we became friends…" She pauses, before adding: "More than friends."

Iris's heart beats hard, swelling with emotion for this woman, and when Anna looks up at her, all she wants to do is plant a kiss on her soft lips. Yet she's afraid to.

"I fell in love with you," Anna says and Iris sighs. This is what she had hoped to hear.

"I love you very much," she says to Anna.

Anna closes her eyes and after a while, Iris worries that she might have fallen asleep. Is she okay? She gently strokes her cheek.

"Things are different now," Anna says. She opens her eyes but avoids looking at Iris.

Iris feels herself grow cold. She fears asking but she has to know.

"Different how?"

Anna's breathing is laboured as she tries to talk, and it takes her a while to get the words out: "I need my husband and my children."

Iris wants to scream. Anna is finally awake and talking to her, and this is what she wants?

"So what are you saying?" When Anna doesn't respond, Iris eventually forces the words out: "It's over?"

Anna pats her hand and Iris can't decide if she's being caring, because it feels patronising.

"It has to be," Anna says.

74

Daniel

Dan is happy. Anna is at home and he was included in her first family dinner. It's a miracle that she has woken up. It's a sign. He is where he is meant to be. What's even better, is that Erik went to sleep on the first floor, Anna on the ground floor and Dan in the basement. He's one step closer...

This morning, he woke up in a house with two parents, two younger siblings and a grumpy grandmother. It felt like something out of a storybook. If people woke up like this every morning, they would definitely want to go into the world, making it a better place.

After breakfast, Erik gets ready to drive the children to day care. Then he will do some errands before coming back to pick Gerda up. He's going to drop her at the bus stop, he says. Dan listens carefully to keep track of Erik's schedule. He needs to be alone with Anna. If he can hide away in the basement until Gerda leaves, then he figures he will have the opportunity he's been looking for.

"Erik, can't you drive me to the train station instead?" Gerda asks. "I don't feel comfortable taking first a bus, then a train."

She's an odd lady; spaced out most of the time and when she does talk, she complains a lot. Dan is happy that she's leaving. He does try to be nice to her though, for Anna's sake.

"I wish I could drive you," he tells her ingratiatingly. "But I don't have a licence yet."

"Thanks, young man," she says. She almost smiles and that's great.

They will obviously have to spend time together in the future. Although, if he's going to cut his mother out of his life, perhaps Anna can cut hers out too. That would be better.

"Do you want me to drop you at school?" Erik asks.

"No, that's okay. I've got my bike."

When they are out of the house, the children in the car and Erik about to get in, Dan pretends to have forgotten something inside.

"See you later," Erik says and Dan waves goodbye to the boys as they leave.

He does plan to go to school later because it isn't worth getting into trouble. The principal might call Frida and that's to be avoided. But he plans to be late. He will say that he had an emergency appointment at the doctors, or that he simply overslept.

Dan can hear Gerda talking to Anna, so he takes the opportunity to slip down to the basement unnoticed. He's lying on his bed, waiting for Gerda to leave, when he hears the doorbell ring. Who the hell is that? More visitors? A nurse? He really doesn't need that today.

A woman is being greeted by Gerda, she says she's a friend of Anna's, and then there is muffled conversation. He strains his ears to hear what is going on but it's impossible now. They must be in the living room. He has to be patient and wait this one out. Sooner or later Erik will be back for Gerda anyway.

While he's waiting, Dan gets off the bed and checks himself out in the floor-length mirror. He's wearing a new T-shirt and jeans and has washed his hair. He checks his breath as well and it isn't bad.

It seems to take forever before he finally hears the door close. First, the friend leaves, then Gerda is picked up by Erik.

Dan counts to a hundred before he tentatively makes his way upstairs. He needs to make sure Gerda won't rush back for something she's forgotten.

The house is quiet when he reaches the top of the stairs. Leaving the dark basement with its wood-clad walls behind, it's like stepping into the sun, being up here. It's warm, light and airy. He heads towards the living room, his moves now quick and alert. Dan doesn't know how much time he has before Erik comes back. Hopefully Gerda will manage to convince Erik to drive her all the way into the city to the train station.

The parquet floor creaks under Dan's sock-clad feet. He looks down, trying to soften his steps. The fishbone pattern on the floor is beautiful. The whole house is. Erik claims it's small but it's a mansion compared to what Dan is used to. He hopes they can stay living here.

Anna looks like she's sleeping, the duvet only half covering her body. She's wearing a thigh-high nightie with a Mickey Mouse print on the front. Gerda brought it for her. Erik thought it was ridiculous. "She's thirty-four!" he said. "Not fucking five." But Dan likes it. It makes her look youthful.

He carefully sits down next to her, which causes her to stir, but she doesn't wake up. Maybe she's just taken her medication? Her face looks relaxed. He places a hand on hers and squeezes it gently. This feels so right. He looks at her heaving chest as she inhales. Transfixed, he feels a deep desire to touch her upper body. He's sure she won't mind. Letting go of her hand, he excitedly places his hands on Anna's round breasts. They're heavy and warm. He strokes them and watches the nipples harden. They actually stiffen under his touch! He feels himself grow hard. She's responding to him. Excited, he leans down and tugs at a nipple with his mouth, the cotton fabric growing damp in his mouth. His heart beats fast, the thrill of being this close to her overshadowing anything he has ever experienced. This is what he's wanted. He's fooled around with girls before but this is different. His whole body wants Anna. It's like he's on fire, his cock is throbbing. He needs to be even closer, this isn't enough; he lies down next to her. She smells of hospital but he doesn't mind, her flowery perfume is still detectable underneath. He snuggles closely, burrowing his nose into her neck, his hands stroking her stomach, sliding down between her legs. She's warm there and he wants to undress her so badly, to feel her skin against his, but first, he opens his fly and lets the hard-on out. It springs into position, leaning against Anna's leg. He looks at it almost in awe: his cock on Anna's leg. If only he had a camera to document this.

Just then he hears Erik's car pulling into the driveway. *Fucking hell!* Why couldn't he stay in the town centre a bit longer? It makes him angry, he's not ready to leave yet. Dan quickly thinks of possible options. Beat the crap out of Erik and go back to Anna? That's what his body wants but his mind is smarter than that. He can't be caught, then he'll be sent packing, and he's not done here yet.

Panicked, he sits up but Anna starts to move and he quickly stands up and forces his fly shut, which isn't an easy task. He should run but he needs to gaze at her for just another second. That's when she opens her eyes, and looks straight at him. *Fuck!*

"Eh, hi," he says, his voice trembling. "How are you feeling?"

Her eyes look alarmed and she scrambles into a sitting position, hiding her body.

"Get away from me!"

He stalls but he hears a key in the door and grabs his bag. Using the patio door, he runs outside. He doesn't stop until he's far away from the house. The anger subsides and is replaced by excitement. He was just lying next to her! He can't believe how close he got, and how incredible that he now lives in the same house as Anna. He's achieved a lot in a short space of time.

*

Several times during the day, Dan locks himself in a bathroom to think about Anna's body and how it reacted. Over and over, he fantasises about what could have happened if Erik hadn't arrived.

He slips his hand inside her knickers and touches her.

She wakes up and looks at him, grateful that someone is making her feel good. She smiles and lets out a contented sigh. "Please don't stop, Dan. That feels amazing."

And with his limited experience he does the best that he

can because that's what she deserves, the best. At least until he's so hard he's worried he might come. He mounts her and with her encouragement, he thrusts himself inside of her. It feels so bloody good!

After school, he wants to rush home to Anna but a nasty surprise is waiting for him in the courtyard. Frida.

"I'm not some fucking toddler you need to pick up," he says.

He walks off but she runs after him. "Dan, where have you been? I need to talk to you."

He keeps walking but slows down. It's not worth causing a scene. He finally has people's respect; he doesn't need them to see this.

"Okay," he says and turns to her. "Not here though. Over there."

He shows her to a quiet area, a meadow with trees and a pond. This is by far the nicest school he has ever gone to. He wants to do his final year here before... before what? Anna will expect him to go to university, she already mentioned that, but he also needs to work to take care of her. Once she recovers fully, they will have to discuss it and plan their future together. A mental flash of her body again, warm and willing.

"I'm not coming back home," he says.

Frida studies her feet: sparkly sandals and chipped nail polish.

"Where are you staying?" she asks after a while.

"None of your business."

"Dan!" Her eyes stare at him in disbelief. How can she not understand that he's fed up with her being such a mess? Her arms hang by her sides like a ragdoll, her hair is uncombed and her make-up smeared. "I'm your mum. I... need you."

"You need the bottle," he says.

He revels in her hurt eyes. *That's right, I fucking hate you.*

"Is this to do with your teacher, Anna?" she says quietly. "Do you miss her or... did..." She takes a visibly deep breath. "Did you hurt her?"

"We've already been over this," he says. "You obviously think I'm capable of such violence."

Maybe she finally realises he's not a little baby anymore.

"Maybe it was you," he says. "Maybe you were sick of being compared to her and you attacked her?"

"I didn't like her, Dan," she admits. "She was trying to take my son away from me, but I'm not a monster!"

"Maybe your boyfriend did it to impress you? It said in the papers that an artist was suspected of her attack."

"He w-wouldn't harm a fly," she stutters.

"Really? Remember how he had your head in a headlock or all the times when he fucked you hard, tying you up and shit?"

He's enjoying this. Her world falling apart, like she has destroyed his over and over.

"That's different, that was harmless fun..."

"You think that's appropriate, especially with your son in the house? It's fucked up, that's what it is."

She starts to cry. "Dan, please! You're my son."

"But I'm never your number-one priority."

"And for her you are? She's only a teacher, Dan. She has loads of other students. You're not fucking special!" She's raising her voice and he can tell where this is going. He needs to exit now, to get away. Back home.

"I'll call you later," he says even though he has no credit on his phone.

"I spoke to the police," she says as he walks off.

He stops and turns to her. "You did what?"

"They had questions about Rolf, about his alibi."

"And what did you say, I mean, about me? Did you mention me at all?"

She bites her lip, delaying, as if she wants to get back at him. He won't take the bait; he will wait a hundred years for her to respond if he has to.

"Rolf didn't do it, Dan," she says. "They let him go."

Fuck, they did?

"That means nothing," he says.

"You need to give him a break."

"What about me?" he says. "Don't I fucking get a break?"

"I told them that Anna was your favourite teacher. They remembered me. Dan, I don't want anything bad to happen to you. You're all I've got!"

He scoffs. Sure. But the dude is off the hook? That's a bummer. He will have to fix this, and he will, because he deserves Anna. He closes his eyes, thinking of her hard nipple on his tongue. No one can take that away from him. No one.

He walks off, leaving Frida behind, and in that moment he decides that when he gets home, he will get rid of Erik. No more games. Forget the guitar lessons. There's no time to scheme and act out a whole plan. He needs to take him out the old-fashioned way.

75

Erik

Erik feels a strong desire for his wife. He likes this calm version of Anna. It reminds him of their younger days. She's not rushing around, trying to do a million things; she doesn't care about colleagues or students or tests. She's also lost weight, which means that, physically, she resembles the old Anna. Now, for the first time since she arrived home from the hospital, they're going to be alone together, and he's looking forward to that.

This morning, he was a dutiful husband; he dropped the children off at day care, picked up a parcel with gear for an amplifier that he probably won't get to use, did the grocery shopping and dropped the mother-in-law-from-hell off. The self-righteous Gerda is finally gone, but only after first declaring herself indispensable.

"How will you cope without me? Who will open the door? Anna had a visitor earlier." She said it as if the queen herself had called on her daughter.

"Who was it?" Another supposedly concerned teacher or parent?

"Her name was Iris," she said.

He had no idea who that was.

"She was a bit older than Anna," Gerda said. "Very sophisticated."

"Must have been a colleague. She has many," he said drily.

He doesn't know half the people who want to see her. All he is there to do is serve them coffee and cake. Ahead of him stretches months of Anna recovering. He is expected to focus on nothing else.

"When is the bus leaving? Do I have to *wait*?" she asked, at which point Erik had enough.

"Would you ever speak to your husband that way?" She looked baffled. "What I mean," he continued, "is that you let your husband walk all over you but when he's not around, you speak to people like they're shit."

"Not to my Anna!" she exclaimed.

"Well, you used to. Her coma has obviously made you nicer, but only to her. You still look at me like I'm dirt on your shoe."

"Not at all!"

"What was it you said on our wedding day? 'He might be a looker but how will he provide for you?' Like we're living in the Stone Age."

"Well, she wouldn't be working so hard if it wasn't for you and if she hadn't been working late she wouldn't have been attacked!"

She started to cry and it was the first time he had witnessed that. Normally, her husband's boot in her arse wouldn't even make her flinch.

Erik still doesn't feel bad. He can't hide that he doesn't like the woman and it bothers him a great deal that she pretends to now care about her daughter's welfare.

Gerda is gone, however, and there are no unexpected visitors, which means they're alone. He takes a moment to deliberate on his next move. Should he be ashamed about his feelings of desire?

He wonders how Anna feels right now. She just about remembers who he is, will she want to get undressed and receive him with open arms? He's not sure. Yet he wants her. Badly. A part of him feels an animalistic need to repossess her after she cheated, even though he pretends not to know. Another part wants to keep the peace until she fully recovers. *If* she recovers. There is still a chance she could get worse.

He walks into the living room, deciding to play it by ear.

"*Hej*," he says jovially.

She's sitting up, cradling her knees.

"What's going on?" he asks. "Are you okay?"

Is she upset about her mum leaving? At least she's not crying but he sits down and hugs her. She hugs him back. That's a good start. Then he kisses her cheek, her forehead, her lips. She doesn't exactly kiss him back but she doesn't pull away.

"I've missed you," he says.

He strokes her back and moves his hands to the front, over her breasts. She closes her eyes so he pushes her down onto the bed, pulling at her knickers.

"Wait, Erik," she says, opening her eyes again and perhaps he's moving a bit fast but at that moment his fingers reach her magic spot and it sounds as if she's letting out a moan, which spurs him on. He rubs and circles for a few seconds before he yanks his trousers down.

"Erik, I'm not…" she starts but he's already hard, she's his wife, and he's waited patiently. Surely he can't be expected to stop now? This will be good for her memory, it will bring them back to the beginning when they were newly married and couldn't keep their hands off each other. He separates her legs and she doesn't stop him, so he quickly pushes himself into her, moving in and out.

"I'm your husband!" he pants but at that moment, she starts to bang her hands on his shoulders, begging him to stop.

"Stop Erik, just STOP…"

But he can't. He's so close, he just needs to…

"Argh!"

He comes hard, releasing his long-suppressed spunk into her. He lies on top of her for a short while, realising that he's heavy and she's still in recovery; he should move. She lies underneath him like a dead person, completely motionless, when he pulls out of her and sits up.

"I'll get some tissues," he says.

He can't look at her right now.

When he comes back with a roll of toilet paper, Anna is sitting at the end of the bed, the wet spot gleaming in the sunlight. He wipes at the bed linen, grateful that his mum isn't there to do the laundry.

"Anna," he says. "I'm sorry if that was too soon."

"You've missed me," she says.

He looks at her, surprised.

"I *have* missed you," he says.

"There's something I need to talk to you about."

She's got an apathetic look on her face and he tenses.

"I need your help," she says. "That boy, Da… David. He needs to go."

"Sure…"

"He was here, Erik." Her shoulders slump. "Just before you came home, he was here. He was *looking* at me."

"What do you mean?"

Didn't David leave for school earlier? Had he come back?

"I woke up and he was standing right in front of me, looking at me. I felt scared."

A protective instinct hits Erik but he also needs to defend David since he's the one who brought him into their house.

"He seems to think you're the greatest teacher on earth," Erik says. "He's a fan. You have a lot of them, remember?"

"I don't care, Erik. It was creepy. I need him gone."

It bothers him that she's ordering him around but perhaps he can let this one go.

"Did you speak to Kent?" she asks.

He shakes his head. "No, but I will do."

"When?" she demands.

He sighs. "I guess, right now."

*

Erik isn't looking forward to seeing Kent after accusing him of being a bit too chummy with Anna, but he does need his help. Apart from Anna's comments just now, he has to admit that David has overstepped the boundaries. He's made himself a little too comfortable. The night before, he even gave Anna a kiss on the cheek before going to bed. Erik witnessed her recoil at his touch but assumed it was because she didn't want anyone to touch her. Now he's not sure. He just wanted to be seen to do the right thing.

"Come on in, Erik."

Kent is always so sickeningly pleasant, it makes it hard to hate him.

"Hi there, sorry to disturb you."

"No problem. How is Anna settling in at home? You must be ecstatic!"

"I know, it's just… she's still recovering."

Kent shows him into the living room and they sit down. No coffee or whiskey like last time, Erik notes. Maybe that's because Märta is absent, or he just wants Erik out of there as soon as possible.

"When do you think she'll be back at work?" Kent asks.

That's all you fucking care about, isn't it? "Not for a while. Anyway, I came to talk to you about one of Anna's students, David." He realises he has no idea what David's surname is. "He's been helping me with the children, babysitting and stuff, but he's, well…" It sounds so embarrassing. "… he ended up staying the night when his place was being fumigated and now he keeps delaying moving back home."

"Did you ask him to leave?"

"Of course! He's just… he's a smooth operator, comes up with excuses."

"Erik, you're the adult."

Erik stares at Kent with contempt. It takes all of his mental strength not to hit him. Through gritted teeth, Erik explains that he is aware of this.

"Right," Kent says. "So, what do you want from me?"

He's so different, Kent, when it's just the two of them. Maybe he does secretly fancy Anna, or he just thinks that Erik is a piece of shit.

"Do you know anything about him?" Erik says, swallowing his anger. "Where he lives? I might need to speak to his mother."

"David?" Kent leans back on the flower-patterned sofa. "I'm not sure I know who that is. I know most of Anna's students, but not all of them of course."

Erik takes out his phone. "I took some photos last night when we were celebrating the boys' birthday."

"Oh, are they six already? Please wish them a happy birthday from me. They must be thrilled to have their mum back."

Erik nods. *That's kind of obvious, don't you think?* "Here." He moves across to the other side of the coffee table and sits next to Kent. He points to David.

Kent looks at him, his eyes growing. "Erik, that boy's name isn't David. That's Daniel, the boy who was giving Anna a difficult time at the beginning of the year."

"What?" *Fuck. He's been taken for a ride?* "Are you sure?"

"Yes, that's definitely Daniel."

76

Daniel

When Dan gets back to Anna's house he knocks on the door but no one answers. He knocks again. Same result. Even though they have agreed not to ring the doorbell in case Anna is sleeping, he pushes the black button outside the main entrance just the same. But nothing. He knows she's in there, so why isn't she opening the door? Perhaps she's in bed, unable to get up. He should have insisted on having his own key.

He walks around the house and looks in through the windows. Anna is lying in her bed in the living room and Erik is sitting next to her, talking. He tries to open the patio door but someone has locked it since he left. Can they not see him? He bangs on the window.

"Hello! Can you please let me in?"

Erik looks up, then he looks at Anna and they nod to each other. What the hell was that about? Erik picks up his phone and talks to someone, and Dan automatically takes a step back. Should he walk away? Are they on to him? Did Anna understand what happened this morning and has she told Erik? Is that what this is about?

Before Dan has made a decision about leaving, Erik looks at him, smiling and waving. Dan relaxes. Maybe Erik had to speak to the hospital about something urgent. Is Anna okay?

Erik gets up and walks across the floor to the patio door. It feels like it takes him a million years. Dan places his hand on the handle, eager to get in.

"What's wrong?" he says when Erik opens the door. "How is Anna?"

"She's fine," Erik says. "Just tired."

"I was ringing the doorbell. I thought you couldn't hear me?"

Erik doesn't respond. Instead he says: "Are you hungry, David?"

Dan looks over to Anna but she's lying down now, facing away from him, the duvet covering her.

"I could eat," he says.

They walk into the kitchen where Erik opens the fridge and pulls out leftovers from the previous night.

He sits down while Erik puts lasagne on a plate and heats it in the microwave. Why is he doing this? Is he just being nice? His body language seems stiff. He gets the feeling he has upset Erik somehow.

"So, you're ready to teach me the guitar later?" he says.

If he can get Erik into the basement, he should be able to overpower him there. Erik is fairly well built but so is Dan, plus he's found a set of golf clubs in the wardrobe downstairs that he can use.

"Maybe not today," Erik says.

"Oh, that's a shame. I was looking forward to it."

He starts to hum "Should I Stay or Should I Go" by The

Clash, but quickly stops. The lyrics don't feel appropriate: he's not going anywhere.

When the microwave pings, Erik puts the plate in front of Dan without a word. He hands him a knife and fork and a glass of water. It feels odd, being waited on like this, but perhaps that's what normal families do? They feed their family and friends.

"Where are Sebastian and Lukas?" Dan asks.

"At a friend's house."

"Right."

Erik keeps glancing towards the door. Is he expecting someone?

"I think Anna had a visitor this morning," Dan says.

"Really?"

Just then, the doorbell rings and Erik runs over, seemingly relieved. Who is it?

With his mouth full of pasta, Dan looks up when two people approach him. It's a woman and a man in police uniforms.

"*Daniel*," they say. "You'd better come with us."

*

It's all very confusing and it feels more serious this time. He's allocated a lawyer of some sort and suddenly, Frida is in the room. She sobs hysterically, lashing out at the police from time to time. "It wasn't him! You have it all wrong! Leave him alone!"

It feels like an action movie or a deranged comic, where the innocent are captured and tortured. They have his notebook. That fucking stinks. It's private. At first he just stares at it across the table.

They expect him to talk, but so far it's mostly Frida's voice that can be heard. He can't stand her pleading but eventually it becomes clear to her that nobody is taking any notice. She changes tack, predictable that she is, bringing out her round sad eyes and her smarmy voice: "I may be a bit stupid and not understand, so could you explain why we're here exactly?"

That's what she said to Anna as well. "I don't understand the stuff Dan is studying. It's going to make me look stupid." It's such bullshit. He already knows she's stupid. All she cares about is men who are prepared to fuck her. They always come first.

"So here we are again," they say.

He doesn't respond. What is it about this time?

"We have found a bracelet of Anna's amongst Daniel's belongings. It has blood on it. She was wearing it the night of the attack. There are also a number of compromising statements about Anna in his notebook." The policeman clears his throat and adds. "According to his own notes, Daniel has also associated himself with someone called Black Adam. It turns out that Anna received a large number of emails from someone calling himself that very same name."

"Bah!" Frida exclaims. "Who cares about emails? Anyone can claim to be someone and send an email these days."

Dan straightens his back. It's just occurred to him that Frida is defending him. He moves his chair closer to hers and she puts an arm around him. That feels good, not demanding but comforting.

"It's not just emails—" the policeman starts, but Frida interrupts him.

"Look," she says. "I think Dan has harboured some very loving feelings for Anna because, well, I probably haven't been the best mother and she is very... I mean, I can see why he would like her."

Hearing Frida speak like that about Anna makes him feel even better. Maybe sitting here, in this room, isn't so bad after all.

"I love Anna," he says, spurred on by Frida's words. "She sees me, she acknowledges me and despite some stupid shit I have pulled on her, she hasn't reported me to anyone."

Frida removes her arm. Maybe he got a bit carried away? Nevertheless, it saddens him that she lets her pride get in the way. She should be happy that someone has made her son feel like this. He can't stop, however. They need to understand how wonderful he thinks Anna is; that he wouldn't hurt her.

"Anna isn't like other teachers," he says. "They take their phone out as soon as a class is over, but I've never even seen Anna with a phone. Her attention is always on the students, on me..." He stops and looks at Frida, but she's avoiding eye contact. "We have moved a lot," he continues. "I mean a lot! And I have tried everything from being the quiet student who makes no fuss to being a troublemaker. And guess what?" He looks directly at the policewoman sitting opposite him whose eyes seem to care. "It makes no bloody difference! When you move, everyone forgets you. This time, I did want to draw attention to myself because I wanted Anna to notice me, and yes, I did email her and I did threaten her but I didn't do anything. I love her."

"You threatened her?"

He buries his head in his hands. He shouldn't have said that. Now what? He's not sure he wants to betray Anna and tell them about her and that woman, kissing. If she finds out he snitched, she will be upset with him.

"I wanted to move in with her family," he says.

Frida bursts out crying and he glances at her pathetic form, make-up running down her face. He feels no compassion. This woman fed him crisps for breakfast and made him clean up the vomit of strangers; she made a fool out of him in front of his friends until he realised it wasn't worth having any. He feels the rage accumulate at the memories of his failed childhood.

"You can't blame me," he says. "I wanted a normal fucking family."

"I'm your mother!"

"Don't even start!" he shouts. He doesn't care where he is; he can't control himself any longer. "Since when do you act like a mother?"

"Since now," the policewoman interjects. "She's here, isn't she?"

They both fall silent.

"Tell me about this bracelet," the policeman says, holding up a picture of a silver chain with two hearts on it.

Dan recognises it. "Anna used to wear that every day."

"Not when she was brought to the hospital," the policeman says.

"Maybe she dropped it somewhere?" Dan suggests.

"Or the attacker wanted a memory of her."

"It wasn't me," he says. "I didn't take that bracelet."

"And yet we found it hidden in your notebook."

His brain explodes. Did he take that bracelet? He remembers being upset with Anna in the parking lot, how she pushed him off and he fell to the ground like a stupid little kid. All he wanted was to rip her clothes off but she wanted nothing to do with him. Yet she hugged him. She grabbed his arm in a loving way and pulled him close. Surely he didn't misunderstand that?

He closes his eyes and pictures Anna naked.

Her expression is calm, her hair falling freely around her face. She smiles at him and stretches out a hand.

He takes it and together they walk into the woods behind the school. She's leaning against a tree and he lifts her up—

"Daniel?"

He looks at them.

"I didn't do it," he says. "I wouldn't hurt Anna."

The policewoman leans over the table.

"Daniel, where were you the evening of March the eighth?"

"I don't know."

"Maybe your mum knows?"

Dan looks at Frida. Why would they trust her? She's a mess.

"He was at home doing his homework," she says.

Frida cries and Dan knows why. She was most likely too pissed to know where he was. The question is: will she still confirm it to save her son? Dan needs to get out of this joint. He has unfinished business he needs to take care of.

Apparently Frida isn't a watertight alibi. Did anyone else see him at home? Did they have a pizza delivered? Frida looks as if she's thinking while Dan slowly feels the hope run out. It seems like he will have to stay here for a long time.

77

Rolf

Rolf is living every day as if it's his last. Mistakes change your life. He's learned that the hard way. No more messy affairs, no more controversy, no more media attention. He would also like to say "no more women" but that would be like cutting off his balls. There are limits.

His bags are packed and the moving van in the courtyard is full.

"Are you running away?" Karin asks over the phone.

His daughter's inherited directness always cheers him up.

"I'm not running away from anything," he says. "The police let me go, remember? It's just time to sell the house and create a life elsewhere."

"What about my childhood memories?"

"They're documented in a photo album somewhere."

"Seriously, Dad? Don't you think it's mean to let me suffer just because the two of you fucked up?"

"Hey," he says. "You might be of age but we're still your parents."

She laughs. "I'm just messing with you. Anyway, I would like to see you soon."

"Really? You don't need money, do you?"

She scoffs. "Since when do I ask for money? You know that I take care of myself."

He does. She has a monthly student grant, a generous loan that the state provides, and on top of that she works in a café on the weekends.

"It's just that I hear parents from your old class complain about their kids needing money."

"I'm not like other kids, and you're not like other parents. Anyway," she says. "You might have guessed that I've met someone and I want him to meet you and Mum."

His little girl with a boy in her life.

"Just bring him to your mother's place," he says. "I'm allowed to visit."

"But first, there's something you should know. He's not my boyfriend… He's my fiancé."

What the hell? Rolf wishes he were drinking so that he could get something caught in his throat and cough loudly. Instead he gasps silently.

"You're too young! Who is he? Did he get you pregnant? Is that why he asked you to marry him? And why didn't you tell us?"

"You done?" she asks calmly.

He sighs. "Yeah." Fuck, he really is losing everyone at the same time.

"Look, Dad. I'm not pregnant and he didn't ask me. I asked him."

She's taking charge of her life and this shouldn't exactly surprise him.

"Congratulations," he says. "I hope I'll like him…"

"Thanks, Dad. You will. And I'm sure Mum will too. So... the million-dollar question... what is Mum going to do now?"

The movers are packing up his paintings, revealing one at the back that he hasn't seen for years. It's of Iris. She's holding a book in her hand but she's gazing out over the garden; a shawl is draped over her legs and there's something sorrowful about her posture. Did he ever make her happy?

"Have you asked her?" he says.

"Of course," Karin says. "You know what she's like, though, she's like a clam. She won't tell me anything. I heard she woke up though, that woman."

"Yes, she did." He pauses as they pack up the painting of Iris. A part of him doesn't want to keep it, but at the same time, he can't bear to lose it. "Look, Karin... I have made a lot of mistakes in my life, I mean, I have seen them as learning experiences of course, not mistakes, but... your Mum, she's a much better person than I am. That woman might not want your mum anymore, so who knows what the future holds. Know what I'm saying?"

"Sure, I mean, my life already consists of an interesting brocade of people, so I'll support you both. So, where are you moving to?"

He's moving to a farmhouse, east of Gothenburg. At least for now, until he decides what he wants to do with the rest of his life.

"Gothenburg," he says. "So that I can keep an eye on you."

"That's cool as long as you don't interfere with my life too much," she laughs.

Rolf is standing in his bare studio, watching the movers pack the last pieces.

"I'm changing my style anyway," he says. "I'm going to paint something I feel passionate about. Nudes."

She chortles. "How original! But I mean, good for you."

He imagines the women lining up, willingly losing their clothes for him. Maybe some of them will be comfortable with him painting in the nude, maybe others won't. Either way, he will live an authentic life, filled with art, sex and strong family ties.

"So you're sure you're not escaping Hågarp?" Karin says.

"Not exactly," he says. "My new motto is simply 'if you find yourself in a hot seat… move seats'."

78

Erik

Officer Johansson has arrived at Erik's house with one of her male colleagues. They're sitting at the kitchen table but have turned down his offer of coffee.

"We appreciate that Anna can't come to the station right now," Officer Johansson says. "So we thought we would come here instead."

Erik wonders if everyone on the police force is as accommodating.

"She still doesn't remember anything about that night," he says.

"If she doesn't," Officer Johansson says, "then we need to assess whether to involve a therapist."

A therapist? More people coming and going in this house?

"Of course," he says. He needs to be agreeable.

"But first, we wanted to talk to you."

"Is this about Daniel?"

Officer Johansson nods. "We had to let him go."

What? No! "Why?"

"He's got an alibi," Officer Johansson says. "He can't have been at the school parking lot at the time of the attack."

"But he's creepy."

"Maybe so, but he can't have attacked Anna."

"What if he's bought his alibi? Kent told me his brother is a criminal."

"Erik," Officer Johansson says, making him feel like a child. "We are following all leads."

He finds himself missing Tina. They're so vague and diplomatic, but he mustn't show too much emotion. The iPhone on the table that is about to capture Anna's conversation might already be recording. He's not the enemy. Can't they see how much he cares about his wife?

"Everyone talks about Anna being dedicated to her work and not having any interests outside of school. She doesn't seem very tight with anyone around here. That must mean you're very close?"

"We are," he says.

"We have also spoken to her family..."

"I bet her father could have something to do with this," Erik interrupts. "He's a violent man." Why hasn't he thought of that before?

"He was at an auto convention with his wife. Anyway, there are people who don't seem to think you had such a great marriage."

Oh. "We do," he says. "I mean, of course we don't always see eye to eye but we love each other."

He starts to cry. It can't be helped. His marriage is under attack and David or Daniel or whatever his name is, has been released. What now?

"We appreciate how stressful it must be to care for your wife at home while she recovers," Officer Johansson says.

"Thank you for saying that," he says sincerely. Thank you. "Just find the person who attacked her," he pleads.

"I think we're ready to see Anna now."

*

Erik brings Anna into the kitchen. She walks by herself now, steadied by his hand. They greet each other and Officer Johansson apologises for the intrusion but Anna says she's grateful for the work they're doing.

"We don't want to bother you," Officer Johansson says. "We just have a few questions."

Anna nods. "Okay."

They look up at Erik and he realises he's expected to leave.

Why do they always make him feel like he can't be trusted? But he backs away. He has no choice.

"I guess I'll leave you to it."

He closes the door and walks up the stairs with heavy feet to signal that he is out of the way. Except he immediately sneaks back down again. The kitchen door is thin enough for him to hear what's going on. Anna is vulnerable; he can't leave her alone. That would be irresponsible.

"Do you know Pernilla Arvidsson?" they ask her.

Wow, straight in his gut. No small talk.

Anna doesn't say anything at first. He presses his ear against the white MDF door.

"The name is familiar," she says eventually.

Erik's had enough of Pernilla. Can't she run off with Sophie's dad and be done with him?

"If you think of anything, let us know," Officer Johansson can be heard saying.

"Okay."

Anna sounds so eager to please and he knows she's frustrated that she can't offer more help.

"We need to ask you something else." The policeman clears his throat. "Did you see your husband at the school parking lot the night you were attacked?"

Pernilla! That lying bitch. He wants to scream through the door. It must be her.

"Erik?" Anna says. "No, why would he have been there?"

"We have to ask."

"No," Anna says. "That doesn't make any sense."

There's muffled conversation and he can't hear them. When it sounds like they're about to pack up, he quickly runs upstairs to avoid getting caught. Then he waits until his name is called.

"Erik?" It's Officer Johansson. Anna's voice isn't strong enough.

He walks downstairs at a leisurely pace. *See, I've been busy up here.*

*

When they have left, Anna turns to Erik.

"They asked if I saw you in the parking lot. It sounds like someone might have seen you there." She looks as if she's trying to remember. "No, hang on, they said that someone *did* see you but that the person isn't necessarily trustworthy. That's why they needed to talk to me."

He leans his head back, sighs. *Shit.*

"Maybe someone is making it up," he says.

"Who?"

443

"I don't know."

"Erik, this isn't a time for secrets." She looks so helpless. "I need to remember. Please."

"I know," he says and places his hands over hers on the table. "But it's got nothing to do with you."

"Nothing to do with me?"

"I'm sorry, I didn't mean…" Maybe it's better to come clean? She will find out sooner or later anyway. "There's this girl who's been really into me and I think she might have said something to the police to piss me off."

Anna nods. "Right. Why would she want to get you in trouble?"

"Because I'm not into her."

"Anymore?"

It's like an alarm going off in his body. Does she know about Pernilla?

"I guess," he says.

"I'm trying to remember, Erik. No guesses, please."

The mild woman who was wheeled into the house a week ago seems to have gained some strength. He wants to lash out at her, tell her how hard these last three months have been, but how would that help? They would argue and he would be labelled the bad guy.

"Erik, I can't do this. I feel like I don't know you."

"What do you mean?"

Every moment since she came home feels like a test. He's not sure what's right or wrong, how to act, what to say.

"Who is she?" she asks.

He won't get into this. What he will do, however, is hold up a mirror and reflect Pernilla's pettiness right back at her.

"Perhaps she was so jealous she decided to get rid of the competition?"

The shocked look on Anna's face makes him regret his words.

"I'm sorry," he says. "I shouldn't have said that."

Pernilla was so sweet initially. Caring. The way Anna used to be. She listened and laughed and joked with Sebastian and Lukas. The way a mother should. Anyway, he obviously misjudged her. *You also misjudged Anna.*

"Why did we get married?" she asks. "I just don't feel... in love with you."

"Please don't say that," he says, injured. "After everything we have gone through, don't say that. You will feel it, I'm sure."

She pulls away and shakes her head.

"No," she says. "I want a divorce, Erik."

79

Anna

The following morning, Anna tells Erik to go to work. She needs to be alone, to think.

"I don't need a babysitter," she says.

"I'm not sure…"

"Please," she begs. "I need to rest and it would be nice to have some peace and quiet so that I can sleep, watch a bit of TV and perhaps even read."

He hesitates and she understands it's because of the previous evening's conversation. Erik hasn't agreed to the divorce yet. He told her that he married her for life.

"We are meant to be together, Anna," he said but nothing about his body language mimicked the passion or conviction that Iris had shown.

She appreciates everything Erik has done and she has tried, but her request for divorce slipped out and when it did, she found it more liberating than terrifying.

Anna remembers Iris. Their bodies entwined, pleasuring each other, moaning and giggling. How effortless it was. She wants to feel that way again but she needs to be on her own now, to get back to her old self. It's pointless telling Erik about Iris; until she has regained her full memory, she can't be with anyone. Anna hoped that Erik would help her fill in the gaps but every day she's annoyed with him. She's not sure why.

"What is it about me that you love?" she asked him.

She felt she had asked that question before, she just couldn't remember when. Nor could she remember his response.

"We have two children together," he said.

"Is that enough?" she asked, deciding to put pressure on him. "What is it about *me* that you love? Help me remember."

She wanted him to tell her that she was the only woman for him, that he loved her laugh, her eyes or her hair. Anything that she could hang onto.

He looked teary-eyed. "I don't know," he admitted. "I just feel like my life has gone down the toilet except for those two boys and I can't be without them, not even every other week if we share custody."

"That will be hard for me too," she admitted.

"I won't do it."

And there it was again. A flickering memory. He had said that before. *I won't do it*. Her memory was still fitting together like a puzzle, the pieces finding their place one at a time. Was it when she was offered the job in Mörna and she asked him to move with her? Or was it when she suggested they have children or when she asked him to take paternity leave? Nothing was ever straightforward with him.

"You have to take some responsibility," she said. "If you're not satisfied with your life…"

"Oh, here we go again," he said. "No, I'm not bloody satisfied with my life, especially not having a wife who wants to divorce me, and oh, I have a dead-end career. So apart from my boys, I pretty much have nothing."

"I didn't tell you to give up your music ambitions," Anna said.

At that point he stormed out of the kitchen and left her alone.

*

By half-past eight, Erik has agreed to leave but there is a knock on the door. It's two police officers.

"We just want to check that everything is okay," they say.

Erik is impatient and tells them he needs to take the children to day care.

"Can we come inside and talk to Anna?"

Erik looks at her and she nods. Of course they can.

"You go," she says to him but he lingers while they step into the hallway.

"We just want to make sure you're all right."

"Thanks," Anna says. She appreciates their concern. "But really, I don't think you need to worry. There still have been no threats."

This has slightly surprised her. If someone so violently attacked her, then he or she must have really hated her. Does that person feel satisfied, just knowing she was hurt? Is that enough? She hopes so.

She promises to call if anything seems suspicious and Erik assures them that Anna is only left alone for very short periods of time. They also show the police their new burglar alarm, with a panic button for Anna.

After they leave, Erik hugs her.

"You see," he says. "You need me to stick around to protect you."

"You're going to be late," she says, withdrawing from his embrace.

She kneels down to hug the boys, pulling them both close.

"Mum, you're hurting us," Lukas laughs.

"I love you so much," she says, breathing in their scent, remembering the baby stage when she tried to nurse them both at the same time. It made her feel like a cow! The sudden memory makes her smile.

"Mummy needs to rest," she explains. "But when you come home, I want you to tell me all about your adventures."

"We will," Sebastian promises.

When Erik and the boys have left, the house is completely quiet. She thinks of her beautiful boys playing at day care today and although she will miss them, she knows they will have fun. They have so much energy. Every time she sees them, she feels abundantly cheerful. That's an emotion she remembers.

She lies down on her bed, to rest and let her mind wander. All she can hear are the trees blowing in the wind outside, birds chirping; the stillness makes her feel content. At least until the previous evening's conversation repeats itself in her head. She's leaving her husband. That's big.

She shuts the thought down. It's too much for her brain to cope with right now. Her thoughts drift to the police instead. Why do they keep checking up on her? If only she could remember that night.

Daniel threatened her. She remembers that. She remembers *him*. He wrote her letters and emails and he was there, in the parking lot. Was it the same night as the attack?

That's the tricky part. She doesn't know. *You will do as I say.* He wanted to live under her roof and somehow he had managed to do that without her knowledge. Was that his plan all along? To attack her, get her out of the way and then wriggle his way in? He kissed her and she rejected him. Had he punished her?

She gets out of bed and walks through the house, to spark those final memories. This is her home but she feels like a houseguest. As soon as she feels better, she will move somewhere else. Maybe even sooner if she can arrange it. She decides to start upstairs. It takes her a while; she must stop on every other step and take a couple of breaths before she can move on. With each step, however, she feels her strength returning and it's a good feeling. She needs to be strong.

Sebastian and Lukas's room is a mess. She smells their pillows, her insides pulling so hard at her, she must steady herself. They are both incredibly pure. What must it have been like for them, seeing her in the hospital, not knowing if she would ever wake up again? The recurring guilt pains her. What could she have done differently? How could she have prevented this from happening? She feels very strongly that she had something to do with it, that it somehow was her fault.

She makes the boys' beds and moves onto the landing and into her and Erik's bedroom. The desk is still a mess and there are clothes all over the floor. She's been upset about this chaos many times before. She can hear her own voice: "Can you please, please pick up after yourself?" Sounding like a mother.

She feels an urge to tidy up. If she can clear up a part of the house perhaps she can also find some peace. She gathers up all the clothes and separates them into the two laundry baskets in the bathroom: white clothes in one and all the rest in the other. Exhausted, she sits down by the desk and stares at the paper pile towering like a pyramid in the middle. She picks one at random. An electricity bill. She puts it to the side. There are a number of bills and she wonders if Erik has paid them.

She knows she should be resting and not worry about mindless matters such as this but maybe something will trigger a recollection of an event that evening. Books always talk about an item or a phrase or a song bringing back a memory.

Seeing Iris made her happy. Nothing had changed. Her body might be bashed-up but her feelings are intact. Has she ever told Iris that she loves her? She can't remember. Yet she ended it because she felt she owed it to Erik to stay. He took care of her, sat by her hospital bed, willing her to wake up. His mother told her on the phone, how he was there every day.

She clears the desk, organising everything into piles. It's cleansing.

Then she makes the bed and lies on top of it. It feels odd, as if this has always been temporary. Her bedside table, a flea market bargain, is empty apart from her alarm clock. Erik's is another story. It's overflowing with glasses, beer bottles and crisp packets. She clears it all away, to make it look like an adult's bedroom, and then she pulls out the drawer in his bedside table.

Ever since Anna returned home from the hospital, Erik has felt like a stranger to her. She remembers their wedding day but the man she has come home to seems different. It's strange, to remember a day filled with laughter and love many years ago, but not being able to remember recent events. He just seems preoccupied. She remembers him as funny, charming and safe. What happened to him? Is it her fault? Has the incident crushed him? She wants to find proof of his love for her, love letters or photos of the two of them together during happy times. Even though she has decided to move on, she needs those full memories to tell her children one day.

There is a neat stack of papers in the drawer and she takes them out: birthday and anniversary cards, a notepad and a white envelope that has been torn open. All the cards are either from herself or the children. She opens all the cards to see what she's written. Most of them are pre-printed with only a line by her: *I love you, hugs from Anna*. The letter is the life insurance paper they signed when they bought the house. It strikes her that Erik thought she might die. That must have been awful. Maybe she should go easy on him? He's been through a lot.

She opens the notepad and finds a list of items with figures next to them. *Deposit for an apartment… new guitar… leasing of a recording studio*. The list is long and at the bottom, there is the total price tag, 2.5 million kronor. That's the value of their house. The value of their life insurance. Has Erik already spent the money he would have earned from her death?

It feels like a stab wound. He's already imagined a life without her.

It seems as if he has done it with ease as well, with enthusiasm even. He was planning to make his music dream come true, and leave this house for an apartment. How could he possibly think that would be better for the boys? Sebastian and Lukas don't even seem to factor into the list. Also, if he is so happy to have a life without her, then why is he against a divorce? It doesn't make sense. She looks at the list again. It's like a shopping list for a new life and it stings.

She puts everything back in its place when a folded page falls out of the pad. It's a different colour to the rest. Pastel green, like the paper provided in the school library. She picks it up and unfolds it. It's got printed text on it and as she starts to read it, she feels sickened.

Anna is cheating on you with a woman who lives or works in Hågarp. If you wonder how I know this it's because I saw them together, kissing. Not just in a friendly way but passionately, with tongues. You should leave her. She doesn't love you. She will never love you again.

Her heart almost stops. Daniel went through with his threat. Erik knows about Iris. Or perhaps he didn't believe the accusations? After all, he wouldn't have known who the note was from. It could have been from anybody; it could have been made up. Erik must have thought it was a lie. There was no proof. No pictures. He wouldn't have paid any attention to it. Maybe he was going to show it to her but then she was assaulted and it was forgotten about?

What should she do now? Tell him that she found the note and explain to him what it was actually about? The very thought makes her sweat. She doesn't feel strong enough; they might argue. She will leave it for now. Having made a decision makes her feel better but her hand is shaking as she closes the drawer.

*

That evening, Erik brings home pizza from the local pizzeria. They eat with their hands. The boys are bubbly but Anna finds it difficult to keep up. All the time, she keeps thinking of the note and the list. *Calvin Klein underwear... Armani jeans... Trips to New York and Los Angeles – visit music studios.* So much detail. And Daniel. He had purposefully tried to sabotage her marriage.

"Not hungry?"

"It's probably the medication," she says.

"So how was your day today?" Erik asks while chewing. He quickly polishes off a slice and picks up another one.

"Fine," she says. "I tidied up a bit."

"Why?"

"I wanted to keep busy."

*

She sleeps badly. Every now and then she switches on a light and tries to read to avoid obsessing. She needs the hours to go faster until morning when the boys will be awake. They are the best remedy for negative thoughts. Her book lies open on her lap. She struggles to absorb the words, thoughts making their way through her head like it's a complicated labyrinth.

When Erik comes down in the morning, he kisses her before heading into the kitchen. The boys jump on her bed. They cuddle and giggle and she feels joyful. There is so much love when they're in the room.

"Time to eat," Erik calls and they all walk in to find the breakfast table loaded with bread, butter, ham, cheese, sliced cucumber and tomatoes, eggs, cereal, milk, juice and coffee. There's even mustard herring, her favourite.

"Wow," Anna says. He has gone all out. She hadn't expected a *smörgåsbord*. Is he trying to prove that he does love her and that he wants her to stay? Either way, she should enjoy this time with her family.

She drinks her coffee, careful not to spill. Her movements are still shaky plus Sebastian and Lukas are taking turns sitting on her lap, wriggling around as they stretch their little bodies to pick up a glass or a cereal bowl. The coffee tastes bitter. It's like it's corroding her tongue. Maybe she's forgotten what it's supposed to taste like? She tries to eat but halfway through breakfast the sleepless night catches up with her. She's so tired she can barely spread butter on the bread.

"Are you okay?" Erik asks.

"I slept really badly last night," she explains.

"Do you want to lie down?"

She nods. Her eyelids are getting heavier. Erik helps her to the bed while the boys finish eating.

Erik tucks her in and when her head comfortably rests on the pillow and the duvet is pulled up to her chin, he leans in and whispers: "Why did you go through my bedside table?"

Her body stiffens within the sheets, her mind hazy. "I'm not…"

"That was very naughty," he says, his hand bearing down on her, slapping her cheek.

The burning sensation momentarily clears the fog, bringing with it a memory.

*

She is outside the school building. It's *that* night. Iris's husband is there. There is something unnerving about him,

455

not only because he has followed her twice but also because of his reputation and his obvious possessiveness of Iris. His being there also annoys her. Who does he think he is, demanding that she leave his wife alone, as if Iris doesn't have a mind of her own? She feels manipulated but her conviction remains strong. Fortunately, Rolf eventually sees that and she manages to make him leave. She heads towards her car, to drive home to Erik. She is going to end her marriage.

Unlocking her car, she leans in to put her bag on the back seat. That's when she hears footsteps on the gravel behind her. She prays it isn't Rolf again. It's pitch black in the parking lot and the encounter was unpleasant enough, leaving her feeling guilty and dirty.

"Hey, wait up."

"Erik?"

She looks up, thankful that it's him. But what is he doing there?

"Are the children okay?" she asks. She holds up her phone, looking for missed calls but finds none.

"They're fine," he says. "Sleeping."

Incredulously, she asks him: "You left them home alone? They're only five…"

"I needed to talk to you."

"Couldn't it wait until I got home? I'm just on my way now…"

"It couldn't wait, Anna." His face looks hard as he continues. "Because as usual I have no idea of knowing when you will be back, since you practically live at this fucking school. And I need to speak to you right now, away from the children because I can't account for my actions."

Her throat tightens.

456

"Okay, what's up?" she says, trying to ignore the dread she feels. Does he know about Iris?

"I know," he says.

His eyes are so intense, she takes a step back. With the car door supporting her, she asks: "What do you know?" Perhaps he saw Rolf and wondered who that was or maybe he has found out that Daniel is blackmailing her. Anything is possible. And anything is easier to talk about than Iris.

"I know about your affair."

He takes a couple of steps towards her until they are only a few centimetres apart. She can smell his coffee breath.

"I'm really sorry," she says. "I was going to talk to you about it this evening, I just didn't know what to say or how to say it." She buries her head in her hands. "I'm so sorry, I never meant to hurt you."

"I find that hard to believe," he says. He moves even closer now, their chests touching. She feels the edge of the car door press into her back. He is upset, which is understandable. "There will have been a moment when you could have pulled back and said 'you know what, I have a husband who I promised to love until death do us part'. But you didn't."

She looks up at him, at once resenting his threatening composure.

"Erik, I am leaving you," she says, as calmly as possible.

"No, you're not," he says.

"Yes, I am."

"And the children?"

"We can share custody. You're a great dad."

"I want full custody."

"Erik, come on. We need to sit down and talk about this in a constructive manner."

But he doesn't back off. "I've been your puppet ever since

457

we moved here," he says. "While you have dedicated yourself to the youth of Mörna, I have put my own life on hold."

"Erik, no one has asked you to do that."

"And now you do this to me? With a *woman*?" He spits the word out and she feels a need to defend her relationship.

"At first we were just friends," she tells him. "But then it became something else."

"When people find out I will be a laughing stock!"

"I'm sorry, Erik. I love her."

That's when the first blow hits her.

She staggers backwards, her back ramming into the car door. There is no sense of time. Instinctively, she puts her hand to her head. There's blood on her fingers. She stares at the dripping redness, amazed. *Erik did this?* Bewildered, she looks around. *Did anyone see?* She hopes not, that would be embarrassing: teacher beaten by her husband.

She looks at Erik, expecting to see remorse but his fists are still tight; the vicious stare alarming her. She's about to speak when another blow strikes her head. Her back bangs into the door again and this time she falls over. She immediately tries to get back up but a boot explodes into her stomach and she screams, or at least she thinks she does; nothing comes out as she gasps. She needs to make him stop.

"Erik." She strains to find her voice. "Please... don't!"

She cries and she senses him getting down on his knees next to her. He brushes the hair out of her face and wipes her tears, almost gently. She relaxes. This was obviously just a freak accident, his temper getting the better of him.

He helps her up, holding her arm just above the elbow.

"Thank you..."

"So, you're not going to see her again?" he asks.

It feels more like an order than a question.

"Ehm…" Not seeing Iris is not an option but maybe she needs to make him think that. It's just… it's ridiculous. This is Erik, her husband for over six years. She knows him; she must be able to reason with him.

"Erik, we need to go home." She catches her breath. "To talk, properly."

"I'm sorry?" he says. "I didn't hear you? Are you going to stop seeing her?"

His tone frightens her.

"Maybe it was a rash decision," she agrees. "I will rethink it."

He laughs.

"Are you saying that because I just punched you in the face?"

He's so obnoxious, and no matter how scary this side of him is, the anger bursts out of her, the words flying out of her mouth.

"Who the hell do you think you are, using violence to control me?"

He grabs her belt and pulls her to him.

"No need for violence," he says. "You need sex? Then how about with me, right now?"

He unzips her fly.

"Erik, please don't," she says, trying to fight him off but he's wearing a big hoody and gloves, she can't scratch him or really hurt him. Instead she pleads with him. "It's me. Your wife."

"Apparently not anymore."

Now he grabs her by the lapels of her coat, and pulls her face so close, spit hits her lips. "You fucking disgust me," he says and then he rams her head into the door. Over and over, she feels the thunderous pain. She tries to fight back but he's stronger, and eventually she realises that no matter what she says or does, he will keep going.

She feels dizzy, her eyes won't focus; they're getting increasingly damp and sticky and she wipes them, only to see her hands covered in even more red. It looks like paint.

"I have nothing!" Erik shouts at her. "You have taken everything from me!"

Another boot and it sounds like something breaks. She hopes it's a tree branch and not her ribs but the agony is unbearable. Despite the pain, she clambers on to her hands and knees. A blur of movement and her head smashes against cold metal. Then everything turns eerily quiet.

80

Iris

Iris has spent the morning in bed. There is no longer a library to go to. Lena has stopped paying the rent and a group of men have cleared out the books to give them to charity. Luckily, Iris managed to save her own private English book library before Lena pettily changed the locks. Iris bought those books with her own money so they are rightfully hers, and she will keep fighting for them to be translated into Swedish. Perhaps this will be her new sole focus?

When Rolf makes his daily morning phone call, he enquires about Anna. She's still upset with him but she recognises that he's trying.

"There has been no contact," she admits.

"I'm not sure if I should say this Iris, but I will: I told you so."

"I'm not in the mood, Rolf."

"Seriously? I'm only joking," he says. "Well, half-joking anyway." He laughs. "Have a sense of humour!"

"I'm just…" She can't do this. "I don't want to talk about it."

"To be honest, I don't either. I'm sick of Anna. If you work it out, great, let me know. If you don't, even better."

"Rolf!"

This was a mistake, but then she thinks of Karin. She can't alienate herself, and so she moves the conversation along to their daughter.

"Have you spoken to Karin?"

"Yes, she has a fiancé."

"I know," she says, pleased that Karin chose to tell her first.

"You do? But we haven't even met him? Well… I guess I hadn't met your mum when I popped the question either."

"We have to let her go," Iris says.

Rolf sighs. "So, what's going on this weekend? Should we go and see your delightfully demented father?"

She's grateful that she won't have to deal with her father on her own, but she doesn't feel ready for a road trip with Rolf. Not yet.

"Not this weekend, Rolf. I'll let you know when I'm ready."

"No problem. Anyway, I have plans so I gotta go… I haven't been laid in a while."

She suspects he wants to make her jealous but he should know better.

"What about that single mother who called me?" she says.

"Actually… her son was brought in by the police because of your teacher friend. He was apparently her student."

The anger comes back.

"I swear I had no idea about his connection to her," Rolf assures her.

Is he telling the truth? Rolf does spread his oats far and wide with little thought for anything but his own satisfaction. Unless... could he have been that calculating? She's not sure anymore.

She opts for silence, not wanting to be pulled into his world.

"I ended it anyway," he tells her. "It's time for a fresh start."

She couldn't agree more and hangs up, feeling a new fire inside of her. There is no longer a "Rolf and Iris". It's only "Iris" now. She's strong and stubborn and she won't go down without a fight.

She drags herself out of bed, showers and puts clothes on. Dressed in the same outfit she wore the day Anna entered her library for the first time, she applies her signature red lipstick, and reviews the result in the mirror. What does Anna see when she looks at her? Does she see an older woman or does she see a contemporary? Does she see someone who's in love with her or who is preying on her? Does she see a woman or a librarian? A woman to be taken seriously or a hippie? She kisses herself in the mirror.

"I don't care," she says out loud. "It doesn't matter."

She heads out to the Golf. Even if Anna's husband is at home, Iris will insist on seeing Anna. She is still a friend of hers; she has rights.

81

Anna

I *can hear them talking about me and feel a tingling sensation on my leg. Something light is being moved up and down my calves. It tickles.*

"Be careful, Lukas. Play with the cars on the floor, not her leg." I pick up Erik's voice. It's uncharacteristically brittle.

"Daddy? Is she sleeping?"

Lukas's words make my chest tighten. I badly want to scoop him up. I'm right here, baby. I can hear you. *But however much I try, my lips won't move. I'm so tired. A tiny finger pokes my stomach and I imagine it leaves a dent in my foamy skin.*

"I want Mummy," says Sebastian and I can feel his warm breath on my face. "I want to hug her."

My baby boy squeezes me and as much as I relish the skin-to-skin contact, it also makes me want to cry. My cheek is burning. That was very naughty. *The look in his eyes, like the man he became that night in the parking lot; pent-up rage exploding out of him, repeatedly slamming my head against the car, his callous words matching his forceful hands.*

Who is he?

Sebastian hugs me even tighter and the love he shows me makes me scared. I can't live without my boys. What has Erik done to me? I try to wriggle my fingers. Maybe I can reach the panic button? But my fingers won't move. Is this how it feels to be near the end?

Sebastian is Mummy's boy, always seeking comfort in my arms whenever he's hurt. If I don't wake up, who's going to hug him and tell him it's going to be okay? He's not like Lukas, who dusts himself off and keeps going.

Sebastian's small body squashes my aching lungs, but I don't care about the pain; I care about my boys, now that I remember them. The labour of bringing them into this world, the failed epidural but the immense joy at seeing them one by one: first Sebastian and then Lukas a minute later. Tears well up. Can they see my tears? Do they slide under my eyelids and down my cheeks? Are they real?

"Get off!"

Erik's cry alarms me. He sounds frustrated rather than angry but soon the weight is lifted off me and my chest is once again hollow. Give him back to me. Please.

"You have to be careful with her." *Erik's voice breaks.*

"Daddy, don't cry."

Erik is crying? You fake bastard! *Enough with the acting. If you hated me so much you could have just left me.*

There's a piercing sound. Over and over, it echoes in my head. I want to know what it is but succumb to the heavy tiredness swaddling me like a tight blanket. In the distance, I hear someone say: "I came to see Anna."

I know that voice and immediately, I fight the sleep. She came back! Despite my efforts to push her away, she came back. Please dear God don't make me fall asleep just yet. Please. Iris, I can hear you.

"Get out."

No, Erik! I want to jump up from the bed, grab him and tell him that it's not her fault. But darkness stretches its arms around me, pulls me in.

Am I dying?

82

Erik

"Will you play with us, Daddy?"

"In a minute," he says.

Anna is lying on her bed. She looks like she's fast asleep and he can't decide whether he wants to be near her until the end, or whether he should just take the boys and leave the house.

He thinks back to the night when he received the note about Anna's alleged indiscretion. Rob had briefly popped in after Anna left for school that evening, and shortly after he went home, someone slipped the piece of paper under the door. At first, Erik thought it was Rob who had put it there, but it seemed too far-fetched. Rob would have told him something like that face to face anyway. He was a simple guy, he didn't play games. Also, the person who slipped it under the door had alerted Erik to it by incessantly ringing the doorbell like it was a fire alarm. Rob had strict instructions from Anna not to ring the doorbell, to avoid waking the children up, and he wouldn't have violated that. Erik stepped into the street to see if he could catch the delivery guy or girl, but there was no one there.

He walked back inside and unfolded the note. He read it a few times, the first time laughing, the second time inquisitively and the third time with concern. Surely it was a lie? But who would want to hurt him like this, was it someone trying to upend his marriage? Pernilla?

ANNA IS CHEATING ON YOU WITH A WOMAN WHO LIVES OR WORKS IN HÅGARP. IF YOU WONDER HOW I KNOW THIS IT'S BECAUSE I SAW THEM TOGETHER, KISSING. NOT JUST IN A FRIENDLY WAY BUT PASSIONATELY, WITH TONGUES. YOU SHOULD LEAVE HER. SHE DOESN'T LOVE YOU. SHE WILL NEVER LOVE YOU AGAIN.

It just didn't sound like Pernilla's words and she didn't know that Anna had been going to Hågarp regularly. Who would know that? Maybe Kent. It was possible, but if he knew anything about Anna he wouldn't tell Erik, especially not in this mysterious way. He was too boring.

Reading the words again, Erik realised that Anna had been different lately. She had been happy, smiling to herself when she didn't think he was watching, and he knew it wasn't because of him. There was something to this note, and he couldn't ignore it.

The sensible thing to do would have been to confront her when she got home but after pacing up and down the kitchen several times, he realised he couldn't wait. The thought of another person's hands on his wife – a woman at that – was disgusting. It was like someone was laughing in his face and he couldn't take it. He had to see her immediately.

Phoning was pointless, he needed to see her reaction when he confronted her.

If she had made a mistake, he would need to punish her, but they could work it out. She had told him she was going down to the school and so he put on a dark jacket with a hood, just like the old days when someone needed to be corrected. He didn't want anyone to recognise him – he couldn't have people thinking he was irresponsible, leaving his children unattended at home. He jogged down past the supermarket and the one-storey school building, which didn't take long. She was already in the parking lot when he arrived and when he saw her he felt better. At least she had told him the truth. She was at school, not with some woman. But he hadn't expected her to confess not only to having an affair with a woman, but that she was planning to *be* with her.

"Erik, I am leaving you," she said.

Her words were so calm and his first reaction was denial. She couldn't leave. She wouldn't leave.

"I'm sorry, Erik," she said. "I love her."

That's when the brain cables overheated. It was a physical reaction. He had never hit her before, but no words could convey how truly enraged he felt. He had lost a sister once, a person who loved him unconditionally, and now he was losing his wife, a person he was supposed to spend the rest of his life with. It wasn't just the loss of his marriage that upset him; he would lose his house and the car and, more importantly, his last hope of being in the music business. She would leave him with nothing. He didn't have a penny to his name. He had dropped out of college when Jonna died and his career had been off-track ever since. Without Anna, he was a nonentity. His name wasn't on anything; he hadn't been approved for a mortgage or a car loan. For each loss that popped up in his head, he banged her head against the car door again. It made him feel better. She deserved this. She was a liar. When they bought the house and the car, she had said that, in the eyes of the law, he owned half of everything but now he was sure she must have scammed him.

"I have nothing!" he said. "I have nothing!"

She didn't respond, which was just as well. The blood made him think of life and death and that's when the life insurance came to mind. Signing it had been smart. It had felt unnecessary at the time but now he saw himself standing in the spotlight on stage. It could help him start over. With that thought on his mind, his blind anger turned to focused bashing and when she finally fell to the ground he stood back and looked at the bloodied mess that had been his wife. It felt surreal, that he could have caused this, but then he corrected himself: she had caused this herself. She hadn't even fought very hard, as if she knew her own guilt.

He went into practical mode. Did he need to worry about evidence? There were no cameras. Anna had repeatedly complained about this after computers had once again been stolen from a classroom. They needed CCTV footage of which there wasn't any. He had still scanned the area when he walked up to her, just in case. DNA wouldn't be under her fingernails or anywhere else, other than where a husband's DNA would be expected. Who knew that TV shows could be so educational? *CSI* and *Dexter* had proven their worth. He wasn't sure whether he should move her body or whether that would be too difficult? He was worried he would leave evidence behind if he did. Thankfully, the parking lot was dark and no houses had been built at the back of the school due to the adjacent land being protected. Maybe she could remain where she was? There was no one around. Finally, there was a perk with the town being deserted by ten o'clock at night. The only sound was the murmur of the ocean in the distance, his only companion.

He decided to leave her there. That's when he noticed her bracelet on the ground, the silver one with the two hearts, one for Sebastian and one for Lukas. It must have come off her wrist. He leaned down to pick it up and tucked it in his pocket, not able to leave it behind.

Her phone was another matter; he couldn't hang onto that, but leaving it was too risky. There could be compromising messages and no one should know that his wife had cheated on him with a woman. He destroyed the phone with the back of his heel, ensuring the sim card was sufficiently damaged, and took the items with him to discard of them later.

He could have told the police about the message under the door but then he would have been suspect number one. He didn't have any other proof of her infidelity anyway, other than Anna's own confirmation. It wasn't until he found the Xeroxwed emails, the shockingly graphic emails that had made it even more real, that he had had some sort of evidence. But even then, he couldn't tie them to this woman whose name he didn't know. She most likely lived or worked in Hågarp, that was all he knew, and he couldn't exactly knock on people's doors and ask them if they had fucked his wife.

He thought about going to the library in Hågarp, where Anna had supposedly been meeting with a book club, if that was even what she was doing and where she was going. He's thought about going to the library many times since but he's been too afraid of what he will find. Plus, he hasn't wanted to draw attention to himself. The moment someone realises that he understands the truth about Anna's affair, it will be trouble. He has no problem with people knowing she cheated – it helps him play the victim – but they must think he only just found out. He had needed someone else to come forward about her infidelity. If only he had better friends.

Erik kept the note in Anna's workbag together with the life insurance papers but conveniently removed the bag from the house, telling Rob he had grabbed it in haste in case Anna should need it. He expected the police to search the house within the first twenty-four hours. Once she was back home, he moved the papers to the bedside table where it should have been safe. Why did she have to spoil it by snooping around?

He had been so careful. The clothes he wore that night had never made it into the house. He stripped down in the garden, grateful for the wild and lush bushes and trees that he was yet to trim, and after getting dressed in new clothes, he put them in a black bag. He almost put the bracelet in as well but he couldn't part with it. Using the gloves he had worn earlier, he put it in a ziplock bag, which he later kept with her laptop. The rest he discarded in a bin in another road. It was his lucky night; the bins were already lining the streets, ready to be emptied by noisy trucks early the next morning, before Anna was found. No one would be out walking behind the school at that time of night and he would wait until the morning to report her missing. He wasn't stupid.

The children were an issue. When he locked the door that night, believing that Anna would never return, his heart ached for them. But they have coped better than expected.

Sure, they're happy that she's home but they also recognise that she's different which makes them wary. He can tell. That makes him confident that the three of them will be just fine.

He's been on edge for months. It unnerves Erik that someone knows about Anna and that woman, but now it's finally about to come to an end. Anna will not be around to remember that night.

He can't let her live. Now that she wants to divorce him, as soon as her memory comes back, she will tell everyone that he confronted her that night. She already knows about the note.

When the doorbell rings, Erik ignores it.

"Why aren't you opening the door, Daddy?" Sebastian asks.

"It's a Jehovah's Witness," Erik says. "Leave it."

But Lukas has already opened the door and let a woman inside.

"She says she's a friend of Mummy's," Lukas says.

Erik gets up from his chair and walks across to a woman.

"I don't think we've met," he says apprehensively.

"I'm Iris," she says, extending a hand. "Anna's *very* good friend."

She looks deeply into his eyes as she says "very" and that's when he understands. What's worse is, she wants him to understand. *This is her?* She's so much older than Anna. He wants to laugh. This is the woman she was going to leave him for? But it's not funny.

"I came to see Anna," she says.

"Get out!" He gestures towards the door. "You're not welcome here. She is *my* wife."

"I know she is. I'm just a friend visiting a friend. How is she today?"

"She's sleeping," Sebastian tells her. Then he turns to Erik. "Is she back in a coma again, Daddy?"

"No," Erik says. "Say goodbye to the lady, she's about to leave."

"But I only just arrived. I would love a cup of coffee." Iris smiles sweetly at him and he wishes the boys weren't there so that he could show this woman who the boss of this house is.

"Why don't you boys go upstairs and get dressed," Erik says. "Let Mummy's friend visit and when she leaves, which will be soon, we can do something fun, okay?"

While Sebastian and Lukas walk upstairs, Erik needs to make a decision. This woman – Iris – is not Anna; he doesn't care enough about her to put his freedom at risk.

When he confronted Anna, he didn't think. Not at first. He was just so mad, and she didn't seem remorseful enough, which made him even angrier. Now it's different. He's already tasted life without Anna and since she's not willing to stay with him, he's decided that being a widower suits him. Especially one with life insurance money.

The sleeping pills he has crushed into her coffee should be enough to kill her. If it isn't, he will simply try again, but according to his research he's given her a deadly dose. He almost killed her once and that wasn't even planned, which caused a great deal of stress. This time he's calmer and more together. This time he will succeed.

"I heard a boy from school was in custody for her attack," Iris says.

Erik nods even though they've let him go, the fools. When

he hid Anna's bloodied bracelet in Daniel's notebook, he *did* think. He needed the boy out and he needed someone to take the blame after the police released the artist. As long as Anna couldn't remember that night, it would work.

"She told me about him," she says. "That he was threatening her."

Did she now? "Then why didn't you tell the police?"

She looks him up and down as if she's in charge.

"I didn't want to hurt you," she says. "But judging by your reaction when I arrived just now, I'm guessing you already knew about us?"

Shit.

Iris walks up to Anna's bed and sits down next to her, resting a hand on Anna's.

"I'll just make some coffee," he says.

Should he crush up more of the sleeping tablets? He just doesn't know. What's the right thing to do? This is not a decision he can call a friend about, not some fifty/fifty choice. He needs to be sure. Does he even have enough left to knock Iris out as well? He might not. Also, two dead bodies will be impossible to explain. The nurse won't be back until after the weekend. By that time, Anna will have died of "natural causes" due to her recent injuries, but Iris can't. He needs to get her out of here.

He pours a cup of coffee for Iris. Later, after Anna's body has been removed from the house, he will need Iris to explain that he was polite and not in any way acting odd.

"I'm sorry about before," he says, stepping into the living room. "I'm sure you can understand that this has been a stressful…" He stops, coffee spilling over his hands, burning. "What are you doing?"

Iris is leaning over Anna's face. Is she kissing her?

"I'm not sure she's breathing," Iris says in a stressed voice. "I've called an ambulance."

"What?" *No.* "I'm sure she's fine. She sleeps very deeply these days."

He walks across to Iris and attempts to hand the coffee over but she pushes him away. "She needs medical attention. Now!"

"Call them back and cancel that ambulance," he says. "You're overreacting. This is *my* wife we're talking about, not *your* fucking girlfriend."

He grabs her by the collar and pulls her back.

"Back the fuck off!" she says and manages to get out of his grip. She's petite and slippery.

This is not good, he thinks. I need to get her out, not bash her head in.

"Please just leave," he says. "I've got this covered." He picks up his phone to call 112 to cancel the ambulance but she snatches the phone out of his hand.

"I don't think you have your priorities right," she says. "That ambulance is taking Anna back to the hospital."

"Who the hell do you think you are, thinking you can dictate what goes on in my house?"

"I love Anna," she says.

He's so close to losing it, to ripping her head off. "Don't say those words about my wife, you predatory old lesbian."

He wants to hurt her with his words instead of his fists but Sebastian and Lukas, who must have heard the commotion, are making their way downstairs. He needs the boys to love him. *I'm a sensible man, I can control myself.*

"I'm so glad you're here," Iris says to them. "An ambulance

is coming for Mummy. Can you please keep an eye out through the window for me?"

They're visibly distressed by the sound of "ambulance" and Sebastian is immediately by his mother's side. Lukas, however, does as he's told, taking up his position by the window. Erik feels the blood heating up again. This woman cannot order his children around.

"Don't talk to my children! Don't you fucking dare. Just get out!"

"Or what?"

She's not afraid of him. At school he preferred to bully than to be bullied, but Iris seems immune to his scare tactics. She's right, though. What can he do to her? Then he realises what will hurt her.

"It's too late for an ambulance," he says.

83

Daniel

There's an ambulance outside Anna's house. Dan gets off his bike and runs through the crowd that's starting to gather around. People are so nosy.

"Anna!"

There's an argument going on at the back of the ambulance. Erik and that woman from the library are trying to push each other out of the way. The boys are there too, crying. Dan walks up to them.

"I'm going in the ambulance," the woman says.

"She's *my* wife. So clearly I'm going."

"You don't give a damn about her. Get away from her."

"*No one* goes with her," the paramedic says and closes the door. "You can drive to the hospital separately but I suggest you set aside your differences before you get there."

"What's happening?" Dan asks the guy. "Is she okay?"

But there seems to be no time to answer his questions. The paramedic gets into the passenger seat and they drive off.

"What's happening, Erik?" Dan asks.

Erik's eyes are burning into him. So he lied about his name, big deal. Surely they can make up?

"Stay the fuck away from us, creep."

Apparently they can't. But the boys, they must still like him?

"Sebastian, Lukas?"

Lukas runs up to him but Sebastian is holding onto his dad's leg.

"Mummy is really sick," Lukas cries.

Dan picks him up and hugs him.

"Come on, buddy, everything is going to be fine."

"Don't touch him," Erik says. "David, I mean Daniel, hurt Mummy."

"I didn't."

The Nissan dude came to Dan's rescue. He had apparently passed by their house that night and he verified that Dan was there. Frida had been Rolf's alibi and now Rolf was his. It was like a full circle of bullshitters helping each other but so what? He was in the clear.

The woman marches across to a red car and Dan runs after her, still holding on to Lukas.

"Are you going to the hospital?" he asks. "Can I go with you?"

She stops and surveys him. "Who are you?"

"Daniel."

"Are you the student who tried to blackmail Anna?"

Oh, shit. "Sorry, yeah, but I didn't mean any harm."

"Really? Well, I have no space for you."

The woman drives off but Erik is still there. He's picked Sebastian up now and he clings to his father like a koala.

"What's wrong with Anna?" Dan asks.

"Don't know."

Then why isn't he driving like a madman to the hospital to find out? Erik seems paralysed. Is he in shock?

"Let's go," Dan says. "You drive and I'll go with you."

"Sorry, pal, not happening."

"Okay, how about we all go inside and calm down then?"

"You're not coming into my house." Erik turns to Lukas. "Come here, son."

Lukas shakes his head sullenly. "Don't want to."

"Lukas. Here. Now!"

Erik's face is stern but Lukas refuses. Eventually Erik comes up to Dan and tries to take Lukas from him but it's not easy with Sebastian still clinging to him.

"He doesn't want to," Dan says. "Leave him be. He's okay. I can hold him."

"I want you to go."

Dan doesn't. They stand on the street for ages, both holding a child, trying to stare each other down. No one interferes but at some point a car pulls up next to them.

"It must be here to get you," Erik says. "After you escaped the last time."

Dan wants to run but he can't leave Lukas. Equally, he can't bring him. That would be kidnapping.

"Erik." It's Gerda, Anna's mother. Her hair swept back in a bun, the glasses heavy on her nose. "Anna called me last night and she didn't sound happy so I have driven *all* the way here."

"Hello," Dan says.

"This is *Daniel*," Erik says. "Not David. Daniel is the student who made Anna's life hell."

What? He didn't do that.

Gerda steps up to them and asks the children to join her.

"Come," she says. "Why don't we get some juice inside with Mummy."

"She's not there," Sebastian says. "The ambulance took her to the hospital."

Gerda looks at Erik. "What happened?"

"Just go inside," he says. "I'll explain in a minute. Everything is fine. I just need to take care of something first."

It's not fine, but the boys do as they're told and Dan is left feeling naked without the warmth of Lukas's little body holding onto him.

"I didn't make Anna's life hell," he tells Erik. "I love her."

"You love her?" Erik scoffs. "That's ridiculous. She would never be interested in a nobody like you!"

That's when Dan loses it, even if it's in plain view of the neighbours. He needs to eliminate this man from earth, this man who stands in his way of happiness, and now also mocks him.

He throws himself onto Erik, but Erik grabs hold of his neck and flings him onto the ground like he's made of paper. Dan is completely shocked; what the hell happened? He can't move. His legs are kicking and his hands are trying to push himself back up but Erik is strong, his grip firm. He struggles to breathe.

"Please…" Dan says. "Help…"

"Leave him alone," a woman shouts and a man grabs hold of Erik's shoulders, but he's strong and easily shakes the man off.

Erik continues what he's started: a knee pushes into Dan's back; a fist comes slamming down on the side of his head. Once, twice, three times.

Someone cries out that they've called the police, but are

they bluffing? Erik appears unaffected, and Dan tries his best to get to Erik using his elbows. *Please stop!*

"You are never going to see her again," Erik shouts.

"I won't," Dan says, but he's not sure Erik hears him.

The blows continue and pinned to the ground, Dan starts to give up. *What's the point? Nobody loves me anyway.* He closes his eyes and imagines what it will be like to be dead. Will anyone attend his funeral? That's when screeching tyres bring him back to the present, a murmur running through the crowd. The pressure on his body lightens and the air flows back into his lungs. Freed, Dan quickly turns around to blue flashing lights and tries to stand up. His legs just won't cooperate. At least Erik is finally being pulled away from him, two police officers handcuffing his hands behind his back.

"Erik Berg, you are under arrest for the attack on your wife, Anna Berg."

Erik tries to break free, grunting, the rage out of control. Like a bear struggling against the restraints.

"I read your disgusting journal," Erik yells at Dan. "But guess what? She's dead."

Epilogue

"Apparently Pernilla writes to him every week. She's not working at day care anymore though. Thank goodness."

"Have the children visited their father in prison?"

"Yes."

"How are they coping?"

"They have to get used to seeing him incarcerated. On a good note, they're excited about moving to a new house and having their own bedrooms, although they're fighting about who should have the bigger room!"

"Have you spoken to him?"

"Well… yes. I felt it was the right thing to do, for the children."

"What did he say?"

"Believe it or not, he felt insulted that the police had been watching him! They told me he had been making enquiries at the insurance company recently, asking about 'what-if' scenarios. The day he drugged the coffee, he also called day care about report cards for the children, should they move abroad. Abroad? Can you believe it? Anyway, he was starting to get overly confident I think, with first Rolf, then Daniel, being arrested. The important thing for me is, that they never completely trusted him. I wish other people had felt that way too, including myself."

"Speaking of Daniel, how is he? Has anyone spoken to him?"

"Yes, he's moving to a small town south of Malmö. His mother is in AA and has a new job. This time, he says, he actually wants to move."

"That's good. What about you?"

"The children are my priority."

"And you?"

"I'm glad to be alive, thanks to you."

A man enters the room.

"Are you both ready to sign?"

The two women nod. Together they say: "One mortgage, no life insurance and no regrets."

"We intend to live our lives to the fullest," Iris says to the man.

"Ehm, good for you," he says. "But I really just need your signatures."

They sign and leave the bank, holding hands. Outside the sun is shining.

"It's good to be outside, but we need to pick the children up."

"I'd better get used to that," Iris says. "When you're running late, I guess I'll be picking them up."

Anna plans to go back to school after the summer. "Don't fix what isn't broken," as Kent rightly pointed out. "You love your job."

"What if your bookshop is busy?" she asks Iris.

"That's the pleasure of owning it. I can close it for thirty minutes!"

Anna stops in the middle of the crowded street. She looks at this woman who makes her feel alive, and kisses her for all to see. Love overshadows pain. She's able to walk, she's able to talk, she's able to think and read and raise her children.

Anything is possible.

Acknowledgements

There are so many people I would like to thank. First of all, my incredibly charismatic agent Luigi Bonomi whose enthusiasm and creative genius never ceases to amaze me. To the very best editor a girl could hope for: the wonderfully talented Sarah Ritherdon who is fabulous to work with. Copy editor Paul King, for his attention to detail – thank you!

I would also like to thank the Emirates Airline Festival of Literature (EAFOL) and Montegrappa for creating the Montegrappa Prize for First Fiction. Thank you to Isobel Abulhoul, Yvette Judge and the whole team at EAFOL, as well as Charles Nahhas.

Thank you to Alison Bonomi, Angela Chadwick and Gwenhwyfar Dunne for reading my book and providing valuable feedback, and to Danielle Zigner for coming up with the brilliant title *When I Wake Up*.

Research for this book was made easier thanks to Jörgen Winberg, Carina Bonde, Camilla Kunstelj, Linda Schönbäck,

Maria Jalakas and Jennie Eng. Any mistakes or liberties with the truth have, however, been made or taken by the author!

Without the support of friends, this book wouldn't be possible. I would especially like to thank Lotta Lindman, Teresia Stedt, Katarina Fröberg, Margareta Lindberg, Anna Janson, Annika Roslund, Anna Bromley, Sara Berger, Tobias Schildfat, Nicola Gregory, Lulu Mahaini, Sigrid Combüchen, Thérese Granwald, Brandy Scott, Mikaela Théssen, Erica Siri, Annabel Kantaria (and the Green Suitcase Book Club), Cheryl Murree, Göran and Kerstin Larsson, for believing that I could do this. Also, thank you to my parents and my brother and his family for cheering me on. If you're not mentioned but you're in my life, that means you inspire me and for that I am very grateful.

To my wonderful husband, Mark, who is always supportive of anything I take on, and to our beautiful children who I hope are inspired to go after their dreams. I love you all.

Finally, to Aria and Head of Zeus – I am so grateful that you believed in this book, and to all the readers out there! If it weren't for you, there most definitely wouldn't be a book. Thank you!

Jessica Jarlvi